THE DETECTIVE
&
THE UNICORN

MICHAEL ANGEL

THE DETECTIVE & THE UNICORN

First Edition Copyright © 2011 by Michael Angel

Second Edition Copyright © 2014 by Michael Angel

ISBN-13: 978-1466369320

ISBN-10: 1466369329

Paperback Edition first printed October 2011. Second edition printed and published in the U.S. by Banty Hen Publishing, October 2014.

Cover art by Annah Wootten-Pinéles, www.annahlouise.com.

For more about Banty Hen Publishing, please visit our website at: www.bantyhenpublishing.com.

Also by Michael Angel

Centaur of the Crime

Dayna Chrissie, the leading Crime Scene Analyst for the LAPD, finds herself transported to the magical kingdom of Andeluvia. She's given three days to solve the king's murder, before war breaks out between Andeluvia and the Centaur Kingdoms. The price of failure? A war that will kill millions.

Hope she works best under pressure.

The Wizard, The Warlord, and the Hidden Woman

When the Caranthine Empire invades the peaceful land of Melusia, the wizard of Darkfell stands ready to repel the attacking hordes.

Ready, that is, until a terrible accident knocks him out of action. Muriel, the wizard's younger sister, sends a desperate call for help to a selfless, immensely powerful heroine she's read about via her magical scrying mirror: Leetah, the legendary Mage of the Rose.

But Leetah exists in only one place: between the ears of California-based fiction writer Jason Summer. Even with special, unseen allies and the help of a wizard's kid sister, it's going to be one bumpy ride.

See the full listing of Michael Angel's works at
www.MichaelAngelWriter.com

Other Books from Banty Hen Publishing

Sagebrush and Lace

Six guns, whips and wild, wild women!

1876: Time to throw away the corsets
and draw down on the Old West.

When Horace Greeley said "Go West Young Man"
he never would have thought that two young women
would take his advice to heart. Striking out against all
odds and risking everything to be together.

Society calls them Sapphists.
Chief Sitting Bull calls them 'Big Magic'.
Buffalo Bill Cody and Wild Bill Hickok
call them friends.
Pinkerton's detectives want them alive.
Clarke Quantrill's gang of outlaws want them dead.

Two runaway women in a man's world
risk their very lives to be together.

See the full listing of J.D. Cutler's works at:
www.JDCutler.com.

See the full listing of Sugar Lee Ryder's works at:
www.SugarLeeRyder.com.

'FANTASY & FORENSICS' BY MICHAEL ANGEL

Book One: Centaur of the Crime
Book Two: The Deer Prince's Murder
Book Three: Grand Theft Griffin
Book Four: A Perjury of Owls
Book Five: Forgery of the Phoenix (Fall 2016)

FANTASY NOVELS BY MICHAEL ANGEL

The Detective & The Unicorn
The Wizard, The Warlord, and The Hidden Woman
I Married the Third Horseman

SCI-FI NOVELS BY MICHAEL ANGEL

Apocalypse with a Side of Grilled Spam: Season One
A Shovelful of Stars
The Adventures of Amanda Love
Treasure of the Silver Star

ACKNOWLEDGMENTS

Special thanks go out to:

Sharon Gorrell, whose insights and edits
made *Detective* shine.

Annah Wootten-Pinéles, whose art
brought Derek, Rachel, and Tavia
to life in a truly compelling way.

And finally, to the man who became
the inspiration for Derek's character.
We all sleep safely at night because
people like you watch over us.

DEDICATION

To Sandra,

When I first began this story, I wasn't sure
whether or not you still loved horses.

So I wrote it for the Sandy I knew from long ago.

The girl who enjoyed everything about those
marvelous drinkers of the wind. Who knew breed
and color like the back of her hand. Who understood
how such a creature fills the void in a person's soul in
a way that none other can.

I later found out that you still enjoy tales about
all things equine.

This warms my heart.

I hope that this story shall warm yours in return.

CHAPTER ONE

The photo of a snow–white Pegasus in the company of the President of the United States had made the front page of the *Los Angeles Times* twice now.

Both times this happened, someone close to me has been killed.

The first time was three years ago, when the President welcomed a Pegasus, a dryad, and a pair of griffins to the White House. Their arrival became a kind of cultural touchstone for everyone, like the Kennedy assassination, the moon landing, or maybe 9–11.

Television networks and the Internet broadcast the event across the planet. I remember thinking that the whole thing looked a little surreal. Between the somber, blue–black suits of the President's cabinet and the colorful, Renaissance Faire medievalism of the group from the newly discovered 'Morning Land', it was Norman Rockwell meets the cast of *Narnia*.

For the next three years, the cable channels ran plenty of documentaries featuring the strange and exotic peoples from that world. I didn't pay a lick of attention. I had nose to grindstone, trying to make a name for myself at the Los Angeles Police Department.

And I was doing the best I could to rebuild my life after losing Beth.

1

* * *

I pulled into the Sub Shack off San Fernando Boulevard and put the unmarked Chevy Impala into park. Next to me, Dorian Martinez squinted into the last rays of sunset. The blood–red cast of the light gave his skin the shade of mahogany.

"And another eight hours of taxpayer–funded time flushed down the drain," he sighed. "Wish we were casing North Hollywood, see a little more action."

"Too much action for my blood." I peered through the store's windows and grimaced. The line of people from the counter snaked out the door and onto the sidewalk. "Think we can get a line jump from your favorite waitress?"

"Derek, I'm shocked." Dorian gave me a look of mock surprise. "Do you doubt my powers?"

"Just get us some dinner, hotshot." I replied with a grin. Dorian Martinez and I had worked Narcotics off and on for the last couple of years. His unfailing good humor made even our last boring, fruitless stakeout bearable.

He went up to the counter and effortlessly charmed the Latina cashier. He'd have been the perfect partner had he not been a dead ringer for a young Antonio Banderas. Dorian—even his name suggested he had a picture up in his attic doing his damned aging for him—attracted women like honeybees to a flower.

Of course, Dorian did his best to share the sweet nectar with as many as possible. He was young. Free. Single. I didn't feel much like that anymore. I fiddled with the battered silver circlet on my fourth finger. I still wore the ring, even after all this time.

Dorian brought back a pair of turkey subs, a crumpled copy of the *Los Angeles Times*, and a couple cans of soda that dripped icy beads of condensation in the dull summer heat. He slipped into his seat and pushed the paper into my hands.

"Check out the picture on the front page," Dorian smiled. "Bet your niece wouldn't mind getting a copy of it. Little girls love horses."

I unfolded the top section and read the headline: *Morning Land Joins President to Select New Envoy to U.N.* The president stood off to one side, grinning a politician's grin and waving to the crowd. To his left, the Pegasus looked as if he'd been sculpted out of fresh snow, from his muscled legs to the downy tips of his wings. His dark, liquid eyes sparkled in the photographers' camera flashes. I couldn't help but think of a proud, young swan.

The car's radio crackled to life. "Victor two–three, this is Eagle's Nest."

I picked up the transmitter and then toggled the button. "This is two–three, Detectives Ridder and Martinez. Go ahead, Nest."

"Victor two–three, we have report of a disturbance at 2200 Durham."

"Copy that," I replied. "Two–three on approach, out."

I put the radio back in its holder and pulled out of the lot. With a mild curse, Dorian crammed our sandwiches in the door compartment.

It only took us a few minutes to cover the distance. The look of the avenues leading up to Durham took a steep nose dive. Streetlights cast forlorn circles of amber. Every third lamp hung askew and broken, knocked out by rocks or neglect. Barbed wire fencing sprang up along empty lots like fresh crops of weeds.

Gravel crunched under the tires as I pulled up in front of a sprawling, two–story place that looked like a flophouse gone to seed. The sun finally sank behind the nearby hills, probably in disgust. The building's hot pink neon signs and a rising full moon provided the only illumination.

The 2200 block of Durham housed the TomKat, a lesser-known nightclub for 'Discriminating Gentlemen'. In this case, 'discriminating' meant that the patrons required a lap dancer to be able to fog a mirror while swaying her hips in a circle.

I killed the Impala's engine. The evening went quiet. Dead quiet. I could see the glow of the club's interior lights, but I didn't hear a thing. No sounds of rowdy drunks, throbbing dance music, hustling bartenders, parties of loud businessmen looking for a way to unwind while on the road. And on a Friday evening, no less.

"Man, I *really* don't like this," Dorian said, echoing my thoughts.

We got out and peered more closely at the building. The swinging, saloon–type entry doors swayed gently in the wind. The windows were open on the second floor. A hazy, blue–white glow radiated from within.

"Better call this in." Dorian nodded and grabbed the radio at his belt.

"Detective Martinez to Nest..." He frowned. "Not working."

I tried my own radio. A press of the transmit button yielded nothing. Dorian leaned into the car and tried the vehicle radio.

"This is unit two–three, requesting backup." Static crackled back. He looked at me, puzzled. "All three on the fritz at the same time? What're the odds?"

I checked my cell phone. The screen read NO SIGNAL.

"Don't think we ever marked the TomKat as a signal dead zone," I said cautiously. My mouth had gone dry, held a sour, metallic taste. "Maybe we—"

A loud thumping came from upstairs. A curious flash of light from the upstairs windows. Something like bluish ball lightning. Then our eardrums throbbed as a high–pitched scream cut the air. It sounded like someone in agonizing pain.

Dorian and I drew our semis. We ran towards the TomKat's entrance. The saloon–style doors waggled back and forth in the wind as we approached.

As if they were the lips and tongue of some enormous creature set to devour us whole.

Chapter Two

I froze as I pushed through the doors.

"Sweet Jesus, what happened here?" I breathed.

It sounded like someone was in trouble on the second floor, but I don't think anyone could have passed up what I saw without pausing. Behind me, Dorian gasped in shock.

Bodies lay in rough tumbles across the room. The bartender rested with his head in his arms by the beer taps. A pair of cocktail waitresses sprawled out one–two at the bar. A group of businessmen from what looked like the National Pocket Protector Association slumped at one of the tables.

But the patrons' expressions were peaceful. Eyes closed, faces in repose.

"All breathing," whispered Dorian. "Sleeping?"

I couldn't begin to explain it. Another blue–white flash of light, this time from the staircase, left a ghostly scrawl across my retina. We didn't have time to speculate. I motioned towards the stairs and Dorian followed.

A wooden staircase covered with dingy, gold shag led to the second floor. A trio of bulbs stuck into a fake chandelier above lit the way. It swayed overhead, making our shadows skitter back and forth across the ratty carpet.

Blue–white light flared from behind the half–open door at the top. As we came to the last three steps, I began to hear a faint murmur. Almost a thrumming in the air, as if a crowd of unseen people around me were going *ahhhhhhhhhhhhhhhhhh*...

Dorian moved to one side of the door. I shifted to the other. Even if we'd felt free to talk, I don't think we could have used our voices.

The volume, the thrumming in the air, increased. Picked up energy, as if the crowd were on their feet now. As if they sought to drown out every other sound in the world not made by their spectral vocal cords.

Ahhhhhhhhhhhhhhhhhhhhhhhhhhhhhhhhhh...

The bulbs in the chandelier flickered. The hair on my arms and the back of my neck stood straight up at attention. Like I was in the eye of an electrical storm. Whatever was happening, we had to go in now.

We went through the door with a crash.

Dorian went in first and to the right. I followed through on the left. Guns drawn at the ready. Into the room and sectioning it off. Searching for threats.

The blue–white light radiated from a congealed pool of mist on the ceiling. I didn't see a power cord. Office furniture had been shoved against the walls to clear the center of the room. Chalky smells of day–old charcoal and burnt sawdust assaulted my nose, made me want to sneeze.

The scents rose from where I thought someone had thrown a fistful of lit cigarette butts on the bare, pitted wood floor. Burning sparks outlined a complex diagram made up of symbols and shapes. The sparks danced along the diagram like a flame following a line of gasoline in a channel of dry sand. The sound, the awful humming sound of the crowd, had gotten so loud that I could see the panes of glass in the windows vibrate.

AHHHHHHHHHHHHHHHHHHHHHHHHHHH...

And then, silence.

Silence as deafening as if someone had just pulled the plug on a rock band's main amp.

Dorian took a step back. The toe of his boot had scuffed out a piece of the lines. The line had smeared, like he'd walked across a kid's hopscotch grid.

"Not again."

It wasn't Dorian's voice. It was the voice of someone older, someone harsh and unforgiving.

A man stepped out of the shadows and into Dorian's line of fire. A weather–beaten black duster hung from his wiry frame. Leather gloves, denim jeans, and Western–style boots with rusted steel tips completed his outfit.

His features jutted out knife–sharp. Bony cheeks under taut pale skin. He had dead, doll's eyes like a shark's. A tattoo shaped like an obscene question mark coiled under his left eye.

The man spoke something in a foreign tongue. The words didn't sound right. Didn't sound human. Ugly sounding. Too ugly to come out of a man's mouth, too ugly to have been formed in a man's brain.

The gut–instinct part of my brain reacted. Told me that, no matter my training, to hesitate now meant a horrible death. I tried to cry out.

Shoot! Shoot, Dorian! He's right in your sights, shoot the son of a bitch!

Dorian didn't move. I didn't either. Couldn't move.

My brain had nothing, no guide wires to make the muscles move. With a sick shock of horror, I realized that the man in the black duster had done this. Somehow, he'd immobilized us. Like insects entombed in a drop of amber.

"I have had enough of you people," he hissed. The man eyed the scuff mark made by Dorian's boot. "I'm going to make an example out of you."

The man leaned forward and whispered something quiet but horrible sounding in Dorian's ear. A sudden wind kicked up through the open windows. It made the man's black duster ripple as he stepped back a few paces.

"Don't want to get my clothes dirty," he said into the darkness. "Go ahead."

Dorian's arm moved. He placed the muzzle of his semiautomatic under his chin. Without any hesitation at all, he pulled the trigger.

A loud *bang!* and the nine–millimeter slug exploded out the top of his skull in a fountain of blood and bone. Dorian fell backward on the floor. His body jerked spasmodically for a second. The stench of his singed hair flooded my nostrils. His dead eyes looked up at the ceiling, a pair of glassy brown marbles.

The man in the black duster turned his eyes to me.

"Now." His voice was calm. "It's your turn."

CHAPTER THREE

The man's boots made a heavy tread on the floor as he made his way across the room towards me. To deliver his poisoned word into my ear like a junkie's dirty hypodermic needle. I couldn't move, but my mind was racing. My emotions shifted like water through rapids, torn between fury and terror.

Something primal tore loose in my brain with a snap! that echoed inside my head. Something awful, fueled in equal parts by rage and despair. Hot fingers caressed my forehead and drove daggers of salt into my eyes. I realized that I was dripping sweat as if I were in a high fever. My hand twitched.

Slowly, I began to raise my gun. Pain lanced through me as I fought to keep moving it. Like I'd plunged my arm into a barrel of boiling pitch. The Glock felt like a lump of metal welded to my palm.

The man in the black duster saw my movement. His eyes went wide with amazement. I heard the sharp intake of his breath.

You didn't expect this, did you? If you like it so far, then you'll just love what comes next, you bastard.

"It can't be." He stretched out one bony hand to grab the gun.

My vision dimmed black around the edges. With a convulsive jerk, I got my Glock up as high as his waist. The man in black was on me. His clammy fingers touched my wrist. The touch of a corpse.

I squeezed the trigger.

The man spun away as if I'd shoved him. He hit the floor. Flopped over, gasping like a hooked fish stranded on the dock. I saw the bullet hole on the lower left side of his torso, an inch above his belt. A crimson stain around the wound started spreading, fast.

I was almost ashamed at my delight when I saw it start to drip.

"You—" he choked out. Stopped as he saw my arm continue to move haltingly, quivering as if it was made of rubber.

The man struggled to his knees and spoke another ugly word. He began to fade away, like the ghost of a picture on a television screen. At the last moment, before he vanished, his eyes locked with mine. Hate and pain filled his gaze.

I returned the look with a hell of a lot of interest.

The hold over my body vanished. I fell. Cracked my head on the floor. Grappled blindly for my radio. My voice came out in a croak.

"This is Detective Ridder. Anyone, please respond."

The dispatcher's voice came in clear. "Victor two–three, come again?"

"Code eight," I gasped. "Officer down. 2200 Durham. Upper floor." My eyes closed. The world went spiraling off into darkness.

* * *

I came to in a hospital bed. The doctors wanted to keep me under evaluation for the night. I had to threaten an orderly with bodily harm if they insisted. Even so, with all the poking and prodding, midnight passed in the rearview mirror by the time that I was able to drive back to my house.

My seven–year old niece Rachel hit me like a cannonball as I walked in the door. I picked her up as she covered my face with kisses and tears. Rachel clung to me stubbornly and wouldn't let me put her down until I paid the sitter and saw the woman out the door.

All I did for the next few minutes was croon, "I'm here, shhh..." to calm Rachel's nerves. Eventually, she let me put her down at the kitchen table.

"What...what happened?" she asked. "Will you tell me?"

I suppose if I'd been a proper dad, I would have said 'this is adult stuff, and you'd better get off to bed'. But I wasn't a dad. I'd wanted to have my own kids with Beth. But that was something from another time and place. When I wasn't a widower who hadn't quite yet seen the end of his twenties.

But I was just an uncle, one who had been roped into niece–sitting while Rachel's mom was away on business. I wasn't sure how to handle a little girl beyond the basics of feeding and tucking in. So I sat quietly with her for a minute.

I'd always been honest with Rachel about what I did in my line of work. Yes, I smoothed some of the edges. But I wouldn't talk down to her. She was too smart for that kind of thing anyway.

I told her about how Dorian and I had answered a call from the station. I told her about the man in black. But all I could say next was that Dorian would no longer be coming by the house. That he had gone on to a better place.

"What do you think that man was?" Rachel asked softly.

"I don't know, honey. I don't know who that was."

"Was he a monster?"

"I don't know." I swung her up in my arms again. "But I'm here to watch over you, no matter what. Got that?"

"Yeah, I got it," she said. Rachel rested her head against my shoulder as I walked back to the bedroom. Her sheets lay all tangled up. I awkwardly pulled them into something resembling a bed more than a bird's nest and tucked her in.

I picked up one of Rachel's favorite stuffed animals, a marmalade–colored doll named Sugar Pony. Rachel snuggled the doll, then looked up and said, "Maybe Sugar Pony needs some of her friends tonight, Uncle Derek."

"Now that's a good idea, why didn't I think of that?" I went down the ranks of animals perched on her shelf. "How about Frankfurter the Dog?" He got the nod, so I put him in the bed.

So did 'Pig' the Pig, 'Harvey' the Lobster, and 'Super Pickle' the Zebra. "Are all the animals on the Ark gonna sleep tight tonight?"

"All night," Rachel said sleepily. I knelt by the bed, kissed her goodnight, and switched the light off on the way out.

I went to my bathroom. Shut the door and locked it. I didn't want Rachel to see me lose control. Not when I'd told her that I'd watch over her. I groped for the sink. Gripped the porcelain sides as tight as a drunk hugging a lamppost.

I stifled a grim laugh. Watch over her, protect her? Yeah, Derek Ridder's track record as a protector looked pretty damned rotten right now.

I'd gotten Dorian killed. I let him go into the building, should have gone myself, should have gone upstairs alone, should have, should have, should have…

I should have saved my wife, too.

That felt like I'd been slugged in the kidneys. I slumped to my knees. A howl of despair threatened to burst from my lips. I twisted a towel into a rat's tail, shoved it into my mouth, and pressed my forehead to the cold floor tile. I lay there, sobbing into the towel I'd jammed into my mouth.

I must have drifted off to sleep then. A cold draft woke me, carrying the scent of morning dew tinged with bath soap. Outside, the sky started to brighten towards dawn. I splashed some cold water on my face to wake up. The liquid from the nickel–plated tap left a heavy, mineral taste in my mouth. I went out the back door and leaned up against the outside wall. The knobby texture of the stucco dug into my back through my thin shirt.

I didn't have much choice, really. I had to carry on. I knew that I had to try and live up to Rachel's trust in me. To do right by Dorian. And for Beth's sake.

I just wished to heaven that I knew what to do.

CHAPTER FOUR

A ghost lay in wait for me back at the station.

I'd been doing plainclothes work out on the street, where the late summer sun beat down like a sledgehammer. I hit the showers and did my best to steam off the sticky layer of sweat. When I came out, I tried to rake my mop of black hair into place. Not that it did much to improve my looks. Even Beth had once charitably described me as a cross between Matthew Broderick and Frankenstein.

I wrapped a towel around my gut and opened my locker. Right then, the ghost fell out from its hiding spot.

"*Ooooo–weeee–oooooo!*" The ghost jiggled at the end of its clear monofilament line. Its black, plastic eyes flashed with colorful Halloween cheer. I snatched the toy up and nudged the 'off' switch on its base.

"Clever," I said, holding back my temper.

I looked around the locker room at the other guys. Several gave me an uneasy laugh back. But a couple of them didn't meet my eyes.

I'd recounted at the formal inquiry what happened to me and Dorian at the TomKat. Depending on what people chose to believe, I was hopped up on adrenaline, wrung out from seeing Dorian buy the farm, or flat–out crazy.

I kept my mouth shut outside the station. We were going with the story that carbon monoxide fumes from a faulty heating unit had overcome everyone at the TomKat. Never mind that nobody in Los Angeles would be running a heater in the middle of August.

The people I'd seen downstairs started coming to about an hour after I'd been sent to the hospital. If they'd been exposed to some kind of poison, it didn't take. No one had reported so much as a headache.

I just finished changing when the desk sergeant poked his head in the door. "Hey, Ridder," he called, "The Captain wants to see you in his office, ASAP."

I stood and ran my fingers through my hair with a sigh. I straightened out my shirt with a brief tug and went to see Birch.

* * *

The door to the Captain's office stood ajar. I could see the broad expanse of his back as he fumbled with something behind and under his desk. I rapped on the doorframe to announce my arrival.

"You needed to see me, sir?"

"Ridder? Come in, close the door."

I took the seat in front of his desk as Birch found the jumbo–sized bottle of Maalox he'd been digging for in his desk drawer. He shook out a couple tablets, chewed them to powder, then washed them down with a sip of coffee.

Captain Alan Birch made an unlikely looking commander. He was tall, almost as tall as I was, with a barrel chest and bulging forearms that would've made Popeye envious. Birch had an affinity for cowboy hats, Tabasco sauce, and antacid, in roughly that order. To top it off, he'd risen through the ranks without having to shave off a handlebar mustache that wouldn't have looked out of place on baseball pitcher Rollie Fingers.

"How've you been bearing up, Derek?" Birch asked.

"Feeling fine, sir. If you think I need some more head–shrinking, that's your call. But I'd rather we spent the money on something else."

Birch steepled his fingers. He paused, then seemed to come to some kind of conclusion about me before he spoke. "Something's stirred up a hornet's nest all the way up our food chain. Is there anything, anything at all that you want to tell me? Something that might not have found its way into your report?"

"I'm sorry, Captain. If there's thunder from upstairs, then I'll be as surprised as you when it starts to rain."

"And as wet," he quipped. He let out a deep breath. "I've been ordered to put you on special assignment. Specifically, the case involving the TomKat."

"Sir, I don't think that will be—" I stopped in surprise.

He nodded, acknowledging my unspoken question.

"Orders signed and sealed by the Governor, Detective Ridder. I'm supposed to give you a copy of those orders and a letter addressed specifically for you. You're to read it and then go directly to the Mayor's Residence in Hancock Park."

Birch pulled out an oversized manila folder and handed it to me. I took it gingerly, then pulled out its contents. There were two memos and a cream–colored envelope. I carefully laid them out on Birch's side table one at a time.

The first memo bore the seal of the Governor's office of California. It listed the Captain's orders in terse bullet points. The second memo also bore a seal—the one used by the United Nations. The text contained a lot of diplomatic lingo—but the gist of it was that someone was asking for the highest degree of confidentiality.

The writer hadn't signed the letters by hand. They had neatly typed their signature at the bottom of the page:

Ambassador Stormwind, Clan of the Osprey
United Nations Embassy—The Morning Land

My first thought was something along the lines of: *Stormwind? You have to be joking! Which member of the flower–power generation got to name this kid?*

Then it hit me.
No, it couldn't be. Could it?

15

I let out a laugh. Birch looked at me, eyebrows raised in query. "Captain, we just got a memo...from a Pegasus! Did he send the letter as well?"

"Not sure," Birch replied. "Your letter didn't come with a return address."

A glistening mass of purple wax held the flap of the large, cream–colored envelope shut. Birch leaned across the desk and handed me a letter opener. I used its sharp edge to break the seal.

The rich scent of wild blackberries filled the room as bits of wax crumbled away. The flap came open. The paper inside felt like fine, stiff cloth.

I took out the letter, unfolded it, and held it in trembling hands.

CHAPTER FIVE

I read the message over twice to make sure I understood it. Wordlessly, I handed the letter over for Captain Birch to read.

Greetings and Salutations Mr. Derek Ridder:
I received your summons this week past. I find that your plight has touched me deeply. I shall come to your aid.
I look forward to the day that we stand shoulder to shoulder against those who would cause you harm.
Very Truly Yours,
Tavia, Daughter of the Warder of Cavilad
The City of Seven Bells
Province of Cavilad
The Morning Land

"What do you make of it?" Birch asked.

"I'm not sure. The large block letters reminds me of when I visited Rachel's elementary school. Like a kid's handwriting."

"That could be a clue as to the age of whoever wrote this. 'Daughter of the Warder'? What grown woman signs a letter like that?"

"Maybe women in the Morning Land sign everything from their letters to their alimony checks that way."

"Or maybe this woman, this girl, doesn't have full command of our language," Birch pointed out. "What's this 'summons' she's talking about?"

And then something caught my eye. A second, tattered piece of paper lay at the bottom of the envelope. I carefully removed it with two fingers and turned the paper over. I let out a sharp exhale. The careful lettering carried the unmistakable scent of Crayola crayons.

This is a note for my uncle Derek.
He is brave and protects us and my famly.
I love him verrrry much and He
needs your help fighting monsters.

Fine examples of crayon art decorated each corner. A bright yellow sun rising over the mountains hung at ten o' clock, my house at two. A police badge nestled in the bottom left. And at the bottom right, Rachel had drawn a person, almost a stick figure, really.

The picture showed a man in a blue uniform. I suppose that it looked as much like me as one could expect from a crayon portrait. Rachel had drawn me as big and strong. But my mouth was a dead black line and my eyes looked very sad.

* * *

The motor pool had lent out the last spare cruiser. So I took a mud–and–bug spattered Ford Ranger pickup that had originally been assigned to our K–9 patrol. When it rained, the upholstery would start to smell charmingly like wet dog.

When I got to the Mayor's Residence in Hancock Park, the rent–a–cop guards buzzed me upstairs to a waiting room outside the mayor's office. I made it up to the top of the stairs when the door opened. A tall, sallow–faced man stepped through and saw me. He looked me up and down for a moment, then spoke over his shoulder in a voice both crisp and cold.

"He's here, Tavia."

"We're almost done," came the reply. "Ask him to wait just a minute, please."

I couldn't see into the room, but I heard the words well enough. Tavia—I mentally noted that the first syllable of her name was pronounced so that it rhymed with 'save'—didn't sound like a little girl. She had the voice of a woman in her mid–twenties. If she'd been American, I'd have guessed that she was a blue–eyed, cornsilk blonde from someplace like Nebraska. One with long, shapely legs that did justice to a tight pair of jeans.

"You're going to have to wait."

The sallow–faced man's words shook me out of my reverie. He wore a charcoal–colored suit and tie with gold cufflinks. He also looked pretty well muscled under the suit. But given the dark bags that hung under his cold gray eyes, he hadn't been sleeping much lately.

"Yeah." My voice returned his words with the same degree of warmth he'd given me. "I heard the first time around."

His hand shot out. "I'm Federal Agent Coombes."

"Detective Derek Ridder, LAPD," I replied. I realized as I shook his hand that he was what we gym rats called 'damn strong'. It felt like gripping a solid oak banister. "Didn't catch which agency you worked for, Coombes."

"That's because I don't throw it out to everybody, Detective Ridder."

Great. Another Fed who thought he was a tough guy. Though with that grip, this one actually had a case to make.

"Okay," I said, deciding to play along a little while longer. "Mind if I ask how you figure in all of this?"

"Tavia's a friend to the ambassador of the Morning Land. She's a high–profile foreign national on U.S. soil, one that needs watching."

"I'm sure you never miss a thing with those peepers of yours. Nice. Bet she feels really safe."

"My job isn't to keep her safe. It's not like this one can't defend herself." He gave me an ugly smile through his teeth. "But it's not up to me anymore. Looks like you wanted the job, you have it."

What job?

19

The question almost escaped my lips when the door opened a second time. The mayor of Los Angeles, a well–tanned man with a wiry frame, stepped into the room with a big smile on his face and approached us.

"She'll see you now," he said, and he motioned to my new best friend, Agent Coombes. "Let's go. She wants to speak with the Detective alone."

Coombes didn't break eye contact with me until he'd gone down the stairs. I turned away and walked into the mayor's office. Sunlight streamed in through the room's window and it took a second for my eyes to adjust to the brightness.

"Hello, Derek Ridder," Tavia said, in that same pretty, feminine voice. "I've come a long way to meet you."

"The pleasure's all mine, Tavia," I replied.

I was just about to welcome her to Los Angeles when my brain finally caught up to my mouth. My voice died in my throat.

Tavia had a mane of long, cornsilk–blonde hair. Her eyes held the dark, icy blue of a Nordic lake. I guess you could say she had nice legs as well, all four of them. They ended in cloven hooves glinting with the same glossy sheen as the spiral wonder that graced her forehead. I blinked, but the vision didn't go away.

Tavia, the Daughter of the Warder of Cavilad, was a Unicorn.

CHAPTER SIX

I'd wager that most of us have had one time in our lives where we've scolded ourselves for sounding utterly stupid. Especially when you knew that you needed to be at the top of your game.

I certainly won't forget the first time I met Tavia. Unfortunately, this was one of those times which fell smack in the middle of 'utterly stupid' territory. In my defense, nobody had told me I'd be having a nice midday chat with a creature that looked like an extra from the cast of *My Little Pony* or *My Friend Flicka*.

"The pleasure is all mine, Tavia," I said. I found myself staring for a couple seconds. When my eyeballs had processed the image and my brain completed its de–icing procedure, I finished by saying: "You're a unicorn!"

She blinked. "Yes," she said slowly, "I am indeed."

I wasn't sure how to read her expression, but I think it registered between surprised and amused. I decided to try and right myself by asking if she'd just arrived, or if she'd been in Southern California for a while.

"How long...uh, how long have you been—"

"Been a unicorn? All my life."

Her tail flicked, once. I looked at her dark blue eyes more carefully. Definitely amused.

I cleared my throat.

"Uh, let's start over." She canted her head to the side, eyes not leaving mine. "It's a pleasure to meet you, Tavia. I'm sorry if I reacted poorly right then. I didn't mean to stare. It's just that no one told me that you were..."

I groped helplessly for a word. She came in to save me.

"An equine."

"An equine," I agreed, with a slight nod and a smile of discovery. She was scoring all the points so far in this conversation, but I was already getting a sense of who and what she was. Tavia had a sense of humor, a sense of compassion, and not only did she know English, she knew some basic Latin as well. "All your letter said was that you were from the Morning Land. And I have to be honest, I had no idea that anyone here had sent a 'summons' to you."

"I thought that might be the case."

"Then if you don't mind me asking," I said carefully, "Why did you come?"

She looked away and tapped her right forehoof on the floor three times. I realized that she was thinking. Perhaps deciding what to say.

"My people are quite different from yours." I sensed that she was also being careful with her reply. "Many of us live by a concept that I'm not sure exists in your world. We call it *amor fati.*"

I shook my head. Again, it sounded like she had said something Latin, but that was all I could make out.

"It means 'to love one's fate'," she explained. "It's a way of life in which one sees everything that happens, even suffering and loss, as something good, something to embrace."

I carefully kept my expression neutral. There had been an awful lot that had happened to me in the last three years that I wouldn't have exactly called good. An awful lot that I would never, ever, willingly embrace.

"In other words, I believe that the power of what we call 'fate' brought me here," Tavia continued. "Your niece's message should never have reached me. There was no way that it should have even gotten to New York. I saw the envelope that arrived at the U.N. She'd drawn a square on the upper right corner and labeled it 'Rachel's Stamp'."

"Rachel understands about stamps, but she doesn't know where I keep mine," I said, suppressing a chuckle. "I guess she thought the matter urgent enough that she just decided to create one of her own."

"And your people's couriers decided to take it? Is that normal?"

"No, it's not. I mean, I know that they'll take letters that kids put out in December for Santa Claus. But to the United Nations? Never heard that one."

"And yet, Rachel's summons got to the U.N., where it was then sent on to me. It is a simple message, surrounded by pictures showing a pleasant land, a symbol of order, and a suffering man. You, I believe."

I swallowed. "Yes, it is."

"But above all, the summons told of a hero who would be overwhelmed by evil were he not sent aid. Given my sire's station, how could I refuse?"

"Sire's station? I'm sorry, Tavia, but I'm not sure how that fits into all this."

"Another difference between our peoples." Tavia's tail made a second silent swish through the air. "In the Morning Land, we adopt our sire's—our father's—named position and duties as our own."

I considered that for a moment. It was different, give her that.

"As the Warder of Cavilad, my father has a duty to guard and protect," she continued. "I am so charged as well. So long as it is a worthy cause, I am allowed leave to defend all who fall under the shadow of evil."

"Our duties are much the same, then. Only we say, *'To protect and serve'.*"

"So we are in agreement, Derek Ridder," she said, adding what sounded like a pleased little nicker. "And like an uncouth filly, I have talked for too long. It is your turn."

"My turn?"

She dipped her horn in acknowledgement. "Your turn to tell me of this evil that Rachel spoke of."

So I did.

I told Tavia about my friend, Dorian Martinez. What happened during the terrible night at the TomKat. I told her every little detail I could remember about the man in the black duster. As I spoke, I watched Tavia in turn. Perhaps it's a habit that all cops have. Maybe it was also due to the fact that Tavia was the most amazing creature I'd ever seen.

I didn't know a lot about horses. But on the surface, Tavia looked like she could pass for an Arabian—similar to the ones I'd seen used for the smaller kids at the local farms. She had a clever–looking face, broad forehead, and a finely chiseled muzzle that dipped elegantly like the turned up nose of a pretty girl. Her large, scoop–shaped ears flicked with her moods and rotated to catch my words as I spoke.

For an earthly horse she was small. I suspected that she was only slightly larger than a pony. I stood six-foot-four, and my eyes were level with the tip of her horn. Of course, Tavia had much more articulation in her face than a regular equine. She also had eyebrows, ones that could rise as high as the stray strands of forelock that tumbled down her face.

She had a deep chest, a short, level back, and a golden, high–set tail with the same silky texture as her mane, plus a hint of curl at the end. Her coat was a shade or two darker than her golden mane and flowing tail, which made her what I was pretty sure was called a 'palomino'.

Her legs shaded into what I later found out were called 'socks'. Her forelegs shifted from gold to pale white above her cloven hooves, while the socks on her hind legs were midnight black, and rose slightly higher than the white pair.

It was the smallest details I found the most interesting. I wouldn't have expected a unicorn to have personal adornments, but to my surprise, she did. Her right shoulder sported a black squiggle of a tattoo. And the small flashes of color I saw in her mane were actually marble–sized red, blue, and green beads.

They had been cleverly threaded into her hair about three inches up from the end.

And when Tavia looked at me, her eyes met mine directly. Earthly horses couldn't do that—their eyes were widely spaced, for better peripheral vision.

Having eyes in the front of the head, like humans, or bears, or wolves—that meant something else. Binocular vision meant depth perception. It meant that Tavia, no matter her initial appearance as a horse, was actually a predator. Tavia wasn't the cuddly, romantic creature seen on medieval tapestries and new-age postcards.

She was a fighting creature, designed for combat.

I concluded my story and fell silent. Tavia regarded me, and her deep blue eyes took on a cold glitter.

"I know who murdered your friend. He is one of the most dangerous men in all the Morning Land. Would you like to know how to hurt him? *Badly?* Because I can show you how."

Michael Angel

Chapter Seven

"The man with the black duster is a warlock. A man who wields magic as a weapon. And he is the former ruler of the petty realms to the north, the kingdoms that make up what we call the Red March. "His birth name is Sir William Teach."

William Teach. I rolled that name around in my head for a couple seconds. To my mind, a person named 'Bill Teach' was someone who coached the local high school basketball team. Someone who got a little loud from drinking too many six–packs of Bud Light. But it also sounded like a guy who you wouldn't mind inviting over for a Sunday barbeque.

It certainly wasn't the name of a man who would kill a cop.

Tavia gazed out the window. From the tone in her voice, she was trying to work through old memories. Bad ones, at that.

"On the first day of the season of High Tend, refugees from the March told us that a tyrant had risen, forging an empire out of the old human kingdoms."

"William Teach," I said grimly, and Tavia nodded. "What did you do?"

"My father the Warder sent me to spy out the land, see if there was anything to be learned. No one, myself included, took Teach's challenge to our power seriously." She hung her head. "We were badly mistaken. I found a huge army of knights and men–at–arms. And Teach could do much more than swing a sword. He had the magical ability to dominate and enslave the will of others."

I leaned forward to speak, but changed my mind at the last second. I needed her to finish her story. She saw me hesitate, and then nodded acknowledgement.

"I see you want to know how I resisted him. Obviously, if I hadn't, we wouldn't be talking today. It was the hardest thing I've ever had to do in my life. It wasn't because I was a unicorn. We learned that the hard way."

"I don't like the sound of that."

"It sounded more than unpleasant to a lot of people. Worse was to come. Teach struck a deal with the *Tengan*." Tavia almost spat the name. She pawed the carpet with one hoof, then continued. "The Tengan are demons, demons who have invaded our world from ancient times. The day war came, the Tengan horde streamed up from the south, burning and destroying our lands as they came. And Teach's army invaded from the north. My people, the humans and creatures allied with us, were caught between the anvil and the hammer."

"But you won the war. You fought off both Teach and the demons."

"At a terrible price, Derek Ridder." Her voice dropped. "Thousands passed under the sod that day. Teach used his power to hold many of my friends while he drew their life from them with cold steel. He only fled when he saw that his army had been scattered and broken. And we thought that we'd seen the last of him these many years."

"Until now," I finished for her. "So, you and I are the only ones that were able to break his hold. Why?"

"This is something that I wish to know as well," Tavia took a few steps forward. I saw my reflection in the liquid blue of her eyes. "You and I must share something in common. Something that allowed us to pass through the warlock's fire unscathed, while others were consumed."

Tavia stopped. Her nostrils flared, and she drew back a step, head raised. She snorted.

"What's wrong?"

"Your clothes, Derek Ridder. They have a scent about them, a scent that troubles me. Something evil. Quickly now, is there anything special about what you wear?"

"No, not that I know of. And just call me Derek, please. I just showered and threw these on. I'm not even wearing cologne."

She cocked her head at me again. "Derek, these clothes are not the ones that Rachel depicted you wearing in the summons."

"That's right. Rachel drew me wearing my dress blues, the uniform cops wear on the street. But if you're a detective, you sometimes go plain clothed."

"What you have on now," Tavia persisted, indicating my long-sleeved shirt, jacket, and slacks with a sweep of her horn. "These are your 'plains clothes' that you wear at work?"

"Actually, no. Those are in my gym bag at the station. These are some of the things I've been wearing..." My voice trailed off.

A feeling of alarm fluttered in my chest. I felt a sudden chill.

"These are some of the things I've been wearing around the house." My voice grew raised and strained. I couldn't help it. "Tavia, please tell me what the *hell* you think is going on."

She raised her head. "I need to see your house. Immediately."

"Of course. Um, I don't know if you're going to be able to travel in my pickup. You could stand in the truck bed, but I don't know how you could hang on if I made a sharp turn."

Tavia surprised me with a neigh that was equal parts laugh and derision. "That won't be necessary. I know where your house is located, and I can travel swiftly on my own if I'm not concerned about being seen. Still, you should get there shortly before me."

"How are you going to travel—"

"Derek, *please*. I'll explain it later if you like. Right now I have the feeling that something terrible is about to happen. Will you trust me?"

I hesitated. The world hadn't given me much reason to trust anyone lately, let alone someone who looked like they belonged on the set of *Fantasia*. But I'd been a detective for far too long to base trust on appearance alone. I believed in the power of the hunch. I nodded curtly and Tavia dipped her horn to me.

I dashed downstairs and out to the parking lot. For a few sickeningly long seconds, I hurriedly fumbled with the Ranger's unfamiliar key fob. I flung the door open, jammed the key home in the ignition.

The motor whined in complaint like a sick dog. I ignored it as I gunned the motor out of the parking lot. I swerved around a pair of slow–moving cars. The Ford jolted as it bounced through a pothole.

The dashboard switch for the roof's light bar had a wedge of duct tape slapped over it. Scribble on the tape read *Under Repair*. So, I pounded the truck's horn with my palm again and again. More traffic ahead. Snap decision. I slung the wheel to the right and powered through the emergency lane.

I dug out my cell phone and speed-dialed my home number. I heard the phone ring over the desperate pounding of my heart.

The phone rang four times.

"Hello," my voice said. "You've reached the Ridder residence—"

I jabbed the pound sign to skip the message.

"Rachel, this is your uncle. Pick up the phone."

No one picked up. I spoke again, almost screaming into the phone. I wanted to make sure that she could hear me over *SpongeBob SquarePants* or whatever the hell she might be watching.

"This is an emergency, Rachel! Pick up *now!*"

The line remained silent.

CHAPTER EIGHT

I hung up and speed–dialed the number of Jenny Kim, Rachel's best friend in my neighborhood.

"Hello?" I recognized the young girl's voice as Jenny's.

"Hey, Jenny, it's Derek Ridder," I said, trying to keep my voice calm. "Is Rachel there? It's *really* important for me to speak with her."

"She's not here, Mr. Ridder," she said, in a sing–song way. "She went back home for lunch."

"That's nice," I winced as the Ranger rolled through another pothole with a bone–jarring jolt. "When did she head home?"

"I dunno, I guess about a half–hour ago." She stopped and said, "Are you okay, Mr. Ridder? You sound funny."

"Oh, I'm fine. But tell your mom and anyone else there to stay inside for now. Cop stuff, you know?"

"Sure thing," she said, though from the tone in her voice, I could practically see her rolling her eyes. "Bye now."

I hung up and scraped the curb as I barreled around a sharp bend in the road. People stared at the rear of the truck as I sped away. I didn't care. I was getting the same sick feeling in my stomach as the night at the TomKat. Jenny lived only four houses down the street. No way would Rachel take half an hour to get home.

I wrenched the wheel around and accelerated up the steeply sloped road. My house was at the top of the first hill. I grabbed for the pickup's radio.

"Eagle's Nest, this is Detective Ridder, I have a code eight!" I shouted, "Nest, come in!"

For a second I thought I heard someone reply. But as I crested the hill, the radio blasted back wall–to–wall static. I checked the cell phone. Again, it picked up no signal. I gripped the steering wheel, knuckles white with tension. Visions of the TomKat flared in my mind as I pulled up to the house.

Everything looked quiet as I shut the engine off.

I checked the compartments in the Ranger's cabin. The cracked–vinyl cargo bins yielded balls of dog hair and a mummified box of nicotine–laced chewing gum. No weapons or ammunition. I hadn't really expected to find much, but having a shotgun on hand would've steadied my nerves.

I left the keys in the ignition as I got out. I pulled my semi from my shoulder holster, held it at the ready. Alert for a dozen kinds of dirty tricks, I jogged up towards the front door.

I noticed a couple of things out of the corner of my eye. Little things. Things that made the icy feeling in my chest drop another few degrees.

The wooden gate to the side yard had been left ajar.

The front door lay half–open.

"Rachel?" I called.

I held my Glock out. Carefully, I gave the front door a push. It swung open with a loud, asthmatic creak.

"Rachel, I'm home early today, come give your Uncle a hug, okay? We—"

I froze as I was about to step on the doormat. The patch of bare soil that ran up the side of the path towards the door had a footprint in it. A deep, heavy print.

No, not a footprint. A *paw* print. Like the track of a giant wolf.

Tiny indentations extended an inch in front of each toe. If it was a wolf, it was one with a gigantic set of claws.

I entered my living room. Nothing was out of place. I went to the kitchen next. Again, nothing. Nothing that should've instilled in me the sense of dread that prickled my forearms into white–fleshed pincushions.

"Rachel?" I turned to face the hallway that led to the bedrooms. "Rachel, come out, you're worrying me."

"Uncle!" I heard a high–pitched voice call, "Uncle!"

"Rachel!" I cried with relief. "Where are you?"

A hulking, low–slung shape padded out of my room. It came into the half–light of the hallway. My nose filled with an earthy, musky smell. The smell of a freshly dug grave.

I felt my stomach tighten as if my guts were in a wine press.

The thing that came out of my room had the height and bulk of an Irish wolfhound. Its shoulders brushed the sides of the hallway as it came towards me. It was covered in matted brown and orange–striped fur, as coarse as hog bristle. The creature had a blunt muzzle and a flat forehead like a badger's. A pair of beetle–browed black eyes glared at me. The neck sloped up to a huge hump of muscle over its forelegs. Each of its large feet ended in a quadruple set of dull black claws.

A loud creak off to my side. I backed up against the refrigerator in horror as a second dog–wolf thing padded through the front door. It stood in the middle of my living room like it had all the right in the world to be there.

The creature actually grinned at me. I saw with a sick shock that its jaws opened as far back as its ears. Needle–sharp teeth lined its mouth, all the way down.

Its muzzle worked with a short snapping motion. Instead of a bark, it made a human sound. It wasn't speech, not exactly, but it did damn good imitation of a person speaking a single word.

"Uncle!" it said, in the perfectly mimicked voice of a little girl. "Uncle!"

And then I heard a long, loud scream. The creatures' ears perked up. I gasped. That was no imitation—it was Rachel's voice screaming in terror. A loud clatter from Rachel's bedroom. The heavy thud of a piece of furniture being flipped over.

Another scream, and I saw a *third* dog–creature come out behind the first one in the hallway.

It had Rachel in its mouth.

It gripped her by the neck of the jacket she was wearing. She hung in its grip, shivering and whimpering. The toes of her sneakers dangled above the floor. Her eyes were blank and wild with panic.

The first two creatures began to advance on me. They snarled in stereo. Their snouts rippled as they exposed their teeth.

"William Teach. Bids good–day to you," the one in front said, its muzzle twitching as it spat out the words.

And then something surprising happened. My fear went away. The searing red–hot taste of anger filled my mouth. Anger that these things could just enter my house. That they'd obviously been casing my place, had been why Tavia had smelled something evil.

That they could come in here and threaten my niece.

"You goddamn monsters," I gritted. My voice shook with fury. "Try dancing with someone who can go a couple rounds with you."

The first one leaped at me. The things were hellishly fast. Much faster than anything their size should have been. I swung around as it came at me. With a horrible flex of its head, it got its mouth around my right hand.

Pain exploded along my arm as crushing jaws bit down.

CHAPTER NINE

Warm stickiness cascaded down the back of my fingers. I should have lost my hand right there. But even in my half–crazed state I realized the damned wolf thing had bitten as hard as it could—into the case of my Glock.

I squeezed the trigger.

The back of the creature's head exploded in fleshy gobbets. Scent of hot iron and singed fur. I tried to pull the Glock out of the thing's mouth. The gun caught on the teeth that clenched it in a death grip.

Another snarl, this one off to the left. The creature in the living room sprang at me.

The living room window exploded inward in a loud *crash!* Broken wood and glass showered the carpet. Tavia dove through, trailing sparkling glass shards like a golden comet. She landed, then took a great bound forward. She held her head low, eyes intent on her target.

Tavia speared the creature in mid–leap on her horn. A blood–curdling howl erupted from its throat as it died. The final wolf–thing took in what happened. Even Rachel's numbed eyes widened as she saw Tavia standing amidst the ruins of the living room. The creature turned and bolted for the front door. It still held Rachel in its mouth.

"No!" I shouted.

With a final effort, I pulled my gun free. I took a shot at the creature. My bullet notched the tip of its tail as it fled.

"What the hell are those things?" I demanded. Tavia shook herself free from the animal that she'd impaled with her horn.

"Yena," she said breathlessly. "We have to catch that one."

I ran to the pickup. I started the motor, saw the thing—the *yena*—bounding down the hill.

"Beware!" Tavia called, as I brought the pickup around. "They're fast, and they hunt in large packs."

I mashed the gas pedal under my foot. I swung the Ranger around and onto the highway as I reached the bottom of the hill. The yena ran ahead of me by no more than thirty yards. There was no way I could lose it now, I was sure.

Then the damned thing began to pull away from me. The sleeves of Rachel's jacket flapped madly in the wind. I stole a glance at the speedometer. The needle passed fifty miles per hour, and the creature was leaving me in the dust.

I shifted, gunned the engine again. Suddenly, the sound of hooves on asphalt clattered in my ear like a flurry of hailstones against a slab of wood. Tavia blazed past my driver's side window to close with the yena.

I had the truck up to sixty now. Both Tavia and our quarry were still ahead. I blinked, but the speedometer stayed stubbornly pegged to the same spot.

Was this even possible? Had any canine—or equine—been able to run at these speeds? Probably not. But now I was dealing with beings like Tavia who were magical. The normal rules just didn't apply.

I coaxed the Ranger up to seventy. I tried the radio again out of desperation. It actually worked this time.

"Reading you, Detective Ridder. This is Eagle's Nest," said the dispatcher. They'd been told that I was driving the K–9 unit's old vehicle. "Come again, unit King–nine?"

I released the transmit button for a moment. My mind raced. Which police code did this situation fall under?

A 10–89 was an 'animal complaint', but that didn't quite cut it. No, this was a kidnapping. No matter if the culprit had two legs or four.

"Code eight. I repeat, code eight. I have a 10–96 in progress. An assisting unit and I are in pursuit. Require immediate assistance."

"King–nine, what is your twenty?"

"Eastbound on highway 136, between Echo Canyon and Topanga."

"Copy that, King–nine, units one–three, one–four, and one–five en route." There was a pause, and he continued. "King–nine, identify assisting unit."

Oh, great. This should be interesting.

I watched in awe as Tavia's hooves moved in a blur. Her mane and tail streamed out behind her like a pair of golden flags caught in gale–force winds. Her blue eyes narrowed to mere slits as she leaned into the run. Her hooves struck a shower of crimson sparks on the midnight black of the highway asphalt.

"Eagle's Nest, assisting unit is a palomino unicorn," I said, feeling foolish as I said it. "Please advise that on approach, the unicorn is an *assisting* unit."

The dispatcher went silent for a second.

"Uh, King–nine, please repeat."

"You heard me loud and clear the first time! Dispatch, alert approaching units of the assist, then inform Captain Birch. He is aware of the situation."

Maybe I was stretching things here. But after all, Captain Birch did know about the message from the Morning Land. He could probably put two and two together.

The yena veered off the highway and onto a frontage road. I dropped the radio. Yanked the wheel to the right. The Ranger tilted dangerously to one side.

We'd been doing over eighty–five while I'd been on the radio. But now, I was quickly catching up. The creature was tiring. So was Tavia. Her sides gleamed with sweat.

The suburban streets gave way to an open-space preserve. Fields of waist-tall grass, now golden in the dry summer sun, lined both sides of the road. Construction signs dotted the lane ahead. I shifted down to a slower speed. Up ahead, our lane disappeared as orange cones and cement dividers shifted the traffic over to the left.

I scanned the road for oncoming traffic as I pulled within twenty–five yards of the yena and its precious cargo. Tavia put on a final burst of speed. She ran side by side with the doglike creature.

Then the yena did what Tavia had been waiting for.

It leaped to clear one of the cement construction dividers. That's when the unicorn struck. So quick, I almost missed it. What I saw almost made my heart stop.

I thought Tavia's horn had only been sharp at the tip. That would've made it a good stabbing weapon but little else. Apparently the horn was sharp along the entire length. She didn't jab at the yena as it reached the top of its leap. Instead, she made a surgically precise, horizontal slash.

Tavia hamstrung the monster in mid–stride.

The yena let out a yowl. Its hindquarters collapsed. The unicorn dove in and to the right. She caught Rachel's jacket in her teeth as the yena let go.

Tavia brought her right hind hoof down on the monster's back. A *snap!* like broken kindling. She stiffened her forelegs, skidded on the loose road gravel, and slid to a halt.

I gasped and stood on the brake pedal. I thanked the powers that be that the truck had antilock brakes. Otherwise, I'd have smashed Rachel and Tavia into pink and golden paste.

The Ranger slewed almost completely around before it finally came to a stop. Breathing hard, I threw open the door of the cab and ran towards the unicorn and my niece.

I saw movement off to the side of the road. A lot of it. Yena began to emerge from the golden field of tall, late–summer grass.

A chorus of growls rippled through the air. Tavia must've brought down their hostage courier right before he reached the safety of the pack.

And now we were in the middle of them.

CHAPTER TEN

This time I didn't hesitate.

I drew my Glock. Began firing into the pack. I dropped the first yena with a shot through its eye.

A second let out a cough as I hit it in the side. It fell to the ground in a foul–smelling heap. A third one yelped and limped off, holding one of its paws high.

The pack wavered, trying to assess how much of a threat I was. Tavia took advantage of that moment and shoved Rachel at me.

Hurriedly, I took my niece from the unicorn. Tavia whirled to face the next onslaught. Rachel's hands pressed into my sides like little blocks of ice. She gasped, weeping and shivering as she clung to me.

"Rachel, listen," I said firmly. "You have to do what I tell you so your uncle and his friend can get us out of this."

"O…okay…" she whispered. Her teeth began to chatter.

"We gotta play piggyback ride right now. You have to hold on to me, no matter what, okay?" I helped her up. She snuffled agreement and I felt her hands lock around my neck.

Tavia whirled into a blur of motion. She parried attack after attack. She bled from a cut to her ear, a slash on her side, but she didn't seem badly injured.

Three yena lay in the dirt around her. She blocked a lunge by one on her left. Slashed the legs out from under one to her right. With a bone–shattering kick from her hind leg, she caved in another yena's head.

And they still didn't back off. One leaped at her from behind. I put two bullets into it. The yena collapsed on the side of the road. Tavia slowly retreated towards us. Her pretty tail lay matted in red. I hoped that it was all yena blood.

"Back to the truck," I said to her. Her undamaged ear flicked and rotated to hear me. "Help is on the way."

"Be better to fight with something at our rear," she agreed. Her voice sounded tired, out of breath.

Tavia and I retreated, step by step. The yena matched us pace for pace. A strange, tense standoff. The four remaining yena didn't want us to escape. But none of them wanted to be the next to take a bullet or a slash from Tavia's horn.

I kept going back until I felt the sun-warmed rear bumper of the pickup against my slacks. Rachel's hands gripped my neck like a rubbery vise. Her gasping echoed in my ear. I smelled the tartness of lemonade on her breath.

One of the yena made a lunge. Tavia slashed it across the face. Howling, the creature whirled about and ran off.

A second tried to get around me to snap at Rachel. I put a bullet in its chest. It went down, paws twitching.

That was when I heard the gun's chamber click empty.

I didn't have a spare magazine. But the yena didn't know that. I kept the Glock pointed at the remaining two canines and they stayed at a distance.

"Tavia, if you cover me, I think I can make it to the truck's cabin." Right then, another chorus of growls sounded behind us. I glanced quickly over my shoulder. A second pack of at least ten more yena approached the front of the truck in a mass.

"Nix that idea," she said. "I can take them. You must handle these."

"Tavia, I don't—" But the unicorn was gone from my side.

I blinked stupidly for a moment. Of course, the unicorn didn't know I was out of ammo either.

I wasn't sure I could get to the truck's cabin in time. The remaining two yena snarled at us from less than a dozen yards. The damned things were so fast they'd be on us in a second. Instead, I kept the gun pointed at them and carefully climbed into the bed of the pickup.

"Rachel, when I crouch down, you have to let go. Your uncle has to find something to hold these monsters off, okay?"

"Okay," she replied tonelessly. She slid off my back as I crouched for a second. The two yena surged toward us with hideous eagerness. I brought the Glock back up.

But they didn't stop. Not completely. They slowed to a creeping step-by-step. One paw, then another. Trying to get close enough to leap at the same time.

Right then, I learned about another of Tavia's talents. With a clatter of hooves on metal, Tavia sprang onto the Ranger's hood. The unicorn stood there a second, looking like an outsized hood ornament. She curled her head around to her flank as if nibbling at an itch.

She bit into one of the green beads wrapped securely in her mane. With a quick flex of her jaw, she yanked it off and took it in her mouth.

Tavia bit down, hard. I heard the *crunch!* as if she'd bitten into a piece of hard candy. With a flick of her head, Tavia sent the bead sailing into the midst of the pack at the front of the pickup.

The bead detonated in an explosion of blue fire. The four yena closest to the impact yowled as their coats broke out in flames. Stench of burning fur and yena soiling themselves in fear hung in the air like a foul-smelling fogbank. Blue sparks arced from creature to creature, lighting up the yena's greasy fur wherever the current touched.

Tavia leaped down into their midst. She stabbed with her horn. Lashed out with her hooves at the enemies around her.

That was when the last two yena on my side decided to rush us.

I hurled the empty Glock at the closest yena. I managed to bean it on the nose. It yelped and ran off. The last one was on us in a flash.

It clambered over the tailgate. Put its two forepaws into the truck bed. Rachel screamed again as its muzzle worked. Making that awful imitation of a human voice.

"Kill!" it cried gleefully. "Kill! Kill!"

I reached down blindly, groping for something I could use.

Anything I could use.

The awful sound of claws raking on bare metal made me cringe. The thing's hind paws scrabbled for purchase on the rear bumper. It lunged at us with a snarl.

All I could see was its quivering red maw, ringed with razor–sharp teeth.

CHAPTER ELEVEN

Toothy white jaws snapped shut just short of my face.

In another second the yena would be in the truck bed with us. My hands closed around a pole of metal. I lifted whatever I'd blindly grabbed. At the far end of my makeshift weapon lay a wide metal spade, labeled *The Poop Scoop Patrol.*

The yena finally got its footing. It lunged forward, teeth bared. Smacked into the head of the spade with a muffled *whump!* The creature fell on its hindquarters with a coughing snarl.

I stood up. Raised the scooper high. Then brought the spade down on the yena's head as hard as I could.

It yowled and tried to rise. I brought the weapon down again. And again. My vision went red. Its howls turned into sweet music for me as I beat it down.

"It's over, Derek." Tavia stood by the side of the pickup. She was grimy and smudged with blood, but she was radiant. "You won."

I dropped the spade. The yena lay crushed beneath it.

"Yes, I did," I said, in a parched voice. "We did."

Tavia nodded, then looked at Rachel. My niece still clung to the leg of my pants. But she gave Tavia a look of pure wonder.

"Are you all right, Rachel?" Tavia asked.

"Yeah, I'm okay," Rachel replied, shyly. "You...you're really a real unicorn, aren't you?"

"All her life," I said quietly.

I heard sirens approach in the distance. My legs began to shake. I sat down, and Rachel snuggled into me. Without a second thought, I put my arms around her, held her as close as I could.

* * *

Later that evening, Officer Lynn Macedo tried to talk with me. But her eyes kept drifting over my left shoulder, towards where Tavia stood in my dining room, head lowered and talking quietly with Rachel.

"You're sure you don't want us to stay? Ray and I could—"

"For the last time, we really don't need it. Tavia says she has the situation well in hand, and I believe her."

Lynn glanced over my shoulder once more. Her face softened, and her lips pursed in a little 'O'. I couldn't help but turn and look.

Rachel had thrown her arms around Tavia's neck. She gave Tavia a bunch of little-girl kisses and stroked the unicorn's golden mane. The sight was sweet enough to send anyone watching into instant diabetic shock.

"Maybe I could—"

"Thanks, but no thanks, Lynn. Just tell Birch that I'll be back in tomorrow."

"Two days from now," Tavia said. She raised her head and Rachel simply shifted to holding one of the unicorn's sleek golden forelegs.

"But—" Lynn began.

"Two. Days." Tavia repeated firmly.

The unicorn's voice remained gentle, but it didn't invite argument. Lynn nodded resignedly and bid me goodnight. I closed the door and watched the pair of cruisers pull out of our driveway. One of the cars rode low. The remains of the two yena we'd killed in the house had been securely bagged or wrapped up in what was left of the rug from my living room.

I wrestled a sheet of plywood that I'd gotten from the garage into place over the smashed living room window. It took me a couple minutes to nail and duct-tape it into submission. I turned back to the kitchen, saw it empty. My breath caught for a second, until I heard Tavia and Rachel's voices coming from my niece's bedroom.

I went over to the bedroom's open doorway. Rachel was happily showing off her stuffed animal menagerie to her new equine friend.

"See, this is 'Pig'," Rachel said, then helpfully added, "He's a pig."

"So I see," Tavia said, completely straight-faced.

"And my bestest friend, Super Pickle the Zebra!" Rachel brandished the stuffed toy so that Tavia could see where she'd tied a red-and-white towel around the zebra's neck to make a simple terrycloth cape. "He fights all kinds of bad guys with his super stripey powers, and he can fly!"

"Really?" Now Tavia's expression was one of sheer amusement. "And which of his powers lead people to call him 'Super Pickle'?"

"Well...none of his powers, really."

Tavia arched one delicate eyebrow. "Then why do you call him that?"

"'Cause it's his name." Rachel said, as if it were the most obvious thing in the world.

"Well, yes," Tavia pressed on. "But why is 'Super Pickle' his name?"

"It just is!"

"But…" Tavia shook her head. "That's not right."

"What isn't right?" Rachel made a puzzled little frown.

All of a sudden, there was an awkward silence. Whatever had just taken place in the innocent chat with my niece had thrown the unicorn for a complete loop. I cleared my throat softly, breaking the quiet.

"Maybe you and Tavia can talk about this later. It's very late, and it's way past your bedtime."

My niece rolled her eyes, which was always a bad sign when I was trying to get her ready for bed.

"But I can't go to bed! I want to stay up with Tavia, I don't feel tired at all!"

I had to admit that Rachel had a point. Getting kidnapped, then rescued by a creature that looked like every little girl's horsey dreams—I'd probably be pretty charged up as well.

"You know," said Tavia, "In the Morning Land, we sing to our yearlings when they can't sleep."

Rachel brightened. "You're going to do that for me?"

She leapt into bed and pulled the blankets up around herself, though she looked more excited and wide-awake than ever.

Tavia gave a little nicker, a sound I now understood was her version of a laugh. "In a manner of speaking. The best sleepy-time music is in *Thari*—the language of the dryads. What you call wood spirits."

Rachel settled into her pillow, eyes wide. Tavia closed her eyes, canted her head forward slightly. Her horn moved in a slow pattern in the air above the bed. She took a breath, and then…

I'm not sure you could call it singing, but it was strange and beautiful at the same time. Tavia's voice began low, as a murmur, a pattern that echoed softly in the ear. Rachel's look of wonder turned into drowsiness. Her eyes slowly closed.

I followed suit. Tavia's rushing, murmuring tones resolved themselves into the sound of wind whispering through summer willows. It wasn't like the sound I'd heard in the air at the TomKat. And yet it was similar in the way that far-off trains can sound like distant thunder in the night.

Tavia's voice rose and fell like an autumn leaf caught in a stray breeze. Liquid, flowing, never quite pooling into individual words. And when she finally finished her song, I opened my eyes. I felt more calm and refreshed than in days.

Rachel was fast asleep.

Tavia and I stepped quietly back into the living room. The unicorn motioned to the front door with her horn.

"We need to go outside. I want to set my Wards," Tavia said. "And it would be best if you took your gun."

CHAPTER TWELVE

"Are you expecting trouble?" I asked.

"No," Tavia replied, "Just preparing for it."

I pulled back my jacket and showed her my shoulder holster. In it was my fully-loaded spare Glock. She nodded approval, and we went outside to the edge of the front yard.

Tavia curled her head to her side, nipped a red bead from her mane, and crunched it in her teeth. She scraped out a shallow hole in the ground, dropped the bead in, and then filled the hole back in with loose soil.

Next, she raised her right foreleg and flexed her cloven hoof, the way a human might bend two fingers. She traced a pattern in the dirt that looked similar to the mark that had been tattooed or branded on her right shoulder. Finally, she knelt and tapped her horn against the pattern.

She got up, and I followed her around to the side yard. The gate still stood open from earlier. I paused to scoop up a padlock from its holding box.

"What exactly are we doing?" I asked.

"The same thing you are doing right now," she replied, as I clicked the lock into place on the side-gate's handle. "These wards seal us off from any magical threat."

We came around to the back yard. Beyond my concrete patio, the yard sloped upwards towards a brush-choked ridge topped with gnarled valley oak. Tavia started up the incline. I had to lean forward and step lively to keep up with the unicorn. Her mane and tail glowed palely in the moonlight.

"I'm placing a special boundary marker at each end of your land, something we call a gyric," she continued. "The symbols on the marker have to be drawn and placed exactly, if they are to protect us at all. It's one of the guiding principles of any type of magic."

"Magic?" I asked. My voice must have sounded skeptical. As we drew closer to the top of the slope, Tavia gave me a curious look.

"Yes, I mean magic." With a wry tone, she added, "Given the fact that you're standing here talking with a unicorn, I would think you'd be more open to the idea."

She had me on that one.

"I guess I'm thinking of magic as something you *are*, not something you *do*. I guess I saw William Teach do magic as well. But it seemed like something that just came from within him, something he was."

Tavia stopped at the ridgeline and found a spot to scrape out a small hole.

"For most magic, the greater the degree of control you want, the more detailed you have to be."

The unicorn repeated her ritual. We turned and picked our way back down the hill. A key turned in my mind as I walked at her side. Specific instructions. The rules of magic.

"So, if you wanted the full benefit of magic, you couldn't just write 'I protect this place' on a gyric," I went over to the concrete step at the house's back door and knocked the dirt from the soles of my shoes. "You would have to write something like, 'I, Tavia, protect Derek Ridder's house', right?"

"That would be correct."

"Then that's why Rachel's calling her doll 'Super Pickle' confused you. In your world, everything has to have a meaningful name."

"You have it right," Tavia said, with a surprised look. "Things and people need purposeful names. As we say, names define someone from the sun-side, and from the shadow-side. Powerful spells can turn on this kind of knowledge. There is even a branch of magic called *delving* that uncovers the hidden names."

I found myself stifling a yawn. I stretched, felt the coming ache of adrenaline-drained muscles.

"Well, I think one of us should delve into some sleep. We can start doing detective stuff when the sun rises."

"I'm tired too. But we can both sleep. My wards are proof against anything that could get close enough to hurt us."

"Then I'll see what I can set up in my room for you," I said.

All of a sudden, I felt awkward again. I wanted to be a good host, but I didn't know what to do next. How the heck was the unicorn going to use my bed?

"I, uh, cleaned all the glass slivers off the living room couch. I'll just use that."

Tavia let out a full nicker.

"Really, I'm touched. But that's hardly necessary."

"I can't just let you—"

"Derek, look at me."

I did so as she continued to speak. The unicorn's irises were twin rings of deep sapphire. The effect was almost hypnotic.

"I know I look like a horse to you. You can't help but think of me as one. But I am a creature of the woods, the plains, the outdoors. I'm much more comfortable out here in the night air."

"But…" I struggled to put my feelings into words, failed. "But what if it rains?" I concluded lamely.

Tavia sighed, though in good humor.

"Do you really think that I've grown up in the wild, as a unicorn, without ever being *rained* on?"

I could hardly argue with that. I unlocked the back door. But before I went in, a thought occurred to me.

"When Officer Macedo left earlier tonight, you were pretty firm that I wouldn't be going anywhere for two days."

"Yes, I was."

"Mind if I ask why?"

"Only one reason," Tavia said, with a scrape of a hoof on the patio cement. "But it's rather important in keeping your niece alive."

CHAPTER THIRTEEN

"All right," I said, "If it concerns Rachel, I'm all ears."

"I know how William Teach operates. I believe he may try to hurt you again. Through Rachel. So we need to be especially watchful, at least for the time she remains in your care."

"If you're right, she'll remain at risk. Rachel and her mom live only a few minutes' drive from here."

Tavia nodded. "I'm hoping to reduce that risk. So long as your niece remains close to you, she'll need protection, magical and otherwise. It would seriously restrict our ability to act."

"What are you proposing, then?"

"That I use the contacts at my embassy to work with the LAPD, to put Rachel and her mother in a witness protection program. This should be done as soon as Emily returns, which will be in two days."

I sighed, then looked out into the darkness. Ran my fingers through my hair. Tavia's suggestion was the right one.

"I agree." A thought occurred to me, and I turned back to the unicorn. "But how did you know the name of Rachel's mom? And that she'd return in two days? Did you use magic to divine Emily's airline schedule?"

Tavia nickered softly in reply.

"Actually, you had Emily's name and her return date marked on the calendar hanging in your kitchen."

I blinked. Again, Tavia's tail flicked in amusement.

"Any more questions, detective?"

"Oh, no," I said, as I stepped into the house. "I can tell when I'm outmatched. 'Night, Tavia."

"Pleasant rest to you, Derek."

* * *

I awoke with a gasp.

I blinked, trying to clear the spots that danced around the edges of my sight. Put my hand out, rested it on the wrinkled sheets next to me. Leaned across the bed and rested my face on the pillow next to mine.

I inhaled, hoping against all hope that I would smell lavender, or the light scent of powder. Hoping that a trace of my wife's scent would be left. Something to convince me that the last three years weren't real.

Nothing but the scent of clean linen.

I groped my way to the bathroom. I ran the water and listlessly brushed my teeth. Even now, three years after I'd lost Beth, there were mornings when I'd wake up and think that she was just out making coffee. Each time reality came knocking, it broke something inside me anew. But the real world was here and now, wasn't it?

Wasn't it?

Yesterday's events flooded into my mind.

I almost swallowed the damned mouthwash in mid-gargle.

I dashed to the bedroom window and pulled up the blinds. The back yard lay empty, quiet. No doglike monsters prowling the patio. Certainly no palomino horses bearing spiral horns and speaking accent-free English.

Could I have just dreamt it all?

I couldn't bring myself to finish the thought for a long, breathless second. Then I cupped my hands and raised them to my nose. I smelled the bleach-like tang of the mouthwash, the mint from the toothpaste. But underneath that, the sharp scent of cordite. The smell I'd only get from practicing at the shooting range.

Or gunning down yena with my Glock.

Yesterday really *had* been real.

I set a new land-speed record into and out of the shower. I pulled a reasonably clean shirt and pair of jeans from the closet. Then followed it up with my shoulder holster before I went out into the living room.

The television flickered brightly. A lot of the outside light had been blocked by the plywood I'd placed over the remains of the window. Rachel looked up from the couch, watching cartoons while she plowed her way through a huge bowl of raisin bran.

"Afternoon!" she said happily.

"Morning, Rache," I tousled her hair as I went by.

"Nope, it's afternoon now. Tavia said to let you sleep."

"Let me sleep?"

Sure enough, the clock above the stove said that it was a little past noon. I rubbed the back of my neck with one hand as I started the coffee maker. I hadn't woken up this late since my college days.

I looked out the back window a second time. Then followed it up with a peek out the front door. Again, nothing.

"So, did you and Tavia talk about anything interesting this morning?" I asked Rachel lightly.

"Yeah, some neat stuff. She's super smart, you know, and really, really pretty for a horse. She even let me help her put her harness pack on."

"Harness pack?" I didn't recall Tavia wearing anything except her beads. "You mean, like a saddle?"

"Course not!" she said, around a mouthful of cereal. "You can't ride a unicorn, she told me that. It's kind of like a fanny pack, only she wears it around her shoulders."

"That's funny. I guess I missed the part where she brought it over."

"She didn't bring it over, the man did."

Rachel looked down. She dug her spoon into her bowl, as if searching for raisins hidden in the milk.

"The man?"

"Uh-huh. I didn't like him. I don't think Tavia likes him very much, either."

Michael Angel

CHAPTER FOURTEEN

"Rachel," I said, trying to keep my voice casual. "Who was the man?"

She shrugged. "I dunno. Tavia told me to stay inside, so I peeked around the wood you put over the window. She waited by the driveway, the man pulled up in a big black van. He got out and started talking to her."

"What did he say?"

"I couldn't hear, they were too far away." Rachel pursed her lips in thought. "I think he was getting angry, he started moving his hands like he was getting fust...fuster-ated."

"Frustrated," I said, helping her out.

"Frustrated, uh-huh. And Tavia kept shaking her head 'no'," said Rachel, as she mimicked the movement. "At the end, she stamped her front foot at him, and he stopped talking and gave her the harness pack before he left."

I heard a rustling sound in the back yard, followed by the sound of hooves on the patio cement. I opened the back door and stepped out into the midday heat. Tavia trotted over with her head held high and tail whisking briskly back and forth.

"A pleasant High Tend to you, Derek," she said, with the tiniest dip of her horn. "I've been out beating the bounds, and no one has tried to break my wards. Did you sleep well?"

"Pretty good." I checked out Tavia's new gear. It fit snugly about her body at her neck and shoulders. The pack's light brown leather had a number of slits and pockets, most held shut by rivet-like buttons. "Interesting gear you have there."

"Thank you. I let an associate through the wards so I could get it."

"Associate?"

"Well, that's how he would like to think of himself," she said, with a dark-sounding snort. "This is my harness pack. When I'm traveling, I keep this around to store small items that could be of use."

"You really are amazing. And I feel like I'm being a pretty bad host. Have you gotten a bite to eat since yesterday?"

"Night feed," she said. When she saw my puzzled look, she added, "When needed, my people can graze while they sleep."

"Oh," I said simply. It didn't make me feel any better that I'd been such a poor host as to simply offer Tavia my lawn to snack on. "I have the fixings for a Cobb salad, would you like that? No, wait—that usually has bacon and chicken breast in it, I can leave that out."

"There's no need to. "Unlike your world's equines, my digestive system can handle small amounts of meat."

I went back to the kitchen and emptied the contents of the fridge's crisper to make a triple serving of lunch. I heaped the salad on a pair of plates and a huge platter, then brought it out to the patio table. Of course, Rachel couldn't resist the opportunity to have lunch with her favorite uncle and a unicorn filly. So, I had her bring out a pair of plastic forks and some iced tea for us.

I pulled the largest bowl I could find out of the cupboard. I filled it with cold, bottled water and set it at the table for Tavia. She dipped her muzzle and drained it immediately. I refilled it for her as she tucked into the mound of greens, much to my niece's delight.

Rachel could be normally pretty reserved around guests, but not this time. She peppered Tavia almost non-stop with questions about the Morning Land. I hated to interrupt, as I was learning a heck of a lot just by listening in.

'High Tend' was the Morning Land's term for 'summer'. 'Solstice' was a gift-giving holiday of theirs that didn't sound too much different from our Christmas. I was about to remind Rachel that Tavia needed time to eat in peace, when all of a sudden she asked something I thought would have thrown our guest for another loop.

"Tavia, what's it like?" Rachel asked eagerly, her elbows on the table.

"What's what like?" Tavia cocked her head a little at Rachel's question.

"You know, what's it like...being a unicorn?"

"Ah," said Tavia, her eyes sparkling, "That's a tough one. I'll make you a deal, Rachel. I'll answer your question, but only after you answer mine."

"Okay, that sounds fair," my niece agreed.

"What's it like," Tavia asked, "Being a human?"

"Um." Rachel sat back in her chair with a little 'thump'. "I think that might take me a while to figure out."

"Take your time," Tavia replied sagely, and went back to eating her salad.

* * *

Rachel volunteered to take the dishes in after we were done. I'd just cracked open a bottle of soda when my cell phone rang. I unsnapped it from my belt and checked the number out of habit. A local number, but one I wasn't familiar with. I debated for a second if I should let it go to voicemail, then pressed 'Send'.

"This is Ridder," I said curtly.

"Derek? It's Birch."

I hit the button for the speaker and put the phone on the patio table so that Tavia could listen in. "Yes, Captain? I know I'm on the duty roster, but I have to be at my house for—"

"I got the story from Lynn Macedo," Birch's voice sounded tinny over the small speaker. "I'm bringing someone who says that you weren't the first to cross paths with our mysterious Man in Black."

"Then that's someone that I definitely need to speak with," I said. Birch signed off and I glanced at Tavia. She nodded, thinking.

"This makes sense. William Teach said 'not again' to you, as if his work had been disturbed before."

"Teach also said 'I have had enough of you people'. Whoever disturbed him before might've been a cop. But no one came forward when I asked around."

Tavia raised her head slightly. She spoke a couple words under her breath, then moved her horn around in a counter-clockwise circle. "Captain Birch is coming. I've dropped part of my wards for a moment to let them through."

I straightened my shirt as I went out to the front yard. Across the valley, dark clouds rose like black anvils in the distance. The day remained sunny for the moment, but the air had the heavy, humid feel it got just before a downpour.

My old Tacoma pickup and a low-slung Pontiac Firebird pulled into my driveway and grumbled to a stop. Birch got out of the pickup, dressed in jeans, a neat, collared shirt, and a broad cowboy hat. He had his battered leather briefcase tucked under his right arm.

"You left your truck at work," he said, as he handed the keys to me. "I took the day off, thought I'd use the chance to talk to you to give her back."

A recent retiree I'd known from around the station named Nick Pozowski got out of the Firebird. Unlike Birch, he looked like he'd finished eating something that had disagreed with his stomach.

"How's it going, Ridder?" Nick asked tersely, as he came up to the house.

"Pretty good. Nice to see you again, Nick," I said. "Thought you were out to pasture, couldn't resist that trailer stocked full of bass lures and beer."

"It wasn't the bass or the beer I wanted." He shrugged. "I just decided to fold before someone else cashed in my chips for me."

I stopped for a second and appraised Pozowski's grim demeanor. I didn't particularly like or dislike the man. He'd been one of the old timers on the force. One who had developed the ingrained cynicism that many veteran cops wore like a set of invisible clothes over their uniform.

I brought them around the side yard. Tavia reclined on the lawn next to the table, looking relaxed and regal. Birch's eyes lit up, and even Pozowski's expression took on a dreamy look.

"Good morning, Miss Tavia," Birch said, and damned if he didn't take off his hat as if he were being introduced to a Southern belle at the society ball.

"A pleasant High Tend to you, Captain," she replied, with a dip of her horn. "And it's just Tavia, if you please."

Birch nodded, and nudged Pozowski with an elbow. "Um, yeah," he said. "Nice to meet you, Tavia. Hope we're not interrupting anything."

She shook her head, and the beads in her mane rustled. Pozowski and Birch settled in at the table as I pulled up my chair.

"Okay, I'll bite," I said. "Nick, what's got you looking like you've just come from an Irish wake?"

"I've been wondering." Pozowski said haltingly, "Whether or not my partner and I ended up getting Dorian Martinez killed."

Michael Angel

Chapter Fifteen

Pozowski's statement stopped me cold. "What do you mean?"

"Gilberto Chavez and I saw this 'Black Duster' guy a month before you ran into him at the TomKat. I haven't been keeping in touch a lot since I left. I didn't get the message when you were asking around. And as for before..."

I traded a quick glance with Tavia. She nodded and stayed silent. There was a time to interrogate, and a time to listen, and this was one of the latter.

"Detective Chavez and I were staking out a meth lab at the Harmony Village trailer park," Pozowski continued. "We're camped out down the road when this white van pulls up in front of the trailer. This guy exits the vehicle, pulls out two clear plastic sacks full of what looks like Sudafed, Vicks, or maybe Kickapoo Joy Juice, in the easy-swallow size.

"He didn't look like nothing special. Five-ten, five-eleven maybe. Caucasian, bald except for some dirty blond hair around the back. Clean-shaven. Blue shirt, jeans, brown leather gloves and cowboy boots with steel tips. Tattoo of some kind below the left eye. Black duster with a hood. Strange thing to wear, since it was hot enough to pucker your ass to a leather seat."

Nick stopped, looked at the unicorn sitting next to him. "Pardon my language."

"No offense taken," Tavia replied.

"The guy goes inside the trailer, goods in hand. We wait a minute, call it in, then exit the car and move in. Chavez gives me the nod, and *BAM!* in we go through the door. I enter this one room, only heaps of broken furniture against the walls. What looks like a white chalk circle on the floor. And there he is..."

Pozowski drummed his fingers on the table before continuing. His voice changed tone. Before, he'd been recounting events that were as real to him as the table under his hand. Now, he sounded tentative, unsure. Like a man trying to find his way over thin ice.

"The guy's just standing there. He's got this look on his face, like some guy we seriously pissed off because we interrupted him on Super Bowl Sunday. And...he dissolves. Not like the witch from that movie with the ruby slippers, the one they threw water on. He faded away, like the ghost of a picture on the tube, you know, when you're trying to pull in a channel that's not on your satellite dish.

Pozowski wiped his brow with a napkin. "What that guy did really weirded me out. And that's why I handed the Captain my walking papers the same day."

I nodded. Digested what Pozowski had said. Birch undid the snaps on his briefcase. "I still have Chavez on the trailer park case. Here's what forensics found out," he said, as he laid the papers out on the table. "The circle was made of the same stuff they found at the TomKat."

"Soft white chalk," said Tavia.

"Yeah, that was it," Birch said, surprised. "How did you know?"

"It's what I would have used. It's easy to get anywhere in my world, and yours as well, I gather. He'd have been using it to set the stage, to draw magical runes and symbols of power."

"I didn't see nothing like that," said Nick. "Just a white circle."

"He didn't have time to do more. He was gambling that you were only there to observe, not to arrest him."

"Well, we could've done that. The capsules were real enough."

"Maybe, but this isn't like him at all." Tavia rose gracefully to her feet. She gave Birch and Pozowski a quick run-down of what she'd shared with me about Sir William Teach, and how only we two had survived against his dreadful power.

I steepled my fingers in thought. "Then why would he want to go draw his magic circles at a meth lab? Was he planning to flip the pills, make some cash? Maybe buy loyalty from the local gangs?"

"Doubtful. There would be easier ways to make money with magic."

"What's he after, then?"

Tavia hesitated for a fraction of a second before she answered. Her tail made the tiniest of twitches. I doubt I'd have even noticed it, had I not been around her for the past day. Had I not been observing her so intently.

What she said next really got my attention in a hurry. Or, rather, what she chose *not* to say.

"Teach doesn't like working with humans not under his magical control. It's why he's still operating alone after all these years."

"Well, so much for the loyalty angle," Birch said dryly. "He seems to work well enough with those yena things, though."

"Yena are native to the Red March. They're not his allies, so much as servants." Tavia's voiced settled back into her normal, calm rhythm.

"Allies or no, Teach is doing pretty damned well confounding our investigation. We weren't able to lift a single print from him at either place. No DNA, either. And not a single damned witness from the TomKat. Nobody remembered someone looking like William Teach showing up."

"Magic could account for this. A spell to suggest that someone forget you were worth remembering. And a sleep spell to knock everyone out while he went to that upstairs office."

"I'm in Nick's camp," Birch stated. "I don't like the way this 'magic' stuff is playing out."

Nick nodded strongly in agreement.

"Warlock magic is seldom pleasant," Tavia acknowledged. "For anyone concerned."

"Then what do you think Teach's next move will be?" I asked. "He's injured, and badly. My guess is that he'll hole up. Lie low for a while."

Tavia shook her head, frowning. A warm, moist wind began to kick up a little. The wispy ends of her mane tossed like little golden motes in the breeze.

"That's not likely. He will be back very soon. We need to figure out where he plans to pop up next."

Birch snorted. "You seem awfully sure about that. But given the size of the hole Ridder put in him, William Teach isn't going to be running marathons anytime soon. I'd guess at least three month's bed rest, and that's assuming he didn't bleed out or pick up an infection."

Again, the faintest of hesitations from Tavia.

"Trust me to know my quarry, Captain Birch. Like a bad-faced coin, Sir William Teach will turn up in this world in one week's time." She accentuated her words with a clack of one forehoof. "That is when we need to take him down."

Captain Birch leaned forward in his patio chair with a creak.

"Well then. I have only one question remaining."

"And what might that might be?"

"What is it," Birch asked. "That you and Derek Ridder share that allows you to resist the warlock's power?"

CHAPTER SIXTEEN

"Tavia, from what you said, William Teach really has hurt you. Taken friends from you," Birch said gently. "Dorian was Derek's friend. Could that be what you and Derek have in common?"

Tavia and I looked at each other, startled. I'd put that question to the side since I'd been so interested in other ones.

"I doubt it," she said. "Teach has killed an awful lot of people. If that was the common element, there would be more people who could have stood firm against him."

"Any ideas on your end, Ridder?" Pozowski asked.

"Not a one. But since Tavia wants me to stay with Rachel until tomorrow, at least I have time to think on it," I acknowledged. I turned and spoke directly to Tavia. "What do you have in mind beyond that?"

"I want to visit the TomKat. I might be able to find something your teams weren't looking for."

"You're in luck," said Birch. "The room at the TomKat hasn't been touched. The cover story was carbon monoxide poisoning, so the health department immediately shut the place down."

Birch and Pozowski talked over a few more points with us, then got ready to leave. Before they pulled out of the driveway,

Pozowski motioned me over to the driver's side window of his Firebird.

"Best of luck to you, Ridder," he said. "This is way outside anything I've ever seen in my time. Tell you what, you nail this guy, you can tell me through the U.S. mail."

The breeze kicked up another notch, carrying with it the heavy scent of raindrops. Pozowski revved the Firebird's motor and backed out into the street. Birch followed suit in the K-9 unit's Ranger. A rumble of thunder followed on the heels of their exit.

A spray of stray raindrops spattered the concrete. I got out my key ring and unlocked the garage door. Though I'd done this hundreds of times before, I took my time. Moved deliberately.

I needed time to process what I'd seen from Tavia. The catches in her voice, the way she'd deflected questions. It all told me one thing: The unicorn wasn't playing straight with me.

And that made me feel uneasy like nobody's business.

"I don't like this," I said, as I rolled up the door with a metallic clatter.

"There's not much to like about William Teach," said Tavia. She watched me drag the patio table and chairs inside the garage so the rain wouldn't rust their frames out.

"I'm not talking about William Teach."

Again, Tavia's brow raised in question.

I looked the unicorn right in the eye.

"I'm talking about you, Tavia. I don't know how humans and unicorns work together in the Morning Land. Maybe they don't. But if so, then it's a lot different than here."

Tavia blinked. "I don't know what you mean."

"Yes, you do," I said curtly. "You're holding back two pieces of information. And it's obvious that you didn't think I'd notice."

To her credit, Tavia didn't immediately deny anything. Instead, she scuffed one hoof nervously on the pavement. Her ears twitched as if tickled by the raindrops carried on the wind.

"You're so sure that Teach will be back in one week. I'd like to know why you're so sure he'll be showing up for round two when he'll still be recovering from the time I plugged him in the gut."

"I've… I've only got guesses. Based on past experience." she said. Her eyes flicked away, then came back to me.

"Let me show you something." I brushed away the cobwebs from one of the garage shelves and pulled out two long, thin metal objects. I unfolded one with a snap so that it became a tripod, then placed the second piece on top. "Ever see one of these?"

"I think so…"

"It's called a telescope," I said evenly. "You use it to look at the night sky. It's one of the hobbies my dad and I shared when I was growing up."

Tavia was quiet now, not sure where I was going with this. I began ticking the events off on my fingers.

"Dorian was murdered by William Teach at the TomKat three weeks ago. Nick Pozowski said that he'd seen Teach at the trailer park one month before that. And you think that Teach will be back in one more week. Now, I'm no mathematician, but I'd say that corresponds to a pretty regular cycle. A lunar cycle, I'm willing to bet."

"I'm sorry, Derek," she said softly. "I underestimated you. That was unfair of me."

"Oh, don't apologize. Tell me the other piece of information you're holding back. Tell me why you think William Teach is in my world now, not yours."

"I'd prefer not to talk about it right now."

"Well, Tavia, this isn't exactly about how much you 'prefer' something." I walked back outside and pulled the garage door down with a bang. "Anytime I'm put on a case, the suspect's motivation is the first thing I need to know."

I walked back up to the porch. Leaves rustled and the tree branches all along the hill swayed, making a series of arthritic-sounding creaks. Tavia followed me, her breath coming a little hard, like she was intensely debating something in her mind.

"Honestly," she said, "I don't know for sure."

"Then can you give me some ideas?" I asked, forcing myself to not grit my teeth. I took a breath, then said, "Tavia, are we a team or not?"

"I can't..." Her head hung sorrowfully for a moment. "We *are* a team, Derek. Please, not now, all right? Maybe later."

With a crash of thunder, the sky opened up. Rain poured down in warm sheets. I turned and walked into the house, leaving Tavia out in the rain.

CHAPTER SEVENTEEN

Rachel refused to eat her breakfast the next morning. Apparently, Super Pickle the Zebra had told her something 'Very Important' last night. That something being: "Growing zebras don't eat oatmeal, they only eat pancakes with lots and lots of maple syrup."

Refusing to eat her breakfast paled in comparison to what happened later in the day. Emily showed up to take her daughter home. Rachel flat-out hated the idea. She plunked herself down on the living room couch and refused to move.

In fact, my niece threw the first real tantrum I'd seen in years.

"I won't go, you can't make me!" she cried. "You can't make me leave Uncle Derek! And you can't make me leave Tavia! She's *my* unicorn, and I'm not going anywhere without her!"

A moment of awkward silence followed. Thankfully, Tavia decided to fill it in. Her voice took on the same gentle but firm tone I'd heard her use with Lynn Macedo two nights ago.

"Rachel, listen to me. I know you enjoy my company, that you want me to meet your friends. But know this," Tavia raised her head proudly, tossed her mane. "No one can own a unicorn. No one in the world. Do you understand?"

Rachel stood absolutely still for a second. Then she ran back to her bedroom, bawling. Tavia looked at Emily and me a little sheepishly.

"That usually works better," Tavia sighed. "Let me talk with her."

Emily waited until the unicorn had left the room. Her dark eyes flashed at me with exasperation.

"Derek, I was going to start by asking what the heck is going on here. But before you tell me, I need to know one thing."

"What's that?"

"Is it..." she glanced over her shoulder, made sure Tavia was still absent. "Is it safe for Rachel to hang around that...unicorn? She looks sweet, but also ferocious, if you know what I mean."

"Yes, she's a little of both," I agreed.

I couldn't blame Emily for her worries or her irritation with me. She'd stepped off the plane at LAX and into the arms of a pair of U.S. Marshals. Then she'd been followed by an official police escort to my house.

When she'd arrived, I'd met her at the door with what was, at least in her mind, a talking horse with a sharp spiral horn. And worst of all, it appeared that her daughter had gotten rather attached to this dangerous looking wild animal.

I motioned for her to sit next to me. I tried my best to explain the events of the last three days. How Rachel had, in a way, set in motion the chain of events that had brought Tavia here. And why the Department of Justice had decided to interfere with their lives by putting them in the witness protection program.

Emily listened without comment. When I finished, she regarded me coolly. She played nervously with a lock of her long, dark brown hair. It was a simple gesture, and yet one that still gave me a *thrum* inside.

Beth had been only two years younger. She and Emily were enough alike in manner and appearance to strike memories from me like sparks from flint.

"This man, this William Teach," said Emily. "He's really done these awful things? Slaughtered people in Tavia's world, murdered Dorian in ours?"

"Yes, it's true."

"Then you have to get him," she said simply.

"You…" I sat back, surprised. "You understand what has to be done, for me to pursue this man?"

"Yes, as a matter of fact, I do." Emily put her hand on mine, grasped it tightly. "You should know better than anyone that my family isn't made up of shrinking violets. If this 'warlock' thinks he can distract you with us, then we need to step aside and let you get to work.

"And Rachel?"

"It'll be hard. But Rachel will understand, in time. She knows you need to get the bad guy. Do you know how she thinks of you?"

I shook my head.

"She says that her Uncle Derek is her 'hero knight'."

"She has an active imagination," I said. "Still, it's nice to know that I'm somebody's idea of a hero."

"It's a heavy responsibility," Emily said, with mock gravity. She smiled, then spoke in a more serious tone. "The unicorn, Tavia…how many of the legends around her kind are true? I mean, she has cloven hooves and a spiral horn, but she looks more like a horse than a goat or a deer. Can she cure poisons, divine the truth of things? Can only a virgin touch her?"

"I don't know. And I didn't know you were into unicorn lore."

"I'm not. If I picked up anything, you know who I got it from."

The name came to me instantly. "From Beth," I said, blinking. "She loved medieval legends."

"That's right." Emily looked at me in amazement. "Derek, that's the first time in three years that I've ever heard you actually say my sister's name."

I let out a breath. "I guess I've been doing a lot of growing lately."

"Good" Emily put her hand on mine. "Then maybe, someday, you'll forgive yourself. For Beth's sake."

I nodded, afraid to speak again.

The sounds of steps in the hallway. Rachel came out, Tavia following closely behind. Whatever Tavia had said to Rachel, it had worked. My niece went calmly over to her mother.

"I'm sorry," Rachel said, in a tiny voice. "I still don't want to go, but I know we have to."

Snuffling, Rachel snuggled into her mother's arms. Emily looked up from her daughter to the unicorn. *Thank you,* she mouthed silently. Tavia acknowledged the words with a dip of her horn.

* * *

Two hours later, and the late afternoon sun did its best to turn the hood of my Tacoma into a makeshift griddle. But the heat didn't get to me. I turned the key in the ignition and the engine sputtered to a stop. I felt a chill skitter up my spine.

The parking lot of the TomKat sat quietly, as it had that first, deadly night. The swinging saloon doors and the front windows had been boarded up. A staple-gunned poster from the health department decorated the outside wall like an especially cheap piece of wallpaper.

I checked my watch. Still had a few minutes to kill before Tavia and I tried out our little experiment. I got out of my pickup and walked to the public telephone booth at the corner of the lot. The crunching of the gravel seemed deafeningly loud in the silence.

A quick dig into a pocket, and I dropped some coins into the pay phone. I punched in the number for Gilberto Chavez's office. As the phone rang, I pulled out my cell. I glanced at the signal strength. It held steady at a nice and strong five bars.

The line picked up after only two rings. "Detective Chavez."

"Gil, it's Ridder."

"Hey, amigo," he said, a smile in his voice, "How's it hanging?"

"A little low, and to the left," I replied. Yeah, it was an old gag, and a juvenile one, but we still used it around the office.

"I hear you have a new partner. And she's a cute blonde."

"You heard right. I already brought her home with me for a sleepover," I laughed, tossing the joke back at him. "I'm in the lot at the TomKat, she's going to join me in a bit. Thought I'd check in with you. Any luck with the leads on Teach?"

"Some. And it's damned odd stuff, I'll tell you that."

I sighed. "Let's hear it."

Michael Angel

CHAPTER EIGHTEEN

The *click!* of a three-ring binder being opened sounded pin-drop clear over the receiver. The rustle of papers being shuffled. As I waited, I propped my cell phone up on the booth's metal shelf where I could watch the display.

"Once we got the detailed description of William Teach from you and Tavia, I got a few hits in my search. This guy started showing up way back in May. First time in Canoga Park. Couple security guards reported him for hanging around their BMW dealership."

"Car shopping?" I asked, incredulous. "Somehow, I can't see a warlock taking a Beemer for a test drive."

"It gets stranger after that. Next month, he's cited for loitering by a mall cop at the Galleria in Glendale. The month after that, Pozowski and I come within an ace of bustin' him at the Harmony Village trailer park out by Sepulveda. And then come August…"

His voice trailed off.

It was up to me to say it. "Come August, that's when he showed up at 2200 Durham, at the TomKat." I leaned back against the sunbaked wall of the booth, felt the dull pulse of warmth in the small of my back.

"Yeah, afraid so. Now, as for the trailer park, there's a tiny bit more."

"Let's hear it," I said.

"The guy who owns the trailer is still in the Kern County slam. He's a freelancer, doesn't care if you want to whip up a batch of meth or some Alice Dee. Claims that Teach called him, wanted to flip some gel tabs. But he never got to meet Teach in person. The night before Pozowski and I were at the trailer park, the freelancer got nabbed at a Bakersfield sobriety check point."

"So the rendezvous didn't come off, but Teach still went in. More evidence that he really didn't give a damn about making meth. Thanks, Gil."

I hung up, checked my watch again. It was time. I looked around, expecting a burst of light, a noise, something.

To my surprise, all I heard was the gentle sound of hoofbeats. Tavia trotted around the side of the building. I waved to her. She made her way over to me and I held up my cell phone so she could see it. The signal strength of five bars had been replaced with the words NO SIGNAL.

"As we guessed," she said. "That's why your phone went out the first time you were here. Same thing when the yena arrived to kidnap Rachel."

"Any ideas on why the—well, the way you travel—could affect a cell phone?"

"I can only guess." Tavia glanced at me, then quickly added, "But I'd like to share my idea with you."

I spread my hands out in encouragement. Tavia hadn't said much to me since last night, but it did seem she was taking our recent disagreement seriously. She still hadn't shared with me what I really wanted. I figured that if I got her comfortable talking to me again, she would finally get off the damned fence.

"The day I met you, do you remember me telling you that I didn't need to ride in your truck in order to travel?" I nodded, and she continued. "The ability to do that is limited to unicorns, a couple other magical creatures, and humans, if they have an artifact that is attuned to the *tellura*."

"Tellura." tried out the unfamiliar word. I put the accent on the second syllable, the way she did.

"A 'tellura' is a natural river of magical energy, which flows through the earth and sea. Casting the right spell allows you to step into one of these rivers, and then step out somewhere else along its banks."

"I follow you so far."

"There's a fair number of tellurae that run through this city. The TomKat is one such spot. Also on the ridge near your house."

"So why aren't these spots always causing problems for phones or radios?"

"Well, that's the part I'm 'guessing' at. Energy sort of 'splashes' out of a tellura for a couple of minutes after someone steps into or out of one. I'm thinking that this is what causes interference with your cell phone and radio signals."

"Interesting." I rubbed my chin with one hand. "So, our friend Teach wasn't interested in the TomKat. Just in what it was built on top of. A tellura."

"Possible. But tellura run for hundreds or even thousands of miles. There would be no reason for Teach to come to this particular spot. He could enter or exit anywhere along the entire length of the tellura if he wished."

"Well, there goes that theory." I sighed. I reached over the edge of the pickup's bed, and grabbed hold of a steel crowbar I'd brought for the occasion. "Time to go see the crime scene."

Tavia waited patiently in the shade of the porch as I pried off the boards holding the front of the TomKat shut. A blast of hot, stale air greeted us as I opened the door. I pushed inside, Tavia following close behind.

Clean-up had been quick and incomplete. Litter lay strewn about the floor and something from the snack bar smelled positively rancid. I turned to the wooden staircase on the right.

Felt my heart pounding in my chest. My mind flashed to the moment when I'd stood here before. When I'd motioned for Dorian to follow me. I leaned against the wall for a moment, knees weak.

"Derek—" Tavia began. Her voice was soft, full of concern. I held my hand up, and she went quiet.

Without another word, we went up the stairs and arrived at the door to the upstairs office. I pulled back the 'X' of yellow crime-scene tape so that Tavia and I could enter. To see where Teach had murdered my partner and friend.

CHAPTER NINETEEN

Teach's dammed chalk pattern still sprawled across the floor. The lines had faded to a dull gray. Smeared in a few spots by boot prints from fellow cops.

"Neither of us saw Teach when we came in the door," I said, swallowing hard. I moved to the far side of the room. "He stepped out of the shadows here."

"Yes," she said, half to herself, "That would have been the logical spot to begin an incantation. But for what, exactly?"

Tavia came to stand by me. She tapped her forehoof on the floor in thought.

She turned to me and asked, "Derek, could you please step away? Let me try something to illuminate what William Teach was trying to do here."

I gave Tavia room to work. She curled her chin to her chest, using her lips to fiddle with one of the pockets on her harness pack. Three silver balls fell out and rattled as they struck the floor. They looked an awful lot like the kind of marbles my dad collected as a kid, the ones called 'steelies'.

Tavia murmured a few Latin-sounding words. Then, using her nose, she nudged each marble into motion.

She didn't nudge them very hard, but they continued to roll long after I expected them to stop. Then, to my astonishment, they began to curve, to follow the outside of the entire room-sized circle. The balls made a faint jingle as they continued to revolve around the pattern.

Little by little, the white chalk lines began to sharpen. To glow with that same creepy, blue-white fire that I had seen burning along their edges.

Tavia cleared her throat, startling me. "This is going to take a couple of minutes. Do you mind if I ask you something?"

"I don't mind," I said. After a couple of days, I was getting better at reading my companion's mood. Tavia was more than a little nervous right now. Her tail made a couple short, sharp swishes through the air.

"I don't mean to pry…" She watched the balls continue their circuit. "But the best sense we unicorns have is our hearing. When I was talking with Rachel today, I heard you chatting with her mother."

"What did you hear?" All of a sudden I felt embarrassed. Emily hadn't exactly been very trusting of Tavia.

"Emily asked if it was safe to keep her daughter around me," she said with a little snort. "She asked how many of the legends surrounding my people are true. And she also said that it was the first time in a long while that you dared to speak your wife's name."

I nodded. I knew where this was going, had thought about bringing it up when Birch had left. But Tavia and I had gotten into our argument right afterwards.

It had been three years since Beth had died. But it was hard—damned hard, as a matter of fact—for me to bring up Beth on my own.

"Forgive me, Derek," Tavia continued. "In my experience, humans don't usually mourn someone for three years unless they were deeply in love."

"I suppose," I said, meeting her gaze. Her deep blue eyes flickered as the light from the floor pattern continued to brighten. "I mean, I suppose for other humans. People. Beth and I…when I wake, I still miss her terribly."

"Derek, perhaps this is the common thread between us." Tavia cocked her head slightly. "To have lost someone you were in love with, romantically."

"I suppose that could be the link," I admitted. And I had to admit that I was suddenly curious. *What or who could break a unicorn's heart?*

A deep thrum vibrated through in the air. Like someone had plugged in a generator. Suddenly, I heard the same damned sound, the sound of a disembodied chorus called up for whatever hellish purpose William Teach desired.

Ahhhhhhhhhhhhhh...

A pair of violet-sheened runes the size of a large dinner plate appeared at the three and nine o' clock positions around the circle. Two more runes blinked into existence at the twelve and six positions. Each had been drawn in the precise hand of William Teach.

"Now I see what he was doing," Tavia said. The unicorn stamped her feet, making the wooden floor shake. "He was trying to build a gate between worlds. But between which ones?"

A final rune started to glow from the heart of the pattern. Tavia leaned forward on all four feet, careful not to break the motion of the steelies moving below. She peered at the emerging lines of the rune, brow furrowed in concentration.

The pale violet light suddenly shifted into the color of freshly shed blood. From nowhere, a violent wind scoured the chalk dust from the floor. The deep bass of the chorus turned into a shrieking howl.

"Teach has set a trap!" Tavia cried, neighing in fear. "Hold on to me!"

The next few seconds took on an awful, stretched feel. Tavia pivoted on one hind leg. She raised her head and took a mighty bound towards me.

I threw my arms around her neck. Clung as tightly as I could. A single, staccato pound of hooves. She leaped straight for the second-story window.

A flash burned our silhouette into the wall. Then a sharp *CRACK!* as the floor and walls shattered. Turned into wood shards and concrete gravel.

I pressed my face to Tavia's golden side as a wave of skin-crackling heat flowed over us.

Chapter Twenty

Tavia and I tumbled in mid-air.

As if from a great distance, I heard the sound of glass shattering, stone crumbling. In one long, dreamless moment the blue sky turned above me. Then came a gray blur, sparks of red.

I felt as much as heard the *crunch!* of gravel around me. Something drove the breath out of me, as if I'd been body-slammed in the kidneys. For a few seconds, the world went black and spotty.

I tried to focus, had to force my eyes to cooperate. The gray blurs resolved themselves into parking lot gravel. The bright-red gleams were chunks of wood burning only inches from my face.

I felt a burst of warmth at the back of my neck. I cringed, thinking it was more burning wood. But there was a moist exhalation, and I knew it was someone's breath.

That someone shouted at me, but my eardrums were still throbbing. As if she called me from a distant mountain peak, I heard Tavia's voice in my ear.

"*—erek! Ush! USH!*"

I blinked. Couldn't understand for a second. Then I realized that I'd been feeling Tavia's warm breath on the back of my neck. Because she had her teeth firmly fixed in my collar.

Whatever was going on, it was pretty important that I help her 'push'.

More out of reflex than anything else, I got my hands under me. Forced myself to do a pushup. My palms tingled as they felt the hot, sharp pieces of gravel underneath.

Then I felt my entire back lifted as Tavia dragged me forward. The weight pinning me fast slid down to the backs of my knees. Then to my calves. And then I was free.

With a moan, I turned myself over on my back. Slowly raised myself up. Tavia stood panting beside me, covered in soot. A few feet away, I saw the wooden roof beam she'd helped drag me out from under. The beam merrily burned, and probably would have smelled of roast Ridder in another couple of minutes.

"Thanks, Tavia." It seemed like such a flat, inadequate thing to say after what had just happened.

She shook her head sharply, making the beads in her mane clatter.

"No, not thanks. I acted like a stupid yearling. I almost got us both killed."

I pulled the radio from my belt, called the fire in. Then, I cautiously patted down or flexed the rest of my body. After a moment, I knew that I'd live. I'd have a hell of a bruise on my lower back, but nothing seemed sprained or broken.

The backs of my hands were red and swollen, but I ignored that and turned to Tavia. Sorrow marked her noble countenance. She stared almost hatefully at the TomKat as the building continued to burn.

"Here, let me—" I put my hands out, stopped. "I've got a couple of burns, and I know you took more of that blast. Let me see if you're hurt."

She nodded. "Top left pocket on my harness. The glass jar is a healing salve. Good for burns if you rub it in deep."

The pocket's metal button still felt hot as I fiddled it open. I took out the jar and unscrewed the top. The bright green gel inside smelled like wildflowers. I checked Tavia over and found a couple of spots on her side that were badly singed. She made only the smallest of winces as I rubbed the salve in as she instructed.

Tavia got to her feet and carefully stretched each leg. She cocked an ear, then said, with a slight quaver to her voice, "Sirens approaching. I should go. Can you...can you please answer their questions?"

"Why—" I began, then I saw the way Tavia hung her head. She was actually embarrassed. I got the impression that this was not something she was used to. "We're still alive, that's what matters. You couldn't have figured that Teach was going to play us that way."

"But I should have!" she said forcefully, with a stomp of a hoof. "I'm the one who knows how he thinks. And he'd have known I was here after him, trying to follow his trail. Some of the yena we fought escaped, they'd have told him right away. It would have been child's play for him to come back here and turn this place into a trap."

"Then I'd better let Chavez know, we need to cordon off the trailer park."

"You don't need to. That was an exploding rune in the center of the pattern. It doesn't go off until you reveal it; read it. No one could have set off that trap unless they could detect it with magic."

"Thank God," I said. Something went 'pop' inside the TomKat as it continued to burn. "All right, I'll take the questions for you this time." I moved to put the salve back in her harness pocket, but she gently nudged my hand away.

"Use the salve for yourself, Derek. It works for humans just as well as my people, and you have wounds that need tending as well."

"Okay." As she began to turn away, something occurred to me. "Tavia?" She looked back, cocked an ear.

"Yes, Derek?"

"Emily was asking about the legends around your people. She wanted to know how many were true. What about the one where only a virgin can touch a unicorn?"

Right then, as I began to hear the fire engines in the distance, I discovered something new about unicorns: they can actually *blush*.

"Yes," she said, and her golden skin on her face acquired a tinge of red. "That legend is sort of true."

"Well, Beth and I never had any children," I pointed out. "But that wasn't for lack of trying. I sure as hell have no claims to sexual purity. How was I able to—"She cleared her throat, her blush now a bright red all over her head and down her neck.

"Well, you see...when it comes to that bit...only *one* of us needs to be a virgin."

CHAPTER TWENTY-ONE

To say that Tavia caused a stir at the LAPD would be an understatement. Even though Birch had briefed everyone on her arrival, people crowded around, trying to get a glimpse of her, usually with a digital or cell phone camera in hand. For her part, Tavia took it all in stride. But I'll admit, it was amusing to see cops I'd worked with on the grittiest of beats gazing at her in amazement. As if watching their favorite storybook character come to life.

I'd commandeered the main conference room in the Homicide department. Partly because it was large enough to comfortably allow Tavia, Birch, and myself to work. Also, because it had a wall map of Los Angeles County mounted on a mural-sized piece of corkboard.

I pushed the fourth red thumbtack into the map and stood back to look at the result. Next, I cleared a spot in the center of the room, so I could lay down a whiteboard on the floor. With a flex of one cloven hoof, Tavia grasped an uncapped dry-erase marker. She drew the five symbols that we'd seen in Teach's diagram.

"These runes open a magical gate between worlds," Tavia said, as she placed the marker to one side. "The fifth rune, the one in the center, marks the world the gate is meant to open. When I saw which rune Teach had drawn, my blood ran cold."

She paused a moment. A shiver ran down her flank, rustling her beads.

"The fifth rune is the sign for the *Tengan*."

"When Teach attacked your homeland, the Tengan's time had also come again," Birch said, recalling Tavia's words. "They were the 'demons of war'."

"The Tengan are why my world's history is written in blood," she said with a sigh. "Every threescore years, they break through the barriers between our worlds, and try to make our lands theirs."

"You mean they use the 'tellura' to step into your world?"

The unicorn shook her head. "Tellura are used to move place-to-place *within* a world. A gate is used to cross *between* worlds. Some spots along a tellura carry a great deal of magical energy. They're the only places one can set up a gate."

"If the people of the Morning Land know so much about gates," Birch observed, "Why did you wait until three years ago to drop by Washington D.C.?"

"Gates only work when two worlds *align*. My sire thinks that it's part of a complex cycle. One similar to how your sun, moon, and earth line up to produce an eclipse at certain times."

"Captain, Tavia explained this to me earlier. The worlds of the Tengan and the Morning Land are on a short, fast cycle. They cross every five or six decades, but the alignment lasts only for a year or two. By contrast, our world and the Morning Land are on a very long, very slow cycle."

"How long?" Birch asked.

"About nine hundred years," said Tavia, with a flick of her tail. "But the alignment lasts longer. Usually for a period of two, threescore years."

"This long cycle explains our popular mythology," I added. "The last time the Morning Land aligned with our world was around the start of our Middle Ages, the era most unicorn lore comes from."

Birch nodded. "So why haven't we seen the Tengan here before?"

"Their world simply wasn't in alignment with yours," Tavia said. She put one forehoof down firm with a clack. "But William Teach may be trying to change that. By finding a place with enough magical energy to hold open a gate for the Tengan to cross."

"And that's why Teach has been showing up once per phase of the first-quarter moon," I said, tapping a finger on the wall map. "He had no luck at the TomKat. As for the trailer park, he just brought the drugs to gain entrance. Teach is testing one segment of the tellura after another, until he finds the right spot to build this 'gate'."

"Probably the last two spots would have been fine," added Tavia. "But each time, the LAPD arrived and disrupted what he was doing. An *incomplete* gate permanently disrupts the energy at the site. Destroys its usefulness to him."

"Each of Teach's appearances move in a straight line, west to east along the tellura," I said, tracing the space between each pin with my index finger. "From Canoga Park to Glendale, and so on. Each segment he pops up to test is exactly seventeen miles apart. We already knew when he would arrive. Now we know the where he'll be going."

I grabbed a marker. With the flick of a wrist, I drew a circle on the map, seventeen miles east of the TomKat. Smack in the middle of a slate quarry in South Pasadena.

"Interesting," Birch said, as he contemplatively stroked the ends of his mustache. "What exactly are you two proposing?"

I gave him an evil grin. "Sir, I'm suggesting that we give Sir William Teach exactly what he wants."

Captain Birch returned it. "And set a trap for him. I like it. What will you two need? What kind of equipment? I'll assign as many squads of men as you think we need for this one."

I traded a glance with Tavia. I was already getting more proficient at reading her body language. She made a barely perceptible motion with her shoulders, a sort of equine shrug. Well, we had Birch's attention.

"As far as equipment," I said carefully, "No guns. I'll need riot gear. Batons, body armor, and Tasers."

"Are you sure that's wise, Ridder? After everything we've seen William Teach do?"

"I'll be happy to explain," I said, holding up a hand. "But only once we get Tavia set up in this room. She's going to need it all day. More likely for two full days."

The Captain crossed his arms and shot us both a look.

"All right," he said, "I'll bite. What does a unicorn need this conference room for, especially for two solid days?"

Birch's eyebrows shot up in surprise as Tavia told him.

CHAPTER TWENTY-TWO

Captain Birch kept glancing out the door of the makeshift armory with an expression that could curdle milk. I did my best to ignore him. Instead, I focused on going through the pieces of riot gear that had been laid out on the room's table. We hadn't pulled some of this stuff from storage in over a year, and I needed to make sure everything was in place, down to the last buckle.

"Of all the ridiculous things," Birch grumped, as yet another member of the Homicide squad entered the conference room down the hall. "Is she serious about this?"

I thought back to my conversation with Tavia, right after the TomKat had gone into self-demolition mode. "Sir, I get the impression that unicorns take most everything quite seriously. And in this case, I'm in full agreement with what she's doing."

"I'm glad you want her hand-picking your team." Birch dug into his chest pocket, found a spare antacid tablet, and popped it into his mouth. "Hoof-picking, in her case. But why does she need to *interview* them?"

"Because we need people who can resist Teach's abilities. Tavia thinks that she and I can resist the warlock's power...because we've each lost someone. Someone we loved deeply, in a romantic sort of way."

Birch turned and gave me a strange look. "Beth?"

I nodded wearily.

"So she's asking some very personal questions. Probably every person on the force has lost a friend or family member over the course of their lives. But not everyone has lost a spouse or a lover."

"Okay, I'm with you so far." He reached out and picked up a shiny, black shoulder plate of body armor. "What about the riot gear?"

"Captain, our resident unicorn expert is pretty sure that William Teach can't do his mind-control thing beyond forty, fifty feet. Unfortunately, that doesn't really help us. I've been to that quarry. It's a single story building surrounded by open fields. No adjoining buildings to the sides."

"Meaning it's going to be difficult to place snipers," Birch said, divining my meaning.

"Very difficult." I popped the battery compartment out of one of the Tasers, checked it for sufficient charge. "Tavia's going to create a counter spell to dampen Teach's ability to control people. But I'm betting that we'll have to get closer to him than I'd like. In case Tavia's wrong, I'm the only one who'll be carrying a firearm."

Birch's face took on a grim look as I slapped the Taser's power cell home.

"You think he'll try a repeat of what he did to Dorian."

My jaw tightened. "It's a winning move of his. I'll wager that he will."

The Captain tossed the shoulder plate he'd been holding back on the table with a clink. "Sounds to me like you and Tavia have all your bases covered."

"Not quite." Birch gave me a questioning look. "Sir, I'm going to need one more thing. Something I don't think Tavia's thought of."

* * *

Three nights later.

The first-quarter moon rose into a warm, cloudless Southern California night. We scrambled during those 72 hours to gain permission from our legal department and the quarry owner. So that the LAPD could prep the area for our operation without giving the game away.

We placed spotters in a two-story warehouse a few blocks away to watch the roads leading to the quarry. Security cameras covered the final approach. A half-dozen police cruisers prowled beyond the spotters' perimeter. Close enough to assist, but not close enough to be easily spotted.

Tavia gave her seal of approval to three other people who'd gone through her screening process. One of them, to my surprise, was Gilberto Chavez. The other two, Ron Hutson and Danny Polanaro, had also been part of Chavez's meth-busting team.

During the lunch break, we'd moved the three men into the workforce by dressing them in worker's coveralls and blending them in during the shift change. When evening fell, and the last of the site's real employees left, I pulled up to the site in a van that had been tricked out with the quarry company's logo. I parked behind some storage sheds by the loading dock and threw open the van's rear doors.

Tavia immediately jumped out.

"Phew! My eyes were starting to water."

"Fumes from the paint job," I explained. "Next time, we should stick with your magical type of travel."

"We couldn't risk my coming out somewhere Teach might see me," she said, missing my joke.

Chavez, Hutson, and Polanaro came out of the shadows to meet us.

"Glad you could make it, Ridder," Chavez quipped.

"So am I," I replied, with a nod at his companions. Where Chavez was getting a bit stout around the waist, Hutson had the build of a short beanpole. Compared to each of them, Polanaro looked like a craggy wall of muscle. "Ron, Danny, it's good to see you."

"Thanks, Derek," Polanaro replied, his deep voice resonating in my ear. "This is wild. I wouldn't miss it for the world."

I started pulling the riot gear out of the back of the van. Began handing it out. We put the equipment on in silence. Tavia turned away from us and closed her eyes, concentrating. She moved her horn slowly back and forth, as if she was using it to dowse for water.

Suddenly, she tapped a forehoof on the dirt with a *clop*.

"The strongest source of magical energy is in the main building," she said.

Tavia led the way through the open loading dock. We picked our way through a labyrinth of industrial equipment, forklifts, and office furniture, all coated in tiny gray splotches of rock dust. That same dust ticked my nose like a handful of freshly ground pepper, made me swipe my nostrils more than once.

Ahead of us, the jungle of machinery and office supplies gave way to a wide-open space. A ten-foot high crescent of blue-gray slate faced us. Shards and chunks of rock had been pried or jackhammered from the wall, but enough of the sheer surfaces were left to glitter at us in the wan moonlight.

I placed Chavez and the other two men in concealed areas, trying to cover every angle of approach. Tavia and I worked our way over to a concealed spot close to the quarry wall. I knelt, checked my Taser, my Glock, and my headset receiver. All was in place.

Tavia recited a stanza of Latinate-sounding words, weaving her counter-spell to Teach's magic. She finished just as the receiver in my ear buzzed. One of the spotters outside had seen someone.

"South side calling in." Tavia said nothing, but cocked an ear in my direction.

"Copy, go." I whispered.

"He's here."

CHAPTER TWENTY-THREE

Two simple words.

He's here.

A terrible chill passed over me.

"Acknowledged," I said.

"He's alone," said the spotter. "Definitely our man. He's carrying what looks like a large walking stick."

"Stand by. I'll call for backup if needed."

"Roger that."

The radio went silent. I stood, made the hand signals for 'one person' and 'approaching'. Gil and the other two men acknowledged the message.

I knelt down. Ran my hand over the cool, reassuring surface of my Glock. But I decided against pulling it. I wanted Teach alive, if possible.

Instead, I took out my Taser. The black and yellow electroshock weapon looked like a wasp in the shape of a handgun. The points of the weapon's twin darts gleamed softly like a wasp's venom-filled stinger.

Moonlight slanted in and glanced off the exposed face of slate. A vein of mica in the rock threw off a rainbow of sparkles. Tavia remained a silent, solid presence at my side.

The sound of a distant footfall.

I suddenly realized I had been holding my breath. Forced myself to let it out slowly. A second footfall. Then the ordinary sounds of a man walking towards us.

Sir William Teach walked into the moonlight.

His ghoulish complexion still looked waxy. Doll-like. He'd stayed with the same black duster, jeans, and cowboy boots. Only this time, he'd paired it with a heavy utility belt and a thick, black shirt.

A pale blue glow at the base of the man's throat drew my eye. Around Teach's neck lay a strand of silver chain links. Dangling from the central link, radiating the unsettling light of a pure morning sky, hung an egg-sized opal.

Teach held a staff made of shiny, black wood in his right hand. At its top, the staff curled back on itself in a shepherd's crook. With a shock, I realized that it resembled the question-mark shaped tattoo that coiled under Teach's left eye like a squashed snake.

I stood and leveled my Taser.

"Hold it right there, Teach."

He froze. His eyes swiveled towards me.

"I know your voice," Teach said. "Detective Derek Ridder."

I shouted the next set of commands. "Hands away from your body! Get down on the ground, now!"

"Oh, please," Teach airily dismissed my command. The warlock blinked, squinted, and then added, "You've managed to surprise me. You have a unicorn with you. And I bet I know which one."

"One more warning, Teach. Down on the ground. Now."

"Detective Ridder, don't you want to know why—"

That was enough for me. I pulled the Taser's trigger.

The weapon coughed. Nitrogen cartridges spat out twin wire-trailing darts. The warlock moved with the speed of a striking snake. Brought his staff up in front, held it up like a shield.

The electrodes smacked into the dark wood with a *chuff*. Teach swung his staff down and to the side. The Taser flew out of my hands. The weapon landed in a dark corner with a clatter.

Teach frowned. His eyes glittered like shards of jet.

"Such insolence," Teach snarled. His lips started to move. His voice rose, filling my ears with that awful, magical language of his.

"Take him down!" I cried.

Nothing happened. Gil, Ron, and Danny stood up. They walked forward a few steps into the open. Like puppets on badly tangled strings.

"Tavia?" I said nervously.

The unicorn let out a low whinny of disbelief.

"How?" she gasped. "How is this possible? Derek, my spell isn't—"

Gil staggered over to Teach's side. Sweat streamed from his brow. His eyes had gone blank with horror. Teach whispered an incantation in Gil's ear, then raised his voice so that we could hear.

"No need for anything fancy. Just kill him."

Detective Gilberto Chavez snapped his Taser forward. He squeezed the trigger. I heard the sound of a child's cough.

The electrodes smacked into my chest plate.

The electrical pulse went through the body armor like water through a sieve. Every nerve ending in my body stood on end and did a nasty little dance.

My skin burned as if it were on fire.

My legs buckled and I fell to the floor.

My heart stumbled like a drunk man on a broken sidewalk.

Tavia darted in from the side. A slice with her horn, and the wires parted. With a cry, she pivoted on two hooves and leaped right at William Teach.

The warlock scrambled back a step. Desperately, he brought up his staff to deflect Tavia's horn. Just in time.

Instead of plunging through his forehead, Tavia's horn sliced through the air a fraction of an inch from his face. Teach shouted to Gil and the two other cops he still held under his control.

"Kill them! I order you to kill them!"

They didn't move.

I realized what had happened as I forced my muscles to uncramp. Teach had forgotten to give orders using his magical language. We'd rattled him. He was making mistakes now.

I rolled to my knees as Tavia slashed at Teach again. Blood flew in a spatter from a small cut she'd opened up on his forearm. He cried out in pain, then grabbed Chavez by the shoulder.

Teach held him out in front like a shield as Tavia dove in for the killing blow. The unicorn barely managed to avert her strike. She hit Chavez with her shoulder and sent him sprawling. But the delay gave Teach an extra second to speak a single, ugly-sounding word.

Robot-like, Danny and Ron raised their Tasers to waist level. They fired blindly. Ron's Taser hit Danny in the gut. The big man crumpled with a groan.

The darts from Danny's weapon struck Tavia in her flank. She whinnied in surprise and pain, then collapsed on her side. Her legs convulsed violently and then went still.

I struggled to my feet. Pulled my Glock and pointed it at William Teach. My gun arm tingled with pins and needles, as if I'd slept on it wrong.

Teach held the butt of his staff above Tavia's neck as she lay on the ground at his feet.

"Put your weapon down," he said darkly, "Or I bash her throat in."

CHAPTER TWENTY-FOUR

I steadied the gun by gripping it with both hands.

"I don't think so," I said, through clenched teeth.

And then, William Teach did the one thing I didn't expect.

"I suppose you have me at a disadvantage," he sighed. "You win."

He moved his staff off to one side, and dropped it. The dark, oily looking length of wood bounced on the cement floor with a clatter.

William Teach put his hands up in surrender.

"Before you 'cuff me', I have a question," he said reasonably. "Has the unicorn ever told you about the partnership of the Rose and the Vine?"

Now that was something out of left field. Of all the things I could have imagined William Teach saying to me, this wasn't exactly on the list.

"No need to answer," he continued, when he saw my puzzled look. "It's what the unicorns call their relationship with the humans of the Morning Land. Would you like to know how the equines treat your people? Your brethren?"

"I could care less," I said. But I had to admit that he had me on that one. Tavia had never raised the subject, not once. "You're hardly in a position to judge the unicorns, Teach. You're the one who tried to conquer *them*."

"Is that what they told you? That I intended to conquer their precious kingdom?" Teach looked at me contemptuously. "I came because the people of the Red March—my people, Detective Ridder—were starving. The March has little rain, long winters, and poor soil. A poor place for crops, a poor place for people. But it's the only place men may live if they refuse to lay down their lives when the equines demand it."

I wasn't ready to believe all that the man said. But something linked up in my head with a click. My mind went back to the evening that Tavia and I had argued.

Tavia had refused to tell me Teach's motivation, and how she knew when the warlock would return. When I'd figured out part of the mystery on my own, she had apologized. She said that she'd 'underestimated me'.

Despite her friendly demeanor and kind words, Tavia had thought that I, a mere human, hadn't been all that intelligent.

"Maybe there's some truth in that," I acknowledged, "but it doesn't matter. You're standing trial for the murder of Dorian Martinez."

I didn't take my gun off Teach for a second. My gun arm finally felt steady, so I dropped one hand. Fumbled at my side for the handcuffs. I took a step forward.

William Teach smiled and spoke a single syllable.

My trigger finger went numb.

The awful, crushing weight of William Teach's magic bore down on me as he spoke a second word. My gun arm shifted off to the side. My brain exploded on the inside with a splash of liquid napalm as I struggled with the warlock for control of my body.

But my anger burned all the hotter. All his words had been designed for one thing. To sucker me into walking closer, into his range of power.

Teach struggled with me in turn. His face went from pale to corpse-white. He threw up one claw like hand. Grasped at the air as he focused his power. As he did, I caught a glimpse of what lay under his black duster.

He'd clipped a hexagonal chunk of yellow metal and plastic to his belt. I recognized the device in an instant. All of I sudden, I knew what I had to do.

"You see, Detective Ridder? I can hold you and the unicorn in my power at the same time," he rasped. "Neither you nor she can move unless I give you leave. And before I dispose of you, I'm going to have you put a bullet in her skull."

I couldn't move my arm enough to point my gun right at Teach, not while he focused his will on me. But I managed to swing my arm back in the direction of my target. It was enough.

With the last of my strength, I forced my fingers to move. To squeeze the Glock's trigger. With a *bang!* the bullet flew true.

I didn't hit Teach. But he hadn't been my target.

The yellow device clipped to his belt shattered.

The suffocating blanket of Teach's power vanished. Tavia leapt up as if she'd been coiled like a spring. The warlock, still whip-fast, threw himself aside. But her horn caught on the chain around Teach's neck. The silver links parted with a snap.

Teach spun away and grabbed his staff. I desperately looked for a shot, but Tavia was in the way. The warlock's opal dropped to the floor.

Without hesitation, the unicorn gored the stone with her horn. The air filled with the sound of breaking crystal. Opalescent shards flew outward in a glassy explosion.

William Teach let out a plaintive cry, as if Tavia had gored him instead of his trinket. He swung his staff at her with all of his might. The crook of the warlock's makeshift weapon struck Tavia's left foreleg.

A terrible, wet sound.

A *crack!* and then Tavia began screaming in agony.

She made a high, equine keening that rattled my teeth in my head.

I fired at Teach in a blind rage. The bullet hit his staff, snapped off the top of the crook. The impact knocked him down.

My next shot went over his head as he fell.

Teach spoke one more nasty word and faded into nothingness.

I ran to Tavia and knelt at her side. She sprawled out, limbs akimbo. Her long front teeth bit into her lower lip as she tried to remain quiet.

Tiny shards of crystal dotted her muzzle with red pinpricks. Blood pooled under her flank. The pool grew alarmingly fast. It spread across the floor in an iron-smelling, scarlet puddle.

Teach had shattered Tavia's foreleg.

Exposed bone gleamed white in the middle of the horrible wound.

"Derek," Tavia said, as she craned her neck. Trying desperately to keep me in her field of vision. "I can't—"

"You don't have to move," I said, my voice breaking.

From a memory I'd thought banished forever, I thought of my wife's final moments. Every fiber of my being wanted to drop everything, to hold her and tell her that it was all right. To comfort her and beg forgiveness for failing her.

"No. Not...move." Tavia was weeping, gasping. "I can't...this isn't a wound...a unicorn can recover from."

Tavia shifted her head. With her horn, she gently tapped the back of one of my hands. The hand that still gripped the loaded Glock.

"If this is to be my fate..." she whispered, "Then you must help me...embrace it."

Tavia's tears flowed like sea foam. Like droplets of quicksilver. Like pure, molten despair. It broke my heart to see it.

I raised the barrel of my gun.

CHAPTER TWENTY-FIVE

Tavia's eyes followed the path of the gun barrel. She watched as I moved it away from her. As I slipped the weapon back into its holster.

The peppery taste of anger filled my mouth. This time, not the anger of blind rage. Something more indignant. Purposeful. I turned away from Tavia and ran back towards the parked van.

"Please…" Tavia's words were delicate and plaintive. A dying girl's voice. "Please, don't…don't leave me…"

I ignored her. Threw open the van's passenger side door. With one hand I reached for the radio while I felt under the seat with the other.

I called dispatch as I found what I was looking for. Per regulations, a first aid kit had been stashed under the seat. I unclipped the case from the seat pad, then got back to Tavia as quickly as I could.

She raised her head weakly as I approached. Her dark blue eyes were clear and focused, but full of fear.

"Listen to me." I snapped the kit's case open. "I don't care whether or not your people would 'embrace' this kind of fate. You're not in the Morning Land anymore. You're in my world now, so you'd better deal with it."

Tavia said nothing. She focused her gaze on me in a mixture of puzzlement and wonder. She didn't flinch as I jabbed her side with the medical kit's supply of morphine.

I bent down, moved to her broken leg. I wasn't sure what to do for her compound fracture. But I couldn't let her bleed to death.

I slipped a tourniquet on her leg above the knee, or whatever the hell they called it on a horse. As I tightened the cloth, the flow of blood at the break slowed to a trickle.

Tavia didn't move through any of my work. She simply continued to look at me. She hardly blinked. As if she was trying to drink in my image.

I put my hand out and rested it on her cheek. She sighed as I stroked her mane, her golden hair now matted with red. Her tears continued to flow, plinking onto the dirty concrete floor.

* * *

The last arrangement I'd made with Captain Birch had been to keep a veterinary clinic's ambulance standing by. And by chance, I knew the vet. Dr. Martin Kimmel owned the San Gabriel Horse Clinic. But I knew him as the Pasadena racetrack's on-site horse doctor.

Martin was as much a California transplant as me, which gave us a lot to talk about after work. He drove a beat-up pickup that looked as if it belonged to the migrant family from *The Grapes of Wrath*. But that night, he and his team of veterinary assistants arrived on scene within minutes of my call.

It took all four of them to gently lift Tavia into a pneumatically powered machine that was a cross between a sling and a stretcher. They had to cut off her harness belt, which I accepted without a word. Without so much as a raised eyebrow, Martin kept up a calm flow of orders.

How to move the unicorn. How to stabilize her. How to keep her from going into shock.

I watched the ambulance pull away in a cloud of dust. I stood there for God knows how long.

Staring out into the darkness.

Feeling as empty as I'd ever been.

Hollow.

One of the officers touched my arm, tried to speak to me. I shook my head savagely and pulled away. I grabbed a spare outfit from the back of the van, shucked my blood-stained clothes, and haphazardly threw on the new apparel.

Fingers trembling, I put the keys into the ignition. I threw the van into motion before I'd even buckled the new set of pants.

I drove to the clinic with one foot on the accelerator and one hand on the horn. Had there been any cops in the area, they'd have been happy to give me a ticket, but I didn't give a damn. I screeched the van to a stop across three open parking spaces and ran full-tilt into the lobby.

Martin must have given yet more orders to the staff. A pair of beefy orderlies manned the front desk. They gently-but-firmly steered me over to a waiting area.

Three hours passed with agonizing slowness. I plowed through what must have been an entire stack of magazines. I barely took note of what I was actually reading. *Horse Fancy*, or something like that.

All the while, I kept circling over to the coffee machine. Mechanically, I drank down cup after cup. I didn't know why I wanted coffee. I didn't taste a damned thing.

My mind was a featureless, formless blur. A whirl of images that did nothing but tell me that I'd failed again. I put my head in my hands. Pressed my fingers against my temples. Took a couple deep, shuddering breaths.

These feelings were all too familiar. I had felt them when I'd woken up in a hospital bed a month earlier. When Teach had murdered Dorian Martinez.

I leaned back and looked at the dingy acoustic tiles in the ceiling. I wasn't a church-going man. Hadn't been in a long while.

I closed my eyes and tried to think of a prayer.

The door opened. Martin came in. His surgical scrubs were badly wrinkled. And his face looked deathly grim.

A part of me inside cried out, *But I didn't even get a chance to pray yet!*

When I spoke, my voice sounded a lot harsher than I meant it to.

"Talk to me, Martin."

"She's alive," he said. "For now."

And with that, he pushed past me to pour himself some coffee. He dumped a packet of ersatz cream into the cup, and then gulped down the entire thing. Poured another, tossed in the cream, stared deep into the fragrant swirl of brown and white.

"That's...good news," I said carefully. "Isn't it?"

"It is." Martin gave me a look. "I don't think she's going to make it, though."

CHAPTER TWENTY-SIX

Martin's words washed over me.

I don't think she's going to make it.

I staggered back a step. As if he'd struck me. Punched me in the gut, robbed me of my air. I met his weary eyes, tried to choose my words carefully.

"Is she...is she in a lot of pain?"

"We've got enough medication in her so that she shouldn't be feeling much," Martin replied. "At least she claims that she's not hurting badly, which is something."

I stifled a bitter, brittle laugh. Shook my head in amazement.

"I can't believe how calm you are about that. I mean, that one of your patients can actually talk back to you."

"You shouldn't be surprised," he said. "All of my patients talk to me. They just don't all speak through the voice box."

It made sense, I guessed. I kept silent and continued to listen.

"The break was a lot cleaner than it looked. Since you had us Johnny-on-the-spot, she didn't go into deep shock from loss of blood. And we're all lucky that the way unicorns and horses are put together is almost identical. It was easy to figure out what to stitch together."

"Then why—" I began, puzzled.

"Why do I think she won't pull through?" Martin stood. He took a long sip of coffee. "Because of what I just said. About speaking non-verbally. Your unicorn—"

"She's not my unicorn," I said, almost automatically. "No one owns a unicorn."

"Well, before I put her under, I told her that we'd do our best to save her. To send her back home to the Morning Land." The vet gave me a quizzical look. "She said that 'we shouldn't bother'. And then she apologized for making so much work for us."

I stared at him for a moment, uncomprehending.

"What are you saying?"

"When a patient arrives on my table, it's often beyond my skill to hold body and soul together. It's up to them to win that fight. Tonight...it was touch and go. And Derek, she didn't fight all that hard." He came over and put a hand on my shoulder. "Do you know what I mean?"

"Yeah," I said, my voice a dry whisper. "I do. I think she needs me now. Or someone."

"Or someone." On his way out, Martin added, "Room nine, at the back."

I went through the lobby and down the main hallway. The rooms I passed smelled faintly of liniment, antiseptic, and horse sweat. Carefully, I pushed through the last set of doors.

Tavia hung half-suspended before me. A series of ceiling-mounted straps ran through a rectangular metal frame, then under her chest and belly. Three of her legs dangled freely, hooves barely in contact with the floor. A clear plastic splint looked as if it had been shrink-wrapped to her injured foreleg.

Her nostrils slowly flexed as she breathed, deep in a drugged slumber. Tavia's head had been placed into a robin's egg blue harness and tethered to hold it upright. Someone had sponged the worst of the bloodstains from her mane, and the strands of her mane, dotted with colorful beads, lay limply against her neck. Small, round bandages pockmarked her face from where the medical team had pulled out shards of opal.

The room didn't have a bedside chair like in a human hospital. I suppose I shouldn't have expected one. After all, how many horse owners would actually stay there, waiting for their mount to wake up?

I went back to the waiting area, then raised a fingernails-on-the-blackboard screech as I dragged one of the half-recliners back with me. I pulled it into the room and did my best to get comfortable. It wasn't until a few hours later, after I'd woken from a troubled doze that I realized Tavia had come to.

She remained silent. A sooty blackness ringed her eyes. Though she was able to focus on me, her gaze was miserable and sad.

"Hello, Derek," she said. Her voice sounded as fragile as spun sugar. But it was clear, not slurred. Whatever drugs Martin had her on, they didn't interfere with her mind.

"Tavia, the doctor says that you're going to be fine. He's worried about you, though." My throat felt swollen, dry. I swallowed, then tried to continue. "I'm worried about you, too."

"I just don't know," she said softly. "I just don't know if you did the right thing, bringing me here."

"And you know my answer to that. You're alive, and you deserve to live."

"Do I? I've made so many mistakes. I led us into Teach's trap, and almost ended up killing us both. I let Teach fight his way out of our grasp tonight." She made an effort to turn her head, to face me directly. "But worst of all, I mistook you for less of a man than you really are, Derek. I should have told you everything. The source for Teach's animosity towards my people."

"There's one last thing," I said. "Do you remember when I offered you my room that first night after you arrived? You said 'I know I look like a horse to you', but that you preferred to be outside."

She nodded. Again, her dark blue eyes didn't leave mine as I continued to speak.

"I wouldn't offer my room to an animal, Tavia. I wasn't thinking of you as a horse. I was thinking of you as a person. As my friend."

Tavia scraped her free forehoof on the floor. Shook her head as a shudder ran down her golden flanks. I realized that she was trying not to laugh.

"This contraption I'm stuck in...it's so...undignified! I cannot bow to you, offer you my fealty."

"There will be plenty of time for bowing after we get you back on all fours," I said, chuckling.

I realized right then that I'd broken out into a happy grin. I felt warm, invigorated. Like I'd stepped into a ray of sunshine after a violent thunderstorm.

Tavia's eyes seemed brighter, somehow. More alive. I realized, right at that moment, that she'd decided she was going to fight harder. That she'd come back with me. For the next round against William Teach.

"That device on the warlock's belt... When you destroyed it, my counter spell worked. What was it?"

"It's a signal jammer," I explained. "Blocks cell phone reception. We have it on a banned electronics list."

"So Teach made the same connection we did."

"And took it one step further. If magical energy disrupts cell phone signals, then he must've figured it could work in reverse. Though I don't know why his spells worked and yours didn't."

She frowned at that. After a moment, she ventured, "The more specific a magic spell is, the better it works. The same could be true for his device. He could have tuned it to block all magic but his own."

"Then we might be in luck. We should be able to reconstruct his jammer, see how Teach set it up."

Tavia let out a great sigh. She shifted in her harness, making it creak loudly. Her tail flicked back and forth meditatively, as if she were shooing away flies. When she stopped to speak, her voice sounded firmer, clearer. Decisive.

"Our enemy got the best of us tonight for two reasons. First, I was wrong about what you and I share that makes us able to fight him. The loss of a loved one was no protection at all."

"What's the second reason?"

"I didn't understand your technology. I had no idea what a 'jammer' was."

I nodded in agreement. "Fair enough."

"If we are to beat William Teach, then we need to know more," she stated calmly. "And if I need to understand technology, then you need to grow as well."

I blinked. "In what way?"

Tavia cocked her head and looked at me intently.

"You're going to need to learn the ways of magic, Derek."

Michael Angel

Chapter Twenty-Seven

Martin held Tavia's X-rays up against the light. He glanced back at her with a frown. Then back to the X-ray. He shook his head in disbelief, as if he had to fight to accept the verdict.

"Of all the damned things," he said. "By all rights, I shouldn't be able to remove you from suspension for at least another three months."

"Indeed," Tavia replied. The sling that curved around her body creaked as she shifted her weight. "But despite your excellent care, a fortnight has been more than enough for me."

Martin threw up his hands. "Then we'll prep you for a mobile splint. Ten more days of physical therapy here before I release you."

"Ten more days?"

"If your magic repairs soft tissue as quickly as bone, then we'll see."

"But Doctor Kimmel—"

"We'll see," he said, in a tone that brooked no more argument. He pushed through the room's doors and called for his veterinary team.

"Go easy on him," I said, suppressing a chuckle. "Martin's worked on horses since he was old enough climb a stable fence. But in treating a unicorn…I think you've blown his mind a little."

"Well, maybe a little," she admitted. Tavia sighed and tossed her mane with a rattle of beads. She'd talked Martin into releasing her from the head harness, but that had been the extent of her freedom.

Tavia hadn't taken Martin's estimate of four months in the suspension sling very well. In fact, had Tavia not been firmly belted into the sling's frame, she'd have hit the floor in a dead faint. Equines of any sort hated confinement, and Tavia was no different.

My apprenticeship in magical lore began that morning.

Tavia asked me to get the healing salve out of her harness belt. I retrieved the belt from where I'd tossed it into the back of the van. The blood-soaked leather strap had been ruined when Martin's people cut Tavia free from it, but the contents were undamaged.

"The salve itself contains a healing energy," Tavia explained. "We need to add ingredients to enhance it, make it into a paste for my wound."

Pausing once in a while to rest, Tavia dictated to me the properties, shape, scent, and look of substances like tree-foil, ground pequod, and night emerald. Armed with copious notes and a fistful of cash, I headed out to the local herbalist shops in Los Angeles' small Chinatown.

I completed my scavenger hunt more quickly than I'd hoped. When I returned, I mixed the ingredients into a slurry of something resembling overcooked spinach. I carefully slathered the mixture around her wound, doing my best to ignore the sharp scents of peppermint mixed with cumin.

Once I'd completed that task, I left to report in to Captain Birch. I didn't get back to the clinic until evening had fallen. But when I entered the room, it took a few moments for Tavia to realize I'd returned. Her head hung listlessly at the end of the harness tether. Her golden forelock drooped over her face. The look of despair on her face sent a stab of pain through me.

That was when I made up my mind. I'd stay with Tavia, no matter what.

I began by stealing one of the clinic's couches from their waiting room. Next, I called in a favor that Lynn Macedo owed me. She stopped by my house to bring me some linens, a travel kit, and a suitcase full of clothes. Lynn also volunteered to bring us groceries and dinner as often as she could.

This time neither of us objected to her visits.

Tavia never lost her temper—not once—during the entire ordeal. But she felt miserable, restless. So on Lynn's next visit, I asked her to make a library run for a stack of books and DVDs.

I decided to tutor Tavia as best I could in basic science: electronics, biology, and chemistry. We quickly learned that it was extremely boring for me to hold the books and turn the pages for her. I'd still have done it, but Tavia shook her head and surprised me with her next request.

"I'd really like it if you read to me, Derek," she said.

At times, we would spend an entire evening with only the gentle light of a desk lamp to illuminate the pages. Tavia would listen intently to the rise and fall of my voice. In return, she'd explain what she called 'herbal lore' to me, and she often compared my chemistry lessons to what she'd learned on her own.

Given the need to keep Tavia occupied, I worked out a system to keep her mind off her confinement. If I needed a break or wanted to take a nap, I'd play a DVD on a television we borrowed from the clinic staff.

One time, when I'd stopped to let my voice rest, I decided to soothe my throat with some ice cream. Out of curiosity, Tavia asked to try some.

That one taste quickly converted her into an ice cream addict.

Bowls and cones proved awkward. So every evening, I would scoop Tavia's portion out onto a platter for her to eat. If her tastes were any indication, then Cherry Garcia promised to be a smash hit with the Morning Land's unicorns.

As I watched, the vets strapped a pair of steel and plastic braces to Tavia's leg. They followed it up by wrapping the braces with what looked like a roll of shiny, blue vinyl. Martin watched them finish the work, then flipped a wall switch.

The grinding hum of an electric motor. And slowly, ever so slowly, Tavia's hooves descended to rest on the floor. Martin's team worked like a trained pit crew, unbuckling Tavia from the frame that had kept her immobile, then respectfully stood back.

Tavia whinnied with happiness as she was released.

She shook her flanks, like a dog after a bath. Then she took a tentative step on the healing leg. Testing it.

Tavia began a jerky, measured pace back and forth as her legs remembered how they worked. It was a far cry from a trot, let alone a gallop. But she tossed her mane with abandon and her eyes shone brightly.

"You have no idea how good this feels!" she cried joyfully. I followed her, held a hand to her side as she stumped around the perimeter of the room.

"Just pace yourself, you headstrong filly." I stroked her mane. "You don't want to give Martin any excuse to put you back in traction."

"Never, never!" she declared. "But we need to keep moving. Need to use these next ten days."

"You think William Teach will be back next week," I nodded.

She shook her head.

"Not this time. We won't be seeing him for at least a couple of months. We destroyed his two magical artifacts. He'll be in my world, trying to replace them."

"His opal," I said, understanding. "His staff."

"Exactly. So we're going to take the fight to the warlock. And you need to study magic beyond basic herbalism."

I blinked. "You don't mean—"

"Yes, I do, Derek." Tavia tossed her head, making her beads clatter. "You're going to have to come with me. To the Morning Land."

CHAPTER TWENTY-EIGHT

The cold wind from the East River scraped at my nose and ears like a dull knife. I paid it no mind. The view of Manhattan at dusk more than made up for the discomfort.

I stood on a palatial balcony that seemed anchored to the sky by a slender, silver needle and to the horizon with a pair of Art Deco eagle heads. I put my hands on the smooth, flat marble railing and looked down. Twenty stories below, a patchy layer of clouds roiled like hot steam.

Behind me, the balcony doors slid open with a hiss of compressed air. Tavia ambled through, her gait still stiff inside the bright blue splint.

"What do you think?" she asked, as she came to my side.

"I'm impressed. I've always seen the Chrysler Building from a distance. Never thought I'd get to cool my heels in the penthouse."

She let out a nicker. "To 'cool my heels'? I haven't heard that turn of phrase before. But the guidebooks don't tell you everything about this place."

"It's the Morning Land's embassy." I thought back. "And where your people placed the portal to cross between our worlds. Beyond that, it would be news to me."

"Most importantly, it's also Ambassador Stormwind's home. Pegasi prefer the highest spots around for their families."

"It's certainly secure," I said, nodding. "Anyone who wants to get up here has to get hold of the elevator. Or climb seventy flights of stairs."

Tavia winced and shifted her leg. "I don't even want to think about stairs."

She paused, and her ears swiveled forward, straining to catch greater scoops of sound. "I can hear the beat of Stormwind's wings. Here he comes."

I squinted, but I saw nothing for a few seconds. Then a shadow emerged from the clouds. A sleek, winged ghost. The shape resolved into the figure of a majestic white horse.

Stormwind drew closer to the skyscraper. Each downward stroke of his wings sounded like the muffled strike of a drumhead. As he drew nearer, I realized that the photos I'd seen of him hadn't done the Pegasus justice.

On the ground, his wings had been folded. And the aerial shots had provided no sense of scale. The distance between his downy wingtips could have belonged to a small airplane.

Stormwind veered to the right. He caught the building's updraft and soared skyward. The Pegasus made a tight spiral around the building's silver needle, then descended towards one of the outstretched eagle heads.

The elongated, art deco sculpture made a perfect landing strip for a horse-sized creature. At the last moment, Stormwind held his wings out stiff, flaring them with the ruffle of soft cloth. He came to a halt, buoyed in the wind for a single, timeless second. Then, with a sharp *tic!* he landed on all four hooves.

I realized that I had been holding my breath the entire time.

Tavia let out a neigh of greeting. Stormwind nodded, but didn't return it. I realized the Pegasus wore what I could have sworn was a World War I era gas mask. The stallion folded his wings like a great bird of prey. With a toss of his head, he indicated that we should follow along.

The balcony doors swung open, admitting us into the wide open expanse of carpeted flooring, chevron-shaped lamp fixtures, and teak wood panels. The apartment looked spartan, but spotlessly clean. Every surface gleamed, and each breath of air held the rich scent of lemon oil.

Stormwind leaned his head against a concave spot in the wall where a little hook projected out. The stallion pulled back and down, and the mask slipped right off. He focused his guileless, coal-black eyes on me for the first time.

"I beg your pardon, but I absolutely *hate* flying in this city," Stormwind fumed. His voice sounded rich and round in my ear. The tones of an annoyed patrician. "The smog burns my eyes and sullies my feathers. I swear on my dam's aerie that someday, I'm going to quit commuting and just do everything online."

Tavia nickered, though I wasn't sure if it was due to Stormwind's words or the sound of my jaw dropping as it hit the carpeted floor.

The Pegasus bowed slightly. "Ambassador Stormwind, Clan of the Osprey, at your service, kind sir."

I returned the bow. "Thank you, Ambassador. I'm Detective Derek Ridder, of the Los Angeles Police Department."

Stormwind snorted, almost meditatively. "Derek Ridder. Your name's been crossing my desk a lot. Have we ever met before?"

"Ah, not...not really," I said. I had to force the words out. I found to my surprise that my throat had gone dry. "You couldn't know this, of course, but I've seen you twice before. Your picture, I mean. Both times I saw you, someone close to me died."

For a moment, I heard nothing but the howl of the wind outside. The nervous shift of hoof on carpet. Stormwind cleared his throat.

"I see," he said, and his voice dripped with wry humor. "Well, that's the first time anyone told me I was a harbinger of doom. I've got a question for you."

I nodded.

"Are you this much fun at parties as well?"

I relaxed. If I'd offended Stormwind, he was enough of a diplomat to let it pass. "I try and keep the ominous predictions to one per evening, ambassador."

"Very good!" Stormwind punctuated his statement with a stamp of a forehoof. "I like that. Now that I think of it, I first saw your name on a child's letter. I'd sent it on to the Warder of Cavilad."

"And that letter is why we're both here now," Tavia chimed in. "We need to use the portal, as soon as possible."

"Yes, yes. I read your reports cover to cover," Stormwind replied. His eyes flicked over me once more, almost furtively. "But we're bringing some sensitive shipments through right now. Sometime in the next seventy-two hours, we should be able to accommodate you."

"Three days?" Tavia said, disbelieving. "Time is of the essence here!"

"Is it, now? Perhaps you need to explain why, then. You claim that Sir William Teach will be stuck in our world, replacing his warlock's staff. I doubt that even the best lore-master could make one in less than a few months."

"You're forgetting about his opal. The one I shattered."

"Yes, about that. I had a delver look at the shards you sent. The stone showed no trace of magic, none at all."

"Teach wouldn't keep a trinket like that around for sentimental reasons," I interjected.

"I agree," Tavia said. "Whatever power the stone had, Teach needed it. We don't want him to find a way to get it again."

"Be that as it may," Stormwind said sternly, "My duties as portal guardian do not revolve around your requests. In fact—"

Suddenly, the *crash!* of breaking glass came from one of the rooms down the corridor.

"Looks like you-know-who is up to no good again," Tavia said.

"He's going to be the death of me!" Stormwind spat, and he trotted forward down the wide corridor.

Tavia chuckled and nudged my side. "Wait until you see this."

"Get back in your room!" Stormwind scolded.

A little boy's voice replied defiantly, "Never! No prison can hold the forces of good!"

The rapid clip-clop of hooves echoed down the corridor. A yearling Pegasus came barreling towards us, his snowy wings unfurled just enough to brush the sides of the walls. Around his forehead, he wore a black bandanna with a pair of eyeholes cut out. Let's just say that Zorro would have recognized the get-up.

"Ta ta TA!" he trumpeted, "I'm Thunderbolt...the WONDER-COLT!"

Thunderbolt spotted me in mid-stride. He braked on all four hooves and skidded to a stop right in front of me and Tavia.

"Whoa!" he said, as his eyes went wide. "Who're you?"

CHAPTER TWENTY-NINE

In spite of myself, I broke into a wide smile as I regarded Thunderbolt. The kid looked ungainly—like a bundle of white-skinned sticks trimmed with feathers and downy horsehair. But cute, nevertheless.

"That's Detective Ridder from the Los Angeles Police Department," Stormwind said sternly, as he rejoined us. "He's here to keep an eye on yearling colts who don't know when to stop playing cops and robbers. He's sent an awful lot of kids like you 'up the river', so you'd better behave."

Stormwind looked over the colt's head and gave me a wink. Thunderbolt cocked his head at me, not sure what to believe. He looked like a carbon copy of his dad except for the shiny black socks on each of his skinny legs.

I took a breath to respond when the gentle chime of a page sounded from a speaker set into the ceiling. A cultured, male voice echoed in the room.

"Ambassador Stormwind, there is a call for you on line one."

"Take a message," he said impatiently, with a stomp of his forehoof.

"Someone's calling about a wildfire, sir."

Stormwind froze for a moment. He half turned and made an exaggerated bow to me. "My apologies, Mr. Ridder. A matter of utmost urgency has come up which I must handle for a few moments."

"Then I will attend as well," Tavia said.

"That's not necessary. It's a routine matter, though it is one that requires...strictly equine attention."

"Last I checked," Tavia replied with a snort, "I still qualify."

"Ah, yes," Stormwind said, a trifle nervously, I thought. "I suppose that you could attend. Mr. Ridder, perhaps you can watch my son for a few minutes? I just don't want him going outside right now."

"Not a problem."

And with that, the Pegasus and unicorn left me alone with Thunderbolt. The colt continued to eye me curiously. He ruffled his wings a little and spoke up.

"So, you're the detective guy from California," the colt said, still sizing me up. "I heard my dad talk about you when he read Tavia's stuff. A lot, actually."

"He did?"

"Yeah, he did." The colt nudged open the door on my left. Inside, a bay window cast light onto a desk piled high with documents. "See what the paper on the top stack says?"

All right. Looking back at it, I was a little slow on the uptake. I actually took a step into the room to get a better look at the paper.

Thunderbolt head-butted me in the small of my back. With a grunt, he shoved me into the room. I wind milled my arms as I stumbled forward. The little colt grabbed the doorknob in his mouth and slammed the door shut.

"Ha!" I heard him exclaim. "Too slow!"

The sound of hoofbeats on carpet. I cursed, fumbled with the knob, and threw the door back open. Back towards the balcony, I heard the French doors slide open.

"Hey!" I shouted, as I dashed after him. "Get back here, you little—"

"No one can catch the Wonder-Colt!"

I ran through the open doors. The wind brushed against my cheek, cold and raw. I came to a stop on the balcony and slowly raised my hands, palms out.

Thunderbolt perched on the balcony's slippery marble railing.

"I know you can fly," I said, trying to sound confident and in charge. "You don't have to impress me."

"Fly? With these?" Thunderbolt flexed his wings, held them aloft. "Nah. I use them mostly for balance right now. Check it out!"

He held his wings out horizontally. Then slowly raised his left hooves in unison, balancing on the right ones.

"Very impressive. Just...get down. Very. Slowly."

A howl in my ears, as a sudden gust raked the balcony. The wind caught Thunderbolt's wings, lifting them. Nudged his hooves off balance.

The colt made a startled whinny and pitched over the edge.

I ran to the edge of the balcony. The colt tumbled head over tail as he fell.

Now's the time he spreads his wings, right? Right? Any time now...

He vanished into the cloud layer below with a tiny wail. My heart pounded in my throat. Cold sweat broke out on my forehead.

I scanned the mist desperately. I called Thunderbolt's name. Only the roar of the wind answered me. The clouds below roiled unsteadily. My stomach did the same thing. Or at least it did, until I realized what was going on.

I took a deep breath. Removed my hands from the railing. I steadied my voice so that it stayed deep and stern.

"All right. You had me fooled. But the game's over."

A voice behind me replied immediately.

"Aw, you're no fun!"

I turned and saw Thunderbolt standing safely on the balcony. His Zorro mask had slipped off a little on one side. Probably during that fall he'd faked, or when he'd zipped around the side of the building under the cloud cover.

"And you haven't been having any fun either."

"I have *not* been having too much fun! I'm—" Thunderbolt stopped. His nose wrinkled as he gave me a puzzled look. "Wait...how did you know I wasn't? Having any fun, I mean. My dad just wants to keep me inside all the time."

"I know how he feels." I squatted to talk with the kid eye-to-eye. "If I was your dad, I'd be tempted to do the same thing."

"You would?" Thunderbolt cocked his head at me again. "What makes you say that? Have you really sent a lot of kids 'up the river' like my dad says?"

"Just one," I held up a single finger. "My seven-year old niece, Rachel. Somehow, I think you two would get along."

"Where is she now? I mean, where did you send her?"

"I wish I knew where she was," I admitted. "Rachel and her mom had to go into the witness protection program. Hidden, where the bad guys can't get to them. So I know the reason your dad wants you inside, safe and bored."

"What's that?"

"Because he loves you as much as I love my niece," I said simply.

Thunderbolt looked down at the balcony. He absently pawed at the marble slabs with one hoof. He gave a cute little snort, then spoke again.

"Those are bad guys you and Tavia are after, right?"

"Uh-huh." I rubbed my hands together to keep them warm, then got up and walked back towards the apartment. Thunderbolt fell in at my side. "That's why Tavia and I are here. To ask your dad if we can use the portal here. I need to visit your homeland, try to learn more about how to fight the bad guys."

"This is too cool!" Thunderbolt said. "My dad will let you use it, I'm sure."

"Best news I've heard all day," I said heartily, as the doors opened and slid shut behind us.

My smile froze on my face at Thunderbolt's next cheerful statement.

"Yup, and I'm going to come along and fight bad guys with the two of you!"

"Wait, what?" I stopped in mid-stride. "I didn't say anything about your coming along."

"Well, of course you didn't *say* that," he said, with a roll of his eyes. "You're not from the Morning Land, and Tavia's a daughter of the Warder. Of course *she* can't ask for help. But it's obvious that you need it!"

Thunderbolt's ears perked up as a nearby door opened with a creak and Tavia rejoined us. Her expression seemed peeved and her tail fairly slashed the air as she twitched it back and forth.

"Your father wants to see you right away," Tavia told the young Pegasus.

"Aw, do I have to? Detective Ridder and I were just talking about—"

"Now," Tavia said sharply, with a stamp of her hoof. Thunderbolt dashed through the open door without another word. It slammed shut behind him.

"Trouble?" I inquired.

"Stormwind just tossed me out of his meeting," Tavia complained. "On top of that, he gave us each a task for this evening. Before we head to my world."

My pulse quickened. "We're leaving tonight?"

"So long as I fill out the right stack of forms. And so long as you pick up your prescription from the drugstore down the block." She nodded at my questioning glance. "Yes, it's medicine. Immune system boosters, mostly. The Morning Land has some nasty germs that even magic won't keep out."

"Right." I dug in my jacket pockets and pulled on a pair of gloves. "Give me a few minutes and I'll be ready."

"We have a couple of hours. Take your time." Tavia walked me to the elevator. "Otherwise, you may end up pony-sitting Thunderbolt again. The last time I was here, the self-proclaimed 'Wonder-Colt' scared me senseless by pretending to swan-dive off the balcony."

"Imagine that," I said, keeping a straight face. The burnished brass faces of the elevator doors slid open. "I'll be back in a bit."

In a flash, the car whisked me down at an eardrum-popping speed. A *ping*. I stepped out and faced the powder-white, marble chamber that made up the sumptuous front desk.

"Sir," one of the clerks called, "You have someone waiting for you in the lobby. He said he was expecting you."

I nodded curtly, hiding my surprise. I turned and took a few steps into the adjoining room, where the white marble shaded into furniture the color of sangria wine and dark coffee. A lone man sat in one of the wingback chairs. Legs crossed, face buried in the folds of a copy of the *New York Times*.

The paper rustled as the man folded it up with a surgeon's precision. His sallow face and gray eyes held no more warmth than the first time I'd seen them.

"Well, good evening, Ridder," said Federal Agent Coombes. "Let's go take a walk down to the corner drugstore. We've got a lot to talk about."

CHAPTER THIRTY

Coombes wore a charcoal-colored suit and tie with gold cufflinks. His expression remained poker-player inscrutable as we stepped outside into the chill air and turned to walk up Lexington Avenue. But given the bags that hung under his cold, gray eyes, he hadn't been sleeping much lately.

"I was wondering when we'd next meet," I said. "Thought you still might be back in Los Angeles, watching my house."

Coombes gave me a wry grin. "Not bad, Ridder. Have you come to any other conclusions about me?"

"I had you pegged as Secret Service. But I asked Captain Birch to do a database search on you. Your name didn't come up."

"Be surprised if it did. My little branch of the Secret Service is 'off the books'. We monitor and protect individuals from the Morning Land."

I rounded on Coombes, fists clenched. "Then what the hell were you doing the night Teach almost killed Tavia?"

"Nothing," Coombes said sourly. "I'm posted out of Pasadena. Could've had a security detail on site in twenty minutes. But we got orders to hold back."

"Orders from who?"

"Tavia herself. She didn't want me talking to you about William Teach just yet. Or about the partnership of the Rose and Vine."

That stopped me. I looked away from Coombes and into the nearby swirl of traffic. Smack in the middle of Manhattan, and all of a sudden, I felt alone.

"All right, I'll bite. Why didn't she want me talking with you?"

"I was in the first group sent to the Morning Land, to act as ambassadors and researchers," Coombes said, as he rubbed his palms together to keep warm. "The partnership Teach told you about is real enough. In Morning Land parlance, the unicorns are the Vines. Humans and other species are the Roses."

"Doesn't sound that bad to me."

"Maybe, maybe not. In many vineyards, vintners' plant rose bushes at the edge of their grape vines. That's because roses and grape vines suffer from the same kinds of problems, like leaf blight. But the roses will always catch the blight first. So, even though the rose bush may be consumed by the disease, it alerts the vintner, to save the all-important grape vines before the harvest is ruined."

It came to me in a flash.

"Teach talked about having to 'lay one's life down' for the equines. So instead of blight, we're talking about the regular invasions of the Tengan, aren't we?"

"Got it in one. If you don't want to do your required military service against the Tengan, you're exiled to the Red March."

"But, if he doesn't want to fight off the Tengan, why try and...well, it looks like he wants to ally himself with them."

"Teach wants to break the existing system, at whatever the cost. I suppose I can't blame him." Coombes shook a finger at me as he added, "Don't think I'm absolving him for what he's done. But he wants humans—with himself in the lead role—to have more of a say in how things are run."

We turned the corner and saw the drugstore's welcoming neon sign ahead. Coombes nodded towards where a little coffee stand huddled in the lee of the building. I didn't protest as he bought two cups of fresh coffee and handed one to me. I shook a packet of sugar into mine as Coombes went on.

"Teach isn't the only one. The whole Morning Land's abuzz with how they might be able to break the cycle of barbarism they've been trapped in."

I took a sip of coffee and felt the liquid do a pleasant burn down the back of my throat. "What are you talking about, Coombes?"

"Every few decades, the Morning Land has to gear up for war against the Tengan. It's slowed their development. The last time the Morning Land was in contact with our world, we shared the same technology. Blacksmith-forged steel. Three-field crop rotation. Water-powered mills to grind grain. But now? Nine hundred years later, and they're still in the late medieval period."

"While we went on to invent the automobile and jet plane," I finished. "We've gone to the moon. Exploded the atom bomb. Magic or no, I can see why they'd want to get their hands on our technology. Particularly the weapons."

"That's why I'm here," Coombes said, as we continued on towards the drugstore at a slow, deliberate pace. "It's why Tavia is here, too. The Warder of Cavilad sent his daughter to our world in order to keep tabs on two people. The two he thinks are trying to smash the partnership of the Rose and the Vine."

"My niece's summons told Tavia exactly where to find the first."

"Correct. And you met the second one tonight." Coombes nodded in emphasis as I turned to stare at him. "Ambassador Stormwind has been doing his damnedest to buy armaments and ship them to the Morning Land. Imagine what someone could do with a case of AK-47s there. Especially if they commanded a few more loyal troops than Sir William Teach."

I pressed my lips together in thought. I recalled Stormwind's furtive looks, his moves to keep me and Tavia out of his meeting. The dark, rich taste of the coffee turned milk-sour in my stomach.

"Why are you telling me this, Coombes?"

"Because I need you to step up and be a good American. I want to know if you've heard or seen anything of interest at the embassy, no matter how small."

I hesitated once more. "Who's he buying weapons from?"

"Anyplace willing to cut a deal. Russian mafia. Venezuelan drug cartels. Some of the rogue elements in the Middle East."

I took a breath and made my decision.

"Stormwind got an urgent page tonight. Someone called about a 'wildfire'."

Coombes' eyes flashed with a predatory gleam for one moment. "Thank you, Detective Ridder. I think you just gave me the piece that Tavia and I were looking for. Right before she got your niece's letter."

"So that's why you were so ticked off at me when we first met," I mused. "Rachel's letter interrupted your investigation. And I'd thought that you were simply jealous that I'd get to work with a unicorn, not you."

Coombes let out a short bark of a laugh.

"You make it sound like I had a high-school crush on the filly!" He stopped, then turned serious. "But there is something to keep in mind. Haven't you noticed the effect a unicorn or a Pegasus has on people? Everyone's in awe; they're almost worshipful when they first meet one. You're only starting to get over it yourself."

"Yeah, you have a point there," I admitted, thinking of my first meetings with Tavia. The reactions of everyone from Rachel to Captain Birch.

Coombes gave me a hard look. "Let me give you some advice for where you're going. The people of the Morning Land tend to think in straight lines. A lot of them make assumptions based on social rank. Rules. Custom. Don't do that. Keep your wits about you. Above all, keep thinking like a cop."

"Thanks, Coombes." I extended my arm and we shook hands.

"No thanks necessary," Coombes demurred. "I'm a little envious of you right now, Ridder. Once you've been to the Morning Land, everything else is just a little...ordinary."

CHAPTER THIRTY-ONE

The sweet, amber scent of apples.

Sunlight warm on my cheek.

A slight jostling sensation that threatened to wake me out of my slumber.

My mind slipped back a couple of decades, to a time when my Dad's Buick bumped over small potholes in the road. Flickers of shadow, cool on my skin as they flitted by like the ghost of a summer breeze. Afternoon on the road to Lake Ariel, where we'd go fishing, or pick up a gallon of farm fresh cider. I'd hop in the back seat to catch a nap, asleep with the certainty of a nine-year old boy that my father would take care of everything.

"Wake up, Derek, we're here," Dad said. Though it was kind of weird how his voice sounded way too high-pitched.

The motion of the car ceased abruptly as I sat up. I expected to see the car's weathered dashboard, cracked like desert hardpan from too much summer sun.

Instead, I sat almost face-to-face with a pretty unicorn filly, one with the oddest blue wrap on her left front leg. The sunlight through the trees dappled her golden side, turning her from a palomino into a pinto. I held a hand to my forehead as a breeze rustled the branches nearby.

"Tavia…" I groaned, "What…what happened?"

"Welcome to the Morning Land. It's normal to be disoriented for a minute or two, especially the first time you make the crossing."

I did feel more than a little light-headed. I remembered stepping through a doorway that looked like it had been made of bubble film and lit up with klieg lights. Then the awful sensation of falling. Falling through layers of mist, falling through a swirl of bright stars. Falling to the end of the universe.

Better watch that first step. It's a doozy.

"Oh, wow," I said intelligently. "If the ride lasted a little longer, you could put it up at the local amusement park and charge admission."

Tavia nickered softly. "Now there's an idea. It would be much better than that awful thing you call a carousel."

"What's wrong with the carousel?" I asked, as I got to my feet. My backpack lay next to one side. I scooped it up. "We used to call it the merry-go-round. I kinda liked riding it when I was a kid."

"It gives me the shivers. To me, it looks like a herd of horses impaled on wooden skewers going round and round."

"I never quite thought of it that way. You have a point there."

I looked around and saw that we'd arrived in the middle of a grove of apple trees. Bright red fruit hung on the branches like strings of miniature Chinese lanterns. The air smelled as fresh and pure as if we were in the mountains. It felt wonderful, and I took in deep breaths of it.

"Where are we, anyway?" I asked, as I slipped my arms into the backpack's straps. "I thought we'd have shown up in the City of Seven Bells."

"We're close to Cavilad's northwest border. It's a couple of hours to our destination, the dryad dwellings of Wyndoon." Tavia looked down and pawed the ground with her good foreleg. "Derek. I always want to be up front with you from now on. So please don't laugh at me, all right?"

I could see that she was serious. "All right."

She pawed the ground again, then looked at me. "When crossing into my world, I decided to arrive at this spot—a rather distant one, at that—for two reasons. I wanted you to help me out of this thrice-cursed splint. It doesn't feel a part of me, what I am, or where we are. It makes me feel alien in my own home, and I hate that."

"Fair enough. And the other reason?"

"I wanted to talk with you about…" Tavia stopped, with an irritated look in her eyes. She raised her left foreleg and chewed insistently at the top of the splint cover. "Ammit, this ishes!"

I knelt to peel off the vinyl-blue cover of her splint. Gently, I touched her foreleg, then opened the catches on the steel and plastic braces. They fell into my palm with a tinny little jingling sound. Tavia sighed, a sound of pure relief.

"That's over and done with," I said approvingly, as she flexed her foreleg. "What did you want to talk with me about?"

"Nothing in particular. And everything." Her tail flicked back and forth as she moved to a low-hanging branch on the nearest apple tree. "If you want to know anything about the Morning Land, I'd be happy to share. And once you're out of questions…I guess I just wanted to talk with you. I mean, about you. Where you grew up, what it was like."

I watched with amusement as Tavia extended her neck. She grasped a ripe fruit in her teeth and plucked it from the branch. With a flick of her jaws, Tavia crunched up her apple and swallowed it, stem, core, and all.

"Well, there's only one fixed gate that goes from my world to yours. The one in Manhattan. But how many gates lead from your world to mine?"

"Three. Well, four, if you count the one a few leagues to the east from here. But nobody uses that one."

"Too out of the way?"

"Too dangerous. It's guarded by a sphinx."

"Are you serious? A human-headed lion thing that eats you if you can't answer her riddles?"

"She's a 'he', and his name is Typhon." Tavia indicated a path worn in the grass at the edge of the clearing. "Let's continue on. The road is this way."

I fell in beside Tavia as she did a bouncy little walk. She wanted to stretch muscles that hadn't really been used while she'd been in recovery. I didn't mind in the slightest, as her gait made it easy to keep pace.

Flat paving stones lined with white gravel marked the course of the road. In the distance ahead of us, the land sloped towards the shimmering emerald mass of an old-growth forest. Around us, autumn colors had just begun to guild the trees. Far off, I heard the honking of geese on their way south.

"I suppose that you called Wyndoon, let them know we're on the way?"

In response, Tavia tossed her mane to the right. She angled her neck so I could see her braids more closely.

"My blue beads. I can use them to speak at a distance to whomever I choose. They're better than your phones, I think. I don't have to memorize those odd groups of numbers your people use. I just need to picture their face."

A thought occurred to me about that. "You can use them anywhere?"

"One can't communicate between our worlds, but otherwise, yes."

"So that's how you've been talking with Coombes," I said. "Did you know that I spoke with him before we went through the gate?"

"Good old Dickie Coombes," she snorted. "I don't like him very much, but at least we're on the same side."

"He's just trying to do his job. Like us."

"That is true enough. He wanted to speak with you before you came to the Morning Land. To tell you more about Teach. And about the Rose and Vine."

"I owe him for that," I nodded. "But that begs the question, Tavia. Why didn't *you* want to tell me?"

CHAPTER THIRTY-TWO

Tavia and I walked on together in silence for a while. The road wound on, slicing ruler-straight through the sunlit countryside like a pale gray knife. The bright sunlight made her horn and hooves sparkle. Finally, she let out a long, sad-sounding breath.

"At the start, I didn't tell you about Teach, or the agreement between our species, because I didn't think you needed to know. By the time I figured that you did, I was worried."

"About what?"

"That you'd be offended. In your world, humans haven't had to share power with another species, equine or otherwise. And I couldn't risk losing your help." Tavia threw me a sideways glance. "You may not realize it, but it's not easy for someone in my position to ask for any sort of aid."

"I'm beginning to understand that," I said, thinking of Thunderbolt's words.

"The only ruler outside of Cavilad who's pledged to assist us against William Teach is the Warder of Wyndoon," she continued. "The Warder is also one of the few who should be able to teach you how to use magic."

"The key there being 'should'."

"I'm sure that it's possible. At least one member of your family is sensitive to magical energies."

I considered for a moment. "You're talking about Rachel, I guess."

"Your niece is a natural delver. And a few creatures in your world are also magically sensitive. For example, there's a type of bee which is so clumsy that it shouldn't be able to fly at all. But it's able to tap magical energy and function pretty much as the Pegasi do."

"You mean bumblebees?" I laughed. "When I was growing up, I used to see them all the time. I'd never have guessed that they were magical."

"It does show that not everything magical has to have a horn, or wings," Tavia replied, with a flick of her tail. She cocked her head at me curiously. "If you would, I'd like to hear a little about what it was like. Where you grew up, I mean."

So I told her.

We talked as we continued on, taking pleasure in each other's company. I didn't think that anyone who'd grown up someplace like the Morning Land would find my childhood interesting, but it appeared that Tavia did. She mostly let me talk, and only asked questions when she didn't understand a term I used.

I told her about my family's roots, which ran through the small towns stuck smack-dab in the center of the great state of Pennsylvania. Where I grew up, you knew everybody by their first name. And by everybody, I meant that you knew the folks who pumped your gas, delivered the morning paper, or picked up your bags of leaves every autumn.

I explained that most of the families I knew when I was in grammar school were solid Protestant Germans. Or Dutch stock, like my family. The kind of folks who valued a thrifty, hard-working, and orderly home life.

Houses were painted white or tan. The curtains in the open kitchen windows were mostly the same red-and-white checkered pattern. And as far as the high school teachers were concerned, kids pretty much fell into two groups: those who had neat haircuts and properly respected their elders, and those who didn't.

Tavia let out a snort. "Here in the Morning Land, if a young human doesn't respect their elders, or get their hair cut properly, they soon learn to. At least when they have to perform service against the Tengan."

"Well, I suppose that battles are fought for lower stakes than here." I grinned. "In my town, whose mom bakes the best peach cobbler is a war fought with grim and not-so-quiet determination."

"Sounds peaceful," Tavia observed. "Too peaceful, perhaps. I think that a unicorn would get fat and lazy."

The air began to feel humid as the sun started to sink in the west. I smelled the moistness of damp leaves up ahead. We crested a small hill and looked down to where the road ended at the bank of a wide stream. On the far bank lay the first stretches of a dark green forest.

I didn't see a way across at first. Tavia pointed out a series of large, flat gray rocks that formed a ragged line across the water. We carefully moved from one to another until we'd safely crossed.

"We're now officially outside the Province of Cavilad," Tavia said, as she indicated the path ahead of us with her horn. "From here on out, we're in the dominion of the dryads."

The paved road had ended on Cavilad's side of the stream, but the dirt path ahead of us remained clear enough. I spotted a couple tracks in the sun-hardened mud by the bank. One or two wheeled ruts, perhaps made by wagons. Several marks were clearly made by the cloven hooves of unicorns.

We continued on into the woods, which were like nothing I'd ever seen. The larger trees resembled arrow-straight red oak, but they had a bleached-looking white bark. In contrast, their leaves were such a dark shade of green that they looked almost black. And despite the oak-like nature of the trees, my nostrils filled with the distinctive, heady scent of pine.

"It just occurred to me," I mused, as we wove our way deeper into the forest. "Neither Cavilad nor Wyndoon had a real border. No crossing, no guards. No paperwork, either. Can't say I miss it."

"We run a few patrols on our side of the river," Tavia replied. "It's just a formality, though. There's been a long-standing peace between our peoples—the alliance of the Plains and the Wood. But you won't find any dryads this far from the heart of the forest. It's impossible."

"Why is that? Do they—"

A buzzing sound. Three small *thunks!*

We froze in our tracks. A trio of arrows stuck in the ground before us. The first, a finger's breadth before my leading foot. The other two quivered an inch from either of Tavia's forehooves.

"Stand where you are or perish," said a cold, stern voice.

I craned my neck up, while making sure to keep my hands perfectly still. I saw the cruel, fanged visage of an iron mask in the tree branches across the glade. If this was the face of a dryad, then they had reacted badly to our showing up.

"What in the seven circles of black magic—" Tavia sputtered. She raised her voice to address the iron-masked individual. "I don't know how you're doing this, but it's...well, it's rude, Sarissa!"

"It is I who makes the manners here, equine," came the reply. The voice sounded feminine. Deeper than Tavia's, and with more than a handful of gravel thrown in for good measure. "I pay never mind to your protests. You know the protocol, daughter of the Warder."

Tavia snorted in reply. But she lowered her head and half-knelt as she recited what was obviously expected.

"We ask forgiveness for violating the harmony of the Woods of the Dryads. We come as representatives of Cavilad," Tavia said, then indicated me with a toss of her horn. "And as representatives of the Other World."

That last part had been deliberate. It got the intended effect. I couldn't see Sarissa's reaction behind her mask, but I heard the sharp intake of her breath.

"Does this satisfy you, Lady of the Dryads? May we pass unto your realm?"

"Aye, you may do so," came the reply.

"Better ask if the other two agree with her," I said tightly. I suppose I sounded harsh. But I didn't exactly like getting shot at.

"Other two?" Tavia frowned.

"I count three arrows in the ground. Unless your friend can shoot multiple arrows with a single pull of her bow, she's got two more archers bracketing us."

Quick as lightning, Sarissa slid down from her perch and landed before us. One hand, gloved in a gauntlet of silver mail rings, held a carved wooden bow. From behind the mask, I heard her utter a single sharp word: *Hist!*

On cue, a pair of dryads dropped from the trees, their faces covered and bows in hand. Sarissa uttered a whispery-sounding phrase.

And then all three raised their fanged iron masks.

Michael Angel

CHAPTER THIRTY-THREE

The dryad named Sarissa stood five-two or five-three, and I doubted that there was an ounce of fat on her. She was skinny, but tautly muscled, with delicate features. A pert nose, narrow hips and chest, and long, slender fingers under a close-fitting glove of chain mail.

From what I could tell, the only armored pieces the dryads wore were those gloves and the fright-mask. The rest of their outfits consisted of a set of shorts and matching short-sleeve top made from soft brown cloth and leather. Each bore a wicked looking blade at their side.

A trace of wrinkles at the corners of Sarissa's mouth and her wide-set green eyes were the only clues that she was older than a woman in her early thirties. Her skin was what I'd have called olive to start out with, but it had tanned almost black from exposure to the sun and wind. All in all, Sarissa reminded me of a female surfer that I'd gone out with a couple of times. Truth be told, she was actually kind of hot, if you liked the girl-jock type.

But all this only registered later, when I stopped to think about it.

Right then, only two things stuck in my mind. The first was Sarissa's hair, which was black with an emerald sheen. Her shoulder-length tresses had clusters of red, blue, and green beads braided in, a couple of inches up from the ends. The second was a tattoo of some arcane mark, placed just below her left eye.

It seemed that both Sarissa and William Teach took their fashion cues from the same person.

I looked for a moment into the deep green of Sarissa's eyes. I had to fight off a disturbed shudder. I sensed that, not only was she older than her early thirties, she was a heck of a lot older.

"It has been nigh on three years since I spoke with someone from your world," Sarissa said to me. "You are one of the few that seems to perceive what is beyond one's immediate fog. This impresses me."

That was a compliment, if an oddly phrased one. I made a small bow. It seemed to amuse her.

"I greet you, Lady of the Dryads, as a mere traveler seeking knowledge. I am Derek, son of Robert, of the Ridder clan."

Okay. The whole 'Son of Robert' thing seemed a little formal to me. But Tavia had counseled me to present myself like that. And I figured it would help the peoples of the Morning Land adjust to my presence a little easier. It gave them a reference point by which to relate to me.

"Well met, Sir Derek. Know that I am Sarissa, Master at Arms and Warder of Wyndoon." She indicated her two fellow dryads, whose features resembled hers enough to look like close cousins. "These are Dory and Magari, members of the senior Wyndoon Guard."

"Ladies," I said, with a nod.

They smiled and whispered to each other in a sisters-sharing-secrets fashion as they looked at me. Well, I suppose I did look more than a little odd to them.

"Hist now," said Sarissa, and the two quieted immediately. She turned back to address me and my unicorn companion with a knowing little smile. "If you would but wait on us for a quarter-hour. When we return, we shall provide you an entrance into Wyndoon like no other."

And with that, she and the two other dryads pulled their masks down. They vanished back into the woods in an instant. I blinked, glanced at Tavia, who looked like she'd had the wind knocked out of her.

"This is all wrong!" she exclaimed. "This is absolutely impossible. Nothing like this has ever been seen in the Morning Land."

"Oh, come on now. The peoples of the Morning Land are pretty socially advanced, at least from what I've read. Is it really surprising that their new Warder is a woman?"

"I wasn't referring to her gender. Sarissa's not 'new' at this. She's been the Master at Arms and the Warder of Wyndoon for over three centuries. And—"

"She's over three hundred years old?" I exclaimed, interrupting. "Well, I never had a thing for older women, but I suppose I could reconsider that."

Tavia let out a loud, derisive snort.

"Males! Always thinking the exact same way. I meant that she shouldn't have been out here. None of the dryads should have been out here. They're symbiotic tree spirits."

"Are they, now?" I stretched my arms out to encompass the forest that surrounded us. "From what I can see, there's a lot of trees around us right here. So I don't understand what you're getting at."

"You're not familiar with the dryads. I am. They're bound to a single tree, their 'birth tree', which they call an *adolenda*."

"Okay, I follow you so far."

"An adolenda is a special kind of tree. They only grow inside the walls of Wyndoon, at the magical core of this forest. A dryad can't travel more than a mile from her adolenda because her life force, the very essence of her being, is entwined with the tree."

"I gather that we're more than a mile from Wyndoon, then."

"A good deal more." She shook her head firmly, rattling her beads. "Which makes meeting a dryad in this part of the forest just flat-out impossible."

"Impossible?" I thought back to the time that Tavia had upbraided me for being skeptical about magic. In a wry tone, I added, "Given the fact that you were just standing here talking with a dryad, I think you'd be more open to the idea."

I never knew what Tavia would have replied. At that moment, we heard a grinding sound in the distance. Followed by the throaty roar of a machine.

"That sounds like…" Tavia began, as her ears flicked nervously forward. "Like something I've heard in your world, Derek. Something enormous. Am I mistaken?"

"No, you're not," I replied.

This was a kind of noise that I knew well. Back home, it wouldn't have caused me to raise an eyebrow. Hearing it here, in the middle of a forest devoted to sentient tree spirits, it sounded completely alien.

CHAPTER THIRTY-FOUR

A second iron-plated *grunt* echoed in the distance. Followed by a dull, mechanical throbbing. I turned to Tavia, astonished.

"That's a diesel engine," I said.

As if to give proof to my statement, a trace of exhaust filtered through the trees. My nose wrinkled at the mixture of pine and burnt diesel oil. The breeze carried the scent off, and the air smelled fresh and pure as ever.

Tavia and I traded glances. We started moving through the underbrush towards the noise. Perhaps a couple dozen yards later, we felt the earth shake.

The vibration reminded me of the shivers one got right in the core while watching backhoes at work in a construction pit. We stepped out onto a crudely graded dirt road. Right then, I saw the giant ore truck slowly making its way down the road.

The truck had been painted in the bright gold and black of a yellow jacket. The name *SUBARU* gleamed from the massive radiator grill. And to my amusement, the license plate hanging below the front bumper read *TREHUGR*.

Tucked upright into the deep truck bed was a stout tree with gnarled looking branches, gold bark, and a profusion of three-lobed red and green leaves. Tavia let out an astonished snort when she saw it. How the dryads had traveled so far from Wyndoon wasn't a mystery anymore.

Even though Sarissa and Magari looked impossibly out of place inside the truck's cab, the dryads seemed to be having the time of their lives. From her seat behind the steering wheel, Magari brought the massive machine to a stop. She yanked on a lever, blasting the flatulent-sounding air horn.

Sarissa saw my expression and laughed as she opened the passenger-side door. Catlike, she leaped to the forest floor and waved us over to the side of the vehicle. Four more trucks lined up on the road behind, each with an adolenda or two tucked into the back.

The base of each tree had been solidly encased in a square transport box. I'd seen builders use these kinds of boxes when they wanted to put mature trees around their buildings. The only difference being that Sarissa's tree box had its own sprinkler system, complete with a portable water tank.

"Surely you know of the link between us and our birth trees," Sarissa said to me. "Thanks to our contact with your world, we've transcended it. Since we would never desire to separate our bond, we simply take our better halves along with us."

"It does make sense," I said, nodding. "I'm just surprised that you were able to put in the roads."

"Trucks are of little use unless they can actually go somewhere, Sir Derek. We dryads have purchased a bulldozer and a road grader from Caterpillar, and we put both to a good amount of service."

"But…" Tavia said, trying to make sense of things. "What about the trees cut down to make way for the roads?"

"The trade-off is a worthy one. What we cut down is made up for when we can protect so much more of the forest." The Lady of the Dryads next indicated a spot she'd set aside for us in the truck bed. "The cab is full, I'm afraid. But for our return, the view is better from back here."

Tavia and I climbed on board without protest. Sarissa gave a double-toot on the air horn and the column of trucks roared into motion. The pace of the column turned out to be nail-biting slow, barely faster than a man could jog. To avoid unduly stressing the trees, I guessed.

The afternoon was well advanced when our convoy wound down the green depths of a slot canyon and emerged along the side of a narrow lake. Steep cliffs of granite on both sides shaded the water, giving it a tranquil hue. Forest fringed the tops of the cliffs on both sides. Along one of the high ridges, I glimpsed a whitish gleam through the green. A huge deadfall of trees, perhaps.

But the gleam vanished as the truck jolted to a halt in the middle of a large glade. Tavia and I stepped off and waited for the rest of the trucks to park.

"I have to give Sarissa credit," Tavia said. "She was telling the truth—that she'd provide an entrance into Wyndoon like no other."

"We're here?" I asked. Tavia pointed upward with her horn. I turned to gape at what I'd nearly missed, hidden in the shadow of the cliff.

Wyndoon had been carved into a cliff face that looked like a layer cake of strawberry red and sugary white stone. A series of ramped switchbacks and steps linked a series of wide terraces. The dryad dwellings clustered thickly together in these open spaces.

Each house had its own bay window and a half-moon shaped balcony. Steeply shingled roofs made of dark wood gleamed with a hard finish or sealer. Boxes of flowering vines cradled every window in a bouquet of little trumpet-shaped yellow flowers. Even at a distance, my nose picked up traces of something luscious resembling honeysuckle.

And most enchantingly, a stream flowed over the top of the cliff face at the far end of the village. The water created a misty curtain that hung in the air like a bejeweled shawl, constantly throwing off rainbows. Far below, the indigo blue of a half-submerged grotto shimmered at Wyndoon's base.

"In case you are curious, that stream is the Naiades, the spring of sacred water," Sarissa said. "The grotto far below is the Pool of Ethra. But for now, I will guide the two of you to your rooms. They are at the summit of Wyndoon."

I squinted against the sun and craned my neck to make out the level she was talking about. A long, steep road to travel. I let out a small groan.

"We could always take the lift," Tavia pointed out.

She tossed her head, towards the far end of the glade. A large wooden platform had been suspended amidst a nest of rope cables. A team of dryads were placing boxes and barrels into the space. The muffled sound of rushing water gave me a clue as to how the device was powered.

"There is a league of distance between 'can' and 'will'. Consider your climb up as the very first part of your training."

"I'm not the one who needs training! That's why I brought Derek."

"Faith, be still before you disgrace yourself!" Sarissa retorted. "Dare you resign your status as a warrior amongst the unicorns to become a mere delivery girl? I alone decide when students need training."

"But—"

"I deem this one such time. There is much doubt and sadness in your heart, equine. Plus, you step too lightly upon one of your legs. Both you and your human companion must make the climb."

With that, she turned on her heel and started up the nearest stone staircase. Tavia and I shared a glance, filled with apprehension.

Then, in silence, we followed the Warder of Wyndoon through the gates of her city.

CHAPTER THIRTY-FIVE

She may have been three centuries old, but Sarissa set a wicked pace up the winding stairs.

I found myself gasping for breath after only a few levels. I did my best to distract myself by paying attention to the sights of Wyndoon. On each terrace lay a grove of golden-trunked adolendas, planted on the inner slope so that they were protected from wind and lightning.

We passed through long, trellised gardens filled to bursting with exotic fruits, vegetables, and barrel-sized white mushrooms with speckled caps. The dryads working the gardens would doff their sun hats and stare at us as we passed by. But the looks they gave us were curious, not hostile.

By the time we reached the top level of Wyndoon, Tavia's coat had sweated through to a shade of dark honey. She favored her damaged foreleg with a slight limp that she did her best to hide. Sarissa unbolted a set of doors, revealing a stone courtyard centered on a bubbling fountain and fringed by a half-dozen rooms overlooking the lake.

"You shall be dwelling here for your time among us," Sarissa said. "I shall summon you for meals and exercises. In the meantime, rest and clear your minds for the tasks ahead."

And with that, Tavia and I had the complex to ourselves. The entire place looked right out of an issue of *Good Housekeeping* for the upwardly mobile medieval lord. The roof beams and furniture were polished satinwood inlaid with ovals of sky-blue turquoise. Tapestries filled with images of dryads battling horrific monsters and sets of freshly sharpened swords decorated the walls.

Tavia and I half-walked, half-staggered out onto the balcony and savored the view. Far below, the lake glinted like a teardrop-shaped sapphire. The nearby rush of the waterfall from the top of the cliffs gave the air a moist, heady scent.

"I have to hand it to the dryads," I said to Tavia, as I pressed my back against the blessedly cool wall. "They know how to put their guests up in style."

"Indeed," Tavia replied, in an exhausted voice. "I think Sarissa just gave us our first lesson. Everything, even the view beyond this room, is going to come at a rather steep price."

Unfortunately, Tavia turned out to be right. Depressingly right.

I didn't end up studying at *Hogwart's School of Witchcraft and Wizardry*. The time I spent was right out of Army boot camp. At the crack of dawn, Tavia and I were summoned to lug buckets of water or rocks from the bottom of Wyndoon back up to our apartments at the top.

Even though the dryads issued me a pair of leather gloves—and Tavia a brand-new shoulder pack—to prevent abrasions, the burdens were backbreaking. The water was the worse of the two. Not only did we have to worry about spilling it, but it was really a useless exercise, since we had a fountain right in our courtyard. At least the rocks were useful when the sun went down.

I found out on the first evening that these were special stones, called *micatum*. Tapping a pair of the rocks together made them give off a gentle, buttery-yellow light. Easy to read by, thank goodness. After the sun set behind Wyndoon's cliff face, I read my assignments: thick, leathery tomes on the history of magic and a veritable encyclopedia of runes. I turned each page gingerly, aware of the book's age and value. The pages weren't so much paper as stiff vellum, held together by a twist of fibrous root, like a spiral-bound notebook.

But even lugging around the micatum was grueling. It didn't make matters any better that every single damn morning, it rained on us as we did the work. Not a drizzle, either. A cold, driving rain only a few degrees removed from sleet.

Afternoons combined yet more physical tasks, interspersed with meditation exercises and something like yoga. These took place on the plateau atop Wyndoon, which was used as training grounds. Sections of the grounds had been equipped to practice archery, mend weapons, or spar with blade and staff.

The Lady of the Dryads had put away her bow after our arrival. Now she carried her wizard's staff, a rod of dark wood, as long as she was tall. Arcane carvings ran all along its length, and the base had been shod with iron.

The other end was hard as well. I could attest to that, since if you messed up in some way, you got a painful *smack!* to the shoulders, head, or back of the hand. Or hoof, depending on who got the discipline. As a mode of communication, it was nothing if not efficient.

The meditation exercises were even harder for me. We would stand or sit in odd postures (modified for Tavia's form but no less comfortable, from what she claimed) for what seemed like hours without moving or talking. I kept getting cramps in my calves and thighs. Occasionally at the same time. Expressing any discomfort earned a smack with the staff.

We were sitting in a variation of the Lotus position as designed by the local sadomasochist club when one of these cramps started. I unkinked my leg and kneaded it. I cursed under my breath as I tried, mostly in vain, to calm the muscles. When I glanced up, I found Sarissa looking at me curiously.

"Are you frustrated, Sir Derek?"

"Yes," I growled, with an emphatic wave of my hand. "I don't understand what we're trying to do here."

"The work I have tasked you has many benefits. The most important, for our purposes, is to rid your body of energies that prevent clearing of your mind." I blinked. "So clearing one's mind is the goal here?"

"The clearing produces a calm state that allows me to sense your potential for manipulating magic. You may also experience a vision of your future. Rare, but not unknown."

"Hmm…" I murmured. Sarissa raised an eyebrow.

"Do you doubt? Or do you feel that you—"

"I see a vision…" I closed my eyes and did my best impression of Luke Skywalker. "I see a city in the clouds...my friends are there...they're in pain!"

That earned me a solid *thwack!* on the head. One hard enough to see stars. Sarissa leaned forward and spoke to me reproachfully.

"Hist now, Sir Derek. Tavia's need for you to see this through is greater than your need to make fun of it." She considered for a moment, then added with a smile, "And I have seen the first three movies in the *Star Wars* series many times, so you are not 'putting anything over' on me."

"Yes, ma'am," I said, and concentrated on putting my leg back into the required place of agony.

Tavia looked innocently away, but I heard her choke down a nicker.

The following week, Sarissa pronounced both of us a slightly leaner grade of meat than ground chuck, so we were ready to learn how to spar. The Lady of the Dryads chose me to start off the day.

"This will be your weapon," Sarissa said, tossing me a plain ironwood staff. "It is not a wizardly stave, but it will do for now."

"You don't think I should have a sword?" I asked.

A frown gathered on Sarissa's face like a thundercloud. "I shall tutor you on how to use a blade, if you can gain but one promise for me."

"What's that?"

"Get an agreement from William Teach to leave us at least one year's time to practice. Until you become more dangerous to your opponent than yourself." I took the hint and shut up.

I easily picked up the basics of both block and attack. I'd been trained by the LAPD on how to wield police batons, which used similar principles.

Eventually, Sarissa gave me a break and let me watch her practice sparring with Tavia. The clearing echoed with the clatter of ironwood on horn. The dryad's staff threw off a blue spark of light as she parried one of Tavia's strikes.

The unicorn and the dryad traded a flurry of quick, light blows. Sarissa changed her stance. She pressed her attacks home, but Tavia parried every advance that Sarissa made.

Tavia deflected the blows from Sarissa's staff. The graceful control of her horn mesmerized me. Just when I thought the contest was deadlocked, Sarissa flipped her staff lengthwise and rapped Tavia's left foreleg smartly above the knee.

Tavia made an equine squeal of pain and danced three steps back. She bent her leg at the knee, keeping the hoof raised. She staggered, desperately trying to avoid sprawling on the ground.

Michael Angel

CHAPTER THIRTY-SIX

I jumped to my feet as Tavia cried out. I took a step forward. She spotted my movement. Made a barely perceptible shake of her head.

No.

I remained where I stood. Sarissa redoubled her attack. She forced the unicorn back steadily towards the edge of the clearing. Their blows stopped as they warily circled each other.

"That was unfair!" Tavia said indignantly, as she gingerly placed her hoof back on the ground. "My leg is still healing."

"It *has* healed, filly. The break exists only in your mind now." Sarissa's green eyes narrowed to catlike slits. "We both know that blow should not have hurt. What is your mind telling you?"

"That doesn't matter—"

"You are right, unicorn. It matters not. It will not matter to William Teach either when you next meet."

"I can take the mad warlock!"

"So sure, are we? He will strike you where he thinks you are weak. Then he will destroy all you hold dear." Sarissa's voice dripped malice as she added, "I wager that he will start by killing Sir Derek."

With an angry snort, Tavia went on offense.

She stepped into Sarissa's next swing. Blocked it. Then struck forward with a half-step. Sarissa twirled her staff to knock out Tavia's foreleg a second time. Tavia turned the blow aside.

In a blink, Tavia slipped inside the dryad's swing. She stepped forward, whole body in motion. She made a vicious thrust with the tip of her horn.

Tavia pressed the point home. Deep into the hollow of skin at the base of Sarissa's throat.

"Yield, Warder!" Tavia demanded.

"I yield, Warder's daughter." Sarissa's staff made a dull sound as it fell into the soft grass.

Tavia tilted her horn away from the dryad's neck. Even as she backed down, I saw a smoldering deep within her dark blue eyes that I hadn't seen before.

"You have an answer to your testing of me. Injured in my mind or not, I still have a fire within me."

"You mistake me, filly," Sarissa replied. "I never questioned your fire. I simply wanted to see what you were willing to fight for."

Tavia let out a breath. Brow furrowed, she remained quiet and did not speak. Sarissa returned the unicorn's gaze with a challenging, mysterious smile.

Tavia and I ate dinner that evening by the light of micatum laid out in a silver reflecting bowl. We'd done this every evening, as Sarissa had asked us to remain in our quarters and allow a dryad to bring us meals cooked fresh from Wyndoon's gardens.

I knew that the isolation had been for a purpose. To force us to study without distraction. And to be honest, I didn't mind. I'd found out that I could bear more hardship with less complaint since I came to the Morning Land.

"I should have expected dryad cuisine to be vegetarian." I scooped out the remains of a bowl that looked and tasted like creamed spinach. It wasn't bad, but even the mushrooms, when sliced and grilled, simply didn't satisfy my craving for meat. "It's about the only thing so far that I expected."

"How do you mean?" Tavia cocked her horn at me. Her mane shimmered in the candlelight-like glow of the magic stones.

"Well, I've never been one to read up on legends and myths. But I did pick up some stuff from movies. Popular culture. But mostly from my wife."

"You mean Beth." The shadows cast by the micatum were such that I couldn't see Tavia's expression.

"Yes," I agreed, with a sigh. "I expected them to be shy types, dressed in gauzy green silk gowns. Maybe look something like the elves in *Lord of the Rings*, live in giant tree houses and sit around playing, I don't know, harps or something."

"What a strange concept. Dryads have always been our land's deadliest warriors. Due in part to their physical nature, and part out of necessity."

"Their nature? You mean their relationship to their birth tree."

"More how they take after it. A mature tree is tough to take down, unless you have the right tools—an axe, or fire. The same for a dryad. They are some of the most difficult creatures in the Morning Land to kill. Had I not withheld my blow against Sarissa's throat today, I doubt it would have done more than inconvenience her."

"Something to keep in mind," I said, as I massaged an aching muscle. "You have me curious now. How was it 'necessary' that they become warriors?"

A gentle knock from the satinwood doorpost. I'd left the door open to allow the evening breezes in. The Lady of the Dryads stood in the passageway, a box held in her arms.

"I could not help but hear your last question, Sir Derek, so I shall provide you with an answer," Sarissa said. "If our tree dies, so do we. If you had that same vulnerability, would you not become expert at its protection?"

"It makes sense," I admitted.

"My apologies for interrupting your dinner," she added, and she hefted her burden onto our table. I spotted an 'Overnight Express' stamp on the side of the reinforced cardboard box. "The Other World has seen fit to send us mail. I have items addressed to you both."

Sarissa pulled out a pair of items that resembled cell phones with attached belt clips. She set them down, then reached into the box a second time to remove a pair of thick envelopes. A plain white one had been marked for Tavia. The large pink envelope labeled To Uncle Derek was obviously for me.

"Looks like Rachel's been busy," I noted, as I felt the weight of the envelope. I set it down for a moment to pick up one of the phone-sized objects. "Cell phone signal jammers, I'm guessing."

Tavia nudged her envelope against the table leaf. With a quick motion of her horn, she sliced it open. She pulled out the papers inside with her teeth, shook it twice, then laid the paper down flat.

"You're right," she said. "Apparently, these have been developed to block all types of magical energy."

"Dare I guess who sent them?"

"You need not. They're from your friend and mine, Richard Coombes." Tavia gave a sigh that trailed off to a nicker as I clipped one of the devices to my belt. "At least he's being useful for a change."

At that moment, the table shuddered. From outside came a muffled *boom*. I jumped to my feet, but the dryad and the unicorn were at the window before me.

I squinted at the base of the cliff, trying to make out what was going on. A flash of light from Wyndoon's side of the lake. Near the guard towers.

A second flash, followed by a percussive rumble from down below. One of the dryad ore trucks exploded in flame, taking the tree with it.

The sound of a woman screaming followed.

The screams cut off with a horrifying finality. In its place came a chorus of howls. It set my teeth on edge and my skin into a rash of goose bumps.

The fire quickly spread to the trees around the parking glade. A ghoulish figure strode fearlessly through circling packs of yena. A man, shouting orders and wielding a brand new shepherd's crook staff.

Explosions of flame blossomed around him. Lit his demonic face with a hellish scarlet light.

Sir William Teach was back in business.

And he seemed intent on burning Wyndoon to the ground.

Michael Angel

CHAPTER THIRTY-SEVEN

Sarissa vanished from my side, Tavia a half-second behind her.

I squinted into the fire that burned amidst the dryad glade. Teach remained clearly visible in the center. His packs of yena circled near like dogs loyal to their master. Once, it looked like one of the yena paused and bit at its side. Then an explosion of flame erupted out in the darkness.

I grabbed one of my practice staves and ran out the door. It may have been all downhill, but my chest was heaving by the time I reached the lowest terrace.

A squad of dryad guards passed by at a quick march. Their grim, armored masks had been pulled down over their faces, and they each carried bows or short swords. As one, they dashed through the main gate with a chilling battle cry.

Another group formed an impromptu bucket brigade, conveying water from a flowing fountain up to one of the burning roofs. I felt the blossom of heat from the largest fire, an inferno that had engulfed one of Wyndoon's storehouses.

Paint curled off the building like old bark. Black motes of ash drifted down and stained my skin. The smell of burning wood, smoldering sap was everywhere. The stench of burnt flesh hit my nostrils, made my stomach turn.

A small team of dryads attended to those who had been bitten or burned. Two patients had been laid out on a pair of crude stretchers. They appeared completely unscathed, but their dead eyes stared out of faces frozen in agony.

I didn't see Tavia anywhere.

Forcing myself to remain calm, I dashed for the main gate. I came up short as a dryad wearing gold-trimmed armor and holding a pair of camo-colored hunting binoculars threw her arm up to bar my way. I swore. The dryad raised her metallic mask. To my surprise, Sarissa glared back at me.

"Stay back, Sir Derek," she commanded. "This is a fight beyond your abilities."

Another flare of fire came from beyond the walls. A second dryad came running up. I recognized Dory's voice from beneath her mask.

"We are undone by Teach's sorcery!" she breathed. "His allies breathe fire, and they do not fall to the shots of our archers!"

Sarissa said nothing for a moment. She pinched a stray lock of her hair with her mailed fingers, then tucked it back under the leather strap that held her mask to her skull. She turned to me again. A look of worry that I'd never seen before was in her eyes.

"Perhaps I have spoken too soon," she said flatly. "Come with me, Sir Derek. Mayhap a pair of eyes from the Other World can penetrate this mystery."

I followed Sarissa through the gate. She stopped to survey the scene, her eyes narrowed with suspicion. Below us, at the base of the wide stairway that led up to Wyndoon's entrance, the dryads had set up a defensive position. The front ranks bore the short dryad sword in one hand, a rectangular shield in the other. Behind them, a greater number of dryads stood ready with their bows.

Sarissa shouted orders in the dryad's sharp, whispery speech to her archers. They took aim at the yena silhouetted against the burning trees in the glade. The doglike creatures couldn't have been more than a hundred yards distant. Definitely in range of their arrows.

With a *twang*, a barrage of missiles winged their way across the open field. But only a single yena dropped. The remainder howled their defiance. Arrow shafts protruded from their bodies, turning them into canine pincushions.

One of the yena packs broke away from the burning grove of trees. They swung towards the line of dryads with that same terrible speed I'd seen before outside my home. A chorus of dry, coughing barks issued from the yena and echoed off Wyndoon's sheer outer wall.

Sarissa shouted more orders. The dryads in the front ranks steadied themselves, ready to receive the yena's rush. But their weapons weren't needed. The yena swarmed across the battlefield and swung back towards the grove and their master.

Tavia burst in from the right. She moved at a gallop, her form a golden blur shaded by the fires with a hellish red. The unicorn sped across the field, in pursuit of the hindmost yena in the group.

Even pin cushioned with arrows, the yena maintained its uncanny speed. Tavia had to strain herself to overtake the canine.

She slashed at the creature's flank with her horn. The yena let out a yelp as it lost its footing. It rolled, kicking up a cloud of dust, as if Tavia had batted it to one side.

Tavia drew up as the yena shook itself and got to its feet. It limped, but growled angrily, baring its fangs. Unsure of what to do, she danced a step back. They circled each other warily.

In the glade beyond, another ore truck exploded with a chest-throbbing rumble. The adolenda in the back crackled like a rare steak thrown on a grill. And then, in the light of the flames, I finally saw what had been frustrating the dryads' weapons.

Pieces of bronze-colored armor plate covered the yena's body, head, and legs. A deep scratch across the plate covering the yena's thigh showed where Tavia's blow had been deflected.

Holes bored in the yena's head plate allowed a few coarse strands of mane to protrude. These hairs been braided together to hold a trio of black beads the size and shape of Brazil nuts.

The canine stopped, made a shrugging motion so that it could snatch one from its braid. With a snarl, it launched itself at the unicorn, at the same time flinging the bead with a toss of its head.

Tavia reared and neighed loudly in return. She leapt over the object the yena had tossed at her. An explosion rippled across the ground where she'd been. The dry grass burst into a circle of flame.

She landed on her forehooves. Then lowered her deadly spiral horn in a charge. She was a magnificent and terrible sight to behold.

As the yena moved to close with the unicorn, the creature's chest plate glinted evilly. Fear gripped my throat in a vice. I had visions of Tavia's horn shattering into fragments against the hard metal.

"Tavia! Don't!"

But she couldn't hear me. Not at that distance, not with the din of fire and battle and howling packs of yena.

Tavia dove forward, her powerful muscles driving her full weight behind her thrust.

CHAPTER THIRTY-EIGHT

Tavia and the armored yena came together in a massive collision.

The sound of their meeting echoed like the crash of two automobiles. A heavy *thud!* Then, the sharp report of something punching through sheet metal.

Tavia pulled back two steps. Then three. Her horn remained unscathed. She watched her opponent warily, waiting to see what he would do next.

A two-inch round hole in the yena's chest plate gushed a viscous stream of red. The creature staggered forward, jaws snapping and convulsing. Then it simply dropped in its tracks without a sound.

I let out my breath in an explosive gush of relief. Next to me, Sarissa placed her palm to her chest for a moment and whispered something that sounded like a prayer. She didn't raise her head until Tavia had galloped back through a gap in the dryad's front lines.

"Sarissa, did you see?" Tavia asked. "The warlock has learned some tricks from us. His beasts are outfitted in armor plate."

"And they're using some kind of incendiary device," I added. "He might've figured that one out by using explosives from my world."

"I saw both developments," Sarissa replied grimly. She held the binoculars to her eyes for a moment, then handed them to me. "Teach is not garbed as well as his minions. Let us press our advantage on this point."

Sarissa gave a spate of orders in Thari. Around us, dryad archers stepped forward and drew. They let fly another salvo, targeting Teach's distant figure.

I raised the binoculars and saw Teach clearly on the far side of the field. I couldn't hear him at such long range, but I saw his eyes track the flight of arrows. His jaw moved as he spoke. He held his new staff out firmly ahead of his body. The arrow storm parted around him like water around a ship's bow and struck harmlessly in the woods behind him.

Sarissa cursed. "Perhaps I should have let you bring your firearm, Sir Derek. We appear to be at a standoff for the moment."

"Which doesn't make any sense," Tavia fumed. "This isn't a big enough force to realistically take Wyndoon!"

"Then what is Teach up to?" I glanced through the lenses again. "It looks like all he's done is set fire to some of the ore trucks."

"Faith, that is enough hurt to us," Sarissa shot back. "Those whose birth trees were in the glade are now dead. But I see through to your meaning. If he does not have enough force, why does he not retreat to safer ground?"

"The 'why' can wait," Tavia said. She pawed the ground angrily. "Derek, do you know a way that we can take the warlock out of this equation?"

I paused, stunned both by the request and the statement of confidence that Tavia had invested in me. But as she spoke, my hand brushed the latest gift from the Other World, courtesy of Agent Coombes.

And I had an idea.

I squinted across the field between the dryad line and Teach's grove.

"I need to get closer," I said to Tavia. "Can you cover me while I do that?"

"You can count on it, Derek."

"Sarissa, at our signal, I need your archers to loose another volley at our warlock friend."

"Aye, certainly," the dryad said, then added, "But how will you signal us?"

Tavia spoke up. "One of my beads can do the trick there."

"Let's do it, then." I handed Sarissa her binoculars and set off down the steps two at a time. Tavia stayed at my side, grimed from the battle's smoke, but with a look of pride on her face.

My heels hit the packed dirt at the bottom of the stairs. Then I launched into a run that would have done my old football team proud on another field of battle, years ago.

Out of our opponent's end zone came a huge pack of yena, growling and snapping. I saw now that they ran with a clumsy lope from wearing all that armor. But it didn't slow them down much.

Tavia accelerated ahead of me without effort. She tore a green bead from her mane. Crunched it in her jaws.

She hurled it out far before us. A flash of emerald flame. The yenas' armor didn't protect them against the magical fire. They scattered with a howl.

One yena's hair acted like a wick, burning down to the trio of black beads dangling from its mane. A triple set of bangs went off like a string of blasting caps. For a single, disgusting second, Tavia and I ran through a spray of wet, musky-smelling red mist.

I could see Teach clearly now without the help of magnifying lenses. He shaded his eyes with his free hand and spotted us for the first time. He saw me, and his face creased in a dark scowl. And then he saw Tavia. His eyes lit up.

The warlock spoke under his breath for a second. Each time I'd met Teach, he never quite reacted the way I thought he would. This time was no different.

He finished his incantation, and then *smiled*.

Smiled in a way that I bet great white sharks did when they were about to carve flesh from their prey.

Another pack of yena emerged from the tree line and began advancing on us. It didn't look like we could get closer without

169

going through them. I snatched the jammer off my belt, gave it a last check to make sure it was on, then hurled it as if I were lobbing a long bomb over the Lewistown defensive line.

The little device sailed over the approaching yena. It bounced off a hard scuff of turf and rolled to a stop only ten yards from where Teach stood.

I shouted at the top of my lungs.

"*Now, Tavia!*"

She came to a halt. Snatched a bead off her mane, crunched it. With a flick of her head, she flung it straight up into the air. The bead exploded like a firework, shattering the darkness with shards of light.

Teach's smile vanished in the space of two heartbeats. From overhead, the whispery sound of arrows in flight shivered through the air. The warlock's face went pale as a dryad arrow punched through the back of his hand and pinned it to his wizard's staff.

He opened his mouth to scream as the cloud of missiles enveloped him. A second arrow grazed his face, leaving a bloody mark. Yet another struck his arm above the elbow. Blood spurted and ran down his sleeve.

Teach stumbled backward, shouting his spells. He must have just stepped out of the range of the jammer, as he was able to do his fading trick just as a second flight of arrows began to rain down around him. His allies, the packs of roaming yena, turned to watch as he shimmered into nothingness and vanished.

They made a skin-rippling howl of despair and fled into the woods.

CHAPTER THIRTY-NINE

Dark clouds hid the sunrise the day after the battle.

Worse yet, they spat cold rain while I was on the morning rock and water run. I wanted nothing more than to scream my frustration at the cold gray sky, but I bit my tongue.

I lifted the two buckets of water I'd drawn from the well. Carefully, I balanced them on the wooden pole that ran across my shoulders. With a glance at the burned-out remains of the storehouse by the main gate, I began my slog up to Wyndoon's summit.

There had been a strange ending to the battle. The dryads didn't act triumphant, nor did they vent their despair at losing eight of their number to Teach's minions. Tavia had said 'They will mourn when the time is right', and it seemed that she was correct about that.

"Sir Derek? A moment, gentle knight," called a feminine voice. I stopped and turned slowly so that the buckets didn't overbalance me.

"Yes?" One of the dryads working in the lower terrace's gardens approached me. She wore a dark green jacket with a hood to block the worst of the rain, and she held a small covered cup in her hands.

"I have something for you to drink," she said, proffering the cup. Like the rest of the dryads, she looked like a slightly younger first cousin of Sarissa's. It took a moment for me to recognize her as Magari, one of Sarissa's senior guards.

"Much obliged, but no thanks," I said, nodding into the gusting rain. "I'm getting enough liquid already to moisten myself from the outside."

"This is a kind of broth we give to those on heavy duty," she said with a smile, then removed the cover from the cup.

A puff of steam wafted out. My mouth watered as I smelled a savory aroma like freshly made chicken broth. I put down the buckets and took what I meant to be a small sip. In the twinkling of an eye, I downed the whole cup. The liquid tingled as it went down, spreading blessed warmth to every part of my body.

"That was fantastic. I feel like I could haul water up the face of Wyndoon all morning, rain or no."

"Aye, that's why you're not given it at the start of your training." Magari looked at the gray sky. Her pert nose wrinkled in distaste. "My garden will be glad when you are not accompanied by the cold and wet that you must now endure."

"What do you mean?" I asked, puzzled.

"It means never no-mind. What I wanted to say was that your training must have taken quite a toll on you over the last few weeks."

"It hasn't exactly been a picnic."

"Then after your evening meal, come back down here and meet me. I have a sure-fire remedy to add spark back to your eyes."

And that's when Magari hit me with what I call *The Look*. I'd been a very lucky man to have seen it a few times, when I'd been training to be the next Jim Brown. Back when I had a set of abs you could bounce a quarter on.

I don't know how a woman generates The Look. They don't have to show a turn of the leg or a flash of what lies under the strapless gown. But they unmistakably send out a signal as loud as the shot from a starter's pistol that they are yours for the taking.

Or, that in a heartbeat, they'd take *you*.

At that very moment I got a not-too-gentle tap between the shoulder blades with an ironwood staff. I sighed and handed the empty cup back.

Sarissa's voice sounded loud and disapproving from behind me. "You and I shall have words about this, Magari. Interfering with this knight's training is fraught with danger. Back to your gardening."

Magari's expression froze. She bowed to both of us, then walked back towards the row of vines she'd been tending. Before she turned the corner, she gave me a last look over her shoulder. One with a surprising flash of raw appetite.

"Shamed I am to have not foreseen this," Sarissa sighed. Her expression seemed rueful, and she leaned tiredly on her staff. "Your bravery and resourcefulness of last night has not gone unnoticed. This has raised your estimation in the eyes of many of my fellow dryads."

"You must be joking," I said, with a nervous laugh. "I don't see how I'm suddenly attractive to a dryad. I'm no dryad, uh, dryad-man."

I stuttered to a stop, abruptly aware that I had no idea what a male of Sarissa's species might look like. The only male tree spirits I could think of were the Ents from *Lord of the Rings*. Simply from the size angle, putting Treebeard with Sarissa would be like mating a Saint Bernard with a toy poodle.

"Ease your thoughts on that count. You are enough of a man for any dryad of Wyndoon. But I wager that your training shall not suffer. There are two, at least, who will see you away from such distractions."

"Let me take a wild guess. You're one of them."

"That is so," she agreed, then faced me. "And I have my own reasons."

Sarissa looked me over as the cold rain pattered down around us. Once again I felt like she was appraising me, but this time with a different set of measures in mind. I felt my face burn. I cleared my throat and broke the silence.

"You said that there were two who would keep me from, ah, such distractions. Who's the other person?"

"You do not know?" Sarissa cocked her head at me. With a smile, she said, "You are a strange man, Sir Derek. The complex you divine easily, and yet the simplest things you sometimes miss."

"What do you mean by—"

"Hist now," Sarissa said, cutting the discussion short. But the ghost of a grin remained about the edges of her mouth. "Despite my words, it is I who must break your training now. Leave your burden, for we have a pair of appointments. Tavia waits for us in the clearing above Wyndoon. But first, there is someone I wish for you to meet. At your dwelling towards the summit."

"All right." I put the buckets and their pole off to the side of the pathway so no dryad would trip over them.

"And I see no reason that I need to arrive drenched in rain and mud," Sarissa added. With that, she raised her staff and spoke a few words. The rain stopped and the sun came out. I stared, dumbfounded. It felt like I'd been on a movie set, and one of the stagehands had flipped the switch to turn off the sprinkler machines.

"You…" I sputtered, trying to get the words out. "No wonder it's been raining every single damned morning I've been hauling these buckets up the hill!"

"Weather working was the first kind of magic I learned when I received my mark of power." Sarissa shrugged eloquently. "It comes easily to my kind."

"Your mark of power." I frowned. "I'm guessing you mean the sign you have tattooed below your eye."

"Only the magically adept can acquire such a sign. I can instruct others in magic because I have mastered many types of it. I favor *Runic Lore*—the study of the signs of power. Another is *Delving*—"

"Where you uncover the hidden secrets of names," I said, recalling my conversations with Tavia. "Seeing a name from the sun and shadow side."

"Just so, hero knight. And I am partial to *Scrying*. You might call it magical divination. I cast such a spell over the battlefield at first light this morning. I thought it prudent. After what you saw the mad warlock do."

"I couldn't hear him," I agreed. "But he did appear to be casting a spell."

"I felt ill to my very core when you spoke of that. How he smiled as he spotted Tavia."

"Was he trying to harm her?"

"I thought as much. I worried that Teach had put a *geas* on her. A kind of magic he could use to control the filly. But he did not do that."

"Then what did he do?"

"He cast a spell, that much is sure," Sarissa said. Her brow furrowed in thought. "But the kind of spell he cast...that is what has kept me up most of the night. Worrying."

Michael Angel

CHAPTER FORTY

A chill gripped me as Sarissa expressed her concern. If a wizard of her power lost sleep over something Teach did, it worried me as well as her.

"The spell that the warlock cast on Tavia was familiar to me," Sarissa said, as we continued up the steep path to Wyndoon's summit. The fresh smell of rain hung in the air, and the sunlight made the adolendas glitter a brassy gold. "In fact, he cast the exact same spell I did. Magical divination."

"Why does that bother you so?" I asked.

"Because unicorns, like we dryads, are magical creatures. As a man of the Morning Land, he knows this. So, if he cast a divination spell on Tavia, he would have learned nothing new."

I mulled that one over. The warm sunshine dried me off and raised my spirits. My muscles had stopped aching, thanks to Magari's drink. So I felt in fine spirits by the time we reached the courtyard where Tavia and I were staying.

All of a sudden I heard a familiar voice scolding his son.

"And keep your hooves off of that! It is sacred to the dryads, and there isn't a single dry cleaner in this world!"

"Yeah, yeah," was the sulky reply. A pause, and then the sudden clatter of little hooves. Thunderbolt cantered into the courtyard, his face bright as he saw us. "Mister Ridder! I thought you'd be here, this is too cool!"

The little colt dashed over to us. I knelt as he rubbed up against me, letting me stroke his brushy mane.

"It's good to see you again, champ," I said, smiling. This time, Thunderbolt's dark eyes were left uncovered by his bandanna. "Hey, what happened? The Wonder-Colt doesn't have his mask."

Thunderbolt rolled his eyes. Sarissa crossed her arms and innocently looked away as the colt motioned for me to lean closer towards him.

"Of *course* I don't have the mask," Thunderbolt whispered. "Can't you see that I'm *under cover* right now?"

"Gotcha!" I replied, just as quietly. "Sounds like your dad isn't happy with you right now."

Thunderbolt snorted. "Dumb tapestry, it shouldn't have been left hanging there anyway. He hasn't been happy with anything, not since he lost his job."

I pursed my lips. It was the first I'd heard of this, but it was hardly surprising. I'd been more than a little out of touch with the Other World since I'd arrived in Wyndoon.

"It so happens that we need to speak with your sire right now," Sarissa said. "As Warder of Wyndoon, can I entrust you with reconnaissance to ensure that our meeting is undisturbed by vile treachery and villainy?"

"Treachery and villainy?" Thunderbolt bounced excitedly. "I'm on it, Lady Warder!"

And with that, he took a coltish little hop onto the carved stone top of the fountain. He spread his wings and got aloft in a handful of beats.

"One cannot help but admire his enthusiasm." Sarissa watched him soar out over Wyndoon. With that, we walked to one of the guest rooms. She knocked, then pushed the door open when she heard the answering neigh.

Stormwind stood next to a drawing table, one raised to a height and angle that allowed him to read comfortably. When the Pegasus turned towards us, his noble face looked slightly drawn.

"Hail, noble Warder," he said, with a delicate bow towards her. "I thank you deeply for allowing my son and I to roost here.

But I do not welcome Detective Ridder. He and I shall have words if he remains."

"Words? What do you and I—"

"Hist, Ambassador," Sarissa said, putting up a hand to quiet me. "You two will be neighbors, and resentments must be treated up front, lest they fester. Furthermore, I doubt Sir Derek knows the reason for your arrival."

In answer, Stormwind pawed the stone floor in anger. He grasped a sheaf of papers from the drawing table in his mouth. Then tossed it to me with a shake of his head.

"Thanks to him, all of my efforts have come to naught."

I carefully unfolded the paper, which turned out to be a copy of the *New York Times*. On the front page, the headline read: *Scandal at Turtle Bay: Envoy from the Morning Land Resigns*. Below lay a color photo of Stormwind being escorted from the U.N. building under guard.

Instantly, I knew that the information I'd given Agent Coombes had been the ultimate cause.

"I'll spare you the reading," he said sourly. "Thanks to an 'inside tip', an investigation tagged me with brokering a deal to ship arms to the Morning Land."

My reply sounded brusque, even to my ears. "Any truth to the charges?"

"My wings are soiled with guilt, I freely admit it. I wanted those weapons, and I was willing to pay whoever stepped up."

"Then you don't have a lot of sympathy from me. For all I know, you could be buying from the same people who put a smoking crater in the Manhattan skyline. And for what? So you can tip the balance of power here in your favor?"

Stormwind paused a moment. He snorted. Then raised his solid, pearl-gray forehoof so I could see it clearly.

"Exactly how are my people going to use weapons designed for humans?"

"By getting humans to pull the triggers," I shot back. "According to the Warder of Cavilad, you want to break the Morning Land's current system. Just like what William Teach wants."

Stormwind stared at me.

"That boneheaded, paranoid equine," he growled, half to himself. "Yes, I want to 'break' the system the Warder has in place. Do you think I want to see my son on the front line against the Tengan someday? With only bows, arrows, and pieces of sharpened steel against the demon hordes?"

"They have served in the past," Sarissa reminded him.

"The Tengan have not come to Wyndoon in a thousand years! If they come again, unleashed by Teach or by the conjunction of our world with theirs, then I want both humans and unicorns to have weapons from the Other World in hand!"

"Hold up," I said, confused. "Both humans—and unicorns?"

"Yes, unicorns," he said irritably. "They could fight in conjunction with humans."

"Stormwind speaks true," Sarissa said from behind me. "Unicorns who bear the wizard's mark are able to change themselves into other forms for a time. Including a human one."

"A human one..." For a second the idea knocked the wind out of me. "You're telling me that Tavia could have such a form?"

CHAPTER FORTY-ONE

"Tavia carries the mark of power," Sarissa's tone was matter-of fact. "Certainly, it is possible for her to have a human form."

"But it is horribly confining to a unicorn," Stormwind pointed out. "It would feel much like the time she spent in your veterinary hospital. Even if she's taken the time to learn the ability, I doubt you'll ever see her use it."

I let out a breath and calmed myself before I spoke again.

"Thank you, Ambassador. As for what happened to your position in New York…I mistook your intent. I can't agree with what you were trying to do, but at least I understand the 'why' now."

Stormwind ruffled his feathers with a soft, birdlike sound. "I will do my best to accept your apology. But mark my words: next time, I hope that you will not be in a position to affect any of my plans. You are Tavia's friend, and that makes you a worthy man, but we shall not touch our wings in friendship."

Without another word, the Pegasus walked out to the balcony. He spread his mighty wings and caught the updraft that wafted up the cliff face of Wyndoon. He rose effortlessly and disappeared overhead.

"He's trying to do his best for his people." I gave a rueful shake of my head. "I suppose his efforts concerned you as well?"

"Indeed," Sarissa agreed. "I have known about Stormwind's radical ideas for some time now. That's why I asked the Warder of Cavilad to put Tavia and Richard Coombes on the case."

I gave her a hard look.

"Something just occurred to me. It seems the Lady of the Dryads is at the center of a lot of things that have been set in motion lately."

"Aye, fancy that." She nodded towards the exit. "And the day is not yet done. Come along now, Tavia awaits us atop Wyndoon."

"More testing?"

"Of a sort. It is time we tested your ability to work magic, hero knight."

I blinked stupidly for a second as what she said sunk in.

All of the endless days of training. Of fighting. Of poring through dusty manuscripts. Each and every morning slog in the freezing rain.

And today was the day that would make it all worthwhile.

Speechless, I followed the Lady of the Dryads up the short, winding path to the plateau above Wyndoon. To one side, a clearing looked over a rocky notch, where the sacred waters of the Naiades poured over the cliffs with a sizzling hiss.

Tavia sat regally on the grass, her golden tail switching lazily back and forth. Sarissa knelt at her side, then indicated that I should sit across from them. With a push of her cloven hoof, Tavia nudged a round pebble in front of me, then drew a circle around it in the dirt. She regarded me with her icy blue eyes.

"Derek. I'd like you to try and move that rock for me, simply by exercising your will."

I closed my eyes. In my mind, I nudged the stone out of place. When I opened my eyes, the pebble was still in the same spot.

"That's okay, Derek," Tavia said hurriedly. "Nobody gets it the first time."

I closed my eyes and tried again. No movement.

And again.

One more time. Beads of sweat began to bead on my brow.

"Would it help if I used some kind of incantation?" I complained. "*Wingardium Levitatesa?* Anything?"

"Not unless one wishes for a firm tap from my staff," Sarissa replied, in a chilly tone.

I sighed. It looked like it was going to be a very long day.

I was wrong about that.

It turned out to be a long *three* days.

Each day, I spent hours trying to move a rock the size of a matchbox. And each day, I had to spend more time meditating. Because it was obvious that I was getting agitated. And it wasn't my imagination that both of my trainers were getting worried as well.

"Screw this!" I said, late in the afternoon on the fourth day. "We keep this up, we'll be sitting here until Teach has us waist deep in yena."

In frustration, I snatched the pebble from the ground and chucked it into the woods. The stone hit a tree at the edge of the clearing. It ricocheted back, bounced off my chest, and dropped back into Tavia's circle with a dull thud.

"I'm puzzled as well," Tavia said. "I can sense magical energy within you most strongly. But there's no way around it. You must be able to tap into it."

We were silent for a moment. I forced myself to be calm, but was only halfway successful. Could we have failed, wasted all this time, because of my magical impotence?

"I must agree," Sarissa said. "Sir Derek has learned to clear his mind. To let energy flow through his system. He's taken in nothing but food and water from the magical sources of Wyndoon. All is as it should be, save for one thing."

The words Sarissa was dancing around hit me in the gut like a sack of bricks. I let out a breath and slowly got up. My feet felt heavy, clumsy. I fought to keep my face emotionless.

All the same, my voice came out in a whisper.

"I don't have the ability to work magic at all, do I, Sarissa?"

"It does not appear so," intoned the Lady of the Dryads.

I turned away and walked out of the clearing without a word.

I heard the soft sound of hoof falls on the lush turf next to me. Felt the warm, velvety nudge of Tavia's muzzle against the back of my elbow.

"Don't be like this," she said gently. "There are other things—"

"Yes, I know." My voice reflected the awful, bitter taste in my mouth. "We've got other options. Maybe I can get close enough to whack Teach on the head with one of Sarissa's glorified walking sticks. I didn't need to waste our time coming here to learn that."

"Coming here was not a waste of time."

"Wasn't it?" I rounded on her, angry. Angry at myself, angry at my piss-poor ability to do anything meaningful. "Teach has a wizard's staff again. Give him another three weeks. At the next full moon, he can return to my world and win this thing in a walk."

Her expression registered hurt, but she kept on. "I...I don't like seeing you like this, Derek."

"If you don't like seeing me like this, don't hang around to watch," I shot back. "Let me be!"

And with that, Tavia halted. Her tail flicked back and forth as her eyes followed me out of the clearing.

My anger didn't abate. I felt like hitting something in my frustration, so I wandered over to one of Wyndoon's combat training areas. The dryad's sparring machine looked like the wooden version of a punching bag with a triple set of arms. The contraption rotated on a kind of ball bearing set into a sturdy base. Any hit would make the arms swing back and bowl over an inexperienced person.

I dug in my back pocket for my leather gloves. Instead, I came up with my niece's letter. I must have read it a dozen times by now, but I couldn't help but read it one more time.

Rachel hadn't written much. She and her mom thought the people in their neighborhood were fun, she liked her new school, and she missed me and her 'secret friend', Tavia the unicorn. *'Shhhhh! I'm not supposed to tell anyone about her!'* the letter helpfully added.

She'd also included a photo of her latest crayon masterpiece. Tavia galloped across a grassy plain in Rachel's idea of what the Morning Land looked like. The waterfalls in the background looked as if they ran with pink lemonade.

I was in the picture too. Much to my amusement, Rachel had drawn me in police dress blues again. I looked like the title character in a Saturday morning cartoon called *Officer Friendly Visits Happy Fun Candy Land.*

A wave of dejection washed over me as I carefully replaced photo and letter in my pocket. Deep down, I'd been hoping that I could write to her about how her favorite uncle had learned his first spell. That he'd been smart enough to master the ways of magic as easily as rebuilding a Camaro's engine block.

So much for dreams. I couldn't find my gloves, so I went over to a storage cabinet the dryads had carved out of a nearby tree. I took out a pair of mailed gauntlets and a practice staff, then began to work the sparring machine.

I started by using a familiar pattern of *thrust—block—strike—block.* In a short amount of time, I started to get into the flow of things. I sped up my attacks, blocking and striking like a snake.

Soon I began adding more power to my blows. I imagined with each hit that I was splitting Teach's head open like a ripe watermelon. In no time, I was dripping sweat from every pore.

That was when I felt a presence close behind me.

I reversed a block to my left and took a half step backwards. It put me safely out of the sparring machine's reach. I turned the staff towards a striking position as I came around.

What I saw startled me.

I brought my weapon to a halt in mid-thrust. Less than a foot away from the first of the trio of unicorns that had entered the sparring area.

Michael Angel

Chapter Forty-Two

A palomino unicorn stallion gazed back at me without a trace of fear or concern. His shoulder and flank bore wicked sets of scars. He carried his magnificently muscled frame like a proud veteran soldier.

The stallion's forelegs shaded into white socks, rear legs into black ones. The mane and tail bore the color of dark chocolate, devoid of beads or braiding. A diamond-shaped patch of black marked his forehead, just in front of his horn.

On the stallion's left, a smaller-bodied filly with a bay coat and a set of four perfectly matched black socks watched me warily. She subtly took a step to stand closer to the stallion as I surveyed them.

While all three shared the body and facial features of Arabians, the filly on the right had an Appaloosa's coloring. Her body shaded from smoked cinnamon to mottled white over her hindquarters, which made it look like she'd draped a spotted, ivory-colored blanket over her rear.

The same white and cinnamon spotted pattern repeated itself in her mane and tail. But what got my attention were the sets of beads braided in her mane and a whorl-shaped brand or tattoo on her shoulder. Her wide, dark eyes were curious and kind.

The unicorns and I stared at each other in surprise for a couple seconds. I couldn't help but wonder what they must have made of me—a rather unkempt, sweaty human using dryad gear. But looking back on it, it was almost a shame that they had to ruin the vision of beauty they presented by speaking.

"You there. Human. I need to see the Lady of the Dryads." The stallion's voice was deep, authoritative. I didn't care for how he skipped over even the pretense of a greeting.

"Take the stairway down into Wyndoon," I said, as I lowered the staff and held it at my side. "I'm sure any of the dryads can tell you where she is."

"I wasn't asking for directions," said the stallion. His eyebrows lowered, along with the pitch of his voice. It was the tone of someone who wasn't used to asking twice for things. "Take us to her. Now."

"Look, I'm kind of in the middle of something right now. When I left her, she was over at the—"

"Then take us there. I don't give a damn about what you happen to 'be in the middle' of."

That rankled me. I wasn't in the mood to deal with this.

"Well, *I* do."

"I don't give a damn about you, either. I've a mind to—"

"Oh, really now," the bay filly said to the stallion, who I guessed was her mate. "Let the human be. I don't see why we have to attempt to hold a conversation with one of these creatures."

"Do you know who I am?" the stallion demanded.

That did it. The smartass in me came out. I looked at each of the females flanking him in turn.

"Forgive me for bothering you, fair unicorn fillies," I said. "This stallion has apparently forgotten who he is. Can either of you help the poor creature out?"

The cinnamon-colored one nickered at the joke. The bay filly turned to her. "Don't encourage him, Aurora. This is a cheeky one."

"I've got a notion to take you down a few pegs, remind you of your station," said the stallion, bobbing his horn in a way that suggested mayhem.

"Then you better get a different notion in that bone head of yours, and right quick," I retorted.

"You think you're funny?"

"You pretty much have me beat in that department."

"Let him be," the filly named Aurora said. "We seek no quarrel."

"I would listen to her," I told the stallion. "It's a healthier lifestyle for the slower equines in the herd. Like you."

With that parting shot under my belt, I turned my back on the unicorns and prepared to resume my sparring.

Bad idea. Very bad idea.

Perhaps I'd been lulled by my experiences with Tavia. But I never, ever expected to feel what I felt next: the sharp dagger of a unicorn horn jabbing me right between the shoulder blades. Even if I'd tried to kid myself as to what I felt, the twin gasps of the fillies confirmed it.

"No, we did not seek a quarrel, but I seem to have found one," the stallion said with his deep, slow voice. "I have an idea to make an example out of you."

Something inside me snapped. Those words he used. The same threat that I'd heard from Sir William Teach when he was about to commit murder: *to make an example out of someone.*

What I did next surprised me almost as much as the stallion. I'm sure it was the only reason I got away with it.

I spun on one heel. Drew my right arm back. With my steel-mailed fist, I cold-cocked the stallion across the jaw.

He let out an *uff!* of surprise that sounded like the air brakes on a big rig. He didn't fall down. I didn't think anything less than dropping a nice-sized boulder on him could have done that.

But he certainly staggered. He wobbled to one knee for a second. Then he shook himself, like a lion whose meal had been disturbed, and got back up. A thread of blood dribbled down the side of his mouth.

"I'm going to carve out my clan's name on your chest," he growled.

I gripped my staff and prepared to fight. I didn't have the slightest notion that I could win. I figured if I was lucky and his friends didn't pile on, I could beat him back long enough to climb a tree or something. And pray that unicorns couldn't use some kind of magic to get me down.

The stallion's horn came down, a gleaming golden sword. I blocked his first blow. My staff shivered like a branch in a gale wind. The strength behind his strike sent a bolt of pain down my forearm.

I heard the sound of galloping hoofbeats approaching. I didn't have time to look. Only time to block. The stallion's second blow came in from the side.

The swing never connected. The high-pitched clatter of horn against horn rang in my ears. Suddenly, Tavia was there, between us. She deflected the blow.

Tavia stepped in front and blocked the stallion's path. She made a series of vicious slashes at him, knocking him back several steps.

Then, from all around us, I heard the whispery sound of bowstrings being drawn taut.

CHAPTER FORTY-THREE

We all froze. I looked around and saw the dryad archers who ringed half the clearing. Bows drawn. Arrows with razor-sharp hunting tips nocked in the strings.

Sarissa's voice shattered the silence.

"Outrage! Abomination!" The Lady of the Dryads stepped out from the trees. Her words crackled with righteous anger. "I gave no leave to pass unto my lands, and you see fit to waylay those under my protection?"

"Lady of the Dryads," the bay filly stepped forward. "We meant no harm, we only—"

"*No harm?*" Sarissa's voice went up a notch. "You bring a great unicorn warrior into the heart of my realm. Then attack a single human like a pack of yena? A human who is my honored guest? Blood has been spilt and wars declared over less than that, Selene!"

"We did not know he was under your protection," the stallion said heavily. "He was unmannerly to me and my companions."

"It is I who makes the manners here, equine. You should know that, Son of the Warder."

Son of the Warder...

My eyes flicked to the stallion's markings. Definitely a member of Tavia's family. The stallion went to both knees, as did his companions.

"We beg forgiveness, Lady of the Dryads, Master at Arms and Warder of Wyndoon," he said humbly. "We came seeking counsel, not enemies, and we offer penance for the return of your friendship."

"I shall exact my penance when I decide on its nature," Sarissa said imperiously. "Rise, and you shall be conducted to your quarters under guard."

She hissed a set of orders. The dryads lowered their bows and took positions along the unicorn's flanks as they proceeded.

The filly named Selene eyed Tavia with distaste, but didn't say anything more. Aurora nickered a friendly greeting, which Tavia returned. Only the stallion spoke to Tavia, in a voice loud enough for me to hear.

"Interesting company you've been keeping. I am curious. Where did you pick this one up?"

"That's not your business, Octavius," was the reply. Tavia followed the line of dryads and stopped at the top of the stone stairway that led to the city proper. She watched the procession as they continued onward.

"Well, Sarissa, I hope that proved entertaining for you," I said, in a biting tone. The Lady of the Dryads lifted her mask, then raised an eyebrow in query. "I don't believe for a second that you would let anyone walk into Wyndoon without challenging them. You withdrew your patrols to ensure that the first person those unicorns approached was me. Just to see how I would react."

She nodded approvingly. "I also hoped that you would take Tavia's brother down a notch or two. Of all the Warder's get, he has always been a blowhard."

"So he's Tavia's brother. Older or younger?"

"Younger, though it should mean little. I was present at his foaling, so I saw him follow Tavia into the world by the space of only a few seconds."

"A few seconds? Then that would make them…"

"Really, Sir Derek. I know you are not a delver, but your books do deal with the meanings of names. The first of the two meanings of Tavia's name is twin."

I felt like giving my forehead a slap with the palm of my hand. It was obvious. Tavia was, after all, the shorter, everyday version of the name Octavia. *Octavia and Octavius.* An obvious pairing for a set of twins.

"Since I don't have sawdust for brains, let me guess the second meaning. Tavia and her twin brother are obviously the 'eighth' of something, right?"

"Correct. As to that something, I shall let you find out from Tavia herself. I need to make sure that our headstrong stallion does not rival Thunderbolt in the creation of problems."

And with that, Sarissa turned and walked down the path towards Wyndoon. The Lady of the Dryads passed Tavia on her way back towards me. Tavia nodded curtly to Sarissa, but continued along and stopped in front of me. The muscles in Tavia's flanks quivered, and her nostrils flared.

"Do you have any idea what you just did?" she demanded.

"I just set an arrogant so-and-so back on his heels."

"You failed to show proper respect to a veteran warrior and son of the Warder of Cavilad. He had every right to maim or kill you without compunction."

That stopped me cold. I hadn't expected Tavia's brother to be an obnoxious twit. But that was nothing compared to hearing Tavia take his side.

"He had every right?" My own voice rose, more in indignation than anger. "You expected me to drop everything and...cater to what that jerk wanted? I'm sorry, but I'd prefer not to play servant to any unicorn, no matter how high-born."

"Well, Derek," Tavia said between gritted teeth. "This isn't exactly about how much you 'prefer' something. You're not in Los Angeles anymore. You're in my world, by my leave, and you'd better damn well show some respect for our traditions, our laws."

"If he's an example of your traditions, I'm not impressed."

"He's saved the lives of many creatures—humans included— under his command the last time the Tengan invaded." Her voice now as angry as mine. "And if you don't like the traditions and beliefs that allow him to act as he does, then you have one other option: *go join Sir William Teach!* Because quite frankly, I can't stand the sight of you right now."

Tavia stalked off into the woods. Her ears swept back against her skull and her tail fairly slashed from side to side.

I leaned against a nearby tree and pressed the heels of my hands to my eyes. I tried to think. And then, a strange thing happened. My anger deflated like a balloon that had been pricked by a needle. It left me with a strange, empty feeling.

I decided to follow her.

I'd seen Tavia move smoothly through underbrush before. So I knew from the path she left that she was still frustrated and angry. Broken branches, tracks in moss or turf, and the occasional crushed bush clearly marked her path.

Her path led away from Wyndoon for a couple miles. At least an hour had passed by the time I came out on the edge of a small, leaf-covered forest pond.

Tavia lay on a large, flat stone that had been warmed by the sun. She'd stretched her forelegs out in front of her and had laid her head on them. She looked pensively out over the stillness of the water.

Tavia's ears flicked towards me as I approached. She didn't raise her head, but her eyes followed me as I stopped a few yards away. I thought of the times I'd tried to make up with Beth after we'd had an argument. I wasn't even sure where to begin.

"I think I said…" I began, then corrected myself. "Actually, I know that I did and said a few things—more than a few things—that I shouldn't have. Tavia, I don't know what to say except that I'm sorry."

Her gaze went back to the pond. A single leaf had fallen, sending ripples across the glassy surface.

"I'm not sure what to do anymore," she said quietly. "You don't know the significance of what you did, you can't. No man has ever struck a unicorn before, not on purpose, not in anger. And I…"

Her voice failed for a moment, and she had to take a breath before speaking again. "I would have fought my own brother. I'd have torn him to pieces…rather than let him lay his horn upon you, Derek. Even though every part of my upbringing told me otherwise. That you were wrong and he was right."

I became acutely aware of my heart pounding in my chest. Not like when I was afraid of the yena, back when it felt like a frightened bird trapped in my rib cage. This was different. I felt a heaviness, a charge in the air, as if just before a downpour. I nodded at Tavia, encouraged her to continue.

"My confusion is wrapped around your being here. You see, my heart has been broken twice in my life. Once by my family, and once by the one who I'd hoped to make my mate. I've wanted so badly to tell you this, but I've never been able to. I don't know why."

"I would like to hear, Tavia."

She turned back to me. We shared a look that communicated more than words. She had seen how it had taken someone—a unicorn, at that—to help me start to heal. To be able to speak where before there had been only silence. Perhaps, just perhaps, I could do the same for her.

And so, Tavia began to speak.

Michael Angel

CHAPTER FORTY-FOUR

Tavia slowly got to her feet. Her hooves crunched on the gravel that lined the shore of the pond. She took a breath and began slowly, hesitantly, as if unsure of my reaction to her words.

"There are two kinds of nobility among my kind. The Deep Nobility, whose offspring are members upon their birth, for they are the most venerated of our bloodlines. Then there are families who are granted noble status *in paternus*. That means their titles expire in the absence of a qualified male heir."

"That doesn't sound quite fair to me," I remarked.

"How much different is it than what your people practice? For many, upon marriage the woman's maiden name, her family's name—is consigned to oblivion."

"All right, you have a point."

"Families gain noble status in paternus when a common unicorn performs an act of true valor. But being part of either of our noble classes confers prestige. Magical power. And titles to land. Some of these titles carry heavy responsibility, to protect and serve those who are tied to that land."

"Such as the Warder of the Province of Cavilad."

"Correct. Through my sire, I am also charged with our family's duties. I have pledged my hoof, heart and horn to protect the peoples of Cavilad for the duration of my sire's life.

And I carry a second oath as well. One that I can break only at the risk of exile or death."

I didn't like the sound of that, but I kept quiet. I didn't dare interrupt and break the rhythm of her thoughts.

"All of the Warder's offspring are dedicated to elevating our family to the Deep Nobility. This can only be done if one of us performs a second act of true valor. Failing that, we must sacrifice everything in order to ensure our family does not lose the title we have in paternus. And our family has been on the edge of losing everything for the last ten years."

"Let me guess," I said flatly. "Capturing or killing William Teach would count as an act of valor to elevate your family to that upper level of snob-hood."

"I know it all seems strange to you," Tavia said. "You can't help that. Your country was founded on an act of revolution that threw out the noble class. But here in the Morning Land, there is a need for bloodlines, for names, for acts of heroism and valor to cement them. And my family's desperation is tied to one of the meanings of my name."

"Sarissa told me that one meaning is 'twin', of which your brother Octavius is the younger half. Even I can figure the second. You stand for the eighth of something important."

"Yes, you have it right. Before it was apparent that my dam was carrying twins, it was known that the colt or filly would be the eighth offspring of my sire."

"That's a big family. Well, at least to me. Do unicorn families naturally have seven, eight kids? Um, colts and fillies?"

"Nay, Derek," she said with a sad little laugh. "It is unusual. My sire's name before he became the Warder was *Destrier*. Do you know what it means?"

I shook my head. 'Des-tree-ay' sounded Latinate or French, but it was outside my recent studies.

"It means 'one who goes to battle'. It's an apt name. My sire has seen off two invasions of Tengan, and he has lost both mates and offspring in doing so. To the peoples of the Morning Land, he is a hero who will sacrifice anything for victory." Tavia sighed. "Of course, he applies this attitude everywhere else in life. It makes it…difficult to measure up as one of his get. We need to be fearless warriors, or talented with magic. If we ask for help, rely on others, we show terrible weakness and dishonor in doing so."

"He sounds like a real hard-ass," I remarked. "You say that he has lost offspring to the Tengan. How many of his 'get' are left?"

"Five of his offspring were male, three female. I am the oldest remaining filly. Of the colts, only three lived to stallionhood. The eldest perished in the Tengan's last invasion ten years ago. I served under the second eldest here in the North, where he died in battle stopping William Teach."

"Leaving Octavius as the sole male heir," I concluded. "But he's a few seconds younger than you. So what happens when your sire dies, assuming that neither he nor one of his 'get' have performed an act of valor?"

"Then our family is stripped of rank, and our name is obliterated," she said. Her face became more downcast as she continued. "My father and I have been…I think your people call it 'estranged'. He hasn't spoken my name since my older brothers passed under the sod. Because I've failed so many times."

"To what, act like a hero? To bring him Teach's head on a pike?"

"More than that. That was the second time my heart was broken. I didn't think a human could understand how that felt, before I met you. I sought after a stallion, wanted him as my mate." She closed her eyes, lost in the memory. "Though I lost him, I fell so deeply in love that running with him across the plains felt like running through heaven."

"And he lies under the sod now."

"Derek, 'lost' does not necessarily mean 'dead'." She shook her mane. "When he learned about my family's situation, he concluded that my pledging to him was just to benefit my sire. None of my words could sway him otherwise. So, I was locked out of the heart of my chosen, and my own family, at the same time."

"Surely your brother wouldn't turn away from you. Just because he didn't exactly take to me doesn't mean he's like that all the time."

"If only that were true," Tavia said quietly. "For the last ten years, I couldn't prove myself in an act of valor. I couldn't turn someone's heart towards me so that my name joined theirs. And I've failed in one last way: to remove myself from our family's bloodline."

"What the hell does that mean?" A terrible suspicion began to take shape in my gut, twisting and unsettling it.

"Only one thing stands in the way of Octavius inheriting the Warder's mantle, to save my family from being outcast. The fact that I am still alive."

My mind flashed to Tavia's request that dark night, so long ago. To end her life. The darkness around her eyes as she hung helpless and alone in the sling. Her acceptance of *amor fati*, to embrace your fate, even when it was a terrible one.

And through it all, I heard Doc Kimmel's voice speaking to me: *When she was on my operating table, it was touch and go...and she didn't fight all that hard.*

"I keep thinking about the night Teach wounded me," she said with a shiver. The beads in her mane rustled gently. "I remember feeling how very cold the floor was beneath me, even as I felt the warmth of my life draining away.

"I remember looking up and seeing your face. Saw you standing over me, guarding me. No one has ever done that for me. No one has even acknowledged that I exist for so very long. And when I was in that hospital, that clinic you brought me to, I felt that I could just slip free, spiral away into the darkness. And then I felt something I never thought that I would feel."

"What was that, Tavia?"

"Regret," she whispered. "I'd thought that I would feel some joy with my sadness. That the loss of my life would at least be my sire's gain. But I felt regret. That I would never see your face again."

Tavia stepped towards me, closed the gap between us. She took her horn, the beautiful, deadly instrument she'd used to slay yena and shatter stone, and laid it gently on my shoulder. It felt wonderful, absurdly wonderful.

I felt the living magic coursing through her. Felt as though she were going to dub me a knight. Felt as though I were a king.

I leaned forward and cradled her beautiful head in my arms.

Michael Angel

CHAPTER FORTY-FIVE

After what could have been a few seconds, a few hours, there was no telling anymore, I let my arms fall back to my sides. Tavia raised her head. She looked back at me with those same dark blue eyes, the ones that made me think of alpine lakes or a clear winter sky.

More leaves fell to the surface of the pond, rippling its surface. I knew we were waiting to see who would speak first, who could figure out what to say. It was neither of us, as it turned out. A rustling came from the underbrush. Sarissa stepped out of the tree line and raised her fanged mask.

"Am I interrupting anything?"

Tavia and I traded a glance. I think I had some kind of lopsided grin on my face. Tavia bowed her head and her tail swished furiously back and forth.

"No, we were done talking," I said. "I think Tavia has forgiven me."

"For now, Derek, for now," she said with a laugh. She flicked my side with a final sweep of her golden tail.

"That's good," said Sarissa, though it was obvious from the way she looked at us that she was curious as to what had just taken place. As a matter of fact, I wasn't all that sure myself.

The Lady of the Dryads took a small cloth sack from her belt and shook it open. Two glass jars containing a dark liquid fell into the palm of her hand.

"Warder's daughter, might I ask you to create a circle of power for me?"

Tavia nodded, then used her cloven hoof to draw a circle in the dark soil. Sarissa sat next to it, placed the jars off to the side, then dropped a pair of pebbles inside the circle. When she motioned for me to sit beside her, I let out a groan.

"Not this again. Come on, what is this supposed to prove?"

"We shall see, hero knight, we shall see." I took a seat as Sarissa continued. "Think back to your readings. Do you recall the rune that stands for 'fire'?"

"Yes, I remember that one."

"Good." She opened the jars, set one on either side of me, then handed me a pinkie-sized paintbrush. "The jar on your left holds plain black ink. But the one on your right contains a potent magic. The concentrated sap of our birth trees, which we call *glessum*."

"You want me to write the fire rune on one stone with the regular ink, the other with the glessum, right?" I frowned. "What is that going to prove?"

"Hist now, do it quickly. Consider me inspired at this moment."

"Fine, if it will get you to stop rubbing my nose in failure," I grumbled. I sketched out the runes as instructed.

Sarissa took the brush from me, then said, "Pick up one rock in each hand."

I did so, as the ink was already dry on both. The pebble in my left hand felt cool and smooth. The one in my right felt warmer. I was about to say so when all of a sudden it turned into a nugget of napalm.

I dropped the rock with a scream. I jumped to my feet as horrific pain rocketed up my arm. Immediately, the searing heat vanished, and it was with disbelief that I touched my unmarked palm. From what I'd felt, I should have had at least a second-degree burn.

Sarissa then motioned for Tavia to touch the same pebble. She flicked it with her cloven forehoof, then started a bit as she felt heat travel up her hoof. She shook her pastern in annoyance.

Finally, Sarissa herself reached forward to touch the pebble. The dryad hissed a curse under her breath as her fingers were burned. Then she beamed with a smile of fierce joy.

"I must beg forgiveness from you both. I have spoken a lie, but only in the service of the greater good."

"What are you talking about?" I asked, irritated.

"The fact that I swapped out the bottle of glessum. Both bottles contained naught but plain ink."

I sat up straight. "But…I thought you said that I couldn't do magic!"

"I said it *appeared* that you could not. There is a league of distance between the two. Now, use the bottle that you thought was glessum on a third stone."

I snatched a nearby pebble and swabbed the paint on. But my excitement turned to disappointment as I held the rock and nothing happened. Tavia and I gave Sarissa a puzzled look, but she nodded, as if this was what she expected.

"I should have figured this out earlier," she continued. "Sir Derek, there is a block in your mind. Part of your inner self mistrusts your ability to use something as powerful as magic."

"Then, when I used the ink I thought was glessum—"

"Your mind believed in the magic of this world, though not your own abilities. Thus, there was no block to prevent your power from manifesting itself."

"Sarissa, your wisdom is without match" Tavia bowed to the Lady of the Dryads. "How did you solve this riddle?"

"I followed what Derek's people might call a 'hunch' after I observed his encounter with your brother." Sarissa turned to address me. "Had you stopped to think about it, would you have struck Octavius when he had his horn at your back?"

"Are you kidding?" Absolutely not. There was no way I could've beaten him. I was angry, frustrated, full of adrenaline from my sparring."

"So you did not think."

"No. I acted on impulse. And almost got myself into a world of hurt because of it."

"The point is, you used your will to act. Your impulse got around a rational block in your mind: that you could not beat Octavius in combat. But the block we must deal with now is likely based on emotion. Emotion and experience that says: *I cannot be trusted with things of importance.*"

Tavia's expression looked hopeful. "You know of a way around this?"

"I believe so, but it will take some time. A fortnight, at least. And it will require Sir Derek to do something he may find abhorrent."

"I want to learn the ways of magic," I said firmly. "That's all there is to it."

"Then know that your block results from a belief. That, at the worst time in your life, you made the wrong decisions. But perhaps I can provide you with a lamp to light that darkness."

I sighed. Deep down inside, part of me had expected it. I knew the day Sarissa was referring to. The exact date and time.

"You mean revisiting the day I lost my wife," I said. "Look, I've gone over this six ways to Sunday with the best grief counselors the LAPD could afford. I understand that I wasn't at fault for Beth—"

"You do not understand! We're not talking about recounting your story. We must visit the Pool of Ethra below Wyndoon. It is a place where we dryads work our most powerful, subtle enchantments." Sarissa gave me a hard look. "What I am asking...is that you relive that dark day. The events that led up to it."

The whole idea scared me. But Sarissa was right. There were things hidden in the shadows of my mind that had gnawed away at my soul.

I wanted them dragged kicking and screaming into the sun.

"I want to do this, Sarissa."

CHAPTER FORTY-SIX

According to the Lady of the Dryads, preparations for the enchantment at the Pool of Ethra would take a fortnight. They started early. Sarissa, Tavia, and several of the other magically adept dryads spent an entire day in the lake's grotto.

When Tavia returned, she looked haggard and worn. I poured her a fresh bowl of water from the spring, which she gratefully drained before speaking.

"It is done, and thanks be for that," she said. "I'd forgotten how involved this kind of magic can be. People think the magical core of Wyndoon are the dryad's adolendas. They forget that the trees drink from a deeper source: the waters from the pool below."

"I guess I'm not understanding this," I ventured. "Why would this be any more complex than creating fire or crafting an illusion?"

"For the same reason that brain surgery is more complex than pulling a tooth. We're talking about opening up a slice of yourself to us. To witness many of your memories. Without the proper precautions, we could alter it, erase it."

I looked down at the ground for a moment. "I don't know if that would be such a bad thing."

"You don't know what you're saying!" Tavia said sharply. Her look softened as she saw that I was speaking innocently, out of ignorance. "I'm sorry. I'm not angry, it's just that...we are shaped by our experiences. By our memories. Altering memories would change and destroy who you are. And I would not change you, Derek. I would never desire that."

"Thank you." I laid my hand on her side, felt her warmth. "I guess that my only remaining concern is time."

She nodded. "I know, you're worried about William Teach. So am I. But we're not going to be idle in the meantime. You're going to learn the basics of the simplest form of magic. Tomorrow, you start on Runic Lore."

I felt a heady rush. Like I'd just climbed to the top of a tall peak and stood in the thin air. Runes could have been something the dryads taught their kindergartners, for all I cared. But I was going to *learn magic*.

Tavia took over my instruction for the next week. I set aside my wooden staff for a bone-handled brush, sheets of fresh vellum, and a pot of fresh black ink. All of the symbols I drew now were based off of a clockwise spiral. I commented on this to Tavia, who looked happy that I'd noticed.

"That pattern is the basis of most runic magic. We call it the Spiral of Creation. Legend has it that we only see it in its entirety at birth and at death. In life, it surrounds us every day, in patterns and symbols.

"Funny, I haven't seen many spirals lately. Unless I inked them to paper."

"Oh, really?" Tavia's tail flicked a couple times, and I could see she was enjoying teaching me. "Look for it in the falling of leaves caught in the wind, or water flowing down a drain. Look for it in seashells, on your world in a creature called a 'nautilus'. And the most obvious example is right in front of you."

She looked expectant, and the light in her eyes told me that she was enjoying my confusion. "Okay," I laughed. "You have me. I'm a slow pupil today."

In answer, Tavia angled her horn directly at me. Seen head-on, I could see her horn itself was a delicate, perfect spiral. Score one for the teacher.

I began learning a carefully selected list of runes selected from the total collection of Runic Lore. The vellum pages I read every night had been pasted together from multiple spell books. It was rather like leafing through a *Reader's Digest* compendium of items taken from *Runes for Dummies*.

To test my accuracy, every other day we'd pick a new rune to create, using a real jar of glessum. The magic worked each and every time. My memory and hand-eye coordination had improved to the point where Sarissa labeled me as having a 'smidgen of promise'.

Fast-forward another week. I began to learn the subtleties of pain wards and explosive runes. Tavia worked carefully with me, as if she were supervising a child who had gotten into a professional chemistry set. I didn't mind at all. The last thing I wanted was to blow up Wyndoon with my bad penmanship.

"Runes can be drawn so they go off at a touch, or even when someone sees the symbol." Tavia paused to inscribe the fire rune on a stone with her horn. "This is one that you know is set off by touch alone. But how would I intensify it?"

"Well, my guess is that you'd add a second spiral. Then lengthen the lines at the ends a little."

"Correct. The stone would then burst into flame as soon as someone picked it up or stepped on it." She touched her horn to a patch of sand and sketched the rune, plus a little tail that looked like a squished question mark. "This is what you can think of as a 'trigger'. Use this and your rune won't work until someone sees the symbol."

"What if I saw it as soon as I drew it? It would blow up in my hand!"

"Not if you blend your name into the trigger symbol, using runic letters. That way, the rune only goes off when someone else sees it." She looked up at me. "Want to give it a try?"

"Oh, you bet."

On a whim, I decided to test out the limits of my knowledge. Instead of a rock, I picked up the ceramic plate that had held my lunch. First, I drew the runic letter for 'clay'. Next, I painted the symbol for the fire rune on top of it, being sure to add the 'trigger' along with my name. Finally, I added the second spiral, but I doubled the length of the lines at the ends.

I went to the fence at the end of the clearing and balanced the crockery on the top of one of the wooden posts. I walked back to Tavia, who had been intently studying the woods in the opposite direction.

"Okay. Take a gander at the dish across the way."

Tavia turned and looked. A little 'fizz' sound came from the disk of ceramic. Then it exploded like a quarter-stick of dynamite stuffed into someone's garbage can.

The sound echoed down the cliff face of Wyndoon, startling flocks of birds into flight. A couple of Sarissa's guards came at a run until I signaled that we were okay.

To say I'd been surprised was an understatement. I'd expected the crockery to go 'pop' the way plates broke when you tagged them with a BB gun at the county fair. But I'd actually vaporized the top of the fencepost.

"Very nice!" Tavia said brightly. "You figured out how to set the rune to work on different things than rocks. And got a pretty nice bang in the bargain."

"Yeah," I said, grinning. "I think we ought to write that trick down somewhere."

Tavia nickered her full agreement.

CHAPTER FORTY-SEVEN

Tavia and I hadn't been all alone on the plateau above Wyndoon. But everyone gave us a politely wide berth. The two fillies, Selene and Aurora, would graze in the outer fields, preferring the fresh greenery to dinner in Wyndoon.

As for Octavius, he kept his distance and ignored me. Except for a single time. One afternoon, when Tavia had been called away, he 'innocently' stopped by the open swivel-spar in the clearing next to mine.

He smacked the sparring arms back and forth with his horn for a while, then backed off a few steps. When he was sure he had my attention, he motioned with his horn to the sparring device, then in my direction. There really wasn't much need for translation: *This thing I'm sparring with here? It's you.*

Octavius spun completely around. He kicked out with his rear hooves. The sound of shattering wood echoed across the valley with a loud *crack!* Still with an eye on me, Octavius stepped over the ruined, crushed stump of the sparring machine and began urinating on it.

When he finished dousing it with a gallon of steaming-hot unicorn water, he nodded in my direction with what I'd swear was a smug little smile and trotted off.

Tavia and I spotted Stormwind cruising by overhead every now and then. He wouldn't land, but he'd acknowledge our calls of greeting with a dip of his wings. Thunderbolt the Wonder-Colt remained undercover, snooping about where he could, though he'd come by to watch us spar in the afternoons.

The kid would also drop by for my lessons in runic lore, though he'd soon get bored and lie near my side. Within a few minutes we'd hear him snoring. I'd put down my drawing brush and run my fingers through his soft mane or rub him between the shoulder blades at the base of his wings. The Pegasus colt actually purred like an oversized kitten.

Life was good.

Of course, you know that it couldn't last.

An early evening, one heavy with moist, Indian summer warmth. Sitting at the courtyard table, I'd gotten halfway through a batch of 'runes of protection' when the gate swung open to admit Tavia and Sarissa. The dryad carried a bundled robe in her arms.

"It's time, Derek," Tavia said simply.

Sarissa unfolded the robe and held it out to me. I put my brush down and took a couple of deep breaths, like I was about to plunge into icy water of unknown depths. I stripped down to my underwear, and then put the robe on. Without speaking a word, we descended to the next terrace. The water-powered lift I'd seen in action upon my arrival in Wyndoon awaited us.

We boarded, and the dryad handling the controls undid a series of coiled vines. A slight lurch, and the lift descended. In a couple of minutes, we reached the base of Wyndoon.

Then, with a rush of warm air, we descended into a rocky chamber below. The lift scraped and bumped along to a stop and we got out, letting our eyes adjust to the muted glow of dozens of micatum that were stacked around the edges of the grotto.

The Pool of Ethra was a wide, Olympic-sized oval, with jagged rock windows at the farthest edge that let in the fading daylight. Mist swirled in from the outside, and I realized that we were at the base of the waterfall which tumbled off the plateau above.

Sarissa led us down a gravel-strewn path to the pool. The water in the pool shimmered with a faint glow, yet it was as clear as glass. The bottom lay mirror-smooth, dotted with luminescent spots of crystal or gemstone. The effect made it look like I was staring into the night sky.

I looked up to see that the roof of the cavern had been left in a naturally rough state. But curiously, the dryads had painted the ceiling with pictures of fish, anemones, and what looked like pictures of finned horses.

Several members of Sarissa's senior guard were in attendance. They set up a kind of chant that sounded like the rustling of a pine forest in a high wind. I shivered to hear it, remembering Tavia's words that the dryads only spoke in Thari when performing their Olden ceremonies or weaving magic.

With Sarissa's urging, I got into the pool. She and Tavia followed. The water in the pool wasn't cold at all. In fact, it had been heated to blood temperature, with the same comfortable, warm feeling of a hot tub.

Sarissa had me lie back, where she held me up from sinking with one hand while keeping the fingers of her other hand on the center of my forehead. Tavia touched her horn to the same spot, while adding her own feminine voice to the chant. I thought about an old friend of mine who was a devout Baptist. For one crazy second, I wondered what he'd have made of all of this.

Warm water entered my ears as Sarissa let me sink in a little deeper. The Thari chanting took on a deep, thrumming tone. I felt incredibly relaxed, like I was daydreaming on a lazy Sunday afternoon. I looked up at the ceiling through the layers of mist that blew in from the waterfall outside.

The patterns painted on the ceiling swayed, like seaweed caught in the grip of waves. The anemones pulsed in turn. The pictures of the fish came awake and swam between the clumps of weed. Soon, the entire ceiling had come alive and moving.

Whether it was real, brought to reality by magic, or by the fancy of my own mind ceased to matter. All was calm and peaceful, and the edges of the images in my sight began to fuzz out. Becoming less distinct even as the thrumming in my ears increased in volume, blending together into a deep hum.

Then, as if someone had dialed down the fuel gauge on a night lantern, the light faded out. My eyes closed. I felt the present wash away, a child's sand castle that had been left out on the beach as the tide came in.

When I opened my eyes again, it was seven years ago. An early summer morning in central Pennsylvania. I stood by the open door of my pickup, next to a woman who I would come to know very well.

And that was when she asked me the question.

The silly, meaningless, random question.

The one question that had set everything into motion.

CHAPTER FORTY-EIGHT

"Are all those muscles just for show? I hope not." The first words I heard Beth say. "I think my dog is sneaking seconds from the food dish when I'm not looking."

"They're not all show," I replied. "And I doubt that he's all that heavy."

I wrapped my hand around the handle of her pet's travel crate. I steadied myself and gave a big heave. My not-all-for-show muscles let out a twinge as I lifted the cage into the back seat of my Tacoma. Damn, had she been feeding her dog buckshot instead of kibble?

"He's a she, actually," Beth said. She reached through the crate's front and immediately got a chorus of whines and a bunch of sloppy kisses from the chubbiest cocker spaniel I'd ever seen. The dog looked like a knee-high, fur-covered snowplow. "Who's a good girl, Winnie?"

"Winnie?"

"As in 'The Pooh'. Winnie's one of those dogs that goes a little crazy when you put her in a car for a while. The crate keeps her calm and out of the way, but it's not like you can bring her on the bus or something."

Beth had also brought along a well-worn suitcase. Hoping that her luggage was lighter than her dog, I lifted it and placed it carefully next to the pet crate. Winnie pressed her cold nose up against the cage, so I rubbed her muzzle. The happy *thump! thump! thump!* of the spaniel's tail echoed in the cabin as I gently closed the rear door.

"I really appreciate you helping me out like this," said Beth, when we had buckled up and I had carefully pulled out into the light morning traffic.

"Oh, anything for a pretty woman," I said gallantly.

That was a little corny, I'll admit. In truth, I'd only found out that Beth was visiting her mom—and bringing her dog along—last night over pizza and a game of quarters with Skinny McCluskie. As for why I was doing the driving and not Skinny, well, who do you think lost the game?

Beth gave me a wry look.

"You're an awful liar, Derek. You haven't even noticed me all year."

I looked away. Beth had me there. She and I had known each other since high school, but we hadn't run in the same circles.

I'd been the fullback on the football team, and my time had been spent with the block and tackle. The odd day out guzzling a cold beer, or the odd night in bedding a hot cheerleader.

We had crossed each other's paths a couple times in the past year at community college. We'd either been buried in books or amidst a gaggle of friends. And now this dark, quiet girl I had 'seen around' had become a doe eyed, raven-haired beauty.

"I'm making up for it," I said, and that really was the truth. "Don't know about you, but I'm kinda glad that I get a chance to, uh, catch up."

"Ah, so that's what they're calling 'getting to know you' these days," she said, not giving me an inch. Winnie whined a bit from the back seat, and she turned to gently shush the dog. "I'm not sure what you'd want to know about me that wouldn't bore you."

"Well, we've got a two-hour drive before we get to your mom's. I'd much rather listen to you than turn on the radio to listen to Captain Trips."

"Mister NASCAR!" she exclaimed. "Five! Thirty-Three! Twenty-five!"

"Thirteen! Nine! Fifty-seven!" I drawled in reply. Beth and I busted up and damn if it didn't feel good to be laughing so naturally with her.

Captain Trips was a popular local radio deejay. Trips encouraged NASCAR fans to call in and shout out their favorite car's number on the air. If anyone on the state highways near Harrisburg turned on their radio during Trip's show, they'd probably think they were picking up Hell's own bingo tournament.

That laughter broke the ice with Beth. We got to talking. She'd skated through high school on the outskirts of all the not-so-popular groups, and only started getting attention two years ago at the senior prom. When she developed what she called her 'B-cup boy magnets'. (I hadn't heard that one before, so I filed it away in that part of the male brain that stores useful innuendo.)

I'd been seeing her around recently because her Biology class took place next door to my English class. I decided to mention it to her.

"Wait, you're taking Robinson's class?" Beth said, surprised. She looked at me skeptically. "But I thought that the only people who took Robinson were…"

"Literature majors," I finished for her.

"Someone like you is into Brit-lit? Or maybe *chick*-lit?"

"Not on your life! I'm doing credits for Criminal Justice. I asked for an extra class in English. I like to read," I added, a tad defensively, "Always have."

"You're full of surprises."

Normally, I'd have made some kind of smart comment in reply. About how, if you're built a certain way, people think you're just a gorilla with a better shave. But I happened to turn to look at her. She gazed at me with a smile. One of those smiles that said: *I think I found something I like here.*

And that felt like I'd stepped out of a dark forest into a clearing. One where the sunlight gently warmed my upturned face.

I dropped her off at her destination without a hitch. From the icy cold greeting I got at the door, it was obvious that Beth's mom didn't exactly cotton to hulking jock types hanging around her baby girl. But when you're young and you're developing a serious case of the hots for someone, you get creative.

I bribed Skinny McCluskie with a Shell gas card and a case of Menthol Lights to get his scraggly butt up to Beth's place and pick her up for 'softball' for the next couple of Saturdays. Skinny would pick Beth up, then they'd stop about three blocks away in the parking lot of the local Pik-N-Save. She'd slip out of his passenger seat and into mine, sealing the motion with a hot little kiss on my lips, like it was the easiest thing in the world.

Now, Beth and I *did* actually go to softball games together. Sometimes I cheered her team on from the stands. Other times, we barely paid attention to the game while we made out in a bleacher box just off the third-base line.

When she got back from her mom's, we celebrated by spending the day at the county fair. Beth got a stuffed bear I won for her at the air-rifle range, and I simply ended up sick from sharing too much of her cotton candy.

Beth got me to try a few books I'd never have picked up on my own. She was into a lot of the Renaissance Faire stuff. Titles like *Medieval Days and Knights*, *The Mists of Avalon*, and *White Magic for Wiccans* jammed her bookcase.

But she didn't fit any of the space-case stereotypes that I had about people who read this kind of stuff. She never tried to align my chakras, feng-shui my room, or tout the virtues of lavender oil over modern medicine.

Even so, I was a little surprised when she handed me a book from off her shelf and said, simply: "Read this. It's the best."

Given its thickness, for a moment I wondered if she'd given me a copy of the Gideon bible. But my eyebrows must've shot up to my shaggy hairline when I saw the cover for the first time.

CHAPTER FORTY-NINE

The cover of the book that Beth handed me looked pretty strange. Front and center was a picture of a castle. From its condition, I guessed that it was located in the part of the kingdom that had been condemned.

"*Lord of the Rings?*" I asked. "You have to be kidding."

"What's the matter?" Beth asked. "You said that you'd read anything except chick-lit."

"Well, yeah...but...I could just go watch the movies."

"The movies have their place," she said, as she placed her warm hands on mine. "But this is special. This book is one that you should read."

And that settled it. We'd been going out for only two months. And already I was losing arguments to her.

Truth be told, I'd avoided Tolkien because a lot of the kids who I knew read Mister J-R-R didn't come to my kinds of games. They were the ones who aced math tests with half their brain tied behind their back. Who scrawled pictures of elves and guns on the back of the school chairs.

Well, never say that I don't admit mistakes. Beth was right about one thing. That Oxford dean could write up a storm. I plowed through the first book and took the next two volumes from Beth's shelf without so much as a wisecrack.

Beth even got me to tolerate shopping for things. I swear that I have never spent more than ten minutes in a clothing store, but it was fine entertainment to help Beth find just the right cut for a pair of skintight blue jeans.

How else could I explain it? When we were together, it was like the world gained another dimension of fullness, another 60 watts of brightness, and all the music on the radio sounded like American Top Forty power ballads.

Life can be funny. Back when I was just old enough to be gunning for my driver's license, if I'd heard someone talking about this stuff, I'd have promptly stuck my finger down my throat. But I knew that whatever we had, it was something I'd never felt before.

And I think—no, I know—that I finally understood what Dorothy must have felt like. When she stepped out of the black-and-white world of the Kansas plains and into the Technicolor realm of Oz.

* * *

Beth lived in a ramshackle two-story she shared with a couple housemates. A pretty sketchy place as a whole, but it had its charm. Among other things, the backyard fence bordered a small park on the edge of town.

On the evening of the Fourth of July, Beth and I hung out in her kitchen, sipping tart homemade lemonade out of glasses made from old Mason jars. Waiting patiently until the violet-hued dusk deepened into indigo, then black. Once the humid darkness descended, we moved out.

Earlier in the year, we'd discovered the loose board in the backyard fence. It was a tight, elbow-skinning squeeze for me, but we both got through. We headed towards the small, raised clearing at the far north end of the park.

I rolled out the blanket we'd brought along. Arm in arm, we lay back under the warm, dark tarp of the night.

That's when the action began.

The park zone fell just a hair's breadth outside the fairground's fireworks viewing area. But where we'd snuck in, the angle was perfect. So perfect. Together, we watched the *bang! boom!* and *sizzle!* of the red, white, and blue starbursts.

The whistles and cheers of the crowds from the fair sounded faint on the wind. They peaked after the last furious salvo, then faded into the sounds of automobile engines starting and moving off. It soon grew quiet enough that the crickets became bold enough to sing into the stillness.

I stretched out on my back, propped up only on my elbows. Beth lay across me at my waist. Her long, fine hair pooled in my lap like strands of soft black silk. She turned slightly to look up at me. Her eyes were coal-dark circles with the brightest stars reflected in them.

"Mmmm…" she hummed in the back of her throat.

"Mmm-what?" I asked softly.

"Nights like this, you don't want them to end," she said, and she seemed to be groping for words. "This summer …well, it's been a very long time since I've been this happy, Derek."

"Me too. I don't want to go home just yet."

"Oh, I know you don't."

"Really? How d'you figure that?"

She chuckled. "Because I can feel your hard-on poking me in the back of my neck."

Beth and I sat up. I took her face in my hands and gently kissed her. Our tongues did a warm, wet dance together. The oldest dance in the world.

Without a word, we stood and rolled up the blanket. I felt her pulse race under my fingers as I led her back to the gap in the fence. As I led her through the back yard, and into her place.

We didn't turn on the light in her bedroom. Not even after we'd closed the door. Our eyes had adjusted to the milky glow cast by the moon.

I felt no need to rush. No need to resort to the clumsy, drunken shucking of clothes like I had on many a night. Those nights with a hot and sweaty woman after an equally hot and sweaty game.

I unbuttoned Beth's blouse deftly, slowly, like I had all the time in the world. And in time, she drew me back to her bed. For me, this was more than the desiring or wanting of a woman. I'd been there. I'd done that.

I'd never dreamt that making love could be so much deeper. So much more fulfilling. But that night, by the wan light cast by the tiny sliver of the moon, I learned, and learned it all well.

And when the words *I love you* were uttered, I couldn't tell if it was she or I who first said them.

Only that it was also said in reply.

CHAPTER FIFTY

Days together with Beth turned into weeks. After she moved in with me, weeks turned effortlessly into months. On the dance floor at the New Year's Eve party I did something foolish and crazy—I asked her to marry me. And then she did something even more foolish and crazy—she said 'yes'.

And it really was crazy, you know. Beth could've chosen anyone she damn well pleased. She was pretty enough that she didn't have to troll for dates, and what's more, she knew it. When she finished her AA in physical therapy, she immediately landed a job at a clinic with a bunch of doctors who all looked like actors on the afternoon soaps.

But she decided, at the ripe old age of twenty-one, to hook up for keeps mind you, with a has-been jock whose glory days were an eternity ago and consisted mostly of smacking down meatheads from Lewistown's offensive line. No doubt about it. I was the one who was marrying up in this relationship.

We had a June wedding where my prayers were answered—I didn't drop the ring or let my voice crack when I said 'I do'. For our honeymoon, we couldn't afford a trip to Niagara Falls, let alone someplace exotic in the Caribbean. So we spent a blissful week at a local B&B.

But even so, I anxiously checked my savings account as soon as we returned. Over the next couple of months, I tried to calculate whether or not we'd have to rely on Beth's salary for the next few months. At least until I made my next career move.

I finished my AA in Criminal Justice and decided that I wanted to join the police. My family had enough firemen in it, so perhaps it was time to add some Blue to the Red. The question was where I wanted to go to Academy. Philadelphia was the obvious choice, but I didn't want to end up there.

That's when Beth's older sister Emily proposed a new idea, during one of our long telephone calls to her condo on the West Coast.

"Why don't you two just move out here to La-La land?" Emily asked. "Yeah, it's a strange place, but you never have to shovel snow in the winter."

"Oh, sure," I said jokingly. "Move out to Los Angeles? On the combined salary of a physical therapist and a police recruit?"

"Look, I know people. I could find you a nice place near the Civic Center, a wonderful, loft-style corner unit—"

I rolled my eyes. My wife saved me from myself by deftly taking the phone and picking up the rest of the conversation. And the idea of uprooting ourselves for sunnier pastures in California didn't go away.

Beth was closer to her sister than her mom, and they missed seeing each other more than once or twice a year. But all I could do was look at my checkbook with frustration, wishing there were a few extra zeroes at the end of the sum line.

And then, you know what happened? Three months after we were trying to settle into the idea that we were married, we won $50,000 from the Pennsylvania State Lottery. Captain Trips, that damned *deejay*, was the key to it.

The clerk at the local 7-Eleven had a radio blaring on the day Beth bought the ticket. Trips' listener base of NASCAR-addled fans shouted out a combination of numbers. So on a whim, she decided to play them.

$50,000 sounded like the ticket to Los Angeles. But really, it was only the entry fee to get a place on poverty row. When the real estate agent finished showing us one of the houses in our price range, I was thoroughly disgusted. Put it this way. Had that house been a dog, I'd have put it down out of mercy.

"Penny for your thoughts," Beth said. "Or maybe a dime. It seems that everything is expensive out here."

"My thoughts?" I snorted. "I'm thinking that if it were up to me, I'd be out of here and back to the airport so quick that you'd see skid marks."

"It's not all up to you," she said. Her voice turned into an angry hiss. "I want to be out here. My family will help us with the money."

"You mean in the way I can't?" I said, my voice rising a little in turn.

"Yeah, pretty much," she said bluntly.

I glowered at her. We'd had discussions around and around this issue, circling it like a pair of wary housecats. But it had never come out like this.

I'll admit, I was a backward traditionalist. It hurt my pride that I wasn't the family breadwinner. And the fact that I couldn't put up the bucks for what was going to be our first house? That stung too. Like a son-of-a-gun.

For the rest of the afternoon, we didn't speak to each other more than the absolute minimum. And that night, we didn't go out to dinner. We didn't make love. We didn't stay up and fight. We just went to bed angry.

But Beth won me over to her side, her way. The next morning, she fixed me a full, hot breakfast. No small accomplishment when you're rooming in a motel with nothing to cook on except an electric hotplate that's seen better days. She also gave me a backrub since I seemed so tense.

I'm a sucker for these things. The backrub turned into something a lot more pleasant and involved taking off more than my shirt. We skipped real estate that day, and never brought up yesterday's exchange ever again.

* * *

We bought a brand-new townhome with cream-colored walls and bright-red roof tile. The idea was to recreate the charm of the old Spanish missions. As far as I was concerned, it made the place look like a jumbo-sized outlet of Taco Bell.

But I wasn't complaining. The mortgage payments were just bearable, the lack of snow in the winter was a definite plus, and even the commute wasn't bad. The subdivision had a light-rail station at the end of the block, so Beth could get to her job at a downtown clinic and I got the family car for the day.

Three years went by. Our transition from a couple of kids who could have auditioned for *The Newlywed Game* into 'solid, married pillars of the community' went without incident. Well, almost without incident. I stayed touchy about Beth being the sole earner for the months I went through the Academy. And she liked spending our way-too-limited budget on antiques and collecting weird things that often as not ended up under dust shrouds in the attic.

Beth didn't bear the monthlies well, and she could fly into tears or brittle feminine rage at a moment's notice. I'm ashamed to admit how petty some of our arguments got. One evening we even had a screaming match over, if you can believe it, the pattern of the damned rug we were going to put inside the front door.

I ended up retreating into work more often than not. Joining the LAPD as a rookie patrolman and working my way up to detective meant dealing with the whipsaw nature of the job. One day I'd be walking through a back alley strewn with spent shell casings and human feces. The next, fencing off a blood-soaked crime scene at a Beverly Hills bistro. And the next, I'd be at a hilltop mansion where the garage was lined with Bentley sedans and the coffee table with Colombian blue-flake cocaine.

Police work in Los Angeles was gritty, demanding. I figured that it toughened a man up. That man being me, of course. But it took only a few minutes one bright July morning to show me what a fool I turned out to be.

I had no protection against what happened. No strength at all.

Chapter Fifty-One

One month after Beth and I celebrated our third anniversary, I stepped out onto the front porch to enjoy the sunshine and savor the scent of newly mown grass. Mornings were the best time to do this. Los Angeles in July can be oven-hot once the sun starts getting traction. I rescued the morning paper—the sprinklers had been turning our morning news into soggy wood mush—and walked out towards the end of our driveway to pick up the mail.

Mister Theo, our neighbor across the street, was out cutting his lawn with his baby-puke green push mower. He handled the mower with care, intent on surgically clipping each errant blade without touching his prized rows of marigolds next to the grass strip. He was an absolute fanatic about lawn care. Perhaps not coincidentally, he was also the neighborhood grouch.

"Morning, Phil," I said amicably, as I pulled the assorted junk mail out of the box. I got a sour grumble in exchange, then a quick double-take as he noticed my freshly pressed uniform.

"I knew it," he said, with an almost dreadful eagerness. "You're gonna take those kids downtown and write them up today."

I sighed. This again.

"For the fourth and last time, I can't arrest anyone for riding their bicycle on your lawn, or through your marigolds."

"Well, I read online that 'conspiracy to trespass' is a crime, and I bet if I set up a camera from your second-floor window…"

I let him ramble, determined not to let him ruin the start of a beautiful day. I usually swapped my civvies for the uniform only when I got in to work. But today I was booked to play Officer Friendly at the local junior high, so I was fully togged out in my dress blues.

That gave me a spark of inspiration.

"You know," I said, interrupting his dissertation on the right to install bear traps on his property. "I'm stopping by West Positas High today. Just to make sure that the boys and girls there have second thoughts before they cross anyone's property. Especially someone's lawn."

That was an exaggeration, to put it mildly. I was actually going over to West Positas to warn about the dangers of doing drugs. And hopefully, to plant some seeds for those students who might want to wear the badge in a few years.

Mister Theo mulled that one over in his mind. I could practically hear the wheel inside his head squeaking as the hamster ran. He gave a satisfied grunt, then wheeled his push mower around the side of his house to give the backyard a dose of the same treatment.

I shook my head. Reminded myself that I was one of the few people on the block of whom he actually approved.

As I walked back up to the porch, I heard the low hiss of compressed air. A couple blocks down from our intersection, morning commuters got on and off the light rail cars. I pursed my lips, considering. Both my wife and the Los Angeles Municipal Railway ran like clockwork. I knew the timing by heart. It meant that Beth would be in the shower for another minute, before she dashed down to the kitchen for her morning coffee.

My fingers twitched, almost involuntarily. I had a minor case of the nerves, in anticipation of having to speak in public. Even if it was just a bunch of kids to whom I was supposed to give a friendly lecture, it bothered me.

So, I went for my best and quickest remedy. I pulled a crumpled paper and cellophane pack out of my chest pocket, shook out a single cigarette, and lit up. The scent of cut grass vanished in a bitter, soothing tang of smoke.

I'd been fighting the urge to light up on and off over the last couple of years, and it was still an open question as to whether R.J. Reynolds or I would come out on top. Beth didn't like it one bit. She only agreed to not make a fuss so long as I didn't light up in the house or in the truck, so I went out of my way so that she wouldn't notice when I did.

It was damned hard to keep the job from prying away at your nerves over the long haul. And there were days—dark, violence-stained days—that could make you question whether you'd be one of the lucky ones who lived long enough to pick up a pension. No matter if you remained simon-pure or smoked like a bag of Kingsford charcoal.

I savored the cigarette, finished it off with a couple of deep puffs, then stubbed out the remainder on the walk under my black-booted heel. Out of curiosity, I unfolded the paper and did a quick scan. The front-page photo was attention grabbing, perhaps worth clipping for a scrapbook.

Beth rushed about the kitchen in a whirlwind of last-minute preparations as I brought the paper inside. A full cup of coffee and a half-eaten breakfast bar lay on the table. "Uh-huh, uh-huh," she kept saying, as she scooped up the bar and turned to face me, cell phone pressed to her ear. Judging from the tone, it sounded like something was up at the clinic.

"Fine, fine, I'll be there, okay?" Beth hung up with a sharp jab of the button. "I swear, every morning that I can't get in before eight, it seems like everything falls apart."

"Your fault for being good at your job." I curled an arm around her slim waist.

She let herself be drawn in, then leaned in to kiss me. For a fraction of a second, her lips brushed mine. Hot, velvety. But she broke away as she tasted the tobacco on my breath.

"Oh, great. Not again," she said, annoyed. "I thought you'd quit the damned things for good this time."

"Think of it as something that keeps me in a good mood."

"I know how to do that," she said, while giving me a naughty little squeeze down below. "You should keep away from the cigarettes, though. Yuck."

"You saying that you don't want to kiss me?"

"I just don't want to kiss a mouth that tastes like a filthy ashtray."

Christ, first Mister Theo, now her. What was it this morning?

"Just drop it," I said, peeved. "I'm sick of hearing you bitch about it."

I could see her bite back a quick retort. With a frown, she pointedly set aside the remainder of her coffee and breakfast bar. Beth picked up her purse and a manila folder full of papers for work. She squared her shoulders and walked out the door.

"Bye," I said absently, as I fumbled in the kitchen cabinet for a cup that hadn't been used.

She said something indistinct in reply, and the door banged shut. My groping hands found one of Beth's favorite mugs, one that had a picture of Eeyore the donkey on it. I poured in some coffee for myself and took a long sip.

I held up the paper's front-page photo to give it a second look. I thought that Beth and I had gotten an eyeful a couple weeks ago when the people from the Morning Land had first made their appearance on CNN. Two of the envoys welcomed in at the White House had been humanoid, at least. But the one pictured on the front page was quite different. Horse-like, save for the wings at its sides.

What was the darned thing called?

My mind had been running through the mental card-sorting file since I'd walked in the door. Nothing went *ding!* in my head until I remembered some silly movie I'd seen a while back on the 'Up All Night' channel. The star was some cheeseball blond-haired actor, and his sidekick was the old guy who'd coached Rocky Balboa in at least two of his movies. *Clash of the Titans*, I was sure of it.

"It's a Pegasus," I said to myself.

I put my drink down and absently let my fingers trace the figure's outline. He—the article said that the envoy was male—was the color of pure talcum powder and tautly muscled like a marble statue.

A 'bang' came from outside. Like a high wind slamming shut a heavy door. Next, the unmistakable shriek of hot metal against metal.

Then a much louder *BANG!* rattled the windows.

The explosion staggered me. Jolted the table. A dollop of my coffee splashed over the paper, obliterating the picture of the Pegasus. Next came a bright light. And the unmistakable, shivery sound of an explosion.

I shook off the instant of shock and was out the door. I skidded to a stop at the end of the driveway.

My little street had turned into a small slice of Hell.

Michael Angel

CHAPTER FIFTY-TWO

At the end of the block, rail cars lay piled like giant Lincoln logs. Twisted metal and debris littered the street. I choked on the stench of burning plastic, gasoline, hot metal. My mind wheeled crazily as I saw where a piece of metal had scythed through my neighbor's front yard, lopping off the heads of two rows of marigolds and burying itself in his mailbox.

Mister Theo's going to be downright ticked off about that.

I shook off the sludgy, shocky feeling and made my way towards the towering, smoky jumble. I kicked away a smoldering chunk of seat cushion that had rolled to a stop by my leg. Screams came out of the smoke.

I saw bodies now. Parts of bodies. Clothing spilled out of broken suitcases on the street.

All kinds of paper—office memos, newsprint, chunks of notebooks—drifted down like snow. As I approached the center of the tumbled railcars, people spotted my dark blue police uniform. They stopped. Turned to look at me, as if I had the power to remedy everything and anything.

Of course. It's Officer Friendly come to save everyone. After all, I'm the only one dressed for the part.

I reached for my walkie-talkie. Just as I did, a pair of black-and-white Crown Vics from the Rampart Division pulled up on the left. A few seconds later, an ambulance rolled in on the right. I'd never even heard their sirens approaching.

I found out later that all three vehicles had been called right before I'd heard the explosion. A man who I'll call John Doe had decided this lovely morning to leave his sorry excuse of a life behind. And he decided to end it all by parking himself—and his ex-wife's pickup truck—on the rail tracks and let the mass transit system finish the job.

He chose a good spot. Practically on a blind corner, so that the fast-moving train would have no time to stop. The southbound train came around the corner right on schedule at thirty miles an hour. The impact crumpled the first railcar like an empty soda can, killing John Doe, the engineer, and everyone on the first car instantly.

The rest of the rail cars flew off the tracks like a set of bowling pins stuck by a wrecking ball. Scattering and breaking into pieces. And they'd been packed with commuters on their way to work.

"Give me your leather belt!" I shouted to a businessman who'd just gotten out of his car, stunned.

He fumbled it free. I took it and pulled it tight around a stump that had been a middle-aged Hispanic woman's upper arm. She screamed once as I cinched it. The river of blood pouring from the wound slowed to a trickle. She began to pray quietly in Spanish.

"Christ Christ Christ…" The businessman said over and over, rocking back and forth on his heels. I shook his shoulder briefly and he came out of it.

"Get the paramedics," I said, and he nodded. "If they're busy, get to the next ambulance that shows up, bring them to her."

I kept moving, trying to sort out who was up and moving and who wasn't. Five more early bird commuters came up to me. Two anxiously clutched cups of coffee, as if the damned things were some sort of talisman against harm.

"Get back," I said, waving them off. "It's not safe here, get back!"

The first one backed off, nodding in agreement. The other four didn't move. One of them, a Latino guy with a goatee and a carpenter's tool belt, shook his head and spoke up.

"No way, I wanna help!" The other three voiced agreement. I didn't have time to argue.

"Too dangerous farther in," I said, coughing as a heavy drift of smoke blew across the street for a second. "You, and you." I pointed at Mr. Carpenter and a woman in a jogging outfit. "Go back ten yards, find anyone injured. Don't move them, bring the paramedics back."

"You two," I said, pointing to a beefy-looking man and what looked like his sister. "Crowd control—keep anyone else coming up away and out of the smoke."

They scattered. I pressed on. I had to grope my way through the smoke, and worst of all was the crazy merry-go-round of thoughts in my head.

Beth wasn't on the southbound train. She must have missed it. She must have been standing safely on the platform. Five minutes ago. Busy fussing with her hair. Busy thinking what a stupid jerk her husband was to start smoking again. So busy that she didn't even think about getting on the damn train.

I spotted a woman's figure on the ground ahead, dressed in what looked like Beth's style of cornsilk-blue skirt and blouse.

Can't be her, can't be her. Of course not. Too tall, too short, too young, too old.

Can't be her.

Can't be her.

But it was.

Beth lay on her back like a crumpled doll. She looked almost like she had been sleeping, in the midst of a bad dream perhaps, but sleeping and sure to get up, right as rain. But the ground around her had turned so wet, so red.

I knelt by her side. Her body and head from the right shoulder up was a warm, scarlet ruin. I tried to put my hand behind her to raise her up, but what should have been firm and bony was all pulpy, soft gristle.

I couldn't feel a pulse. Didn't think I saw her chest move, but all of a sudden there was a disjointed, shuddering clench of her muscles. She took in a gasp of air.

Beth's remaining eye opened. The sounds of the flame and sirens faded in my ears. All I heard was the frightful whamming of my heart.

"Derek."

She said my name with no force, no sadness, no fright, with nothing but a flat, declarative tone. She could have been asking me to wash the dishes or sharing an article in the morning paper with me.

I don't know if she really knew what was happening, if she felt any pain.

But she saw me. She saw my smudged, tear-stained face. I could see the look of recognition for that last second.

Then, as Beth let out the last breath she would ever draw, I swear that I saw stars. Stars reflected in the deep black of her pupil. One by one, each of the lights winked out.

And all that remained was utter and complete darkness.

Oh, God.

Oh, God.

CHAPTER FIFTY-THREE

I came back to the present with a howl of despair. My throat struggled with the inhuman sounds that burst from my mouth. I struggled mightily. My arms and legs thrashed the waters of the pool into sparkling foam.

All in vain. Sarissa held me tightly. Her inhuman strength kept me still until I collapsed in exhaustion. My vision blurred as tears filled up and streamed down the sides of my face.

The dryads surrounding the pool changed their song. Their voices sounded like the patter of raindrops before a storm. The sound seemed to penetrate my fog of emotions. In time, I returned not only to the here and now, but to the world of the rational.

"I…I can stand on my own now," I said, though my voice sounded raspy, as if I'd gone on an all-night bender.

"I will trust that you can," Sarissa replied, but she and Tavia stood close by as I climbed out of the pool and made my way to a flat, cushioned bench that had been placed next to the pool.

A dry towel and robe lay neatly folded on the seat. I took advantage of them as Tavia and the Lady of the Dryads moved to join me. At a gesture from Sarissa, the dryad chorus completed their song, then left the grotto.

"Derek," Tavia said gently. "Are you…whole?"

"I'm whole." I shook my head tiredly. "I feel like a rag that's been in a tug-of-war between a pair of pit bulls."

Sarissa went to a vessel that sat in the nearby corner of the grotto. She pulled out a bowl, ladled some kind of liquid into it, and brought it back.

"Drink."

I brought the bowl to my lips. I drank, recognizing the taste as the same kind of broth that Magari had given me earlier, on my morning exercise. As before, it worked wonders. I felt color and warmth return to my cheeks. My spirit revived, and the weariness I felt drape me like a wet cloak fell away.

"You saw everything…" I said, my voice shaping the statement into a question. Both unicorn and dryad nodded.

"We did," Sarissa stated gravely. "Sorry I am to have asked you to go through this."

"Don't be. Horrible though it was…I don't regret it."

"You do not?"

"No." I grasped my left hand in my right. Felt the firm, cool hardness of my wedding band around the ring finger, as always. "Whatever else…I got to fall in love with Beth again. One last time."

"And she did fall in love with you," Sarissa said. "Of that I have no doubt. Whether or not you come away with the ability to work magic, I believe you have at least solved part of Tavia's riddle. Why you were able to resist William Teach."

Tavia snorted, thunderstruck. "I had all but given up on finding the answer."

"You weren't the only one," I added. "How did I solve anything?"

"The Warder's daughter followed the right trail," Sarissa said approvingly. "But it was not the loss of a loved one which protected you. Rather, it was something that a loved one did."

"I don't see what that could be."

"Sometimes, it takes a fresh set of eyes to see the path. I saw into all of your memories, hero knight. Even ones you may not be proud of. Such as the argument you and your wife entered into—about the rug she wanted at the front door."

I frowned. "You're right, I'm not proud of it. Beyond that, I'm not following you, Sarissa."

"Then I shall strive to illuminate." She knelt, then used her fingers to sketch out a whorl-shaped pattern in the sand before us. "This is the pattern on that rug she wanted. The one she picked out. Does it not seem familiar?"

Tavia let out a sound between a gasp and a whinny. I continued to stare without comprehension. And then it dawned on me as well.

"The spiral of creation," I said, in a voice just above a whisper. "Beth must have known about runes. Magic. At least, what she could glean from her books."

"Indeed," Sarissa agreed. "Runic lore survived in the centuries after the Morning Land lost contact with your world. In some of your people's languages, in your Tarot cards, and the like."

"The symbol on the rug was the one we call *Salus*. A potent rune of protection," Tavia chimed in. "Could she have inscribed this rune somewhere else in order to...protect Derek?"

"I believe so," Sarissa said with a nod. "Were I to attempt this, then I would seek to inscribe the rune on something you would normally carry about."

I pulled off the silver band of my wedding ring and turned it to the light. Along the inside curve lay an engraving of the same spiral shape.

"If Beth gave me a protective talisman, what about Tavia?"

"We dryads are the ones who carve the beads of sorcery," Sarissa said, gesturing towards the selection braided into Tavia's golden mane. "Even though any with the wizard's mark may make use of them. When Tavia received her wizard's mark, her braids, and her beads, I was asked to add an extra one to her set. The request came from Cavilad's roan stallion."

"The one I loved," Tavia said, closing her eyes. "He had a special bead made for you. The dryad who braided your mane would have put it high up, so that you would not use it. May I?" Sarissa motioned to Tavia, who lowered her head without protest.

Limber dryad fingers went through the first braided strand of Tavia's mane. She turned over a red bead at the top. Again, the small spiral shape of Salus appeared, carved in miniature into the soft wood.

"He did this out of love for you," Sarissa said to Tavia. The unicorn nodded mutely. "And so, we have solved two riddles today. There remains only one more."

The Lady of the Dryads reached under the bench and pulled out a wooden tray. On it lay a sheaf of parchment, a jar of ink, and my drawing brush.

"You want me to try this...right now?"

"We need to know," Sarissa said simply. "Delay benefits no one here."

I reached for the tray, placed it next to me. Acutely aware of the eyes on my every move, I opened the jar of ink. Took a deep breath, as if I were about to dive from a high precipice into water of unknown depth.

I grasped the brush. Dipped it into the oily, black surface of the ink jar. The hairs on the back of my neck stood on end as I pulled it free and touched it to the parchment.

CHAPTER FIFTY-FOUR

I thought for a second which rune to draw. I wanted something to test whether the power worked, of course. But this time, I'd prefer to do it without burning my hand. So although I felt mostly restored by Sarissa's drink, I decided to scribe a rune of 'wellness'.

I began with a set of four lines to express the rune for 'parchment'. Next, I quickly sketched the spiral base of the wellness symbol. Then added a flurry of cross-strokes to complete the pattern. I blew gently to dry my design.

I touched my fingers to the ink marks.

A feeling of tranquility rushed through me, like a burst of mountain air, like a plunge into a powdery snowdrift. I shivered, not with cold, but with a sensation of pleasure. Pleasure from the pattern, of course, but also from the knowledge. The knowing, deep inside, that something had changed.

It had been a steep price to pay.

But now I could work *magic*.

Tavia and Sarissa touched hand and forehoof to my work in turn. Their smiles told me all I needed to know. The dryad and unicorn inclined their heads and bowed slightly.

"I greet the arrival of a new student to Runic Lore," Sarissa intoned.

"I too," Tavia said. "May the power serve you and us well."

"Thank you," I said softly. "Thanks to you both."

A jumble of sounds echoed through the cavern from the stone rafters. We looked up to where soft footfalls and the clatter of hooves came from one of the stone passages that led into the cavern. Two of Sarissa's senior guards emerged from an entryway above us. They flanked a single snow-white Pegasus as the group made its way down towards us.

"What's Stormwind doing here?" I asked Tavia.

"That's not Stormwind," Tavia said, with a snort. "This one's wings have gray tips. A mark of the *Tabellae* clan."

"It doesn't sound like you like them very much."

"Yes and no. One could argue that they have their role. The Tabellae are neutrals. It makes them useful as messengers and heralds for all in the Morning Land."

As the Pegasus drew closer, I saw that he had on a harness belt similar to the one that Tavia had worn. The courier's belt had fewer, larger pockets, lined with dark fur. The yellow mark of a burning torch adorned both the equine's belt and one powder-white cheek.

Sarissa frowned as the trio stopped before her.

"I gave orders to not be disturbed," she said.

Her guards bowed without reply, then allowed the Pegasus to step forward.

"Forgive my intrusion, Lady of the Dryads," the Pegasus said. He knelt respectfully before her and spread his wings. "I have come through great danger to convey messages of utmost importance."

"Very well." Sarissa held out her hand expectantly.

The courier curled his head in to grab a set of parchment envelopes held shut with blobs of purple wax. Sarissa took the bundle and cracked open the seals. She began to read silently to herself. The courier sighed, and I suddenly realized how travel-grimed and tired he looked.

"Be praised," Tavia said. "You have made it through the darkness safely, delivered your entire load of messages without fail."

"Have I?" A look passed between Tavia and the courier. Her eyebrows rose for a brief moment.

"This Pegasus has come a great distance for good cause," Tavia said to Sarissa. "I will escort him to the guest quarters."

The Lady of the Dryads nodded absently, her mind still intent on her letters.

"Tavia," I said. "What about—"

"This errand should not take much time," she replied, her voice curt. She led the way up and out of the grotto. Tavia traded a few words of conversation with the Pegasus of the Tabellae that I simply couldn't catch.

Instead, the sound of crumpling parchment rippled in my ear. Sarissa's knuckles were white where they gripped the messages. She spoke, and for the first time since I'd arrived in Wyndoon, her voice sounded harsh, dissonant.

"These words tell me that the darkest of times lie ahead." She addressed one of her guards, the tone of command back in her voice. "Dory, we must prepare for these messages of doom with the Olden ceremonies. Spread the word to all. By nightfall I must address the dryads of Wyndoon and share what must be done as its Warder. Make ready all the arms and armor that we have."

"By your will, Warder." Dory touched her brow in salute and hurried back up the stairs.

Her steps faded away in the distance. Sarissa stood perfectly still, eyes half-closed, as if she were rooted to the ground. Although the atmosphere in the grotto pulsed with moist warmth, I felt a shiver race down my spine.

"What's going on?" I asked.

"Sir William Teach just made the first move, long before we thought he would." Sarissa rustled the papers in her hand irritably. "And these messages tell me naught that I would hear."

"Surely, it can't be that bad," I reasoned. "Not after we beat him back from the gates here."

"Hist now!" She made a frustrated, downward slash with her hand. "These parchments are a bundle of bleak tidings. They tell me that the Warder of Cavilad refuses to marshal the unicorns to help us. They tell me that we in Wyndoon are on our own as surely as if the bond between the Plains and the Wood never existed. And they tell me…"

Her voice failed for a moment. It was then, right then, that I felt the first stab of fear.

"…And if the last report speaks true, they tell me that the death of our world is upon us."

"What are you saying?" I asked, dumbstruck.

Sarissa looked at me grimly. "Sir Derek, I am saying that we have no choice. We go to war now. And we are fated to take this plunge *alone*."

CHAPTER FIFTY-FIVE

The quarter moon gleamed above the light of dozens of torches. A chunk of iced milk against black velvet. I sat off to the side of a raised dais where Sarissa stood, wizard's staff in hand, beautiful and deadly at the same time. Arrayed above and around her, ranks of grim-faced dryads sat upon the steep slope of a hill atop Wyndoon.

Tavia, her brother, and Stormwind stood nearby, their attention locked on the Lady of the Dryads as she spoke. Sarissa began with a line of greeting in Thari that was echoed by the dryads present like a wind through pine boughs. She then switched to words I could understand. Words which held little comfort.

"I have sworn many times at the Council of Warders that I would sacrifice everything, lay our lives down for the sake of this land," Sarissa began. "Even so, I dared not dream that we would have to carry this oath out."

If ever there was a sure-fire attention getting line, that one was it. The collective sound of dryads murmuring to each other in hushed, urgent tones rustled through the assembly. Sarissa waited until everyone had digested that bit of news before continuing on.

"Ill tidings have come to us. That the army of the mad warlock, Sir William Teach, is on the move once again. We do not know what evil magic he has at his disposal. A taste of it he gave us some weeks ago. And a taste of defeat is what we gave him in return!"

Some applause, mixed with sounds like cracking branches that I guessed was a dryad cheer. Sarissa let it go on for a while, then held up her hand for silence.

"We have prepared steadily, and well. We have learned how we can take the fight to the enemy beyond our woods. I have concluded that we must do this. And we must do it alone, for no help shall come from the Council of Warders. No assistance from the Court of Cavilad."

Shouts from the audience now.

"Betrayal! Treachery! Oath breakers!"

Again, Sarissa held her hand up for silence.

"I have bent every ear as I would bend a bow, with the help of the ambassador," she said, indicating Stormwind. "None shall listen. They rely upon the known, to await the blow where they are strongest, at their own borders."

"Not all the valor is thinned from Cavilad's blood!" said a deep male voice. Octavius stepped forward. "I at least shall honor the bond between the Plains and the Wood."

"Well spoken, son of the Warder. Your help may well be needed, for I have saved the darkest news for the last."

A murmur went through the crowd and Sarissa went on.

"I have sent my mind far afield, seeking ever the spoor and source of our enemy's strength. The deep magic of our pool shows us the same thing. That spells have been cast to break open the world of the Tengan."

This time I heard widespread commotion. Not panic, but genuine alarm and cries of 'Tengan!' and 'Sit fast!'. This time Sarissa pounded the stage with the butt of her ironwood staff for quiet to return.

"The fate of our world may lie in what remains of Teach's rational mind. For even he knows that the Tengan seek not to rule but to reduce our world to ash. He must know something of their control, and he must move with caution. The Tengan are a force that could slip off a leash with the least error."

Another dryad's voice came from the audience. "Then why not wait, Warder? Why not wait until Cavilad stirs its army?"

Sarissa nodded wearily.

"A fair question, which I shall answer. A fire can be snuffed out if it is caught at its source, before it turns into a blaze that consumes us all." Sarissa held her staff aloft. Her eyes flashed. Her voice swelled with a terrible beauty. "Dryads of the Sacred Wood! We go to war upon the morrow! Pledge that we shall return victorious against the warlock! To end him once and for all, or pave the road hence with our blood to make it so!"

A roar from the assembled dryads, a great clatter and rumble as they rose and stamped their feet. They banged their mailed fists against their iron shields. A fierce chorus of voices rang out, a choir of Amazons raising their voices in a song that sounded like thunder in the mountains.

Through all the noise and clamor, I only saw one thing. Tavia had watched silently, said nothing. Her expression had been one of pensive thought the entire time. And she'd looked positively shocked when her brother had spoken.

While the dryads sang, she cast me a final, inscrutable look. I returned her glance with a questioning one of my own. But she turned away, slipped out of the torch lit clearing and into the woods.

I followed her. Perhaps, I thought, she wished to speak with me alone. But as I came out into the coolness of the night, she was nowhere to be found.

A rustle in the dark. I flinched, startled, as I felt a hand rest on my shoulder.

Sarissa's voice sounded warm and gentle in my ear.

"Be at ease, Sir Derek. You left the gathering, and I wanted to know why."

"I saw Tavia leave. I'd thought that she wanted to speak with me. Her behavior puzzled me. She's not normally one to keep quiet. Not when something so big is on the line."

"If she did not wait, then you shall not catch up with her. Not at night." She paused, reflecting on my observation. "Her silence puzzled me as well. Mayhap she felt ill-at-ease with my decision to take combat to William Teach."

"She's not the only one," I said.

Sarissa came around to my side. She looked up at me, eyes glinting.

"What troubles you, hero knight?"

I let out a breath. The thrum of the dryads' songs rumbled through the night. The fragrant smell from the torches, the aroma of white sage, hung in the air.

"More than anything else, I want to take out William Teach. But I didn't come to your world to be part of your war. How could I even help? I'm barely literate in your magical lore. I don't know if I could ever live up to what you would expect of me."

"That you have qualms means you care about doing the right thing."

"I suppose."

"Faith, do not 'suppose'. Men like you can turn the tide of a battle. And that is most important. Let me show you something." She led me towards the edge of the cliff. "Look where the moonlight strikes the glades across the way."

I peered into the dimly lit night. At the edge of my vision, I saw a gloomy deadfall of trees. The same ones I'd glimpsed the day that I'd arrived in Wyndoon atop Sarissa's ore truck. I grimaced. The clusters of ragged stumps looked like jagged teeth sticking out of rotted gums.

"Those are the remains of the first sacred grove of this forest," Sarissa said. "The Tengan burned them to ash thirty centuries ago. Can you guess as to why?"

I shook my head dumbly.

"Because no one chose to stand up to the Tengan when they first swept through the land. Now they come again, when we are but a shadow of ourselves. When I need every dryad, every equine, every man of courage to stand with us. Not out of fear or obligation. But out of duty and love."

Sarissa shifted her weight. She stood tiptoe and placed her forehead under my chin. Pressed herself warmly against me.

"Will you finish hearing me out, Sir Derek?"

"Yes." What else was there to say?

"I must be present for the Olden ceremonies, now that I have let loose the fury of the dryads. But later, perhaps I may visit you. To show you how much this land means to me. How much care can lurk in the most surprising of hearts."

With those mysterious words, she vanished into the darkness. I looked over the vast deadfall across the way. The vast trunks of adolendas lay out, a pile of bleached bones. Not just dead trees. Dryad graves.

I thought of Stormwind's desperation. To give his son a chance against the Tengan. I thought of the bargain between human and unicorn, the Roses and the Vines. That awful arrangement that had driven William Teach to madness. I thought of the cycles of invasion and devastation that had plagued this land.

Right then, I realized something. As if I'd been granted the sight of a delver, a knower of names. This magical place, where pegasi flew and unicorns galloped, had a second meaning to its name. It wasn't just the Morning Land.

It was the *Mourning Land.*

Michael Angel

CHAPTER FIFTY-SIX

I couldn't keep the gloomy thoughts of war, both past and present, from my mind. My head still spun from the day's events. I retraced the path to Wyndoon and returned to my room.

I undressed, but couldn't bring myself to lay out a set of clothes for the next day's training. Instead, I snuffed out the light of the micatum on the nightstand. With a deep exhalation, I lay back on the bed in the blessed dark.

When I awoke, the moon had moved far along its skyward course. I'd dozed off, but it was rare for me to wake up so early before the dawn. Then I heard it again. A soft, insistent knock.

"Come in," I said quietly.

The door swung open. I could make out the figure of a woman, her presence only announced by the heavier darkness that marked her outline, and her gentle intake of breath. She stepped into the room. I heard the rustle of beads in her hair.

"Sarissa," I sighed. "I thought you might wait until morning. Here, let me get the light."

I reached to brush my hand against the micatum, to give the room some illumination. But she took my hand, held it in hers. I felt her long, supple fingers lace with mine. She brought my hand to her body as she sat down next to me on the bed.

To my surprise, I felt warm, bare skin under my palm. Gently, I reached out to her. Glided my hands over the flat, muscular firmness of her belly. I circled her wrist in my forefinger and thumb. Felt the wild pounding of her heart through her pulse. I wasn't sure whether that came from desire, or nervousness.

She shivered as I sat up. The Lady of the Dryads reached out, cradled my head in her delicate arms, drew me in towards her. She held me in a warm, soft embrace. I raised my head and our lips met, greedy kisses turning into the sweet heat of melted sugar.

Sarissa shuddered and whispered my name under her breath.

I let out a ragged breath of my own. Had to force myself to remain calm. It had been so very, very long since I'd truly desired a woman. Been intoxicated with the very essence of her this way. Raw need overtook me and I pulled her in to me roughly, draping her body over mine.

She was much shorter than I, of course. Her toes brushed against the tops of my shins as I gathered her against me, wanting to touch every place together. Her long hair, which flowed down to the small of her back, feathered out around her shoulders like a soft shawl. I greedily ran my fingers through its silken softness, rubbing my knuckles against the clusters of beads tucked into her braids, smelled her unique scent.

It was that scent that transported me. It wasn't what I expected. Not a mixture of 'female' scents from the Other World. My world. No fragrant ghosts of perfume, shampoo, or conditioner. Those scents were sterile, laboratory based. Utterly disconnected from sky and earth and anything else alive.

Sarissa's hair held the aroma I'd noticed when I'd first come through the gate. The simple, clean smell of the outdoors. The green, grassy scent of an open plain.

My mind touched on what Sarissa had said to me earlier.

I may visit you. To show you how much this land means to me. How much care can lurk in the most surprising of hearts.

With a flash of insight, I knew what she meant. She'd shown me what it was to work with, to gain the trust of those from the Morning Land. But now she was showing me the difference between being there—and expressing love for it.

I opened my mouth to speak, but she put a finger to my lips. She sealed them shut with the warmth of another kiss. At long last, I gave in to my desires, gave in to her.

Sunlight poured through the window when I finally awoke. I found myself alone. I was more than a little surprised about that.

I dimly remembered, after our passion had been spent, how Sarissa had refused to let me go. Instead, she had burrowed deeper into my arms, if that was possible, seeking to enfold as much of herself as possible in my warmth.

A knock at the door. I pulled the sheets up to cover myself.

"Sir Derek?"

A dryad's head, still clad with a raised iron mask, popped into the door's open space. She grinned a little as she saw how disheveled I looked as I sat in the rumpled bed.

"The Lady of the Dryads is holding counsel with all of her visitors at the terrace room below. She would like you to join her as soon as possible."

"I'll be there in a few minutes," I said.

I quickly rinsed off in the room's washbasin and dressed as well as I could from the limited stock of clothes I had available. I took the steps down to the next terrace at a jog. One of the courtyard gates had been thrown open so that four rectangular tables could be placed together to make a hollow square.

Sarissa, a couple of the senior guards, and the appaloosa unicorn named Aurora were at one table. Stormwind and his son were at the next one. Across from them stood Octavius and his filly, Selene. At every spot in front of the guests was a cup or wide-mouthed bowl of the rejuvenating dryad broth.

I came over to the first table and sat next to Sarissa. She gave me a tired, but pleasant smile. Her hair shone a lustrous green and black in the morning sun. She looked indescribably beautiful to me, and I told her so.

"You flatter me, Sir Derek," she said, pleased. "I had a very long night."

"Yes. It was. And you were very...convincing about your love of this land, of the care that can be found in one's heart."

"Is that so? I hadn't thought that my words had made such an impact."

"It wasn't so much what you said. It was everything else. I understand a lot better now, I think. Thank you, Sarissa."

And with that, I leaned over and kissed her.

The Lady of the Dryads blinked a couple times. She looked at me. "I see."

"Where is Tavia? She should be part of your counsel."

"Agreed." Sarissa spoke to one of the dryad guards in attendance. "Please bring our last guest. Let her know that the news this counsel must impart is the top priority right now."

The dryad guard bowed and left.

"It sounds like you have something new to share," I ventured.

"Indeed we do. Something we were watching has vanished from our sight as surely as mist in the wind, and it is greatly troubling."

"What's gone and vanished on you, Sarissa?"

She grimaced as she spoke. "The army of Sir William Teach."

CHAPTER FIFTY-SEVEN

Sarissa's news hit me like a punch to the gut.

I leaned back in my seat, took a breath to steady myself before I spoke. "Teach's army has disappeared? How could that be? How do you know?"

"Remote scrying," Sarissa reminded me. "We dryads have that ability. And fair Aurora is the most powerful seer the unicorns have. Without her help, we could not have searched such a large area, and so far away."

"You're too kind," the appaloosa filly said, with a tired nicker. "This is what we three came here for, to live up to my family's pledge to support the union of the Plains and the Wood."

"You three?" I asked.

"That was the reason for our visit to Wyndoon," Octavius said, in his deep, brooding voice. "Selene and I were escorting Aurora. She is a daughter of the Deep Nobility. The families who carry blood of noble stock. Unlike any human I can think of. Present company included."

"Listen, stud-muffin," I shot back. "The next time I want your commentary, I'll ask for it."

I didn't think equines could growl. But Tavia's brother made a passable imitation. Out of the corner of my eye, I saw Aurora suppress a smile.

Thunderbolt nudged his sire to get his attention.

"Dad," he whispered. "What's a 'stud-muffin'?"

Stormwind cleared his throat and murmured, "We'll talk about that later."

"Enough," Sarissa said firmly. "Among the messages I received yesterday was a report that Teach had assembled an army. An army of men and yena, from deep within his homeland of the Red March. Yet, when we cast our minds out that way, we found little. Some signs of yena on the move. But naught else."

"Could he have hidden his army? Transported it somewhere else?"

"No single warlock has the power to transport entire armies of men. Not all at once. As for hiding...it is true that one may move an army under cover of wizardry or darkness. But any number of men will leave traces of their passing."

"No tracks," Aurora added. "Of supply wagons, siege equipment. No signs of fields and houses ransacked for food."

"It's been about a decade since Teach invaded," I noted. "Tavia told me that Cavilad annihilated his forces. That would make a big dent in the supply of available manpower. I don't think that could've changed in only ten years."

"That would be correct," Octavius acknowledged grudgingly. "The Warder of Cavilad disagrees with me. But I have traveled through the dark land of the March. The will of the enemy's people has not grown back yet."

"Then let us pursue that line of thought." Sarissa brushed her shoulder-length locks back from her eyes and drummed her mailed fingers on the table. "Let us assume that Teach doesn't have an army of men, only of yena. If so, he must know that he cannot prevail by strength of arms. He must be prepared to advance his cause with magic."

"But what does he plan to use?" Aurora asked, with a feminine snort. "A wizard's staff is a slender reed to break the will of the Tengan, if that's what he has in mind."

Sarissa's reply was cut short by the breathless arrival of the guard she'd sent to bring Tavia to the counsel. The dryad stood for a second, trying to catch her breath. Sweat glistened on her brow, and she held a small bundle of papers.

"The filly you sent for isn't here in Wyndoon," she said. "I checked her quarters, then received a report from the guards at the front gate. She left right before dawn."

"So we will recall her," Sarissa said curtly.

The Lady of the Dryads plucked a blue bead from one of her braids, then cupped it in her hands. She closed her eyes, spoke Tavia's name, and from the cup of her hands rose a little puff of white mist.

Sarissa's eyes opened in surprise. "I cannot contact her."

I sat up straight. My pulse began to race.

"What do you mean? When we arrived in the Morning Land, Tavia said those beads could reach anyone in this world."

"Nevertheless, I cannot contact her, Sir Derek. She is either beyond where you two arrived, or she is blocking us for some reason." The dryad guard cleared her throat. Sarissa spoke, annoyed. "Very well, what is it you bring us? I doubt those pieces of paper have transported our equine friend out of here."

"Forgive me, Warder. I have breached etiquette by taking something from a guest's room, but I felt that you should see this," the guard said patiently, holding up a single envelope. It was unremarkable save for that it was the color of drying blood. The top had been sheared off by Tavia's horn, her customary way of opening letters, and part of the paper inside stuck out. "I would not have touched a guest's property but for the fact that the bottom flap of the letter was showing."

"Yes?"

"Warder, the letter was signed by Sir William Teach."

There was a collective intake of breath from those around the table. Sarissa snatched up the envelope and opened the pages within. I could see the large, rather spidery writing of the man over Sarissa's shoulder, but she read the contents out loud for all of us to hear.

Salutations, Eighth Daughter of the Warder.

If you have not thrown my letter into the fire, you know that I require no introduction. I have lurked amongst the shadows of your land these long years and heard much of what is said about me. It seems that parents scare their children by telling them stories about me. "Behave, or William Teach will come and get you!"

As a boy, under the harsh tutelage of my father, I also heard stories. One of them was a tale that spoke of a gem of great power, one that could control spirits and demons. Of course, I asked my father to read me this story every night, so that I might remember all of its details.

Many years later, my star had both risen and then fallen on the battlefield against the Court of Cavilad. Your troops forced me to flee, but I remembered that old story. Deep in the lands to the far south, I found legends of a great jewel called the Seithr stone that confirmed everything that my father had heard.

Through my own genius and magical skill I obtained it. I spent months in study, discovering that it helped me control demons like the Tengan. And that the stone contains enough power to breach the walls between their world and any I so choose. All I needed was the right site with the correct magical properties.

How ironic it was when I found such a place, only to have you shatter the magical gem with your horn. But magical energy is difficult to truly destroy. I reasoned that that your horn could have taken on the properties of the Seithr stone.

My scrying told me of your return to the world of our birth. I brought my army to the very gates of Wyndoon just so I could find out how much of the stone's magic you have retained. It turns out that you are radiant with it.

You have what I want: the power to remake the world in the image that I choose, by providing both bridge and leash for the Tengan demons. I dare say that I have what you want: the power to raise your family to the highest levels of the nobility. Could the ruling clans do no more if you, the daughter of the Warder, were able to banish the Tengan from the Morning Land, forever?

With my direction, you could seal the borders between our world and that of the ravenous Tengan. All I ask in return is that you let loose the demons where I need—into the Other World, where there are no magical weapons that can harm them. It is a place where I can carve out an empire and a homeland for any human who wishes to trade the rule of equines for mine.

We have drawn blood from each other, true, but I give you my most solemn word as part of the Deep Nobility—the only true clan of the blood, *which you wish to join—that I shall not harm you unless you act against my interests.*

Partner with me for but one night and you shall not be treated as a prisoner but an ally, free to leave unharmed after our work is done. And it must be this coming night, for in the slate quarry of the Other World, the site of our victory has been prepared and the moon is in the right phase for everything to proceed.

If you agree to my terms, meet me at the far side of the dryad's sacred lake at dawn. A tellura runs there. It will take you to where I have opened a portal to the Other World.

Worry not about being seen. I have made preparations to ensure that you shall not be followed.

- Sir William Teach

Michael Angel

CHAPTER FIFTY-EIGHT

Sarissa looked up at us. Her face had gone pale, porcelain fragile. Any of the good feelings I'd carried with me this morning had vanished.

"Why would Teach spell out his plans like this?" I demanded.

"Because he thinks we can't stop him," Stormwind replied.

"And because he wants to rub it in my face," Sarissa said, sitting down heavily on her bench. "The warlock has outfoxed me. His mark lies behind everything in yesterday's letters. Casting magic that made it look like the Tengan would be coming to the Morning Land. Giving me clues that the blow would fall here, close to Wyndoon. Even sacrificing his loyal yena in a futile attack on our gates. He planned all along to invade your world, Sir Derek, not mine."

"Maybe your magic could bring the dryads to my world again—"

"It took weeks to craft a spell that allowed a pair of dryads to go to your world. And the passage nearly killed them," Sarissa stated, with a shake of her head.

"I am curious," Selene piped up. "Why would Tavia agree to be Teach's pawn in all this?"

"Who said that she agreed to do anything?" I asked, my temper flaring.

"Hist now. Let's not jump to conclusions just yet," Sarissa said. She turned to address the guard. "There were smudges on Teach's letter. The residue feels like rubbing wax. Were there any signs that her drawing table had been used?"

"Yes, milady. I brought all the papers and parchments I found on it." The dryad spread them across the flat surface before us. Sarissa picked up one of the sheets with a pleased sound.

"If one wishes to duplicate a letter in our world, Sir Derek, one must place samite paper on top, then move a nub of wax over it." Sarissa held up a thick sheet of parchment and rubbed it with her thumbs. "I can tell by the residue that Tavia did this. You must know why she would bother to make a duplicate of Teach's letter."

"Yes," I said. "She'd figure that we would eventually find Teach's original. She would only make a copy if she were sending it along to someone else."

"If so, she would also send that person a letter of her own, to explain what she was doing," Sarissa said. She grasped a second sheet of parchment. It was thinner than the samite paper, and it carried clear impressions of writing upon it.

"Could this have been resting under the parchment that Tavia used to write her letter?" I asked, hoping against hope.

"We shall see." Sarissa blew across the surface of the parchment, whispering a couple words of magic under her breath in Thari. "I am calling back the last impressions made by Tavia's brush strokes on this parchment."

As she spoke, the thin loops and swirls of letters re-formed on the page before my eyes. Eventually, Tavia's entire message became clear.

Father,

The samite pages I enclose here are an offer from William Teach. They explain much that remained clouded to us, and they also seal his doom.

Teach's one weakness is that he has sought power all of his life. He does this so single-mindedly that he believes everyone else thinks the same way. It has tempted him into bargaining with me.

I leave at sunrise to join him and his army. This will bring me close enough to strike him down once and for all. I hold no illusions about what is to come. William Teach probably has ways both cunning and foul to ensure that it will be difficult for me to strike cleanly and swiftly.

Nevertheless I must try. It is time that we unicorns stop relying on others to do our dirty work for us. I know that my chances of returning are slim to none. But whether I succeed or fail, I do so at the cost of only one life—mine.

William Teach says it was ironic that I took his stone's magic when he found the right spot for working his evil. He knows nothing of irony, nothing at all. For only now, as I go to my likely death, have I found a reason to live.

Goodbye, my sire, and know that even in my failure, I have always served, honored, and loved you faithfully.

Octavia

A moment of silence held the table fast as Sarissa finished reading. Stormwind looked frozen in shock. Octavius bowed his head, hiding his expression. Aurora's eyes had gone blank, as if she were staring into space. I jumped to my feet, hands trembling. I felt like I could come apart at any second.

"Hold, Sir Derek!" Sarissa commanded sternly.

"Hold for what?" I demanded. "We have to stop her before she—"

"How?" Sarissa said, "Do you plan to chase after her on foot? Bide a moment. Whatever else, Teach will need her until moonrise in the Other World. That gives us a little more than eight hours to reach her. Alas, it appears that Teach will have taken her back to your world already, Sir Derek."

"I thought that a wizard skilled in magic could open a gate between the worlds," I said. "Are there none in Wyndoon?"

"The only wizards that we know of who can perform that level of magic are in the Court of Cavilad."

"Then...we should be able to travel along a tellura to get there. Or to one of the three gates to my world that Tavia spoke of. Perhaps—"

The rattle of beads cut me off. Aurora shook herself, tossing her mane. She blinked, and her eyes returned to normal.

"That's not possible right now," Aurora said sadly. "While you read Tavia's message, I cast a scrying spell on the tellurae. The warlock has put up a barrier of magical energy. It may take us the better part of a day to burn through it."

"Teach did say, 'Worry not about being followed'," Sarissa said grimly. "Now we know how he planned to cover Tavia's tracks."

My throat tightened, as if a noose were drawing about it. I did my best to shake the feeling off. "Then can we travel physically? Get to any of the gates before the deadline, without using magic?"

Sarissa and Aurora exchanged a look. Not one of resignation. One of fear. I didn't care one way or the other. I forced the issue.

"Come on, tell me. What's the story?"

"Gentle knight," said Aurora. "There is but one alternative."

It came crashing down on me in an instant. There was a fourth gate. The one Tavia had told me about the day we'd first arrived in the Morning Land. The one nobody used because it was simply too dangerous.

"The gate guarded by the sphinx."

Sarissa nodded sadly. "It lies twenty of our leagues south. But that is no option. Typhon, the creature who guards it, is immortal and nigh invulnerable. Not a single person has ever prevailed against him to pass his gate."

"Not a single person," I pressed on. "But an army...an army of dryads—"

"*Think*, Sir Derek. My dryads, the ones who are geared up to move away from their birth tree, can only travel at ten miles per hour. And that is on the graded roadbeds in our woods. We wouldn't be able to get to Typhon's gate until well after nightfall."

A snort from across the room. Octavius looked back at me with a smirk of contempt. When he spoke, his tone was completely flat and even.

"Why don't we just let her go? It's not like this should concern us."

"You son of a bitch!" I snarled.

I exploded from my seat, my hands curled into claws. All I wanted to do right then was beat him bloody. I don't know what would have happened if I'd gotten within reach. As I leaped forward, one of Sarissa's guards grabbed me from behind.

They held me fast as I raged at Octavius. "I'll rip that goddamn smile right off your face!"

"Try it! Go ahead, you pitiful creature, try it!" Octavius spat back at me.

Tavia's brother had also leaped forward. Selene had thrown her horn across his chest, restraining him as best she could.

Octavius' horn slashed deadly figure eights in the air. His voice sounded hateful, taunting.

"You get the first shot, human, but then I get to end it. End *you.*"

Michael Angel

CHAPTER FIFTY-NINE

The slithery sound of a weapon being drawn out of a leather scabbard rang in my ear. A bright ribbon of steel appeared in the gap between me and Octavius.

"This sword goes into the belly of the one who strikes first," hissed Sarissa. "By my word as the Warder of Wyndoon."

There was no sound except my heavy breathing and the stallion's. Thunderbolt watched us all, his eyes wide and staring. Sarissa lowered her sword as we both backed off.

"Shamed I am, shamed!" Sarissa raged. "Never before have I seen two warriors come to blows like this. Who do you charge as your enemy? I dare say that if William Teach saw this childishness that he would laugh at us all."

My eyes burned. I looked down at the floor, trying to think.

"You're right," I said. "There's nothing else I can do here. Look, give me one of the dryad ore trucks. I won't be carrying an adolenda, so maybe I can drive it faster. I might be able to get to the gate in time."

"And how do you propose to defeat Typhon?"

"I have no idea," I said, resignedly. "My odds of success are probably as low as Tavia's with William Teach. But I won't stand here and do nothing."

"Then I have something to give you," Sarissa said.

The other dryads gasped as Sarissa gave me a handful of blue beads, then knelt slightly, offering up her wizard's staff. I hesitated. So she took my hand and wrapped it firmly around its shaft.

"This staff is carved from a branch of the ironwood trees that grow amongst the adolendas. It has no magic of its own, but it is strong and will serve you better than a practice staff."

The Lady of the Dryads stood and turned to the rest of the group. She looked each of them over in turn with her calculating emerald eyes before she continued.

"It is well that I give tokens to Sir Derek when I cannot pledge my person to his cause. Is there any among you who has enough valor to join him, knowing the terrible odds that he must surely face?"

Octavius merely snorted his dismissal of the idea. Selene stood next to him in quiet support. Stormwind stood silent, unmoving. Thunderbolt fidgeted, looking up at his sire in puzzlement, then back at me. Someone cleared their throat and spoke up softly.

"I will go with Sir Derek," Aurora said, in her gentle voice. "Perhaps my magic can be of some use."

"Thank you," I breathed. "Maybe we can—"

"No," Octavius interrupted. "I forbid it."

"Forbid it?" Aurora's voice was sharp. "You overstep your bounds, son of the Warder. I far outrank you."

"You are mistaken. There is one time that I may place myself above you, Aurora. And that is when I am so charged by a Warder. My sire has ordered me to keep you out of harm's way at any cost. Charging head-on into a meeting with Typhon is suicide, and best handled by the 'son of Robert'."

"I'd like to see you try and stop me," Aurora said, and her horn weaved a pattern in the air, making it shimmer with power. "I could enchant you so that I can leave at any time."

"You are young, and only recently come into the world of the wizard," Octavius said, and he stomped his forehoof hard enough to make the tables rattle. Aurora's pattern winked out with a little starburst of sparkles. The filly gasped. "Just because I can't practice magic, doesn't mean that I can't resist it. Or snuff it out."

"You dare!" Aurora breathed. She turned to Sarissa. "Lady of the Dryads, I beseech you, as Warder of Wyndoon, detain this stallion so that I might help Sir Derek."

Octavius' voice dropped even lower as he spoke before Sarissa could reply. "That will not avail you, Aurora. For one Warder to cross another is expressly forbidden, and would shatter the alliance of the Plains and the Wood. I doubt that the Lady of the Dryads will take Wyndoon to war with Cavilad for your sake."

The filly and the stallion glared at each other. I heard the scuffle of small hooves on the floor. Thunderbolt nudged his sire insistently. His voice was little more than a whisper, but he finally got Stormwind to acknowledge him when he spoke loud enough for all of us to hear.

"Dad, come on! Listen to me, please?"

"Later. Let us go now."

"No!" The colt shook his head. He looked back at me, then glanced beseechingly at his father. "Dad, help him! Why don't we help him?"

"This isn't our place, my son."

"Dad, is Sir Derek a good guy like Sarissa, or a bad guy like William Teach?"

Stormwind glanced at me, and at Sarissa. The dryad stood by my side, her sword still unsheathed. "He's not like William Teach, Thunderbolt."

"Then if he's not a bad guy, he's a good guy, right?"

"I suppose."

"Dad, are we also good guys?"

"Of course we are." Stormwind said with a snort.

Thunderbolt stepped in front of his father, looked up at him with impudent defiance. He spoke slowly, emphasizing each word like it weighed ten pounds. "Then...*why don't we help him?*"

"I don't..." Stormwind fidgeted. "Thunderbolt, a Pegasus can't stand up to a sphinx. And we can't fight William Teach by ourselves. We can't help."

"You're wrong, Dad! You could fly him to that gate a lot faster than some old truck can roll there." Thunderbolt squared his shoulders, set his jaw like he was about to do battle with a dragon. "And you know how you can help Derek fight Teach's guys, maybe even the Tengan."

"I don't know what you're talking about! When I say that it's time to go, I mean—"

"I do know what I'm talking about," Thunderbolt said proudly. "I'm Thunderbolt the Wonder-Colt, and I've been undercover around you all along! We can help, 'cause I know you had magical weapons made there. Ones that can hurt the Tengan."

"You impudent colt! Keep your mouth shut or I'll—"

"Or you'll what?" Sarissa interjected. She crossed her arms in finality. "I may not be able to cross the will of the Warder of Cavilad, but I can overrule *you*, Stormwind. And I say, let the Wonder-Colt speak. His voice has been the only sane one I've heard here yet."

CHAPTER SIXTY

Stormwind looked at each of us, his eyes haunted and resigned.

"There is no need." He sighed deeply, ruffling his feathers. "Detective Ridder, my son has shamed me to act. I can get you to the gate. If you win passage, there is a cache of weapons which may tip the balance in your favor."

"I'm listening," I said.

"I had crates of special ammunition made for the weapons I was shipping to the Morning Land. Your tip led Coombes to this cache. He confiscated the lot and has it stored at his agency's offices in Pasadena."

"What's so special about the ammunition?"

"The head of each bullet has been stamped in silver plate with runic symbols. It will breach magical armor, and I believe it will hurt the Tengan."

"That will help you if you get to the Other World," Aurora pointed out. "But maybe I can help you against Typhon."

Octavius looked as if he were about to speak, but Aurora cut him off with a shrill dismissal.

"Keep quiet, Warder's get! You may have charge of my person, but you have no say over who I gift my magic to!"

Aurora tugged a large green bead off her mane and crunched it in her teeth. She dropped it into my palm. The bead was made of the same ironwood as the rest, but I felt a strange sort of pulse come from it. Looking closely at it, I saw a powdery substance swirl within.

"Legend has it that Typhon is proof against a purely magical means of destruction," she said. "Taking an indirect approach may be best. Squeeze this in your palm three times and place it on the ground before you approach him. It's a sleep spell, one that I've created to leave you untouched. With some luck, it will lull the sphinx to slumber."

"Thank you, Aurora," I said gratefully. "Stormwind, allow me to get my pack, then we'll leave immediately."

But Sarissa took me by my shoulders. She gently lowered my face, kissed me on the forehead, then described a spiral in the air before me with her fingers.

"Best of luck to you," she said sadly.

"My thanks, Lady of the Dryads. I appreciate your casting a good luck charm on me."

"That wasn't for good luck," Sarissa replied. "It was to help your soul find its way to the Spiral of Creation without too much pain. For the odds are that you will meet your doom before this is all said and done, whether at the claws of the sphinx or the blade of William Teach."

* * *

Once I mounted Stormwind's back, I had plenty of time to mull over Sarissa's words on the way to the gate. It didn't put me in any happy place. I steadied my backpack and shoulder straps as Stormwind banked to the left, beginning his descent.

I didn't have much with me: the ironwood staff, a jar of healing salve, Coombes' cell phone jammer, a plastic sandwich bag stuffed with the magic beads from Sarissa and Aurora, and my dryad mail gauntlets. Yet, even with that small load, I felt Stormwind struggle to take flight. The Pegasus' skin ended up drenched with perspiration as we drew close to the gate.

The ride was quiet, save for Stormwind's warm breath sounding in time with the beat of his wings. The constant buffeting of wind chafed and burned my face, and my legs ached from being held in one position. But I didn't pay much attention to the scenery as I kept obsessively checking my watch. By the time we began our descent, almost four hours had gone by.

We landed in a small wooded glade. Stormwind trotted over to a nearby lump of rock so that I could get off easily. I swung my leg over his side, teetered for a second on my feet, and then promptly collapsed.

My thighs seized up in a double cramp that was way beyond anything I'd felt during Sarissa's meditation exercises. I muttered curses under my breath as I feverishly dug into the pack, fumbled with the jar of salve, then slathered it on like a layer of sunblock. Stormwind watched me, his expression inscrutable.

"I'm sorry, Sir Derek," he said.

"No need to be," I said, between gritted teeth. "Equine backs aren't exactly fitted for human butts and legs."

"That's not what I meant," he said, fidgeting a little. "I meant to say that I am sorry that I didn't volunteer to help. That I can't help you any more now."

"You did more than I'd have hoped, ambassador. You're a diplomat, not a warrior. And you have a son who needs you."

"I think it is *I* who needs *him*, sometimes," he sighed. "Typhon and the gate are in the large clearing beyond this copse of trees. Luck to you, sir knight."

Stormwind bowed and spread his wings. He leapt lightly into the air, and I watched him until he disappeared over the hills. My cramps had abated by then and I felt whole and hearty again.

I took off my pack and shoulder straps, then crammed the beads into my jacket pocket. I slipped on my gauntlets and held Sarissa's staff at the ready. With a deep breath, I moved as quietly as I could into the trees.

I had only gone a short way when I saw a dim gleam of blue light through the saplings and underbrush. My stomach tied itself into a knot as I got close enough to see what it was coming from.

The light flickered like a candlewick from an oval of blue glass suspended about two feet above the ground by invisible cable. The gate was placed in the exact center of a circular clearing. And sitting in front of the oval shape, his features darkened in the shadow cast by the glow, was the sphinx.

Typhon had an intelligent, human face with a light complexion, rosy cheeks, and a long, Roman nose. It was this normal-seeming face on the gigantic body of a lion that made him look all the more monstrous. And 'gigantic' was the proper word. Not counting his long, muscular tail, Typhon was the size of a small truck.

He sat quietly, like a cat waiting for his owner to place a plate of milk in front of him. His tail, complete with lion tuft, curled around his feet and flicked lazily back and forth. My poor brain was only able to compose a single thought.

How the hell am I supposed to fight that thing?

Typhon's golden eyes flicked unerringly to where I stood in the trees. I felt someone pump ice water through my veins. He spoke in a deep rumble.

"I know you are there, human. Stop pretending that you are actually hidden from me and come forth. I will not harm you. Not *yet*, anyway."

The power in that voice made me freeze. Had to force myself to move. I began by digging Aurora's spell bead out of my pocket. I squeezed it three times and dropped it on the forest floor. I moved out into the clearing as instructed, holding my hands out so that Typhon could see I had nothing except my staff.

My fear turned to horror as Typhon got to his feet. The sphinx grinned wolfishly, showing a set of teeth that looked like an entire line of freshly sharpened steak knives. Talons dug into the turf and the earth shook as he moved towards me with the lope of a predatory cat.

Chapter Sixty-One

The sphinx's lope slowed to a walk as he got closer to me. It took all my willpower to not run away screaming. And then, I saw that his teeth were bared, not in a ferocious snarl, but in a wary smile. He stopped a few yards away and gave me a puzzled look.

"So," he said, in that magnificent bass voice of his. "Did you bring me anything to read?"

"Uh…" I said, trying to think of something intelligent to say.

So far, Derek Ridder was zero for two when it came to witty opening lines. At least when meeting new magical creatures. Make that zero for three.

"Well, no," I said. "Nobody told me that you had asked for anything."

"Typical," Typhon grumped. "You let someone go without eating them, and see how they repay you. Gratitude, I tell you."

"Why, uh, do you want something to read?" I had no idea where this was going, but I wanted the sphinx off the eating thing, and fast. "How in the world did you learn to read in the first place?"

"When I was created to guard this gate, the powers that be gave me intelligence. Alas, that's made the job boring for me. For centuries, whenever someone showed up to challenge me, it always went the same way." The sphinx rolled his eyes as he did a passable imitation of a knight-errant. "'I am here to smite you, foul creature.' I'd reply with something like 'Roar! come ahead then, hero'. And then in with the swordplay."

"Ah. Swordplay."

"Not as fun as it sounds, I assure you. Since no one can defeat me, I'd at least get to eat lunch. Then go through their baggage. Over time you start gathering a nice collection of books, but the subject matter's pretty limited. You wouldn't believe how many people just keep diaries."

"That sounds nice," I ventured, though Typhon hadn't exactly moved off the 'killing and eating' subject yet. "Bet those diaries helped keep you up on what was going on in the world."

"Meh. Usually it's about who in the royal court was screwing who," he said with a shrug. "That's why I did the riddle thing for a while, it helped keep things interesting. But even that lost its charm after a while. So I had to figure out something else to do."

"Let me guess...instead of just blindly attacking travelers, you ask if they'd bring you books instead."

I hoped that all this small talk was going to help improve the odds of Aurora's sleep spell working, but so far I didn't see any effect.

"Smart man. I like to talk to people. So long as they don't cross a certain boundary, I leave them alone. Or I ask them to pay me tribute in books or scrolls."

"Well. If you let me use this gate, I could return and bring you more books and magazines than you could ever need."

"Not happening," Typhon said, with a truly horrific grimace.

"Look," I said, and my fear of Typhon went down a notch as I thought of Tavia suffering at Teach's hands. Of him breaking her leg anew with his staff. "I need to use that gate. A lot of lives depend on me getting through."

"I am sorry, because you came a long way. But you've failed. However, since you'll be dead, at least you won't have long to feel bad about it."

"Whoa, hold on there, Typhon. Maybe we can work something out."

"I don't think so," the sphinx said, and a rivulet of sticky white drool ran down the side of his chin. "Remember, I said that I leave people alone, 'so long as they don't cross a certain boundary'. You crossed it a couple feet back. You really should have stayed at the edge of the clearing."

"But...look, you called me over," I said, and I slowly moved the staff to where I needed it. "Why don't you just let me take a mulligan on this one, and go take a nap or something?"

"Someone should have told you that I'm immune to almost all magic. At least, before they told you to use that sleep spell you cast. Yes, I called you over beyond the point of no return. Sorry about that. But you see…" Typhon's eyes became golden slits and his voice faded into a feline growl, "…the fact is, I'm *really* hungry today."

He opened his mouth and let out a roar that made the hair on the back of my neck stand on end. He moved forward with a terrible eagerness, becoming all sinuous motion and appetite. I desperately swung Sarissa's ironwood staff across his face.

A deep, wet *crunch!* and blood spattered over my arm. Typhon howled, jumped back in surprise. With one paw, he gingerly touched his face.

"That actually hurt," he said, astounded. "I think you broke my nose."

"Let me pass, Typhon. I won't stop until you let me pass!"

In response, he let out another roar and pounced. I jumped back as he snapped at me. I swung the staff at him again.

A glancing blow caught him above the ear. He hissed, grabbed at me with one paw, then the other. I barely fended him off with the staff. Each time giving him a sound rap on his golden-furred knuckles.

"Wait a minute." he paused. "Sarissa's a pretty odd name for someone like you. Were your parents expecting a girl? A dryad girl?"

"Sarissa? Why do you think—"

I turned beet red.

My big, stupid mouth.

"Well, now. Since you don't know the name that's inscribed on your wizard's staff, my guess is that you're not Sarissa. Or a wizard. So if you can't use magic, you're probably not good at blocking it, either."

Typhon spoke a word in what sounded like a cross between a purr and Tavia's Latinate tongue. Blinding light flooded my field of vision. I gasped, swung wildly into the blank haze around me.

In an instant, my staff was flung away. The heavy cuff of a paw knocked me onto my back. Talons flashed a deadly white, landed on either side of my chest.

A crushing weight bore down on me. My ribs creaked. Breath whistled out as Typhon let out a roar of triumph.

CHAPTER SIXTY-TWO

I gasped for breath as Typhon's paw pinned me to the ground. Two of his terrible claws gripped me like a vise on either side of my chest. I beat my fists against his foreleg with no effect.

All he had to do was clench his paw. My guts would go squirting out between his talons. He let out a pleased-sounding mewl.

Then bent towards my face, mouth open for a bite.

"Hold, Typhon!" came a deep, familiar voice.

The sphinx growled, but raised his head to see who was calling to him. I did the same. Tavia's brother approached from the edge of the clearing. I thought that he looked tired, sweaty, like he'd been part of a long race. But it was hard to tell when I was looking at him almost upside-down.

"Octavius, good to see you," Typhon said, in a pleased voice. "Mind my boundary, please."

"I know where it is, I've been here before," the unicorn replied.

"I was about to have a bite of lunch. You might want to come back later. You know I'm a messy eater."

"I wouldn't dream of interrupting your lunch," Octavius said. "I just came by to twist the knife a little deeper into your main course. This human insulted me, and I'd like him to acknowledge the depth of his mistake."

"Oh, you're a cruel one, you are! Very well, if you wish to tell him to his face, I'll give you leave to cross my boundary this one time."

"I owe you," Octavius said. He stepped across whatever the damn boundary was that Typhon had tricked me into crossing over. The stallion cocked his head, looked at me curiously. "You're no 'Sir Derek', no matter who's chosen to tack that title on to you. I rather like your other name, 'Ridder', since I'll be rid of you soon enough."

I tried to say something. But all that came out of my mouth was a squeaking sound. The pressure from Typhon's paw kept me from drawing breath. My vision began to dim, going black around the edges.

"The problem with you humans from the Other World is that you don't even know how ridiculous your kind even looks," the stallion continued in a mocking tone. "I don't carry a wizard's mark, but I'm going to show you one of the tricks I've learned over the years. One that even Sarissa doesn't know about."

With that, Octavius spoke a few words under his breath. His body shimmered, shifted shape. Typhon let out a low whistle.

"Wow, I didn't know you could do that," the sphinx said.

Where the stallion had stood was now a tall, well-built man of fair complexion with hair the color of freshly brewed espresso. Octavius had shaggy eyebrows, a rugged, haughty look around his eyes, high cheekbones, and golden beard stubble.

He wore a light-colored jacket with no sleeves, which showed off his bulging muscles and scarred shoulders. Tavia's brother also had on a pair of dun-colored pants and thick-soled black boots. He walked closer, stood next to Typhon's paw, then knelt down next to me.

"Now do you understand, Ridder? How we magical creatures can put any one of your kind back where you belong—underfoot?" Octavius leaned back on his heels, looked up at Typhon as the sphinx hunched over us, watching my last moments. He returned his attention to me. "Finally, you understand how we do things here in the Morning Land."

My eyes began to flutter. My vision dimmed as the last of my breath was crushed out of me. The final blackness began to creep in from the edges.

A golden blur passed across my field of vision.

The *crack!* of ice during a glacier's spring thaw.

Warm, sticky fluid cascaded over my face. I coughed. My chest heaved and I half-turned. Typhon's paw lay atop me as simple dead weight.

An iron taste filled my mouth as I wriggled out from between the sphinx's ivory-colored cat talons. I gasped as I felt those talons shiver, then fell backwards to a sitting position. I grabbed the bottom edge of my jacket and wiped my eyes clear of what I now realized was Typhon's blood.

It took me a while to regain my breath, to figure out what had just happened. Typhon lay on his flank, his gaze frozen in a look of surprise. A ragged, bloody hole had been punched into his forehead, smack between his eyes.

Tavia's brother had shifted back to equine form. His horn dripped bright red with gore. He stood dejectedly over the sphinx's corpse.

"I used to spar with Typhon," he said. "He got quite chatty. One day he let slip that he didn't know much about unicorns. He didn't know how quickly we can shift shape. I knew that I just needed a way to get close enough so I could finish him with one thrust of my horn."

"Octavius, I don't know what to say."

"What to say? You need say nothing, just listen," he fumed. His shoulders shook with barely contained fury. "You saw what I just did? Well, I *liked* Typhon. You, I *don't* like. Do you understand?"

I got shakily to my feet.

"I think so, but I should still thank you."

"Shut up," he spat.

I did so as I retrieved Sarissa's staff.

The stallion turned away, refusing to look at me. His head hung low. He let out a long, sad exhalation. Octavius' voice dropped to a choked whisper.

"Save her. Do whatever it takes. But save her."

I nodded wearily.

I walked to the shimmering blue mirror of the gate. The hairs on the back of my neck stood on end. I placed one foot into the gate's flickering maw, then stepped inside.

CHAPTER SIXTY-THREE

Richard Coombes halted as he walked in the door at the Pasadena Horse Clinic. His face went pale as he spotted me. His hand went for his cell phone.

"Jesus, what the hell happened to you, Ridder?" he exclaimed. "You need an ambulance!"

"No, I don't," I said, motioning for him to put away the cell.

I'd already scared the crap out of the clinic's receptionist. It wasn't because I'd appeared out of nowhere in their parking lot. Rather, it was because my face and chest were drenched in Typhon's blood. I'd managed to clean some of it off with my jacket, but I still looked like I'd been in a knife fight.

"You sure?" he asked, in a disbelieving tone.

"Look, I got into an argument with a sphinx. Tell you about it on the way to your office."

Say this for Coombes: unlike a lot of people, he didn't delay any further by asking stupid questions. Instead, he led me towards a plain, brown Buick sedan with government plates. I got in the passenger seat, then fumbled with the seat belt clip for a couple seconds like it was something foreign to me.

He pulled out into the early afternoon traffic. I gripped the armrest by my seat with white-knuckled anxiety. The sheer number of cars, the incessant, crazy motion of the world struck fear into my heart.

It was too hot. Too bright. And much too noisy. Everything smelled like gasoline, tar and smoke. My head began to throb. I rubbed my temples, trying to will the pain away.

At the next stoplight, Coombes fiddled in the door compartment on his side. He tossed me a bottle of extra-strength aspirin. Then indicated a sealed bottle of Evian spring water he'd stuck into the cup holder in the center console.

"You're going to feel like crap for the next couple of hours," he said sympathetically. "Take the painkillers, it helps."

I nodded, then popped a pair of pills in my mouth. I opened the Evian, chugged down a swallow with the medicine. On the second swallow I almost gagged. The pure spring water tasted like melted plastic. Coombes grinned ruefully and nodded at me.

"Trust me, I know how it feels, Ridder. You've acclimated to the Morning Land's pace of things. The purity of their air and water. Maybe the atmosphere has a higher oxygen content than here, I don't know. But everybody who's spent more than a week there comes back with an awful headache on the first day. It's easier if you sleep it off."

"Can't do that," I said, grimacing. "We only have four hours…"

"Until what? Your message wasn't exactly clear, Ridder."

"Until the end of the world. William Teach has brought his yena here, to the Other World. I mean, our world. The world of Los Angeles. He wants to open a gate to the world of the Tengan war-demons. He's either going to run this place, or turn it into a desert wasteland."

Coombes digested the information with a firm set of his jaw. The news shocked him, though. He had to jerk the steering wheel to the right, try to keep us in the proper lane.

"So why'd you call me, not Birch at the LAPD?"

"Because you operate under the radar, Coombes," I pointed out. "You know about the warlock's powers, and that I'm telling the truth. I'm hoping…God, I'm praying that you can send some men out with me to stop Teach before he makes his move. And because…"

"Yeah?"

"Because I learned from Ambassador Stormwind that you have his special ammunition locked up in your office's armory."

The Secret Service man mulled that one over with a soft curse.

"That winged horse has good intel. I don't know, Ridder. Why would you need it, anyway?"

"Think back to the last time I fought Teach. Tavia destroyed a magic stone with her horn, which Teach needed to open a gate for the Tengan and to control them, make them do his bidding. Turns out that Tavia's horn absorbed that magic, so she's the key to it all right now."

"Okay, I follow you so far."

"Coombes, Teach has Tavia. He offered her—" I took a deep breath and forced myself to go on. "He offered her something her family desperately wants, in return for her help. She's gone with him under false pretenses, hoping to kill him or die trying."

"Damned unicorns. They always go for the high drama. It's like they have a martyr complex or something."

"Teach needs Tavia to work magic tonight. At moonrise, which I figure to be around six-thirty. He needs her on hand to open up the gate, probably to control the Tengan he lets through. So, I need that ammo tonight. If you'll lend me a team of guys to take him out, so much the better."

"You're asking for a hell of a lot, Ridder."

"This sure as hell isn't a normal situation. Even if you're not concerned about Tavia's life, consider that Teach showed his hand to everyone in Wyndoon before he left. He knows that he's got to strike fast, to take this city while we have nothing to stop his demons, not one damned thing."

He frowned at my words. But his expression remained neutral as I spent the next few minutes telling him about my training in Wyndoon. What the warlock had done to set the final pieces into motion.

And Tavia's last letter.

Coombes pulled up to a nondescript building a block from Pasadena City Hall. An attendant directed us down a ramp and into a gated underground garage. We pulled up next to a big black van. Coombes got out of the car, threw open the rear doors of the van, then rummaged around until he found a shrink-wrapped bundle of clothes. He tossed it to me as I got out of the Buick.

"This is all I've got around here that'll fit you on short notice." He pointed over my shoulder. "Bathroom's that way. Get that blood off you and come down the end of the hall when you're done. My office is the last one on the left. I have to figure out a way we can do this without getting my ass canned and shipped to Alaska."

He stalked off and I gratefully pushed through the door to the bathroom. Empty, thank god. I put the package of clothes down, then went over and wrenched open the hand-towel dispenser. I pulled out the entire roll and set it by the sink as I turned the hot water tap up all the way.

I pulled off my ruined shirt and jacket, got some soap and started wiping my face down. Once I'd completed that, I sorted through the jacket pockets and threw away the blue bead I'd used to contact Coombes.

Since the closest place I knew to downtown was the clinic where Tavia had been treated, I had simply thought of that location as I stepped into the gate between our worlds. When I'd stumbled into the clinic, I'd pulled one of the blue beads out of my pocket. I cupped it like I'd seen Sarissa do before, and fixed an image of Coombes' face in my mind.

It had worked, at least enough to tell him where I was.

With a grunt, I pulled open the package of clothes. I shed the last of my garments for something that looked like a bank guard uniform. I threw away the tie and cap, but kept the windbreaker, which had a bunch of useful zipper pockets. At least it fit, which was all I cared about.

I went down the hall Coombes had indicated. I passed a couple offices with doors bearing government seals and 'Happy Halloween!' cards. I stepped into the one at the end. Coombes was in the middle of a conversation with someone on his office phone, so I took a seat.

It sounded like Coombes was trying to persuade someone. I looked around as he continued to speak. I recognized a couple items from the Morning Land on the shelves. I spotted a small pile of micatum, a drawing with runes, and a dryad carving.

But I stopped short when I saw the picture Coombes had on his desk next to his day planner.

Michael Angel

CHAPTER SIXTY-FOUR

Coombes hung up the phone. He looked at me calmly as I picked up the frame so I could see it fully. I knew I was being rude, but I wanted to know what a picture of Emily and Rachel was doing on his desk.

"What's going on here, Coombes?" I demanded.

He surprised me by gently taking the frame from my hands. He set it back down on his desk, then paused to wipe off the thin film of dust that had settled on the glass.

"I was given the task of settling Emily and Rachel in a new community. To keep them safe from your mad warlock, remember? I've been checking in on them, making sure that they were safe. Emily and I…we've been seeing each other for a few weeks now." Coombes looked slightly abashed by my reaction. For some reason it made him seem more human to me than before. "You're not the only person who's entitled to feel protective of someone, Ridder."

I started to say something, but failed. Coombes nodded at me, and I couldn't help but shake my head. Life hadn't stopped just because I'd left for parts unknown on a unicorn filly's coattails.

"You're right," I admitted. "I'm not the only one."

"Now we've got to focus on what you need to do tonight. A lot of people owe me favors here. They'll let me move while they wait for the upper echelons to sort through the paperwork." He took a deep breath, then added, "But do you have any proof that we're up against this hard and fast deadline?"

I began to protest, but he held up a hand to cut me off.

"No, I'm not questioning your word. But I haven't seen this letter Teach sent. You don't know for sure if he's bluffing or not. Give me something more concrete, Ridder."

"Teach can't just pop in and do what he needs to bring in the Tengan," I said, thinking fast. "He has to be moving on the slate quarry to secure it. Let's put a call in to the company working out there, see what's going on."

"They're shut down for the season. Not much call during the holidays for decorative slabs of rock," Coombes said. He added, "But we can confirm if anything's going on. I figured if Teach popped up here again, we should know. So I got two of my best men hired as their security guards. They switch off as the day and night shift watchmen."

Coombes opened his desk's bottom drawer and pulled out a solid-state walkie-talkie. He switched it on, turned it to the right frequency, then pressed the transmit button. His voice resonated in the confines of his office.

"Checkmate-One to Nelson. Report in."

The reply came in immediately. The voice was curt. "Nelson here."

"Nelson, give me a status report."

"Everything's fine."

"Specifics, Nelson. Seen anything suspicious in or around the quarry site?"

"Everything's fine."

Frowning, Coombes said, "I asked for specifics. Do you need assistance?"

"No. Assistance. Everything's fine." I motioned for Coombes to take his finger off the transmit button.

"Who's Nelson's relief for the night shift?" I asked.

"Agent Call," Coombes replied. He got what I was driving at and pressed the button again. "Nelson, has Agent Johnson arrived on site yet? He's been your relief for the past two weeks, he should be there."

"Yes, Agent Johnson here. Right now. Everything's fine."

Now the voice sounded not-quite human, like something trying very hard to make words that were new to it. Coombes switched off the equipment with a defeated look on his face.

"Nelson's dead, isn't he?"

I nodded. "Probably. I don't think yena take prisoners."

"Goddamn yena. Goddamn those talking dog things." He struck a fist on his desk with a bang. "I've been to Nelson's house a bunch of times for dinner. He's got a beautiful wife, two baby girls…" His voice trailed off.

"I'm sorry, Coombes."

"Don't be. Maybe that was the kick in the ass I needed." He stood, then came around the desk. "Give me a couple hours to call in a team of guys I trust, get the ammo out of the sub-basement and de-greased. We'll meet in the main conference room."

"That'll cut us a little closer than I'd like. We still have to get over there, and we don't know for sure what kind of resistance we'll be facing."

"Best I can do. If you're so worried about what we'll face, why don't you help us anticipate it?" He nodded at the ironwood staff in my hand. "I don't believe for a second that you've been anointed as a wizard, not even if your name is Harry Freaking Potter, but if you know any magic that can help us, get it ready."

"I will." Coombes was right. This would be our one and only shot, and we could only move so fast.

"Stay in the building while I send all of our office worker bees' home. Oh, and one more thing." As we left his office, Coombes pulled out his wallet, thumbed out ten single-dollar bills, and handed them to me.

"What's this all about?"

He jabbed his thumb towards an open door down and across the way. "The vending machines are in the break room. You'll know what to do. Remember, I came back from the Morning Land too."

And with that remark, he left me alone while he strode off. Puzzled, I went over to where a dingy room held a Formica table with two folding chairs, a triple set of vending machines and a microwave that had seen better days.

I set my staff down on the table, wondering what Coombes was talking about. And right then, a whiff of freshly brewed coffee hit my nostrils.

I was at the first machine in an instant, trying to force-feed it a dollar bill.

When the little paper cup slopped down in the holder and the nozzle dispensed the liquid, I knelt in front of the machine in near reverence. I burned my tongue as I gulped the coffee, black and steaming, from the cheap paper cup like it was liquid ambrosia. That was followed by a chocolate bar with nuts and caramel. And that in turn was followed by the thing that I was craving more than anything else after weeks of dryad cuisine in Wyndoon.

The microwave cheeseburger that came out of the vending machine had the consistency of terrycloth wrapped in grease. And yet, it was like the best prime-aged meat from a five star Texas steakhouse to my taste buds. I washed it down with more coffee, then a Coke.

As I settled into my junk food high, I cleared the table of the wreckage of wrappers and began to go through the room's supply cabinets. I was luckier than I dared hope. In the third cabinet I looked into was a pack of fine-point permanent markers.

I muttered an apology to Sarissa and began defacing her ironwood staff. I felt like I was vandalizing it, even though she'd gifted it to me. I meticulously drew pressure-activated pain runes up and down its length, stopping only to add my name in runic letters to each spiral-themed drawing.

I had two of Sarissa's little blue beads left. I didn't know if I could use them for more than just communication. Instead, I decided that I needed to create some more magical equipment. My second search of the cabinets turned up a 24-pack of drink coasters. Each had a cheesy 'Corporate America Approved' motivational word on one side like *Persistence* or *Leadership*.

But each had been carved out of sandstone. Carved into pieces small enough to fit in the pockets of my dorky looking bank-guard outfit. Light enough to carry, but heavy enough to throw. I got busy with the markers and started inscribing each coaster with my name trigger, then a pressure-sensitive explosive rune.

I decided to use the mirror that hung over the break room's small sink. I stood in front of it and opened my jacket. I carefully traced the rune of Salus on my chest. I didn't know if it would help, but I was in uncharted waters right now, and I had no choice but to experiment.

I snapped Coombes' cell phone jammer to my belt, then pulled on my dryad chain mail gauntlets. I took a deep breath and looked at myself in the mirror. Unbidden, a bunch of ugly thoughts swirled in my head.

You look ridiculous. There's no way that this is going to work. Teach will just whisper in your ear, tell you to exit stage left like Dorian Martinez.

"No. That won't happen, I swear."

And right then, an idea came to me.

I uncapped a marker to draw one final rune.

Michael Angel

CHAPTER SIXTY-FIVE

"Let me get this straight," Coombes' second in command said, in a disbelieving voice. "You want us locked, loaded, and ready to wipe the slate with this guy who's threatening the world, and you *don't* want us to engage."

"You got it, Manny," said Coombes. "We simply deliver Detective Ridder through the zone of hostiles, get him close enough to engage Teach."

"Come on. If Teach needs something that this Tavia chick has, he'll be focused on her. All I need to do is get close enough to draw a bead on him."

"Tavia's no 'chick', she's a filly," Coombes said, straight-faced.

"And I've seen William Teach's work, up close," I added. "Your bullet would either miss, or he'd convince you to put it in your own skull."

Manny grunted at that. He folded his massive arms and looked at me, supremely unimpressed. I'm not small, but wherever Manny stood, it looked like someone had erected a black-suited brick wall.

"We wear the jammers we made, use the special weapons," Coombes continued. "But we can't really count on any of it working."

"Why not?" asked another of the agents.

"Because Teach isn't crazy, and he isn't stupid. Every time he's been encountered he's changed and updated his tactics. Armor for his yena friends. The ability to deflect projectile weapons." Coombes held up his cell-phone sized jammer. "You want to bet your life that he hasn't figured out a way to dampen the effect these have on his magic? Especially after Ridder almost pin cushioned him outside Wyndoon?

Coombes drummed his finger on the map that he'd laid out on the table and held fast with a dozen office paperweights. Then he took a pencil from where he'd secured it behind his ear and scratched a line next to the quarry's main building.

"That's the five-yard line, gentlemen. We get the van up behind the line of storage sheds, convey Ridder to the building, then set up a perimeter between the van, the walls, and the doorway."

A third agent spoke up. "What about inside?"

"It's a confined space, lots of equipment and machinery," I said. "Yena are fast on the straight and narrow, but they're not agile. Especially if they're going to be wearing that armor that Teach gave them. I'll be able to handle them."

Manny and the other five men in the group traded glances. Each of them looked lean and muscled, like they had been Rangers or SEALS before joining Coombes' team. I watched them pull on their body armor and clear faceplate covers, and I could see that they knew their way around the equipment.

Despite the odd looks they gave me, I took a marker and stenciled contact pain runes on the pads of their shoulders, the collar at the rear of the neck, and on the backs of gloved hands. I thought of the fire-grenade beads the yena had worn at Wyndoon, and decided to follow up with runes of fire protection.

Out back by the van, Manny and Call wheeled over a large dolly stacked with equipment they'd pulled from the confiscated crates. I let out a low whistle. Reading about the haul on a manifest was one thing. Seeing the pile of assorted black market firearms and silver-tipped bullets was something else.

"What can we use out of all this?" I asked.

"Bits and pieces," Coombes replied. "Our Pegasus friend bought anything and everything he could, no matter the condition. We've cleaned up and matched ammo to these, at least."

He indicated a dozen snub-nosed weapons with the sweep of a hand. I frowned. I'd seen this weapon more than once on gang-related drug busts.

"Uzi submachine guns, with double-size magazines," Coombes explained. "Illegal as hell, but we've got plenty of ammo, if you want one."

"Thanks, but I don't need a bullet hose. I'm sticking with what I know best."

I reached out and selected one of the other guns off the pile. It was the same type of Glock semi-automatic pistol I'd used on the force, save for the rune stamped in silver on the side. The difference in weight was barely enough for me to notice, and the gun felt familiar and reassuring.

"You've got guts, Ridder, give you that," Coombes said, once we'd gotten into the van. "I'd want more than a semi in hand when there's a pack of yena coming at me."

"At least I have these," I said. I held up one of my rune-marked drink coasters. And right then, of all things, I wished I had a camera to capture Coombes' puzzled look.

* * *

The big black van wallowed through the bumps that led up to the quarry gate. We jostled uncomfortably. A sliver of autumn moon peeked over the horizon, looking huge and yellow like the waxy skin on a cadaver.

I looked anxiously over Manny's shoulder where he sat jammed in the passenger-side front seat. We pulled up to the chain-link fence that surrounded the quarry site. I could just make out the quarry buildings.

Sixty yards of chest-high grass separated the front gate from the buildings.

Hiding who-knew what.

"I'm seein' a chain and padlock on that gate," the driver said, as he slowed to a stop. Coombes frowned and looked at me.

"Ridder, can you tell if anything's booby-trapped? Maybe see what's up ahead?"

I shook my head.

"Okay," Coombes said. He leaned forward and gave the order. "We're just about out of time. Ram it."

The engine roared. We churned up gravel as the rear wheels spun. The van easily smashed through the chains holding the entry shut.

The vehicle slewed to the side on the soft dirt. The driver muttered a curse, then jerked the wheel to get us back on track. The motor revved again and we sped up the road.

Manny let out a small gasp of surprise. Coombes and I leaned forward in our seats to look out the windshield. A beam of blue-green light erupted from deep inside the main quarry building.

It illuminated a cloud of dust that boiled from the surface of the road up ahead.

"What the hell is—" the driver began to say.

I saw it for a heart-stopping second. The glow of hellishly red eyes in the dark, racing directly at us. Yena eyes. The creature charging at us made a mighty leap, head tucked into its chest and plated with solid armor.

The yena cannonballed through our windshield. The air inside the van filled with sharp daggers of glass. The driver screamed, once, before the animal wrenched its torso through what was left of the windshield.

Whip-fast, it tore his throat out. Blood fountained everywhere in a crimson spray.

With a rubbery squeal, the van slewed off the road and into the tall grass.

CHAPTER SIXTY-SIX

The van's passenger-side tire hit a rock hidden in the grass. With a *bang!* it blew out. For one sickening second, the vehicle went up on two wheels and threatened to flip. Manny shoved his arm underneath the belly of the yena. He wrenched the steering wheel to the right. The van came back down upright and we crunched to a halt.

The yena turned and bit Manny on one meaty bicep. He cried out in shock. I pulled my semi. Stuck it into the gap between the yena's head shield and its chest plate.

Squeezed the trigger twice.

The shots were deafening in the confines of the van. The air filled with the iron scent of human and yena blood, the stink of cordite. I pushed the yena's lifeless head to one side, then placed my hand to what was left of the driver's neck. Coombes gave me a look.

"Had to check. But he's gone."

"I'd have done the same." Coombes raised his voice. "Manny, you okay? Everyone okay?"

"Yeah," the big man said, and the rest of the men followed suit.

I squinted through the glass. "We're still twenty, maybe thirty yards out. Don't see any more yena, but that doesn't mean they're not out there."

On cue, a choir of the creatures sent up spine-tingling howls from the grass all around us. Red eyes glowed in the darkness outside the windows. Suddenly, the sound of small *thunks* came from both sides of the van, like kids throwing cherry bombs.

Fire erupted in the grass by Manny's window. A canine face snarled at him from just beyond the flames. More sounds of little beads bouncing off the vehicle's metal sides.

One rolled off the roof. It landed on the yena's body that lay on the van's hood. With a puff, it ignited. The flames caught on the thing's oily fur. Cursing, Manny unbuckled his seat belt. I helped him half-slide, half-crawl out of his seat.

"They're gonna try and roast us here," Coombes said. "Lock and load, pocket all the extra ammo you can. Exit and form a hedgehog with Ridder at the center. Back to the road, then we move up to the buildings."

"Might be able to cut directly across here, save some yardage," said one of Coombes' men, as he looked out the back window.

"No. Too much high grass. Can't see a thing. And they'll try to burn us out again, count on it." Coombes looked around, saw we were all ready. Sweat rolled down his forehead as the yena let out another ungodly chorus of howls.

Coombes counted to three. Then signaled his men to kick open the van's rear doors. The grass around them burned brightly.

But my fire runes worked. They waded through the knee-high flames and cleared the area with sweeps of their weapons. It was a close thing. A pair of yena had been hidden in the grass almost next to the van. They were struck down in mid-leap by the curtain of lead the guns put up.

The team fell into position. We slowly retraced the skittering route that our van had taken off the main road. I kept the Glock in its holster, while I tucked my wizard's staff under my arm. With my free hand, I dug out the drink coasters.

A terrifying howl greeted us as we reached the main road. Then the yena hit us from all sides at once. They lunged out of the grass, jaws snapping.

Coombes' men mowed them down. But they kept coming. The submachine guns sounded like a factory full of asthmatic sewing machines.

"Keep! Moving!" Coombes bellowed, and step-by-step we advanced. With a shout, I flung a pair of coasters into a mass of yena ahead. One of the stone pieces detonated with a deep-throated *bang!* Bits of canine flew twenty feet into the air.

The other of my rune-covered coasters skidded to a halt in the dirt, symbol side facing up. Then one of the oncoming yena stepped on it. The little piece of sandstone turned the yena and two of his pack mates into gobbets of raw flesh which rained down among us.

Coombes let out a cry of disgust. He pulled out a chunk of meat that had stuck in his collar and flung it away.

I cleared a path with my makeshift grenades, blasting bloody holes in the swarms of yena. We were now among the bodies of the slain canines. They lay in smoking, twitching heaps. The ground grew red and soggy.

The man next to Coombes slipped, fell on his back.

In an instant, three yena burst from the red-stained grass. Coombes shot one down, while Manny blew away another. But the third one leaped forward, brought its deadly jaws down on the man's thigh, tearing at it like a haunch of meat.

The yena touched the pain runes, yelped, then fled back. Bullets whizzed over it, riffling the fur on its back. Only the coaster I skimmed at it touched the mark. It and three other yena that stuck their heads up at the wrong moment vanished in a scarlet flash.

"Come on, Kenzie, get up!" Manny shouted, doing his best to pull the wounded man up by his shoulder while keeping his gun ready.

"Sling him up on your arm," said Coombes. "I'll cover you. We get Ridder to the building, get a wall to our backs, we can treat him."

At a limping pace, we drew close to the storage shacks at the end of the quarry complex. Yena swirled in the grass, always just out of sight. The mix of tawny orange and blood red vegetation looked surreal in the blue-green glow coming from the building. Coombes and his men started to conserve the ammo, only firing when a clear shot presented itself.

The yena sensed this, and pressed us again, hard. I heard the sound of breaking glass. Another group of yena crawled through a shack's skylights and onto the corrugated metal roofs.

"Above us!" I cried. Yena fire beads landed among us. Again, my fire runes protected the men around me from the flames.

Coombes raked the roof with his Uzi, clearing it.

Another five yards, and we made it to the side of the main building, gasping for breath. Coombes and three of his remaining men formed a perimeter, blasting away at anything that stuck its head out of the field. Manny and I stayed in the center of the group. He put Kenzie down and I reached for the big man's medical kit on his belt.

"No need," he said sadly, waving my hand off. "No pulse in the wrist or neck. Bled out."

He slapped one of the rapidly diminishing spare magazines into his gun, and turned back to the perimeter.

"What the hell are you waiting for, Ridder? An invitation?" Coombes shouted above the din of the weapons and the yena snarls. "We can't hold them forever. Get going before it's too late!"

I'd used up the last of my coasters. So, I pulled my Glock and held the gun tightly at the ready. I leaned against the entry door's push handle and slipped inside.

CHAPTER SIXTY-SEVEN

The inside of the building glowed with the same awful, blue-green light. It flickered with a sinuous, rippling motion that made my stomach queasy. I moved forward into the mass of machinery, office furniture, and stacks of stone slab work, listening to the sound of intermittent gunfire from behind me.

I recognized the space ahead as where I'd posted Hector Chavez and his men to ambush Teach. The hair on the back of my neck and my forearms stood at attention. Turquoise-shaded arc lightning crawled along the tops of the metallic presses and tool cabinets.

The air moved with an unpleasant, hot breeze. Like desert wind over a graveyard. I felt my chest tighten as I saw Tavia and Teach standing together, side by side.

The unicorn and the warlock worked together to draw a massive door on the rock face. Tavia with her horn, Teach with the tip of his wizard's staff. The stray hairs in Tavia's mane shimmered and crackled.

Her horn and her wizard's mark glowed with power. Her eyes were blank masses of shimmering blue-white. She moved clumsily, as if she were in a deep trance.

The outline of the door was almost complete. It was really more like the tracing of a four-lane tunnel to be bored into the rock. But instead of the blackness of a tunnel, the rock face itself

303

was changing. Shifting from solid, dense slate into a glassy, transparent substance. A substance which would turn to smoke any minute.

A hellish light began to shine through. I saw shapes. Horrible, nightmare shapes, moving inside that glow. Like hideous creatures stirring inside a birthing sac. A sac about to spill its contents.

"The Tengan…" I whispered to myself.

A gelatinous head on a scaly neck scraped the barrier with a distant, rubbery sound. It let out a tinny shriek from a mouth filled with needle-sharp, slime-covered teeth. It sounded like something horrible that had fallen into an open grave. Something that was now, finally, starting to claw its way out.

I shook myself out of my horrified daze. Set my jaw and considered. The Lady of the Dryads might have been shocked at what I was about to do. But I wasn't in their world anymore, and mine was at stake.

I took careful aim at Teach's back with my Glock. I squeezed the trigger three times. I didn't think it would work, but it would have been foolish to pass up the chance to end things quickly.

I hate it when I'm right.

The bullets slowed to a stop a foot from their target and then tumbled to the floor like misshapen steel marbles. Teach heard the clatter, then turned to look at me.

"That was quite underhanded, don't you think, Detective Ridder?" Teach called out. "As bad as hitting below the belt? Or kneeing someone in the tender spots?"

"You and I threw out the 'fair fighting rules' last time," I replied evenly.

He laughed. "I suppose that you have me there."

I kept the gun pointed at his face. Tried to think of something to do. At least Tavia seemed to have heard me. One of her ears flicked.

"What's wrong with Tavia?" I demanded.

"The filly? Why, she's helping me, of course. You did read the letter I sent, didn't you?"

"If she's helping you, let her speak to me," I replied.

"Oh, I'm afraid she's a little busy right now," Teach said, with a ghoulish grin. "You know, I did promise not to not harm her. That is, unless she acted against my interests."

I took a step closer towards Teach. I watched for any sign that Coombes' signal jammer had any effect. The glow near the tip of the warlock's staff wavered like a candle in a high wind. But otherwise, I saw no effect on his magic.

"Unicorns are really such staid thinkers," Teach said. "She was actually shocked—shocked!—that I would cast a scrying spell on her thoughts the moment she came along. When I saw that she was planning to impale me on her horn—well! Obviously from that point on, the deal was off."

Behind him, Tavia's horn ground to a halt in mid-air. She slowly shook her head side-to-side. As if she were trying to wake up. Perhaps if I could keep Teach's attention off of her for a few more moments, it would make all the difference.

"What have you done to her?" I demanded.

"I've enslaved her to my will. Once I get my gate, it shouldn't be too hard to separate what I need—her horn—from the excess: the rest of the unicorn."

And with that, Teach made a gesture with his staff. An invisible force slapped the gun out of my hand. He hissed a set of words. I felt the weight of his will bearing down.

I fought him. I held one hand against Coombes' jamming unit. I felt the pulse of the rune of Salus on my chest and inside the curve of my wedding band. I shook him off with a strange, tearing sensation in my forehead. The blankness in Tavia's eyes wavered. She shook her head again, this time making the beads in her mane rattle.

"Impressive," Teach said, panting.

He reached out and touched Tavia's wizard mark.

Tavia's eyes went well and truly blank. Her muscles locked rigid again. But his compulsion over me had vanished.

Teach spoke a phrase of ugly words. His staff shifted shape, and then hardened into a wicked looking longsword.

"Fine, if you want to play it out this way," he spat. "Let's see how much the dryads taught you, Detective Ridder."

Michael Angel

CHAPTER SIXTY-EIGHT

Teach charged at me, swinging overhand to cleave my head in two.

I threw up the ironwood staff and blocked it. A blue-white flare exploded like a flash bulb as the staff and sword met. Teach slashed at me viciously from the side. I blocked, fell back a pace.

I parried one sweeping thrust that took a chunk out of a table next to me. Ducked his backhand swing. Teach pressed each attack with a flurry of slashes. I blocked or slapped aside each of his attempts.

But he relentlessly brought the point of his sword back towards my chest. I had the slight advantage of reach, but he was faster. Each of his thrusts came too damned close to the mark.

I feinted, drew his attention and then spun my staff around. It missed its target but grazed his hand. He cried out and shook his fingers.

"Pain runes?" he said, disbelieving. "Pain runes are children's magic, Ridder. You think you can beat me with those?"

"All I need to do is stall you until you can't perform your little gating spell."

That was pure bluff. For all I knew, Coombes would run out of ammo in the next minute and the yena would flood the room. But I wanted to see if I could keep rattling the warlock.

"I don't think you've thought this through," Teach said. "You're going to have to hold me off until the moon sets. Think you can keep this up for the next nine hours?"

He leaped at me, his duster billowing out behind him. I parried his blade, held up my staff to block him. The two weapons spat and popped, continuing to throw off blue sparks.

Teach pulled a knife from inside his duster with his left hand. He leaned in, turned my staff away with his sword. He stabbed at my midsection with the knife. The knife blade slipped through my clothes and into my skin. The point burned and I heard a crunch! as it lodged against the bone in my hip.

I cried out, more from outrage than pain. He twisted the knife viciously. I felt it tearing through my skin, ripping through the heavy leather of my belt. He had my staff pinioned to the side.

I butted him in the face with my forehead.

Teach fell two steps back and dropped the bloody knife. With a yell, I brought the staff down upon his head. But the warlock had just enough presence to block my strike to finish him off. A section of my torn belt fell off and rattled on the floor. A trickle of warmth dribbled down the outside of my leg. He hadn't hurt me badly, though it hurt like a sonofabitch.

"Still standing," I said, my voice a dry rattle. "Best you could do?"

"It was all I needed," he replied.

He feinted towards me, drove me back a step. His foot kicked away Coombes' jammer. And then Teach's power hit me like a hammer blow.

He held me still. Lunged forward and drove his sword into my right shoulder. I let out a desperate cry of agony. Pain, more pain than I thought possible, shot down my arm.

Teach bore down. He shoved me against one of the wooden work cabinets. His blade pinned me against the wood like a collector's prized butterfly.

I reeled, barely able to hold my staff upright in front of me. "Throw that down, Ridder. Don't draw this out any longer."

I spat at him. Snarling, he spoke a single sinister word. The nimbus of blue fire that ran along the staff's ironwood surface went dark.

He swung his free hand in a broad horizontal arc in front of me. The staff flew from my weakened grasp. Teach smiled as he watched the dryad's staff roll into the darkness with a clatter.

I took the second that Teach was focused elsewhere to bring my left hand to my mouth. I bit into the dryad chain-mail gauntlet I wore with a grimace. My mouth filled with the taste of burnt iron. I spit the steel glove onto the floor and balled my hand into a fist.

Teach picked up the knife he'd cut me with. He stabbed it into the cabinet next to me. His power of command sank its tentacles into my muscles, forced me to move my hand closer to its stained handle.

"Your friend had it easy compared to you," Teach said. "I ordered him to use a gun to end it all. But you? You're going to have to use a knife."

I struggled, felt the agony inside my head as if I were being held against a white-hot steam boiler. But I was only held immobile when I thought about turning the knife against Teach. He wasn't guarding against anything else my will could come up with.

"Your life ends like you lived it—falling short at the final stretch," Teach said. His voice rose as he took a final step closer. Just beyond the reach of my arm. "You've failed at protecting everyone close to you. That's been the story of your life, Ridder. You're just not very good at this, are you?"

Through a haze of torment, I pulled my hand away from the knife. I held my clenched fist up in front of him. I smiled weakly, then spoke my last words through parched lips.

"I'm good enough at it, dead man."

I opened my fist. Held out my palm right in front of his nose. Sir William Teach's eyes went wide with fear as he saw the explosive rune I'd drawn there.

One that only went off when someone read it.

My forearm vanished silently in a white-hot flash.

So did Teach's head. The blast's concussion rolled over me, lifted me back off my feet. I fell backwards and away from the cabinet I'd been pinned against.

The sword tore out of my wound with a horrible, grinding sensation. I landed on my back. Gasped as pain rocketed through my body.

It took most of my remaining strength, but I raised my head. A last flicker of light came from Teach's gate. The snarling, snapping heads of the creatures within writhed in frustration. As the doorway vanished, I heard a last, frustrated howl. As if from a beast imprisoned down a deep well.

A few feet away, Teach's charred, headless body lay limp. I forced myself to refocus. Saw a tattered, bloody stump below my elbow spurting bright red arterial blood in pulses like a lawn sprinkler.

My thoughts came slowly now, like molasses on a Pennsylvania winter morning. Two kept repeating in my brain, like spiked horses on that carnival ride that Tavia didn't like.

Good thing I'm going into shock. Otherwise, losing that arm might really bother me. Good thing I'm going into shock. Otherwise, losing that arm might really bother me.

Good thing I'm going into shock–

Someone broke the merry-go-round my brain had been stuck on. Someone was calling my name. I looked up and saw Tavia's face, framed by her disheveled, singed golden mane.

"Derek," she said, pleading. "Stay with me! Please. Please."

Tavia went to her knees. She touched her horn to my stump, spoke magical words under her breath. The wound shimmered, but it didn't close.

"Regrets," I said. My voice came out as a hard, brittle whisper.

Tavia looked at me. Her expression held a wild, strange mix of fear, of longing, of desperate, fixed determination.

"No more regrets," I breathed. "Now that you are here. With me."

Her eyes welled up with tears. But I could see a galaxy of stars deep within. I felt the distinct sensation of falling through something emptier than air.

Whatever it was folded around me like a blanket. Pulled me deep.

I slipped away into the cold of that outer darkness.

Michael Angel

CHAPTER SIXTY-NINE

I felt a prickly sensation. One that ran from the side of my cheek all the way down to my shins. Cold, like a rime of dirty ice.

I pressed the palms of my hands against the ground and tried to lift myself up. I felt horribly weak, as if I'd been bedridden after a long illness. I shivered, not from the cold, but from some kind of bone-deep weariness. I got about halfway up when the little strength I had gave out. I collapsed to my knees and elbows.

It hurt to think. It was as if the circuits in my brain had been packed in grease. The first thought that came to me was: I don't think this is a hospital bed. The second was that I could still feel my left arm, intact and whole. And then, only then, did it occur to me to open my eyes.

The light was steady and dim, as if someone had thrown a heavy burlap cloth over a lantern. My eyes adjusted slowly, and I saw my left thumb, whole and undamaged, resting on a surface made up of polished river stones. I wiggled the thumb to be sure. It obeyed my command stiffly.

In time, a little more strength came back to me. I levered myself into a sitting position. Raised my head and slowly leaned back. The stony surface lay parched and still like a desert at night as far as I could see.

And high in the dark-before-dawn color sky was a diffuse, sparkly mass. It looked at first glance as if it were made of stars. But I saw the individual sparks move. What I saw resembled a cup of milk and a handful of sparkles thrown into a gently stirred pot of water.

Then I realized that I was looking at a pattern. Like one of those trick paintings, once you saw the image hidden within, it wasn't quite possible to 'unsee' it. The sparkling lights in the sky formed a slowly rotating spiral. And all at once I knew where I was. What I was seeing.

We call it the Spiral of Creation, Tavia had said. *It's tremendously subtle and powerful. Legend has it that we only see it in its entirety at birth and at death.*

Now I heard a soft thrumming. Or rumbling. Like a train chugging past along a faraway railway track. It came to me after a moment. The sound came from a distant, vast herd of horses on the move.

My heart skipped a beat as I saw something move, some dark, shadow creature, slip down from the heavens. While it made no sound, I sensed it land somewhere out on the ground ahead of me.

Part of me was afraid that it was some avenging spirit, come to claim me. Part of me was afraid that it would pass me by and leave me here in this place for eternity.

The light was still too dim to make out much. The figure stopped moving, and I saw that it was the outline of a woman.

I shuddered. There was only one person that could be, here in the land beyond the realm of the living.

I tried to call out. But my voice refused to work. Instead, I felt my thought itself cast out through the air like a rippling wave of sound.

Beth? I thought. *Beth, is that you?*

The figure hesitated, kept its distance. *If you wish that, Derek.*

For some strange reason the idea offended me.

No, I thought firmly. *Who are you? I want to know.*

In response, the figure raised her hand and traced a complex pattern in the air. All at once, it was as if someone had taken a dimmer switch and cranked it up. I felt some real strength enter my body.

I got to my feet. The gravel faded away and was replaced by a well-polished hardwood floor. Walls of fresh, eggshell-white appeared around me, punctuated with bookshelves and windows with diamond-shaped patterns of leaded glass.

I stood in the drawing room of a large English manor house. Red carpets and landscape oil paintings adorned the floor and walls. Heavy beams held up a high ceiling. Along one wall was a classically styled grandfather clock. The light resolved itself into the merry crackling of a fireplace in a white marble hearth. A pair of paisley-patterned wingback chairs nestled in front of the fire.

A pretty young woman stepped out from behind the high back of one of the chairs. She was small, delicately featured, with the pert nose, high cheekbones, and wide-set eyes of a dryad. But her eyes were dark, icy blue instead of green, and her hair was the golden blonde hue of the sun as it came out from behind a storm cloud. A cluster of braids festooned with multicolored beads hung down behind one ear.

Her skin was cream-colored, and a sleeveless sun dress of bright yellow hung from her slender frame. She wore black high-heeled shoes and an elegant pair of white satin gloves. Above the edge of one of her gloves was the brown mark of a recent scar, and on her bare shoulder some abstract symbol had been tattooed in dark ink. She smiled at me uncertainly, as if she were unsure how I was going to react.

"Tavia," I said, my voice heavy with emotion, of sadness and joy in equal measure. I held out my hands, and she took them in her own. I felt her warm, firm fingers under the satin fabric of the glove. "Tavia, what are you doing here? How are you…I didn't expect to see you. In this form, especially."

"I am here with you, Derek," she said, and I couldn't take my eyes off of her as she spoke, no matter how hesitantly. To see her face—her human face—was a miracle beyond anything I'd ever dreamed. "But what you see here, what you see of me?" She held up one delicate hand, laid it against her chest. "All this is a construct of your mind. To give you a way to relate to what is happening, to interact with me."

"Then how is it that I see you—like this? As a human, not an...equine?"

"I think it's because, deep down inside, maybe right before you go to sleep, you think of me as a woman, not a unicorn. And this is how you envision me to look." Tavia smiled, and the pearl-white gleam of her teeth seemed to make the room even brighter. "You should see what my mind is making of all this, it's pretty interesting for me as well."

I was sorely tempted to ask her, but I put the question aside for a moment. More important things were going on. I took a deep breath to calm myself. Tavia absently took my hand in hers again, intertwining our fingers.

"Tavia, I died, didn't I? And if I did, what are you doing here? Did I fail to save you? Did Teach somehow survive, or did the yena overwhelm us after I lost consciousness?"

Tavia shook her head, then looked up at me. I had to fight the urge to kiss her berry-colored lips.

"Those are a lot of questions. First off, you didn't fail. It's over. We won."

I let out a breath. That somehow made things easier, knowing that whatever else, Emily and Rachel would survive. That everyone in Los Angeles wouldn't be slain in their beds by the Tengan.

"The breach to the Tengan's world collapsed. Teach is no more," she continued. "You slew him, and your family's name will be sung in praise throughout the Morning Land. *The Son of Robert, the Warlock's Bane.* And don't worry about the yena. They knew, they knew somehow, that Teach had fallen. When that happened, they slunk off into the brush. Coombes and his men are all wounded, but alive."

"But...if we won, then why are you here?"

"Derek, what I'm doing has never been tried before. In killing Teach, you also gave yourself a big push along the road that leads under the sod."

"I follow you so far, Tavia. But you haven't answered my question."

"I'm trying to. It's difficult. Let me try to explain it a different way."

Michael Angel

CHAPTER SEVENTY

Tavia pointed to the grandfather clock on the wall.

"Derek, you and I are inside a sliver of time. In the fractions of a second such as exist between the swings of that clock's pendulum. It's a rare, subtle magic, one that can catch a moment as if to fix it like a grain of pollen in amber. By doing so, I have reached the ember at the core of your spirit. By being here, I can help anchor you, guide you. So you can find your way back."

"I think I understand. But...Christ, Tavia, if I get what you're saying, you're playing a very dangerous game. You could end up trapped here yourself. End up...under the sod, and for what reason?"

"For a very good reason, I think," she said firmly. "I know what the odds are. But I'd rather risk myself in this than do nothing and let you slip away into the darkness."

"And I'd rather you let me go and *live*, you headstrong filly!" I said, angrily. "Coombes was right, you unicorns have a ridiculous flair for the dramatic. You'd rather die for your family than live with uncertainty."

She scowled. Her dark brown eyebrows were like gull's wings in a storm-tossed sky. But the moment passed, and she looked at me intently.

"Derek. You're still trying to protect me. For someone who's lived the life I've led...it takes some getting used to. But the fate of my family is not on my mind. I came for you, and you alone. The way you came to me, to save me from enslavement and death at the hands of the mad warlock."

"Tavia, this isn't something you should have done," I said, as I held my arms out. She stepped in closer to me. "I'm no one special. I'm not worth that kind of sacrifice."

"You're wrong, son of Robert."

"What makes you so sure?"

"Two things. My heart, and your name. I think you're aware of how we in the Morning Land put great stock in names. And whether you knew it or not, you've had three people who know the magic of delving near to you. Ones who can see the true meanings of your name."

I chuckled. "My ancestors were Dutch. They're not stock from Cavilad or Wyndoon. Do you really think it applies?"

"You tell me." A hint of a smile played across her face. "Do you know what the name 'Derek' means in your family's native tongue?"

"It means 'King', or 'Ruler', I think."

"That's right. Of course, since the king is the 'father figure' of his country, he is addressed as 'sire'. And the root of the word 'sire' is?"

"Sir," I replied. I shook my head, amused. "Which is why Sarissa would always call me 'Sir Derek'."

"Sarissa was able to see that clear enough," Tavia said, and she brought her hand up to caress my cheek. "But I was the second delver, one who saw the hidden meaning when I first became aware of your name from your niece's letter. I wasn't sure if I was right, for I know less delving lore than the Lady of the Dryads. But as soon as I spoke with the final delver, I knew I was right, and that you were someone very, very special."

"That last delver being Rachel," I acknowledged. "Her natural talent, the attunement to magic that runs on Beth's side of the family."

"Even so. She knew intuitively what it took me a while to figure out." Tavia cocked her head at me. Although she was in human form, I could see the same equine mannerism in her movement. "It's in the remaining part of your name."

"Ridder?"

"Your *full* name."

Although I never used it, I did have a middle name, one that came direct from the old country. "It's 'Helden' Ridder."

"I'm pretty sure that you know what your family's surname means in Dutch. But the meaning of 'Helden' is 'hero'."

I thought for a second. My dad had told me about the surname before. 'Ridder' was taken from an old military word for 'Rider'. And during the Middle Ages, that meant...

"Knight," I said, blinking. "And that's what both Rachel and Sarissa called me: the *Hero Knight*."

"They're right, you know," Tavia said. "It's one of the ways I see you."

She looked up at me, her eyes shining. I couldn't fight it any longer. I drew her in slowly, not wanting to startle her, and placed a kiss on her lips. Tavia may have been equine, and this representation of her purely a mental image taken from my dying mind.

But she felt warm and sensual and fully human. I felt the heat rise between us. She returned my kiss, just as passionately.

She wrapped her arms about me, snuggled in as close as she could. Softly, as I stroked the golden locks of her hair, I asked, "If that was one of the ways you see me, what is the other way?"

She looked up at me with a playful grin. "Do you really want to see?"

"Of course."

She reached up and placed her fingers on either side of my temples. Her voice whispered a magical phrase, and my eyes closed. I felt her finger's touch leave the sides of my head, but I still felt her warmth against my side.

"You can look now, Derek."

I did as she said. To my surprise, I found that we were no longer in the manor house. Tavia had returned to her equine form.

We stood on a rolling expanse of plain covered in dark green grass and patches of tiny purple wildflowers. Bounding us on one side was a mountain range, tall enough so that the highest peaks were tipped with snow. A lazy river meandered in watery blue coils all over the landscape.

One of the river's arms lay a few yards away downslope. Tavia trotted towards it, halted, and turned back to me. She motioned to me with her horn.

"Over here, take a look. You'll find this interesting, I promise."

As I joined her, I heard a hard, clattering sound as I stepped on the rocks that lined the river's bank. I pushed through a strand of thick-stemmed reeds at the edge and joined Tavia as she stood gazing at the water's glassy surface. I stared for a moment, puzzled at the reflection.

My breath whistled out in a whicker of surprise.

CHAPTER SEVENTY-ONE

A powerfully built unicorn stallion stared back at me from the surface of the water. He had a deep, rounded chest, elegantly dished face, and a closely cropped mane. His flanks were silvery, with a metallic sheen that tapered down into the dark pair of socks on his hind legs. His mane and tail were the exact same shade of midnight black as my hair.

I peered more closely at the reflection. As I moved my head left to right, right to left, the stallion's head followed suit. I lifted one silver foreleg, examined the dark cloven hoof, then brought it down into the water with a splash. I craned my neck, looked back at my long, muscled flanks with amazement. I tried to flick my tail. Sure enough, it bobbed in place as it should have.

"Is...is this really how you see me?"

I realized now that we must have been speaking in whatever magical tongue that the unicorns used. Only a third of the words were really 'spoken'. A great deal of the communication was done with the expressions of the face, the stance and positioning of the body, the tail, the placement of hooves.

"Oh, yes," Tavia said, and her laughter was like the tinkling of little bells. "As much as the way you saw me, back in that room with the clock and the fireplace."

She gave a small leap up away from the bank, motioned me with a flick of her tail to follow her. "Come with me. You need to stretch your legs."

I followed at a walk, abruptly aware that I was trying to figure out how to work four legs, not two. I took a deep breath, tried not to think about it, let the body do its thing.

Maybe moving to a different pace was like shifting gears in a car. Before I knew it, I was trotting along at a rapid pace. I felt the strong beating of my heart moving in time with the pistoning of my legs.

I came up to Tavia's side like I'd been moving at her speed all my life. We moved across emerald hills, leaving the mountain range farther behind. We crossed dales speckled with more purple flowers, and then ran through a vast green plain.

And it truly did feel like running through heaven.

"This is wonderful!" I said, as I worked to smooth my gait out like hers. "I never thought…I never dreamed it could be like this."

"Well, now you have another reason to return," she said, arching a single eyebrow at me. "You can tell Rachel what it's like."

I let out a nicker, and was surprised to hear that sound emanating from my chest. "Like I would need another reason besides you."

We slowed, came together and our sides touched. Tavia nuzzled me, and I returned the gesture, showing affection the way that equines did. Our horns touched, and I felt living energy flow through the connection like an electrical circuit.

Tavia broke our contact and snorted. She raised her head and looked back at the mountain range behind us. I turned and followed her gaze. I felt a tremor, like an earthquake rumble through the ground. A curtain of black dust began to flow down the distant mountain slopes.

The sounds of mass numbers of creatures on the move. The wind picked up with a howl, and along with it came a screech that sounded like ragged claws on metal. Like the sounds I'd heard beyond the gate that Teach had been building to the world of the demons.

"What is that?" I asked. My head came up in equine alarm. "Tengan? Here?"

"In the way that I am here with you, yes. They're the image that my mind has manifested."

"For what?"

"For the last test. To get out of here—or not." Tavia said, and I saw her set her jaw. She spoke quickly. "Derek, listen to me. Ahead of us, at least seven leagues distant, is the river we call the *Keheilian*. We must get to it. If we falter, if we fall to what comes behind us, then we remain in that rocky desert you saw, the place that exists between life and death, trapped forever."

"How is a stretch of water—"

"It's not like any other river," she said, interrupting me.

With a toss of her head, we quickly shifted to a trot, then into a loping canter. I looked down, tried to watch where I put my feet. To make sure they didn't end up in some chuck-hole or tripping over themselves.

I found myself breathing hard, not out of fatigue, but stress and fear. I had to learn this body's gaits better than this, but I couldn't figure out how to break the three-beat gait and move faster. Tavia spoke to me again, and I flicked one ear in her direction to listen.

"The Keheilian is a magical river, one that binds evil so that it may not pass. Legend has it that there is a ferryman there, one who bargains the price for those who need to cross."

"That legend exists in my world too. The ferryman to the underworld. Does this, uh, equine body come with a pocket of coins to pay him?"

Tavia snorted again in derision.

"Pay? I think not. My people have never paid for passage, and we never will," she said proudly. "When a unicorn comes to the river of the dead, we have the strength of mind and body to swim across on our own."

"I should have expected that," I said, with a shake of my head.

I bore down and focused on my gait again. Tavia pulled ahead. I tried not to pay attention to the gathering storm of sound that was creeping up behind us. I dared not slow, but tried to follow Tavia's path. For my troubles I stumbled as we crossed a small dip. Tavia had seen the dip coming up and shifted her path the slightest bit to the right, but I simply wasn't used to moving at these speeds in my new body.

I heard a trumpeting from behind me. From some approaching creature that had spotted my misstep. Another chorus of howls, and gnashing teeth from the nightmare horde that was coming up behind. I didn't fall, but Tavia must have seen me stumble out of the corner of her eye. She fell back and nipped my flank with her pearl-white teeth.

"Move! You have to move faster, stallion!"

I bit back a reply, knew she was right. I could hear the individual steps of our pursuers now, the unsettling scrabble of hundreds of clawed feet. Tavia pulled ahead again, her mane and tail flying like a golden banner. Her hooves moved like the wind, and she almost seemed suspended in air. She moved like a wave in the ocean, with a grace and beauty that I could never hope to match.

Or could I? I now had the same musculature, the same body structure. I watched her movements, the beat and placing of her gait. For a breathless second, it was almost as if my body responded with a 'so that's how you do it, why didn't you say so?'

And with a single, smooth movement, I shifted from a three-beat canter and into a full gallop. I drew alongside Tavia, who blinked and flicked an ear in surprise and encouragement.

We ran side by side, like a pair of thoroughbreds at the track. Our hoofbeats pounded together in a blindingly fast rhythm. We came to a drier section of the plain. Together, we threw up twin rooster tails of dust and clods of dirt as we galloped on. I still heard the clashing, growling pack of demons. Their sounds no longer grew louder, but only seemed to hold pace with us.

Tavia and I began to sweat. Our flanks glistened as if we'd been running through a squall, and our necks started to lather.

My breath came hard, but I knew I could continue, could hold the pace a little longer.

The land started to slope down again. The wide, dusty plain gave way to a kind of lumpy short grass prairie. I didn't like the look of it. This was the kind of landscape that could hide a pothole or trip-worthy root to someone as inexperienced as me.

I glanced at Tavia, hoping to follow her lead. For a heart-stopping second, I didn't see her at my side. There was movement in my dust cloud. I saw the tip of her horn sawing the air as she struggled onward. I fell back a body length to run beside her.

"What are you doing?" she demanded. "Go on! You'll make it! Can't be more than a couple leagues now."

But I saw what slowed her. Tavia favored her foreleg again, the one Teach had broken. Her eyes watered, her breath came in ragged gasps. It was all she could do to avoid pitching over at each step.

"Your leg," I called to her, as we ran on. The beasts behind us roared, saw that we'd slowed. I heard them pick up the pace accordingly. "This is a sliver of time, not the real world!"

"The break exists only in my mind now," she panted. "Sarissa was right...and this is how my mind is interpreting it."

She angrily gestured with her muzzle.

"Derek, go on! Don't make my sacrifice in vain!"

Michael Angel

CHAPTER SEVENTY-TWO

"Quiet yourself, filly," I said, my stallion's voice sounding deep and stern. "We go on together, or we fall together. There are no other choices for us."

"You headstrong, arrogant—" she sputtered, cursing between the beats of her gallop. "No wonder I always saw you as a stallion!"

I let her use her anger. Hoped it distracted her from the pain in her leg for another few seconds. Yes, Tavia saw me as a unicorn, as a stallion, but I was a man from the Other World.

I kept coming back to what Richard Coombes had told me. That the one advantage I had was to not think like people from the Morning Land. To not think in terms of rules, of straight lines.

This race is a straight line, I realized. It's how Tavia thinks of it. Her mind is setting up the rules here. She thinks she's going to lose it since she can't gallop for long, not with a wounded leg. But she also thinks I'm going to win it. So how do I stack the deck in our favor?

It came to me in a flash. It was obvious.

Tavia finished cursing. Her breaths sounded dangerously like a tea kettle getting ready to burst. Her gait rocked back and forth, only seconds from coming apart.

Some ghastly thing that must have been the size of a house let out a roar behind us. Only this time, I could feel the dim, wet heat of some cavernous mouth exhaling. I gagged as I smelled the stench of rotting carrion.

"Tavia, listen!" I said, nearly shouting to be heard over the din of the chase, "You can't win this race, not as a unicorn. You're going to have to finish it...as a *human*."

She glared at me as best she could without turning her head. Spittle flicked the side of her face. "Are you stark raving mad?"

"Hear me out, filly! In your mind, your form is injured. Mine is not!"

Tavia kept quiet except for her tea-kettle gasping. She was listening.

"We can't stop now. So when I give you the word, I want you—" I coughed through a patch of dust as the wind kicked up a notch. "I want you to leap forward as high as you can. Shift to human form, land on my back."

"This is insane!" she protested. "No one—no one rides a unicorn of the Morning Land!"

"Well, *this* unicorn was born in Saint Joseph's Hospital in Philadelphia!" I furiously shouted back. "*And I say you can ride him!*"

Without another word, I moved ahead of her so that she was right on my tail. I heard a gnashing, crunching sound of teeth snapping on air. Tavia whinnied with fear.

"*Now*, Tavia!"

A final cluster of hoofbeats behind me.

A split second of silence.

And then a weight came to rest on my back with an oomph! of air being forced out of a pair of lungs. A pair of strong, small hands entwined themselves in my mane. Tavia's legs hugged my sides, her cold heels dug into my flanks.

Another snap of jaws closing around air. Something moved, cast a shadow to one side of us, almost drawing even. I sensed more than saw the swing of something massive, a clawed arm the size of a telephone pole. It whistled overhead. Tavia cried out, flattened herself against my back.

I threw all my remaining strength into my run. The hills in the distance to either side of us slid back. My hooves felt red hot with pounding friction.

My eyes teared and squeezed half-shut with the wind. Tavia's knees pressed up against my rib cage like a jockey's. She nudged me left or right to avoid tiny obstacles ahead. So I could sacrifice everything—even vision—for this last run.

A gleam from up ahead. Through slitted eyes I saw a narrow, steep-banked river the color of puddled steel. I put my head down, squeezed the last breath from my lungs.

My muscles ached and burned like one big bruise. My ears echoed with the combined shriek of hundreds of creatures dredged up from a score of nightmares as they closed in for the kill.

The ground fell away beneath us.

I had time for one final breath before we plunged into icy water. I thrashed, throwing my hooves out in all directions. I looked up at the gray surface.

Above the boiling foam I saw terrible, shadowy shapes circle, then vanish.

I broke the surface, decided resolutely to not look back, and struck out for the far shore. Tavia coughed. Her fingers remained firmly entwined in my mane.

In a few minutes, I found the sandy bottom of the river. From there I was able to make it to the soft grass above the far bank before we collapsed.

Tavia leaned against my side. She ran her finger along my jaw line. Her sun dress was ruined, stained with mud and plastered to her wet skin, but she didn't seem to particularly mind. She sighed, then put her arms around my neck.

"What happens now?" I asked.

"Now we go back. There's no tarrying for mortals in this realm."

She held up her gloved hand. It started to fade, like morning dew in the sun. I saw the same thing happen to my forelegs. Our bodies slowly turned to nothingness and rose up into the empty, cloudless sky.

I still sensed Tavia's presence with me, though. Our bodies were no more, but our voices sounded together as we continued to move, soundlessly accelerating into the whiteness above.

"You saved me," she said, "Again."

"And you saved me," I replied. "Nice, the way that worked out."

"Yes. You'd think it came naturally."

"I don't think," I said. "Now I know. I'm in love with you, Tavia."

"Yes," she said softly. "And I'm in love with you, Derek. I've loved you for some time now."

"Tavia, we're, ah, not exactly each other's type."

"I know," she said, and I could almost see her shaking her head. "What we feel for each other...this is impossible."

"Really? Given the fact that we're here and both saying 'I love you...'"

"Yes," she agreed. "We really should be more open to the idea."

We shared an intimate little laugh together. It was the kind that lovers keep and treasure in their hearts. The space around us continued to brighten, and I found myself continuing on a little ways alone. I sensed that the journey had stopped, that the heavens had solidified into the color of cream speckled with little black spots.

The smell of clean linen, rubbing alcohol, and the faint scent of blood flooded my awareness. I squinted, then saw the creamy, spotted colors of the acoustic tile that made up the ceiling. I tried to look around.

On one side I saw the green face of a heart monitor next to the metal railing on my bed. At the other side hung an IV drip. The sheets were green and papery, but they were comfortable enough for now. There was a warm, comforting weight on my chest, and I raised my head as best I could.

Tavia stood at my side. The bed had been raised to its highest position so that she could lay her head on me fairly comfortably. Her warm golden cheek rested against the sheet, and her flowing, braided mane poured over the covers like rivulets of gold studded with smooth, colored jewels. Her horn was angled so that it just touched the tip of my bandaged left arm. The arm gave me no more than a dull ache. For some reason its loss bothered me less than I would have thought.

I looked back at Tavia's face. Her eyes were closed, and she seemed to be in a light sleep or trance. Her eyelashes, as lush and curly as a beautiful woman's, were just as I had seen them, back when she had worn a yellow sun dress and had talked to me by the fire.

I let out a deep breath with a shudder. I felt, oddly enough, like I had the first morning after Tavia had come into my life. The morning where I simply didn't know if what had gone before was real. Whether I had truly experienced something beyond anything I'd ever known or felt or held in my heart. Could I have dreamt it all? Could I?

I didn't want to wake her. But I had to know.

"Tavia," I whispered, and I saw her stir slightly. "Was it any of it real? Do you love me?"

Tavia opened her eyes. She gave me a look that made me shiver inside with pure joy.

"Yes, it was," she said softly. "And yes. I do."

Michael Angel

EPILOGUE

"I wasn't sure if I should have sent you the bottle," said Birch. Even over the phone, I could hear the awkwardness in his voice. In my mind's eye, I saw him tweaking one of the ends of his mustache. "If it doesn't work out, I don't know, I suppose you could return it."

"I have other guests here who can use a corkscrew, but I've been getting enough California Zinfandel to stock a regular wine cellar," I replied. "If you don't mind, it might come in handy for me under someone else's tree. Only a week left before Santa comes down the chimney, and I'm not sure I'm up to fighting the crowds at the mall."

"No problem at all. I'm just glad the mayor's office came through for you."

"I suspect that the ambassador from the Morning Land stepped up to lobby on my behalf," I said, shifting the phone to my other ear. I opened the bedroom door to see what was making the noise in the other room. "Hey, I'd better check on my guests."

"Sure, don't want to keep you. Merry Christmas to you, Derek."

"Same to you, Alan."

Rachel and Thunderbolt tore around the living room, giggling and carrying on. I wasn't too concerned—I'd emptied the room of anything breakable. Rachel zoomed back and forth with Super Pickle the Zebra in hand. Thunderbolt was just being himself.

"Hey!" I said loudly, though I really had to fight to keep a smile off my face. "What did I say about flying in the house?"

Thunderbolt came to earth, his black Zorro mask a little askew. Rachel immediately pounced on him and wrapped her arms around his neck with a purr. I couldn't blame her. If anything could top the little-girl fantasy of having a unicorn in the house, it was a made-for-my-size Pegasus.

"Aw, come on, Uncle Derek," said the colt. "I'm Thunderbolt—"

"The Wonder-Colt!" Rachel added proudly. "He's a real-life superhero!"

"Just...no bouncing off the walls," I said with a sigh. Thunderbolt had learned from his adoring fan Rachel that calling me 'uncle' was a good way to get out of trouble. Maybe I was getting soft in the head as well as in the heart.

The doorbell rang. I opened it without too much concern. Because of my guests, I had a double set of magical wards around the house. And Coombes' men were in position to watch out front.

The young man at the door wore a dark blue jacket emblazoned with the FedEx logo. As I signed for the delivery, he peered around me as unobtrusively as possible, clearly curious as to what a miniature flying horse was doing in my living room. I took the two soft-pack envelopes from his hands, wished him happy holidays, and waited until he tipped his hat and went back to his van.

I leaned out the door and waved at the white Jeep Grand Cherokee parked down the street. It was dark now, and by the dim glow of their dome light I saw one of the Secret Service agents acknowledge my wave by raising his styrofoam coffee cup. I made a mental note to send over some hot chocolate to them later on. I'd been on enough stakeouts and watches to understand just how much something like that meant.

My service on the LAPD was what Birch had been referring to when he mentioned the Mayor's office. The question was whether I was acting as a member of the Los Angeles Police Department on the night that Coombes and I went out to the quarry. The connection was pretty slim. I'd been out of uniform, off duty, out of jurisdiction, you name it.

On the other hand, we had pretty well saved the place from alien—or demonic, if you wish—invasion. Once the yena fled, Coombes had called in a fleet of ambulances. They'd found Tavia holding her horn to my chest, invoking a long and complex incantation. At the hospital, Tavia insisted that the nurses raise the bed to its maximum height. Then she absolutely refused to let anyone come near me until I regained consciousness.

My survival made me a potent political symbol, at least to the Mayor of Los Angeles. His Honor wanted his name associated with someone who'd saved the lives of millions of registered voters. So it looked like I was going to get a 'disabled in the line of duty' discharge, with all the benefits I was entitled to.

I walked back to the bedroom and placed the two packs on the desk. I held them down awkwardly with my new artificial hand while I tugged the opening strip off. I was still trying to come to terms with the disability.

The hip wound where Teach had stabbed me was trivial. The damage to the muscle of my right shoulder was not. Between that injury and the loss of my left arm below the elbow, I wasn't even going to be able to feed myself for a month.

Tavia's healing salve cut that awful period to a week. But while the salve could close cuts and speed the healing of burns, it couldn't re-grow limbs. So, I'd been fitted with something called a 'transradial prosthesis'. It looked fairly real, with flesh-toned plastic fingers. A set of electrodes strapped to my upper arm allowed the hand to open or close. But I was still far from mastering that skill.

Both of the soft-packs from FedEx contained letters that had been pre-screened by Coombes' office in Pasadena. I smiled as I opened the cards. Many were from friends and relatives back in Pennsylvania.

A scroll marked with the purple seal of the Court of Cavilad turned out to be two pieces of parchment wrapped as one. The first thanked me for my service to the Morning Land and discussed how my family would officially be honored in song.

The second was a bland but firm denial of my request to visit the Morning Land again.

Coombes had been right about what to expect. Things did seem smaller, more ordinary to me now. It might have depressed me but for the fact that the final letter I opened came from the Lady of the Dryads.

Sarissa wished me well, then told me that she was working to convince the Warder of Cavilad to approve my request for a visa. Actually, she used the words 'I'm trying to get that bonehead equine to think straight for once in his misbegotten life.'

But best of all, she had enclosed a single pressed leaf from an adolenda. I sniffed it and smelled the heady fragrance of another world. One that sprang from the sacred Pool of Ethra.

I put the leaf away for safekeeping, tucked the cards under the crook of my arm, then picked up the bottle of wine Birch had sent me. I ducked through the game Thunderbolt and Rachel were playing now. Whatever it was seemed to involve a lot of running through the house and screaming.

The aroma of roast turkey filled the air. Separate pots with mashed potatoes, squash, and green beans sat on the stove. Emily and Coombes sat talking at the kitchen table, oblivious to the din in the adjoining room. She appeared to be coaxing him to try a piece of fruitcake.

"Ah, there you are," Emily said merrily. I put the bottle down on the table and tacked the cards up on the fridge with a bunch of magnets shaped to look like holly wreaths. "Will you please tell Mr. J. Edgar Hoover here that my fruitcake isn't poisoned?"

"Wrong branch of service," I pointed out. "Hoover ran the FBI. And I think Richard and I have had enough trouble with fruitcakes over the course of our careers to want to eat any."

Coombes laughed. It was the first time I think I'd ever seen a genuine smile on the man's face. It looked like, in time, he might even get comfortable with one there on a regular basis.

"Thanks," he said. "I owe you one, Derek."

"No problem. Where'd Tavia go?"

"Just out back. She said she wanted to talk with you when you got off the phone."

I nodded, and headed for the back door.

"Not too long, you two," Emily called. "Dinner's going to be ready in a few minutes, so tell her not to spoil her appetite by nibbling on the local greenery."

"I'll be sure to mention it." I threw on a jacket and went out into the night.

Tavia stood at the edge of the patio. Her long, lush tail idly flicked back and forth as she looked up at the stars overhead. I walked over and joined her.

I put my hand into my jacket pockets to keep it warm. Southern California hardly ever got a hard frost. But tonight, it was chilly enough to fog a window by breathing lightly on it.

"Looking for something?" I asked, gazing up at the heavens with her.

"Yes, and no. Maybe I'm just feeling restless. Out of sorts."

I nodded. I had noticed the same thing. Tavia had been pleasant with everyone from Coombes to Emily—who seemed to like Tavia now that Rachel was playing with a safer-looking creature like Thunderbolt. But she had been quieter, more distant from everyone, including myself. Often I would catch her gazing at me sadly from a distance, though she would brighten up whenever I spoke with her.

"It's funny, Derek. Sometimes, when I'm not thinking about it, I can almost see a spiral shape high up by the northern stars. But whenever I turn to look, it vanishes."

"Optical illusion, maybe. Or maybe not. Now I understand what you meant when you told me that, in life the Spiral of Creation is all around us. That it only gives us hints as to its existence."

"And yet we're among the few who have seen it in full and returned," Tavia said. "I guess it's made me aware, more than ever, of the time we're given here. Before we see it one final time."

"Why has that been on your mind, Tavia?"

She sighed. "Because I've been putting something off for a while now. Saying goodbye to you."

I kept quiet. I had known this was coming ever since I'd gotten out of that hospital bed. I'd seen the summons that she'd received. I'd heard her talking to people when she thought I was fast asleep. The Court of Cavilad and its Warder wanted her back in the Morning Land.

"Can't they cut you some slack as thanks for your recent service? Or to keep good relations with the 'Other World'?"

"Stormwind's the one they have for good relations, not me," she said. Tavia tossed her head slightly, making the beads in her mane rattle. "As for the rest, what service do you refer to? I didn't stop William Teach. You did. The few yena that escaped are being tracked by Coombes' folks and the National Park Service, for goodness sake. There's no need for a unicorn here."

I need you, I thought desperately.

But I couldn't say that. I had no idea how she would react.

"You sound like you're trying to convince yourself that their judgment is the right one," I said gently. "What do you want, Tavia?"

"What do I want?" She looked up at the sky again, into the woods, then back at me. "What I want...in the end...is to be with you, Derek."

We were silent again. We looked out over the cold winter night together, heard the creak of the bare tree branches in the cold wind. I watched the mist from our breaths mingle together as we exhaled. For some strange reason, it occurred to me how very intimate that was. I felt the moment's tick by like slow drops of rain, each one a jewel in time that I didn't want to see end.

"What I want and what I need to do are different things," Tavia said. "Remember the oath I swore to my family, to the people of Cavilad. Those aren't things I lay aside easily."

"I know." I thought of something she'd told me back in Wyndoon. "Changing that piece of you would destroy who you are. And I would not change you, Tavia. I would never do that, nor stand in your way."

She bowed her head, and the moonlight sparkled along the length of her horn. She nodded, acknowledging what I said.

My next request surprised her. More than a little of what I had read in Sarissa's books had rubbed off on me. And I had thought out each phrase carefully. I knew that Tavia would pay extra attention to words taken from the speech she had heard all her life in the Morning Land.

"I would ask a boon of you, fair unicorn filly," I said, using the archaic word for a request that was serious, but not as binding as an oath. "You do not accept your death anymore, as a simple way to relieve the risk that lies upon your family?"

"I hereby renounce it," Tavia said, with a little nicker. "I have been corrupted in a way most foul by the Son of Robert, the Unicorn Filly's Bane. I can no longer accept fate, amor fati, for what it is without challenge." She turned serious as she spoke again. "But I cannot refuse to risk, to challenge myself should an act of true valor appear to me."

"My boon is simple. When you see the time for an act of valor, restrain yourself from rashness. I ask you to consider that your death—" I had to swallow, to hold my emotions in check. "That your death is no longer an easily paid price, tendered by you and you alone. For you hold another's heart in your care as well. Will you accept this request, fair unicorn?"

"I shall," she breathed. Tavia turned, faced me fully. "I will find a way to fulfill my oath, in the way you wish me to. And I will return to you someday, Derek. Know that in your heart, as sure as the love I hold for you."

It was all I could do not to fall to my knees, to beg her to stay. I put my hand up to touch her, but she shied away.

"Best not to," she said quietly, and her eyes were liquid blue crystal. She was so beautiful to look at that it hurt me inside. "Fare thee well, Derek, son of Robert."

"Fare thee well," I choked out, "Octavia, daughter of the Warder of Cavilad."

Tavia slowly trotted up the hill, away from the house. Moonlight frosted her golden withers and tail. I saw her look back, once. Her face had an expression of complete and utter longing. She turned towards the tree line, and with a ghostly gleam, she was gone.

My eyes brimmed up with tears. I sobbed quietly. I waited until they stopped, felt the emotions that swirled through me settle. And, oddly enough, I felt a kind of happiness. I realized then that life would go on. That Beth would not only have forgiven me, but maybe she would have even been proud of her husband. That she would have been happy for me to go on, living with her memory, but not only for her sake.

I walked back towards the house. I stopped for a second and closed my eyes in reverence. I listened to the happy sounds of Rachel playing with Thunderbolt, the laughter of Coombes and Emily.

I dried my eyes on the sleeve of my jacket and let out a breath. In a way that I never could have guessed, I felt whole again. With a smile on my face, I opened the door and stepped back into the warmth and the light.

Michael Angel

Enter the World of Michael Angel:
Centaur of the Crime, where fantasy and forensics meet for the first time.

Dayna Chrissie, the leading Crime Scene Analyst for the LAPD, enjoys nothing more than finding the one clue that can solve a crime.

The day she finds a golden medallion on a body that's been dumped at a downtown construction site, she doesn't think much about it. Until that medallion transports her to the magical kingdom of Andeluvia. Dayna discovers that she's been summoned to solve the murder of the realm's king, before war breaks out between Andeluvia and the Centaur Kingdoms.

When the trail of evidence leads from Andeluvia, back to LA, Dayna must bring all of her forensic skill to bear in order to solve the case. The price of failure? A war that will kill millions and devastate both lands.

Hope she works best under pressure.

The pages that follow provide a glimpse into
the world of *Centaur of the Crime.*

Print and eBook Editions available
at all major eBook retailers.

Michael Angel

CENTAUR OF THE CRIME:

MICHAEL ANGEL

CHAPTER 1

Just my rotten luck.

In the movies, when crime scene analysts arrive at the site of a murder, it's usually deep in some dark, woody glen. Or, if the murder takes place in an urban area, cops from film-land know enough to hang around on the edges, quiet and respectful like mourners at a funeral. Call it in, set up the yellow tape, and get-the-heck-outta-the-way so my work space stays pristine as fresh-fallen snow.

That no-touchee mojo wasn't working for me today.

I couldn't get something as simple as a body lying up by the Hollywood reservoir, or down one of Topanga's blind slot canyons. The crime scene I'd been called in to work had enough cops snooping around to put on a St. Patrick's Day parade.

I parked the van at the curb and squinted through the grimy windshield and the glare of the noonday sun, trying to make sense of the site. The body of an adult white male had been discovered lying atop a heap of rubble, smack in the middle of a newly demolished city block.

The rectangular piece of property was an ankle-turning warren of shattered concrete blocks, tangled steel rebar, and patches of common mallow. The weed's flowers filled the air with a dusty, nose-tickling scent like ragweed pollen.

California low-rise buildings bordered three sides of the block. Two were clinker-brick apartment buildings that sported rickety metal cage balconies jammed to bursting with curious onlookers. The third was a decrepit office building that some thoughtful ethnic Angeleno had decorated with a multicolored spray-paint mural of the Aztec God, Quetzalcoatl.

Quetzo appeared to be giving everyone at the crime scene the finger, but then I've never been good at interpreting urban art.

I got out of the van, went around back, and threw open the rear doors to finish suiting up. I slipped a disposable jumpsuit-style jacket and pants over my civilian clothes, and then sat on the rear bumper. A dull summery warmth radiated from the metal. I hoped that the plastic pants wouldn't melt in the heat.

I tucked my long black locks into a dingy gray hair net for that oh-so-attractive cafeteria lady look and then jammed the lot under a dark blue Dodgers baseball cap. Finally, I kicked off my flats and slipped into a pair of zip tack shoes that I'd nicknamed my 'stompy gothic boots of doom'. They wouldn't win any awards on the fashion runway, but they'd keep corpse juice out of my socks.

The shoes also gave me almost three more inches in height. I'm already pretty tall, at least for a woman, but when you're dealing with cops, men who each think they're as tough as Clint Eastwood and hung like Mr. Ed, every extra inch counts. Don't ask me why. I think it's a dominance thing. We really are still primates at heart.

I grabbed a heavy aluminum case by its textured plastic handle, heaved it up to my side, and slammed the van doors shut. I stepped over the worn side of the curb and picked my way through the mallow flowers and gravel.

Broken glass and dry twigs snapped under my feet. The cops milling about the scene looked up and watched me approach. They looked unsure as to whether I was there to help clear things up.

Or just muddy the waters a little more.

This wasn't like a bunch of construction workers ogling a tight-bloused secretary on her way to work. Believe me, *nobody* looks sexy in crime scene gear. But show me a beat cop, and I'll show you a frustrated wanna-be detective. If there's less than three cops at a murder scene, they'll sidle up to you to offer their pet theory on how it all happened. Three or more, and they'll hang around, hoping to overhear something they can gossip about to their buddies back at the station.

The debris formed a gentle slope of loose material that'd have been hell to walk through in my flats—let alone high heels—but my stompy boots handled it just fine. One of the guys separated himself from the mass of the LAPD's finest and waved as he came towards me. Hazel eyes, close-cropped hair, and a friendly face that shone through a perpetual haze of beard stubble.

I recognized Alanzo Esteban from working a couple of these joyful little scenes. One of the few detectives in Homicide who I actually liked. Judging by the bashful way he snuck glances at me when he thought I wasn't looking, the feeling was more than mutual.

"Why, señora del acero," he said with a smile. He wasn't a good looking man, but his warm Latino accent sent a thrill down my spine. "So good of you to join us, Dayna."

"Yeah, but I'm sure no lady of steel, no matter what you say," I replied. I fought to keep a grin off my face and lost. "Fill me in. What the hell's going on here, Alanzo?"

Esteban had worked with me enough to know that I wasn't asking about the crime scene, at least not yet. I wanted to know why so many cops were wandering over the site, making my job harder and more miserable by the minute.

"What's going on is that some *pendejo* dumped our dead guy in the middle of this demolition zone," he said. "Construction's due to start here on one of the mayor's pet projects. So you have politicos falling all over themselves to jump into everyone's soup. And when the Chief heard…"

I held up a hand. "He sent McClatchy out, didn't he?"

He nodded. I let out a groan.

"Esteban, I'm not done with you yet!" came a harsh voice. We traded a glance that spoke volumes.

"Speak of the devil," I said.

I followed Esteban across the tumbled surface of concrete and rebar. The sun beat down on the exposed city block and I pulled my cap brim down as far as it could go. Perspiration already stained the inside of my jumpsuit. No wonder I was always able to keep the flab off my hips and the cottage cheese off the thighs. I carried my personal one-size-fits-all sauna around with me. I licked a stray bead of sweat from my lips and came away with the gamy taste of body salt.

We came up to a barrel-chested, red faced man busy shouting orders at the officers towards the far end of the field. His salt and pepper hair was balding, his jowls were threatening to sag, and he clenched a red and black-tipped toothpick between his teeth. A snazzy gray pinstripe suit tented over his wide frame. Office wear for field work always marks you as one of two things: a rank amateur, or a politically appointed desk jockey.

Deputy Chief Bob McClatchy fell into both categories.

"Esteban, see what you can do," McClatchy said, with a wave of one hand. "You know, tell these scene techies to hurry up. We've got real work to do."

"As it happens, you can pass the message on directly," Esteban said, indicating me with a nod. McClatchy squinted at me like Esteban had brought him a new kind of bug to look at.

"Dayna Chrissie, Office of the Medical Examiner," I said. I put my hand out. McClatchy stared uncomprehendingly at my open palm for a moment, as if I were offering him a dead fish. Then the automatic courtesy I was counting on kicked in, and he gingerly shook my hand. "We've met before, in passing. Phone booth shooting in Northridge."

"I remember," he said. "Not you. The case. Took your people eight days to go over a crime scene the size of a shower stall. Real pain in the ass, if you'll pardon my French."

"I pardon and parlez French," I said wryly. "But crime scene processing is always a pain in the ass if you do it right. You don't just run in, scoop up a handful of DNA, and boom, you're finished. And you're going to make it harder for me to do my work if you keep using beat cops to comb the area for evidence."

He scowled at me. From the pattern of wrinkles on his face, I could tell that the scowl was one of his favorite expressions. Maybe he practiced in front of a mirror every morning before he went to work.

"Fine, anything to speed this mess up." He spoke to one of the nearby officers and sent the man off to round up the boys in blue. He shifted the red and black toothpick in his mouth and then jabbed a finger at me. "You're going to perform your initial report with me present, got that, Chrissie?"

Esteban coughed. McClatchy stared at him.

I pointed at the Dodgers insignia on my baseball cap. "I'm not LAPD, McClatchy. I'm a non-com private contractor, like most of your Crime Scene Analysts."

"A lot of the M.E. offices are moving that way," Esteban added. "Gives people like Dayna here more flexibility while it saves the city money."

"Well," McClatchy huffed, "I still want to be there—"

"Then come along," I said brusquely.

I turned away and started hiking towards the yellow and black scene tape markers. I heard the two men follow in my wake, but I didn't turn to talk with either of them. My meager store of patience had run bone dry. When you come down to it, I think that's why I got into this line of work in the first place. Compared to the living, dead people are so much more agreeable, in no small part because they don't try to pull rank— they just smell it.

Esteban stepped quickly to keep up at my side. He said, "You got lucky. Hector Reyes got here ten minutes before you did. Before the rest of the local police division arrived."

"Really? That is good news." Hector was the best crime scene photographer in the department. If he got here before too many extra footprints were set down, we'd have more to work with than a smeary blur of shoe marks.

"Somebody called the body in around eleven this morning," Esteban added, as we each slipped under the yellow tape perimeter. "No eyewitnesses to the killing, or, if the body was dumped here, any reports of suspicious people, suspicious vehicles."

We crested a small rise where the mess of concrete blocks and rusted iron gave way to a pitted gravel surface. I didn't see the body at first, but my eye followed a little trail of red droplets that dotted the ground. Several little trails, actually, that led back to a patch of mallow that'd been half-crushed by a pair of feet, clad in a pair of worn leather boots.

The stench of the body hit me then. The corpse hadn't been lying out too long. Insects were just beginning to gather, and even in the burning heat of the Southern California summer, it smelled only of newly decomposing flesh. On the Chrissie Scale of Stinkiness (patent pending), our guy still only rated a five out of ten. But it still made Detective Esteban pause and His Highness McClatchy reel back as if someone had punched him in the gut.

I stepped up and took my first look at the body. Let my reptile brain sift through the images to pick out any curious, out of place details later. The corpse belonged to a man in his late thirties to early forties. Caucasian with sandy blonde hair. Well built. Looked like he'd been in good health and pounding the weights at Gold's Gym.

And that's when I saw something that really got my attention, got my pulse pumping like I'd gone down to Starbucks and mainlined a Venti espresso.

The skin on the man's arms was covered in little white scales like a snake.

CHAPTER 2

I knelt a couple meters away from the body, set down the aluminum case I'd been lugging along, and cracked it open. I hurriedly slipped on a pair of shoe covers over my stompy gothic boots of doom, a surgical mask over my face, and finished the outfit off with a pair of latex gloves. I chewed my lip in thought for a moment, and then looked up at Esteban.

"You up to taking some body pics for me?"

"As long as I don't have to get too close, I'm okay with it," Esteban said, with an expressive shrug.

I dug out a second mask for him, another pair of gloves, and then pulled out my trusty old Pentax out of one of the case's padded compartments. Esteban had to hold out both hands as I gave it to him. The Pentax had all the grace, subtlety, and weight of a black plastic brick. But nothing beat a digital single-lens reflex camera for minute detail.

I grabbed a set of forceps, took a couple steps forward, and knelt by the body. I waved my hand through the holding pattern of flies that circled above the corpse and began my observations. The smell of decaying flesh hung heavy in the air, like a wet curtain.

"Alanzo," I said, "snap me a set of photos starting at the feet up. Individual body parts, left-to-right. Close up shots on any wound pattern or blood spatter."

Esteban began clicking away with the camera. I looked over the man's brown leather boots. Nice ones, too, by the look of it—hand stitching that would've done justice to the kind of Italian loafers you'd find for sale on Rodeo Drive. The footwear had seen heavy use, judging by the wear on the soles. His dun-colored trousers were made of some kind of rough cloth, and a light blue sleeveless top that looked like—well, to be honest, it looked like what my hippie niece would've called a 'peasant shirt'. A very simple kind of tunic.

Something strange about his clothing made me frown. Suddenly my brain did one of its weird little *clicks* and it snapped into focus: the clothes really were simple. Too simple. The boot straps were adorned with a heavy iron buckle. So was his black leather belt. But his trousers were perfectly smooth, both on the sides, and in the crotch. No zipper teeth, no Levi's button-fly. Instead, John Doe had a kind of rough leather lacing holding his split together.

My mind raced. When was the last time anyone made clothes without zippers and buttons? Hell, when was the last time anyone made a pair of everyday-wear men's pants without pockets?

I kept quiet a moment longer as I looked at the strange wounds on the body. Deep, jagged cuts or slashes of some kind marked the corpse in a couple of spots. One on the left-hand palm, a second on the forearm. Another on the side of the head, where an ear dangled by a strip of pasty flesh. The worst of the slashing injuries yawed open in a fleshy red mouth that cleaved open the right-hand shoulder and exposed a compound fracture of the collarbone.

I spotted a fleck of black against the white edge of bone. I snatched it out with a nimble flick of the forceps.

"What's that?" McClatchy demanded. His voice was muffled. Sounded like he'd pressed his nose into a pocket handkerchief. I heard the man fumbling in his pocket for something but I didn't waste the time to look up.

"Chip of metal," I said, as I turned the object over to get a better look. It was the size and shape of a pinky nail. "Whoever sliced open our John Doe here like a side of beef may have left us a clue."

"Part of a blade?"

"Maybe. These slashes sure as hell didn't come from a twelve-gauge." I caught Alanzo's eye and nodded towards my case. "Pull me a specimen bag out of there, would you?"

Esteban got one and brought it back, holding the edges open with his gloved fingers. I dropped the sample in and went back to work. The shoulder wound was definitely the nastiest of the cuts.

But that probably hadn't killed the man.

No, what probably did the dirty deed was the fist-sized hole in the center of the chest. Actually, it wasn't so much a hole as a fleshy, bloody *crater*. Whatever this guy'd been hit with, it had blown right through his shirt and smashed the sternum into bone powder. Blood pooled in a sticky, half-clotted mass in the cavity. Using the forceps, I pulled the tattered, burned-looking edge of the shirt away to see the edge of the wound.

The remaining skin on his chest also looked like it was made of tiny white scales. I shook my head again in amazement.

Who is this guy? Is he related to Persephone?

Persephone belonged to my college roommate, back around the time that I'd lucked into a scholarship at the University of Chicago. Funny, now that I thought about it. I couldn't recall the name of my *roommate*, who I usually called 'the bitch who keeps mooching my vanilla-bean and coffee ice cream'. But I did remember Persephone, her albino king snake. Pretty creature. And like this guy, the snake's scales were a perfect mesh of little ivory crescent moons.

I was still struggling to figure out whether this guy was some freak of nature when I took another look at his face. His features were strong, generically masculine. The eyes stared out into nothingness like glassy brown marbles. But then I saw something that short-circuited the idea of calling up the FBI to see if they really did have someone to cover the 'X' files.

The 'scales' stopped at the base of the man's neck. They weren't the mark of some snake-human hybrid. It was a pattern that had been etched into the skin from some kind of pressure. Of course, that did jack squat for me, given that all it did was replace one mystery with another.

I leaned in closer to the body to get a better look. The itty-bitty hairs on the back of my neck stood on end as my nose caught the ghost of a scent. Something layered underneath the rotting-meat miasma of the corpse itself. I fought the nausea, rode it out like a wave on a choppy sea. I closed my eyes and inhaled, seeking that elusive scent, and found it.

Sulfur. Mixed with charcoal. Once I found it, the smell seemed to leap down my nasal passages, dig into my tongue, and dance around on it like a lit match. I moved my head back and forth, continuing to trust my senses. The sulfur-charcoal smell was strongest from the chest wound. And then, I smelled something else underneath the charred-sulfur smell. Dry, like fine gin, delicate like lace.

It vanished in a heady rush of menthol that wiped out my sense of smell and buried it under a tidal wave of Vick's VapoRub.

I came within a hair's breadth of a snarl and looked up. That's what McClatchy had been digging for—a tube of menthol to protect his delicate sinuses. Judging from how he kept wiping the snotlike gel under his nostrils, it wasn't helping him much. All it really did was throw an effing monkey wrench—and a dozen extra monkey tools, as far as I was concerned—into my analysis.

My eyes snapped back to the red and black toothpick in McClatchy's teeth. My brain did another one of its weird little flips. I saw that McClatchy's toothpick was done up to look like a miniature lacquered chopstick from Chang's Mandarin Five-Star. McClatchy liked Chinese food. I turned back to the corpse and began to speak, trying my best to sound casual.

"This your first time close to a corpse, McClatchy?" I asked.

"Unless you count the ones in the morgue," he replied. I nodded to myself. That meant he'd only been exposed to the chilled, scent-reduced versions of dead humans.

"It's something that takes time to get used to. I still run into things I never expect to see," I continued. "For example, this one guy we found in the desert near Bakersfield. His intestines had dried up and shrank, like those crispy noodles some Asian places put out on the table for you to munch on."

"Um," McClatchy said. His face had taken on a distinctly greenish cast.

"Then there was this one time I came across a fresh corpse, a gang-banger who'd been gut-shot. So his stomach's been ruptured, and the yellow of the stomach acid and the red of the blood all ended up mixed together. Just like the yin and yang symbol they do at some restaurants, you know, when they put the yellow hot mustard and the red sweet n' sour sauce in a dish and make that little swirl for dipping your chicken egg rolls?"

McClatchy didn't respond. He dry-heaved, held his index finger to his lips, and abruptly walked off. Esteban shook his head.

"Remind me never to piss you off, Dayna."

"You just have to know how to get rid of extra people at a crime scene," I said. "Back in Chicago, the winters made it easy. If there's snow on the ground, you just hand someone a shovel and ask them to get ready to do some shoveling. You turn around and they're gone, because now they realize that they might actually have to do some *work*."

Esteban let out a snort.

I still couldn't get the damned menthol smell out of my nasal passages, though. It hangs around, binds itself to the soft tissues of the sinus like eucalyptus-scented superglue, and the only cure is time.

"I'm almost done," I said, as I probed the meaty pink pit of the chest wound with the forceps. "Might be good to call up the trace techs and then get our John Doe bagged up."

"You got it."

My forceps hit something deep within the chest wound with a clink. Frowning, I felt around under the layer of blood with the prongs. I grabbed whatever it was—it felt hard, oddly ridged, and flat—and pulled it out into the light of day.

I held up a golden medallion the size and shape of a Sacagawea dollar coin.

It gleamed like a polished yellow button. Esteban let out a low whistle. Instead of a Shoshone maiden, the medallion bore the imprint of a horse's hoof and a series of grooved letters.

"I'm going to need another bag," I said, abruptly dry-mouthed.

Esteban stepped away from me to rummage in my case. The reflection of the bright sunlight off the metal made it hard to make out the marks, and it didn't help that they were streaked with sticky, rank fluids from the corpse. I could tell that whatever language it was written in, it wasn't English. Latin, maybe? I pivoted slightly on my heels so that the coin wouldn't reflect the sun into my eyes.

That's all that saved my life that day. Blind luck.

I heard the *CRACK!* of a rifle shot.

The brim of my baseball cap exploded into feathery chunks of cheap cloth fiber. I stared dumbly at the floating blue and white shreds as my mind tried to get the switching gear working again.

Someone was shooting at us!

"Get down!" I heard Esteban scream, "Dammit, Dayna, get down!"

A second *CRACK!* and something bright and deadly buzzed past my ear.

Correction. Someone was shooting at *me!*

Finally, my brain completed its de-icing procedure. I moved, trying to dive to my right and get as flat as humanly possible. I heard the sounds of people screaming, the shouts of the cops all around us.

My side crumpled in pain and everything went dim.

CHAPTER 3

My side burned where I hit the ground.

I fought for breath. Coughed and got a mouthful of sour-tasting concrete dust for my trouble. The scent of male sweat and sport deodorant blotted out John Doe's stench. My left eye pressed up so close to Esteban's silver badge that I could only make out half of his name.

I heard him shouting orders. The crackle of gunfire. More shouts, curses.

I squirmed, and the detective let me up from where he'd thrown his body across mine. I coughed again, then turned to the side and spat out the mouthful of dust. Esteban looked at me, his boyish face a mixture of pride and embarrassment, a sort of 'ohmigod-I can't-believe-what-I-just-did!' kind of look.

I probably owed him my life about then. But his expression just sort of busted me up inside, made me actually say the first thing that popped into my head.

"So," I said, "was it good for you?"

Esteban actually blushed.

He got to his feet, extended a hand, and helped me up. His palm was warm, smooth, and strong. I squeezed it in appreciation.

"I'm sorry," I said quickly. "I mean to say...thank you. For doing...that."

"De nada, Dayna."

McClatchy pounded back up the rise and came to a stop before us. "Either of you hurt?" I shook my head. The detective followed suit. "Dammit! Now I'm going to have to detail even more of my manpower."

Nice to see that even a professional bureaucrat cared. Thanks, jerkweed.

"Love you too, Bob," was what came out of my mouth.

* * *

Actually, the extra security proved a pain in the neck. I refused to leave the crime scene until they'd lifted some prints and bagged the corpse. McClatchy practically had me clapped in irons and shanghaied back to the Medical Examiner's office in the company of two beat cops who looked like they'd been kicked off the Chicago Bears for steroid abuse.

The day hadn't been a total loss, but at times it teetered right on the effin' edge. The bagging people unceremoniously dumped the John Doe on my examination table without so much as a thank-you-ma'am. I swabbed the surfaces of the metal chunk I'd taken out of the body's shoulder, the gold medallion, and the inside of that odd chest wound and sent the samples off to the tox-box experts.

Then I sent samples of Doe's clothing to the fiber experts, sterilized the medallion, stuck it in my pocket, dumped the jumpsuit, left a note for Hector to email me his crime scene photos, pulled the Pentax's memory card, and had just started prepping for Doe's autopsy when something went *sproing*, and all the adrenaline I'd been running on petered out and left me feeling like I'd taken a swan dive off the edge of a cliff.

The two guys from the Bears' defensive line escorted me home and parked across the street from my house. I thanked them and walked unsteadily up the long, freshly paved asphalt driveway. I live on the north side of Los Angeles, up near Griffith Park. It's a tony neighborhood stuffed to the gills with pretty, upscale homes, but my place wasn't among them.

Think of a Santa Fe themed shoebox. Surround it with a lawn that looks more like a well-tended sand dune, and you've got it. I've got a brown thumb powerful enough to kill anything with leaves and roots at up to thirty paces.

I fished the door key out of my purse, stumbled my way inside, and began pulling down all of the blinds. Security or no, I didn't like the idea of anyone watching me in my own home. I left only one window alone—the backyard view that ran right up to the edge of the park. Perched at the top of the highest ridge was the Art Deco dome of Griffith Observatory.

My fingers begin to shake. I started to run a warm bath for myself, and then dug around in the cabinet below the sink for some bath salts. Of course, right when Dayna Chrissie needs something, that's when she runs out. Calgon wasn't going to be taking me away tonight.

So I did the next best thing. I turned the shower to *hot*, scrubbed myself down with a pair of exfoliating gloves until my skin turned bright pink, swaddled myself in the vast white folds of my oversized Egyptian cotton bathrobe, and padded over to the kitchen freezer.

I pushed aside the frozen cauliflower, the rainy-day pack of microwave taquitos, and dove for the pint-size container of my favorite ice cream—a milkfat-laced smart bomb of a dessert called Chunky Chocolate Coma. I curled up in a corner of my beat-up leather couch and proceeded to do the windmill thing with my spoon through the layers of chocolate-coated almonds and soft brownie chunks until I scraped the bottom of the carton.

My fingers began to quiver again. I flung the empty container and the spoon away with a clatter. They bounced off the wall and left me a pair of brown chocolate streaks to clean up later.

I felt a wracking, chest-tingling cry finally break loose inside like an iceberg calving off from a glacier. I buried my face in my hands and just sobbed, sobbed with relief that I was alive—*alive*, dammit!—and that I was going to see another sunrise.

It felt heavenly. It felt as if a rubber band had snapped inside of me.

I'd always been so good, so damned good at holding everything back. Everything that would've marked Miss Dayna Chrissie as someone who just wasn't professional enough to be in forensics. Someone who couldn't control their emotions, who couldn't stay detached, who couldn't be trusted to run an investigation. Who knew if the girl might break down on the stand, when some hotshot defense attorney focused all of his powers on wrecking her carefully built case?

But I'd held it together today. Even had to remind myself to thank the guy who'd put himself in harm's way to keep me safe.

It made me feel good.

So good, it almost made me forget that someone had tried to kill me.

Almost.

* * *

I didn't make it to bed. I stayed curled up on the couch like a lanky, black-haired, green-eyed cat. A cat that someone had stuffed with ice cream and then wrapped in an oversize bathrobe, to be precise. I watched the evening turn into night. The city had lit up the road to the observatory tonight, so that if you squinted, you could imagine James Dean, clad head to toe in shiny black biker leather, gunning his motorcycle up the steep asphalt slope and up to the tinted spotlights that gave the observatory dome the gentle amber shade of a Malibu sunset.

My weary, drowsy brain settled on the round spotlights. Then the lights changed, became darker and more ragged at the edges as I felt my eyelids grow as heavy as marble slabs. I thought of the crime scene today. The drops of red at the scene near the body.

Splashes of blood on concrete.

That's when my mind spiraled back to something I call 'The Dream'. It's a recurring vision-memory thing that comes back to me at the oddest times. To be honest, it took place so long ago, that I wasn't sure if it was real, or if it had been some awful fever dream brought on by eating too many slices of holiday fruitcake.

Yeah, someone was definitely being a fruitcake here.

My eyes closed and the vision of the dusty gray concrete softened and turned white. It was a frigid December in the woods of Pike County, Illinois.

I'd just turned seven.

The blood trail stood out in a pattern of scarlet splashes against the snow. Cold wind bit at me with wolves' teeth and made a low-pitched howl through icicle-coated branches. It raised goosebumps on my arms, even through the fleece of my ballet-slipper pink jacket and mittens. The bare trunks of the birch and hickory trees around me jutted out of the ankle-deep snow like picked-over bones.

I wasn't scared. Not much, anyway. If I squinted through the withered remains of the underbrush, I could still make out the red-green glow of the Christmas lights that rambled along our front porch as if it were some strange, wintery vine. The scent of a wood fire billowed out of our house's skinny brick chimney and skimmed past my nose like a passing phantom.

Curious, I decided to follow the blood trail.

The line of droplets meandered drunkenly between the trees. Dark, heavy shade of red, like fistfuls of ripe chokeberries. My little wigwam boots sank into the snow's icy surface with the crunch of someone biting into stale crusts of bread. Once, the droplets became a splatter, and off to the left, at the level of my head, was a bright gash against the papery-thin bark of a sugar maple tree. Then the trail of blood drops changed direction.

Now it headed towards the house.

I walked faster, let my breath fog up against my eyelashes. I brushed the wetness aside with one pink sleeve and saw the blood trail run up along the side of our driveway, past where Daddy's beat-up station wagon sat like a wood-paneled display of dents ringed with rust. I followed the trail up to the garage's side door. It was wide, built to swallow furniture and auto parts and maybe little girls.

Lime-green flecks of paint clung to the door's wooden surface by faith as much as anything else. The blood pointed the way. Inside. One circular drop lay smeared halfway under the door's bottom edge as if it had tried and failed to squeeze under the worn gray weather stripping.

My breath echoed hollow and empty in the recesses of my hood. The noises from inside the garage were soft but unmistakably clear. The scrape of flesh on concrete, a grunt, as if someone was lifting a heavy object, something falling with a thud against metal. Then the blubbery, snot-choked sounds of sobbing.

I grasped the doorknob, turned it, pushed in.

The all-weather bulb inside the garage hung from the rafters by a single paint-spattered cord. Daddy's orange hunting vest was streaked with red. Dark, chokeberry red. An iron smell rolled off him and filled the room. His rifle lay propped up against the wall. Something that looked like a grayish-white nub of bone jutted out of the darkness of the garage chest freezer. Daddy knelt before the white, coffin-shaped chamber, shaking his head as he cried. A single tear hit the side of the freezer and slithered down over the raised silver letters on the side: *KELVINATOR*.

"Oh, God, forgive me, forgive me," Daddy sobbed. He clasped his hands together clumsily, trying to pray.

I stepped forward into the garage. Daddy hadn't noticed me yet, he was still talking to God. Now I was worried. What could be causing him such pain?

"I'm so sorry," he whispered. "I killed her. Dear God, I *murdered* her."

Whatever Daddy was concerned about, it had to do with whatever was in the chest freezer. The lid lay open, but the lip of the freezer was high up for my seven-year old frame. I stood on tiptoe, grabbed the top edge, and gazed down into the Kelvinator's depths.

My eyes went wide at what lay at the bottom.

CHAPTER 4

I woke with a start. The gray light of dawn came streaming through the window. No fog on the horizon, meaning that it was going to be hot enough to do a sidewalk pizza bake in downtown Los Angeles. I let the coffee brew while I showered again, and then dug into my closet for a not-too-badly ironed pair of Ann Taylor pants, a violet top, and some shoes in a color that wouldn't clash. I considered for a moment, and then pulled out my favorite long-sleeved open cardigan. It was going to be a scorcher today, but I planned to work inside.

Winter lives in the morgue.

I poured myself a cup of Colombia's finest and inhaled the blessedly caffeine-infused steam that curled up from my cup. I eyed the cordless phone on the kitchen counter, fingers itching to pick up the receiver. To give Daddy a call, ask him what he remembered about that day, that strange wintery day when I found him in the garage, bawling his eyes out.

I couldn't bring myself to do it. Like I said, it was a long, long time ago. Maybe I even dreamt that he'd been wearing a hunting outfit. We'd moved to the Chicago area when I was eight or nine.

I never saw him express the slightest interest in sport hunting once we'd settled into our new home.

I mean, for chrissake, he'd been an on-again, off-again vegan since I'd been in grade school. Why would he even *want* to go hunting? He had lots of other hobbies to occupy his time. Maybe I had dreamt all of it, the entire thing, out of whole cloth. I took a sip of coffee, determined to enjoy the rich burnt-umber flavor of the freshly ground beans.

Then my mind did that weird *clicking* thing again, like it was some kind of spongy telephone switchboard that took its own sweet time connecting things together. Lots of hobbies to take up one's time. The John Doe's scale-patterned skin, which looked as if it belonged to Persephone, my roommate's albino king snake.

My roommate—whose name, I recalled, with a tingle of satisfaction, was 'Joan'—had several hobbies. But her favorite one involved dressing up as a 'wench' for some medieval historical society. She hung out with the folks who ran the Renaissance Faires off the college campus.

It wasn't exactly my kind of crowd—give me modern dental care and indoor plumbing any day over Ye Olde Middle Ages— but I did enjoy the few times I went to their events. Jousting, carousing, medieval swordplay done by the men to impress the women. While I got a lot of attention from the guys, I lost interest. I think that happened around the time when I realized it was against the rules to get men to fight to the death for my favor.

But here's the deal: the makeshift knights didn't go in for the museum-piece plate armor suits. They went for body-length chain mail, or vests and a kind of metal skirt. Mail was cheaper, easier to move in, breathed, and since it was just clothing made up of little metal rings, it was lighter as well.

I was willing to bet a year's salary that at the time of his death, John Doe had been wearing chain mail.

Okay, but did that get me anywhere? Again, it looked like I just replaced one mystery with another. I paced the length of the kitchen and stuck my hands in my pockets. Something cold tingled against my index finger.

To my horror, I pulled John Doe's damned gold medallion out of my pocket.

My mind whirled back through yesterday's events.

Okay, I sent samples of Doe's clothing to the fiber experts, dumped the sweaty jumpsuit, sterilized the medallion, stuck it in my pocket...

Oh my God! What the hell was I doing? I'd just tampered with—I'd just stolen evidence from a murder case! I'd robbed a corpse!

Breathing hard, I pulled open a kitchen drawer with one hand. With the other, I moved to put the medallion in the drawer.

The hand holding the medallion put the damned thing back in my pocket.

I blinked. I took the medallion out, tried to put the thing away, and a second time, into my pocket it went. The little hairs on the back of my neck stood at attention as if someone had just run their nails over a chalkboard.

Okay, now this was getting just plain spooky.

I took the medallion out and examined it again. To be perfectly honest, I don't think I'd have blinked if I'd seen the phrase *One Ring to rule them all, and in the darkness bind them* stenciled on one side.

Instead, clear imprint of a horse's hoof dominated one face of the medallion. The strange lettering on the other looked like a cross between Latin letters and Nordic runes. My arms goose-pimpled as I considered what was going on here.

One, I could be losing it.

Two, something effing strange was going on.

I didn't believe in voodoo or witchcraft or Wicca or any dopey new-age version of an Earth-Mother. Hell, I didn't even go to church on Sunday to partake in any of the local religious denominations on order.

I went out the front door in a rush. Of course, I'd completely forgotten that Deputy Chief McClatchy had put me under surveillance for my own safety. I badly startled the half-asleep pair of cops that had taken over for the Bears' linebackers. I gave them an apologetic wave as I hopped into my car and thanked whoever was pulling the strings upstairs that no one had yet tried to take a potshot at me for my absent-minded spate of stupidity.

I drove to the M.E.'s office at the sizzling Southern California highway speed of twenty miles per hour in bumper to bumper traffic. I didn't mind this time. It let me think more on the medallion. I could feel the cold lump of metal in my pocket. Tugging at me like it had its own gravity field.

"Okay," I said to myself, "John Doe didn't get shot with this little golden marker. So how did it get into his chest wound?" The answer was obvious, and it almost made me miss the highway off-ramp to the Medical Examiner's headquarters.

It got into his chest wound because someone planted it there.

Fair enough. Why would someone do that? Knowing even the basics of forensic examinations meant that whoever put the thing in the most obvious wound expected it to be found. In other words, someone planted it there for a single reason.

Whoever it is *wanted* me to find it.

With that happy thought dancing in my head, I pulled in and parked in my assigned garage slot. My police escort parked nearby, in a spot where they could watch the entrance.

The Office of the Medical Examiner was a long, low-slung trapezoid of smoky black glass and long corridors lined with gray carpet. Compared to the 'well tended junkyard' look of a lot of labs I'd worked for, the high-tech look of the place was a welcome change.

I clipped my badge identity card to my belt, pushed through the lobby's king-sized revolving glass door, went through the security checkpoint's metal detector, and then set off down the long gray-shaded corridor for my office at a pace just under a run.

"Dayna!" a familiar voice called, "Wait up!"

A matronly woman with a frizz of hair the color of weak tea and pince-nez glasses that would've warned a librarian to keep quiet half-walked, half-ran to catch up with me.

"I'm sorry, Shelly," I said, as she puffed her way over to my side. "I've got a lot on my mind."

"Figured that as soon as I saw you break the new land-speed record through the door. Any faster, and you'd set the carpet on fire," she said. Her soft Texas drawl spun out her last word into 'fahr'.

Shelly Richardson and I had started out together as junior medical examiners. I'd swapped the M.E.'s green gown to move over to Crime Scene Analysis, but Shelly had stayed and prospered over the last couple of years. Like me, she loved pulling the bizarre and puzzling cases, the ones that could give you a bad case of the shivers, or make you stay up late chewing on your split ends in frustration.

"Maybe if I keep moving, I'll be a more difficult target."

She made a disapproving tsk. We were friends, but she didn't always appreciate my dark sense of humor. Shelly's tastes ran more to reruns of *The Brady Bunch* and comic strips involving cats who hated Mondays and loved lasagna.

"News spreads quick," she said. "Someone gunning for you? Or was it just some punk who up-n-decided to take a couple pot-shots at the cops?"

"It sure seemed like someone was aiming for me," I replied, as we started walking again. "But I can't think of anyone who'd want me dead."

"No jealous ex-lovers? Boyfriends?"

I sighed and shook my head 'no'. It'd been a while since I'd been out with a man on an honest-to-goodness real live date, but that didn't stop Shelly from trying to get me married off. We turned up a second corridor, one which bore a white plaque with an arrow: Forensics Department. Some joker had taken a marker and written *Labs n' Slabs* on the plaque's bottom edge. Well, it was graffiti, but at least it was accurate graffiti.

"I haven't heard from McClatchy about an arrest," I added.

"Because there wasn't one. I asked Esteban. They swarmed the building the shots were fired from. The boys are swearing on the Good Book that nobody could've slipped past, but all they found was four spent rifle casings on the roof."

"More good news," I grumbled. "Well, I mostly came to see what's up with the John Doe we picked up downtown."

"Oh, Connor McCloud? I worked it with the tox-box folks last night. Hector sent me his photos, too."

"*Connor McCloud?* We actually got a hit on that goofball name?"

Shelly rolled her eyes. "That's 'McCloud' as in *Highlander*, dear. We're calling him that 'cause of that little metal fragment you gave us."

"You're kidding me!" I exclaimed, as we reached the glorified broom closet they'd repurposed as my office.

"Read the reports for yourself. You'll find it right peculiar, I think."

I turned the worn brass doorknob and pushed my way inside. Dusty teak bookshelves fairly groaned under the textbooks that took up the bulk of two walls, while the window on the remaining one looked out over the grassy expanse of the building's rear lawn. The mess of paper on my desk was bad enough so that a hamster would've considered the place in prime move-in condition. But I kept a spot on the front left corner for a bright red cookie jar that I always kept stuffed with fresh brown-sugar ginger snaps. The picture on the front of the jar came from one of my favorite Disney flicks. It showed the Mad Hatter and White Rabbit at a tea party, holding up a wooden sign that proclaimed: *Have One!*

I slid into my office chair with a creak of dry springs and opened the first of the folders that lay atop the pile of paper I'd been meaning to properly organize someday. Shelly took the visitor's chair, lifted the top of my jar, and grabbed one of the cookies. I suppressed a grin. I didn't actually like ginger snaps that much, but their sweet-spicy scent gave me a nice tingle in the nostrils. Not coincidentally, it also told me who'd been visiting my office on any given day.

The reports were terse but clearly laid out. No immediate hits on the fingerprints, but the FBI was checking their database as well. 'Connor' had been in excellent health before his death, about six hours before we'd found him. Clean living, too. Zero hits for drugs from cocaine, heroin, aspirin, or even aspartame in his body fluids, stomach contents, hair follicles, and subcutaneous fat.

Findings like that are unusual. But Hector Reyes' photos moved the case from unusual to head-scratching. He hadn't found any shoe prints at all. But he'd seen the same curious thing that I had—multiple blood trails leading to the body. He'd systematically put together a montage of pictures from 360 degrees around the body and then spliced it into a combined image. The blood trails radiated out from the body in a perfectly symmetrical pattern.

There were no traces of someone dragging or carrying a body across the jumbled terrain of broken concrete to leave him in the middle of the lot. None. That had to be wrong. Connor would've been more than two hundred pounds of dead weight. Hard for even a bodybuilder to handle. But Hector's photos showed that we weren't looking at blood trails. We were looking at a splatter pattern.

It was as if someone had simply dumped poor, dead Connor from a platform ten feet in the air, let him fall straight down, and then vanished. Taking the platform with them as well, I might add.

Effing im-poss-i-ble.

And then the report got *really* interesting.

Michael Angel

CHAPTER 5

My office chair squeaked in protest as I leaned forward. Shelly looked up expectantly as she popped the last of the ginger snap in her mouth with a spicy-smelling *crunch*. I closed the report she'd done on the metal fragment.

"Are you serious about what you found?" I asked.

"As serious as a Baptist in church, hon."

The metal chip from the massive shoulder wound was a piece of medium-grade iron called 'blister steel'. But the tox guys had run the metal's impurities against hundreds of possible metal implements. Their conclusion: Connor had been wounded by a genuine antique. The steel shard came from a sword that could only have been manufactured during Europe's High Middle Ages.

"Okay," I acknowledged, "at least I'm getting the *Highlander* joke now, sort of. So our guy got attacked by a nut with a medieval sword. Any recent thefts from museums, private collections?"

"Nope." Shelly leaned back in her chair to give the hallway a long look in both directions. When she was sure it was clear, she continued. "Let's head on over to the slab, take a gander at Mister McCloud. We need to talk. Private-like."

I started to ask a question. Then shut my mouth with a snap. I'd only seen Shelly get serious about stuff like this once or twice, and when she said 'we need to talk', she meant business.

We walked down to the chiller rooms, where we actually kept the bodies. The cold chambers were windowless rooms coated with cheery yellow-brick tiles that looked like they belonged in Oz, not a morgue. The light came from a combination of harsh fluorescent bulbs and a special kind of skylight that bounced the sun down to us indirectly from a reflection panel on the roof. Different kinds of light helped throw different kinds of dyes or marks into sharper relief for us.

Shelly and I didn't chit-chat as we did the surgical hand-wash routine and gowned up in a matching pair of pale green scrubs. A couple pieces of paperwork later, we rolled the body out of the cold chamber. The gamy smell of rotting flesh was muted here—the low temperature slowed decomposition—and there was a background scent of formaldehyde that curled up in the nostrils and plastered the back of the throat.

The man I now thought of as Connor—funny, how easily we can attach names, even to dead things—didn't appear to be much worse for wear. Shelly had performed a modified Y-shaped incision for the autopsy. Normally, we started the cut at the top of each shoulder and ran down to the front of the chest, switching over to shears or bone saws when we reached the sternum. Since our boy's sternum had been powdered, the cut continued around the wound and down to the pubic bone. But Shelly didn't pull the flaps back. Instead, she directed me to Connor's hands as she spoke.

"I'm wondering if our friend really *was* attacked by a medieval knight, or someone pretending to be one. Because he might have been into the same game himself." She touched the man's bare left hand with her gloved one, and then looked questioningly at me.

"You're right," I acknowledged, looking at the wound there and above, on his arm. "Classic defensive wounds. Probably against the same weapon that cut his ear, his shoulder."

Shelly nodded. Next, she grasped Connor's right palm and turned it over. The inner side of the thumb, fingers, and the palm itself showed callus buildup.

"Exactly where someone would hold a sword by the handle," I noted. "This ties up with what I've been thinking about. The guy's weird skin pattern comes from wearing chain mail. Maybe this is some kind of dueling club? One that's into, I don't know...medievalism? Live-action role play?"

"If so, they ain't doing it right. You want to know what caused that awful wound on John Doe's chest?"

I nodded. Shelly smiled as she spoke again.

"So would I. The boys in the lab have no clue."

No clue? What the hell blew open this guy's chest?

"I read your notes, Dayna. Your nose is pretty darn good. The lab backs up your findings of sulfur, potassium nitrate, and wood ash. And get this—the wound was almost completely cauterized. High heat, charring of surface tissues. No way was this done with a conventional firearm."

"No way it could've been..." I mused. My voice trailed off as Shelly's voice dropped a full octave lower and became deadly serious.

"There is one more thing," she said coolly. "It's why I wanted to talk to you in private down here. Detective Esteban said that you found a small artifact on the body. Something made of gold. But you didn't list it on the exhibits turned in to us. Care to fill me in, before department security gets involved?"

I looked at her helplessly and wrung my hands for a moment. I still wasn't sure what was going on with that damned medallion. But Shelly was my friend, my ally. If anyone could help me save my job over this snafu, this bit of black magic, it was her. I drew the medallion out of my pocket and held it up. It glittered warmly in the bright rays that streamed in through the skylight.

Then the medallion did more than glitter.

A delicate ringing filled the air, echoing off the walls of the morgue. It began to get brighter in the room, much brighter. In a few seconds, the medallion blazed with a white-yellow radiance like I was holding a miniature sun in my hand.

"Oh my lord!" Shelly exclaimed. "Dayna, what are you doing? What's going on?"

"I'm not doing this!" I shouted back, but my voice seemed swallowed up by the ringing, by the radiance of the star in my palm. The light wasn't hot, not really, but I could feel pulses of energy coming off the medallion like the heavy swells of an incoming ocean tide. I didn't dare move—I was worried that if I tried to get rid of the medallion, that I'd end up putting it into my pocket, and right now I didn't want the effing thing *anywhere* near my crotch.

I squeezed my eyes to slits, but the brightness penetrated right through my lids. Right then, a horrible, ticklish sensation crawled up and down my skin. I let out a scream that would've done credit to a Hollywood B-movie actress who's found herself in a horror movie. One with a scene where she gets a boatload of spiders dumped on her.

And then it was as if the floor itself melted away under me. Like it turned into a bottomless void of white light. I fell into the void as I continued to scream, tumbling end over end into a nothingness that seemed to stretch on forever.

* * *

Laundry taken off the clothesline.

That's the first scent I encountered as I swam back to consciousness.

I lay on something that was feather-soft. A mattress, I guessed. I felt the slick coolness of sheets covering my body. I didn't open my eyes. I remembered falling, that I must've taken a tumble. What's more, I was a week behind on my wash, so the fresh linen smell meant I wasn't in my bed. I listened for the tell-tale electronic beeps and hums of a hospital room. Nada. Zip. Zilch. Someone nearby coughed gently. I froze. A sigh, and then a voice spoke from somewhere above and to my right. The voice sounded deep, chesty, and yet surprisingly gentle.

"Are you awake yet, perchance?"

That got my curiosity going.

Perchance? Did I hit my head and end up in a Jane Austin three-act play? I half-expected to see a brooding, darkly handsome Byronic man with wild locks of hair and a stylish nineteenth-century jacket.

I opened my eyes.

I lay under a set of satin sheets the color of fresh cream. The sheets were neatly tucked into the sides of a four-poster bed. The room was an elegantly done up affair, with a vaulted ceiling, eggshell-white stone floor, and a pair of ornately carved wooden tables that squatted on either side of the bed. Tapestries made of brightly colored fabrics done up in whorls and stripes draped each of the walls, save the one closest to my bed. Instead, a triple set of bay windows let in bright wedges of sunlight. The edges of the windows, like the furniture and the tips of the four bed posters were marked with gilded fleur-de-lis accents.

Let's just say that Louis XIV would've found it homey.

The man standing next to my bed—looming over it, to be precise—was a brooding, darkly handsome Byronic man with wild locks of hair. He wore a stylish cloth jacket the color of sangria wine, punctuated with bell-shaped silver buttons.

That was from the waist up. From the waist down, he had the body of a well-built chestnut draft horse.

I squeezed my eyes shut again.

"Whoever you are, you're not going to believe this," I said, trying to keep my voice from shaking, "but I think I must've hit my head. Like, bad."

"I'm certain that I would believe you," the man said.

Man? Or would that be 'stallion'? No, a centaur? A centaur stallion?

"I somehow doubt that."

"Relinquish your doubts," he said. "My name is Galen, of the House of Friesain. I was tasked with summoning you."

"Yes, you certainly did a good job, I am most definitely summoned."

I cautiously opened my eyes. Yup, Galen still looked like a centaur.

My gaze flicked down low. Very low. Not ladylike, I know, but see where you look the next time you wake up with a centaur standing next to your bed.

Whoo. Galen really *was* a stallion.

"I swear," I said, as I sat up and rubbed my eyes with my knuckles, "Galen, if I find out that someone laced one of my ginger snaps with lysergic acid, I won't rest until I've hunted them down and…I don't know, keyed their car, shaved their cat. This is really wild."

"Surely you'd think so," Galen said agreeably, "but you're not under the influence of any substance, fair or foul. This is reality. One should accept it."

I looked down at myself. Someone had thoughtfully removed my scrubs, but I still had on the violet top and open cardigan I'd started the day wearing. That probably convinced me more than anything else that I wasn't tripping on acid or having any sort of nervous breakdown.

To triple-check that I wasn't dreaming, I pinched myself on my arm. Hard. Yeah, it hurt. I blinked again, shuddered, and then rubbed my arms as I looked at the rest of Galen, House of Freeze-Sane a little more closely.

His equine body and tail matched the dark brown color of the hair on his human head. Muscles bulged under the skin of the horse body like bunches of the kind of rope they use to keep ocean liners tied firmly to the dock. Interestingly, all four of his legs were fringed with long, silky black hair below what I think they called the 'knee' on a horse.

"Okay," I said cautiously, "I've really got no choice but to accept what I'm seeing here. I'm…well, I'm sure as hell not in Kansas anymore, I guess."

I threw the covers back and got shakily to my feet. Galen reached out to steady my shoulder, and I accepted his help. I placed my hand on his for a moment. His skin felt warm, dry, and completely human. Though the clip-clop sound of his hoofs on the stone floor as he took a step back was utterly alien. It was a real mind-bender.

"No, you are not in 'Kan Sass' anymore, Dayna Chrissie," Galen said with a smile. He gestured towards the windows at the far end of the room. "You've been summoned to Good King Benedict's palace, the capitol of the land of Andeluvia. For the moment, you're the honored guest of Grand Duke Kajari."

For the moment. I pushed that thought aside and asked the more pressing questions on my mind.

"How'd you know my name, Galen?"

He shrugged. "It was printed on the badge hanging at your belt."

I sighed. "Okay. So, how did you bring me here?"

"I set a pair of enchantments on a medallion of King Benedict's reign," Galen replied. "One was to bring you here, to our world. The other was a *geis*, what we call a 'spell of obligation'. To ensure that the medallion wasn't lost."

"Yeah, about that," I said wryly. I fished the damned thing out of my pocket and held it up in my palm. "Can you, I dunno, revoke that? I don't want to have to carry this thing around like pocket change for the rest of my life."

"Certainly." Galen covered my hand with his. He spoke a word or two of some guttural, Nordic-sounding tongue. I felt a tingle in my palm, and then I felt the strangest sensation yet. A 'snap' like a cord of filament line around my wrist had just been cut. "There, now you should be able to throw the medallion away."

I cocked my arm as if I was about to fling the little golden disk away—and then I curved my arm so that I stuck the medallion back into my pocket. Galen started. His nostrils flared and he flicked his curly chestnut tail. I pulled the coin back out and tossed it to him.

"Just kidding," I said. Galen stared at me for a second before breaking into a grin. I returned it. "So, you're the magic guy here, are you?"

"I'm the wizard for the court of Andeluvia, yes."

"Well, then I suppose that you were 'tasked' to bring me here. Care to fill me in on what King Benedict had in mind?"

"That would be quite difficult," Galen said, and his face took on the brooding aspect that I'd expected to see from someone who could've stepped off the set of *Fantasia* and into the world of *Wuthering Heights*. "You see, that's goes to the heart of why you've been summoned."

"Oh?" I didn't like where this was going.

"You see, Good King Benedict's been slain."

"Slain. Ah."

"Yes. He met his end two days ago." Galen gestured with a sweep of one mighty arm. "It's imperative that we unravel the mystery and expose whoever murdered him."

"Imperative?"

"Oh, yes!" He stomped one of his black forehoofs in emphasis against the stone floor with a loud *clack*. "Why else would we need the services of a crime scene analyst?"

It figures. No one ever invites me anywhere for the sparkling conversation.

To read the rest of *Centaur of the Crime*,
please visit your favorite online bookseller
for the eBook or Print edition.

ABOUT MICHAEL ANGEL

Michael Angel's worlds of fiction range from the unicorn-ruled realm of the Morning Land to the gritty 'Fringe Space' of the western Galactic Frontier.

Michael currently resides in Southern California. Alas, despite keeping a keen eye out for griffins, centaurs, or galactic marshals, none have yet put in an appearance on Hollywood Boulevard.

See the full listing of Michael Angel's works at:
www.MichaelAngelWriter.com

'FANTASY & FORENSICS' BY MICHAEL ANGEL

Book One: Centaur of the Crime
Book Two: The Deer Prince's Murder
Book Three: Grand Theft Griffin
Book Four: A Perjury of Owls
Book Five: Forgery of the Phoenix (Fall 2016)

FANTASY NOVELS BY MICHAEL ANGEL

The Detective & The Unicorn
The Wizard, The Warlord, and The Hidden Woman
I Married the Third Horseman

SCI-FI NOVELS BY MICHAEL ANGEL

Apocalypse with a Side of Grilled Spam: Season One
A Shovelful of Stars
The Adventures of Amanda Love
Treasure of the Silver Star

Made in the USA
Middletown, DE
09 December 2021

54738246R00231